EVERYTHING HAPPENS FOR A REASON

By Jacqueline Harvey

Strategic Book Publishing and Rights Co.

Strategic Book Publishing and Rights Co., LLC
USA | Singapore
www.sbpra.net

For information about special discounts for bulk purchases, please contact Strategic Book Publishing and Rights Co., LLC. Special Sales, at bookorder@sbpra.net.

ISBN: 978-1-946539-53-3

Acknowledgements

I would like to thank Jesus Christ, my Lord and Savior for giving me the idea for "Everything Happens for a Reason" and the wisdom and ability to write it. I would also like to thank God in advance for the wonderful plan He has for "Everything Happens for a Reason".

I want to thank my mother, Geraldine Harvey for all of her love and support.

Chapter One

Fear equals: False Evidence Appearing Real, yet the fear of losing could still consume you sometimes. Eat you up in one fleeting, ferocious bite. "But, in Christ, I always win!" Holly said aloud to cast down those thoughts that were contrary to the gospel. "When afraid, locate the area of unbelief," she muttered, knowing that fear, according to the Bible Scripture in 2 Timothy 1:7, was not of God. She released a long sigh as the attention she was giving to such inquiries like: Are you absolutely certain the deposition you've obtained was completely accurate? Could we just go over that one more time? and so on, and so on entered her mind. One of those button-pushing questions could never be answered without becoming speechless unless you had the knowledge to back yourself up, Holly Reed told herself. "Or more importantly knew exactly who you were as a child of the Most High God," she said as she sat in her office Friday afternoon, sifting through the files and paperwork from the case she had supported a few days ago. This coming Tuesday would make it exactly one week. Her efficient fingers turned the pages of the thick transcript, slowly. She didn't enjoy revisiting the two grueling months of the Moore vs. Moore trial although she had to. The photographs of that child's damaged face almost made her lose the sushi she had eaten for lunch that day. Holly had assumed while she sat, viewing the case, the display of the shocking prints would have guaranteed Jeanne Landers, the prosecuting attorney, an immediate win on day one of the startling unveiling. The photographs had been aired on every major television network, during the live coverage of the trial and they also made it on the front page of every primary newspaper in the city. One of the captions read, "Is this going to become the new face of America's children?" Even the gasps coming from that crowded courtroom were universal, telling Holly that the trial would soon be over. Another triumph she would be involved in. She remembered hearing herself whisper, "Thank you, Jesus!" once realizing that their victory was inevitable. People of different nationalities were assembled, waiting for the obvious outcome. Some were seated and others lined the mahogany-wooden walls of the symposium in representation of the society they all had in common. Every opinion you could have imagined was among them. There in the flesh or watching by way of TV. Collectively their in-house faces were in agreement, silently calling the boy's father a demented criminal who deserved to be put away. Everyone from the prettiest to the ugliest, fattest to the skinniest, tallest to the shortest, oldest to the youngest, smartest to the dumbest knew what time it was. Leroy Moore's pay-day.

Holly frowned at the images of young Stephen spread across her desk. He had black eyes and a busted lip in one shot, dark blue bruises highlighted with shades of green covered his torso like a tie-dyed T-shirt in the second photo. Leroy Moore had taken the belt buckle of the belt to the small child's upper body and in the third photograph he had a knot in the center of his forehead the size of a golf ball. Not exactly Kodak moments.

Falling into the support of the chair she sat in, Holly brought herself back nearly three and a half months ago, to the time Mary Bell King called her, asking for help. It was a rainy mid-March day and the defending attorney had come into the office early that dreary morning for no reason at all. Just a hunch she thought at the time, but since it turned out to be a situation that she could be of help to, Holly now knew it was a prompting from the Holy Spirit. She had awaken suddenly out of a deep sleep and could not go back so she rose out of bed and decided to get a head-start on her work. She entered the office, steadying a tall cup of hazel-nut flavored coffee in one hand, her briefcase in the other one. She wore a silver rain slicker and matching hat. Climbing the stairs quickly, the thirty-three year old attorney made it into her office, answering the phone that had begun to ring. It was one of those piercing rings, warning you of the potential trouble on the other end of the line. "Hello," Holly said into the receiver. She was trying to catch her breath, the law firm name not making it out of her mouth. "Is this the law office of Reed, Benjamin & Mann?" asked the uncertain Louisiana-based voice. "Yes, it is," Holly said, asking the woman to hold. The attorney placed the cup of coffee on the desk before her and tossed the briefcase, she held clamped against her rib cage with her arm, into one of the chairs opposite the one she utilized. Clearing her throat, Holly removed her rain hat and coat as she picked the receiver back up. "Thanks for holding," she said, taking a deep breath. "Now," Holly smiled, feeling more relaxed and together, "can I be of some assistance?" she asked the caller. "I hope so... um... who am I talkin' to? Are you a lawyer, sweetie?" "Yes, I am. My name is Holly Reed and you are?" The woman paused. "You mean Reed like the title of the firm?" "Yes, that's correct. What could I do for you, Ms..." "Oh. Name's Mary Bell King," said the woman. "Well, can I help you, Ms. King?" "I'm hopin' somethin' terrible that you can. You see it's 'bout my nephew, Stephen. He, um. I mean his daddy's hurtin' him real bad. Doin' all kinds of ungodly things to the po' boy. Anythang and everythang from beatin' him to the pointa stealin' the breath clear out his lungs, to makin' him do thangs he 'pose to be do'in wit his wife." Compassion as well as shock overwhelmed Holly. Although she and her two partners, Vanessa Benjamin and Tracy Mann were criminal defense attorneys, Holly felt compelled to do something on the childs behalf. This was why she had been awakened out of such a sound sleep, she reasoned. "My goodness," Holly mumbled under her breath. "Before you go on, Ms. King," the attorney told the woman. "I will not be much help. However, I will do my best." Holly asked the woman if she had a pen and a piece of paper, giving her the name and telephone number of the Manhattan District Attorney's office. She instructed her to ask for Jeanne Landers and tell her that Holly Reed, Esq. told her to call her. She was an acquaintance of Holly's as well as an extraordinary lawyer. "I hear your deep southern accent. Where are you located?" asked the attorney. "We are all in the New York City area," said the woman. "Okay, great. Please give Ms. Landers a call." Mary Bell King thanked the lawyer profusely and hung up.

Holly picked up her coffee and leaned back in her chair. She took two sips, put the cup down again and reached for the phone. After checking caller ID to retrieve Ms. King's number, she called her back.

"Hi, Mary. Is it all right for me to call you by your first name?" Recognizing the lawyer's voice instantaneously, the woman answered. "Don't mind at all." Holly smiled a little. "I know this is going to sound a little strange, but... I'd like to help." Holly's Christianity spoke louder than her profession. She knew she was being led by the Lord. "I want to be there for you and the boy, a support at least. I will take this situation into a meeting with my colleagues as soon as possible". The attorney continued to tell the woman, who was so thrilled she began to weep. Deep sobs poured out of her as she thanked Holly for her kind heart. "Oh, it's my pleasure," the attorney said." She reached inside of her desk draw, grabbing a pen and pad to take notes. "You will still need to call the D.A.'s office. I just want to be there on behalf of... did you say the childs name was Stephen...?" "Yes, sweetie. Stephen Moore." Holly nodded, writing it down. "How did you hear about my law firm?" "I found you on the internet. I typed in best lawyers in New York City and the three of you popped up. You and yo' two partners." Holly smiled and nodded again."So, tell me everything," the attorney said. Mary Bell blew her nose and proceeded. She explained to the attorney how her sister, Rochelle and her brother-in-law, Leroy had never wanted children. The only thing they wanted to do was run the streets and live a fast life. Stephen was a hindrance to the couple. Mary Bell had been asking them to give her sole rights to become the boy's legal guardian but they denied her request, allowing her instead, to keep him at her apartment until the unction to pick him up rose in them. "Have his parents ever been arrested for their mistreatment of Stephen?" "No. This the first time I'm tellin' anybody 'bout what they doin'. Rochelle ain't never touched the boy in a ill manner, but to me she just as guilty since she don't stop what Leroy be doin' to him. You the only's one I ever called, Ms. Reed." "What do you or they tell doctor's?" "I," Mary said, stressing the point as she spoke to let Holly know that she was the only one taking Stephen to the doctor's. "tells the ones that ask that the boy's accident prone. A gluten fo' punishment when he get to playin'." "I see. Holly. Please call me Holly," said the attorney. "Uh-huh, thank you, Sweetie. I mean, Holly. I'm so sick and tired of what they doin'. That baby's 'fraida everythang. Can't even go da school." "How old is he?" "Be five next week." Holly closed her eyes, shaking her head. "Okay, Mary Bell. Let's back up for a minute."

Holly told the woman that she would have to collect as much information as possible on what the offender was doing to the child. Go overboard, she said. "The more, the better. Do whatever you have to do, Mary Bell. The boy's well-being depends on you... by the grace of God. Take pictures of the physical abuse, if you can." "Already did," said the woman, her tone angry at the evidence she had obtained, yet she answered as if she were checking off a list. Holly smiled and nodded her head. "Excellent! Very, very good."

Taking a deep breath, the attorney came back to the here and now, continuing along. She had a habit of making positively sure, once any of the firms cases or the ones they had been involved in, were mistake-proof. She did not want to miss a thing. But, later when she was certain that all was well, Holly would be able to push this circumstance toward the far reaches of her mind, just as she had done the others, and she would find herself somewhere with a smile on her face. Because the thought of knowing she was a part of taking that small boy out of his awful household and put into a loving one, would be all the accolades she needed. Jeanne Landers did a phenomenal job. She told the jurors' during her closing speech that Stephen's mother and father weren't close to being fit to parent the child. She stared into each and every welcoming eye of the twelve deciding factors'. Holly remembered how tough it was to abate her own frustration toward the individuals in that courtroom box. It had taken them weeks to deliberate over a case that could *not* have been more conspicuous. The testimonies alone gave the boy's undeserving custodians a guilty verdict. Stephen Moore's father basically gave himself up. Practically put his own handcuffs on with this statement alone, "Every child needs a good beat down, oh uh, 'scuze me, Your Honor, but they needs to be whipped every now and then. All these little hoodlums runnin' 'round thankin' they bad, tottin' guns and what not. It gots to stop!" Leroy Moore shouted, like he was preaching a sermon. His perilous eyes piercing through Holly's like a laser once they left first the judges face then the prosecutor's in search for hers like he was saying something profound in the midst of exonerating himself.

Supporting the Moore case made Holly think about little Jo Jo Thomas. Jo Jo lived across the hall from her as a child. Whenever she would step foot into the courtroom during the Moore trial, she would see Jo Jo's face somewhere. But he was no longer afraid, his body no longer bruised. That was a great consolation. She could vividly remember her mother telling her to wait in the doorway of their shabby apartment while she crossed the dark, dingy, offensive-smelling hallway to the Thomas residence. Her mother would stand out there in her nightgown, robe and makeshift slippers. She was walking on the backs of her three-year old ninety-nine cent store bought bright red sneakers, banging on the door of apartment 3-F until one of Jo Jo's parents' let up on him long enough to open it. The boy's gut-wrenching screams for refuge made Holly's heart flutter. Skip numerous beats. She had supposed they made her mother's as well. Because if she wasn't mistaken, she could recall seeing Cynthia Reed's hand covering her own chest, pressing up against it as she threatened, in a fed-up voice, to call the police. Sure, her daunting served its purpose most of the time. When Mr. or Mrs. Thomas would finally snatch open the door and tell her that Jo

Jo had been bad in school or that he was simply too hard headed for his own good, finishing it up with a smile and a, "you know how dat go, Cynthia?" Jo Jo's father would always glimpse Holly after saying that and her mother would say to them both at different times, "Beaten him that way ain't gone solve the problem!" Cynthia told the couple. "Try talkin' to him first. I knowd what the Bible say in Proverbs 23:13. Been raisin' my chile on that verse since I been walkin' wit the Lord, but it don't say nothin' 'bout doin' whachu doin'! Go on an look it up. You claims ya'll are Christians!" Cynthia Reed paused and quieted herself down for a second. Her daughter guessed her mother didn't like the sound of her voice being so loud. The young girl continued to watch. Cynthia swallowed, lowered her hand from her chest and continued in a meeker manner. "Try to find out why he actin' the way he actin', fo' you whip..." Holly witnessed her mother trying hard to get the couple to understand even while the door came slamming in her face.

Sighing, the attorney could feel the tears demanding to fall. Back then she didn't try to stop them. She remembered throwing herself across her twin-sized bed, crying. She howled as though she, too, were being punched and kicked. Her tears fell until the sun rose the next morning after she had heard later on that evening that Jo Jo had died. His father had killed his own child for throwing away a piece of bread that had accidentally fallen to the floor. Holly remembered how the police handcuffed both of Jo Jo's parents that night while the EMS workers wheeled a completely covered up Jo Jo out into the rainy night, putting his dead body into the ambulance. The sirens on both the police cars as well as the ambulance spun their red lights in silence. It was a quiet that seemed to be respectfully giving the small boy's death a few moments of silence.

Leaning her head back, Holly forced the tears to stay inside of her eyes. Reminding herself of what her mother told her. "Everything happens for a reason, baby." Cynthia Reed said that even though she continued to assure her child that Jo Jo's death was *not* the will of the Father. "It's our job to only believe as Christians,

Sweetie. Like the Lawd commanded us to. Said won't nothin' be impossible for Him, if we do dat.," Cynthia Reed said, raising her hand to God in worship as she went on, "All the power He put inside us soon as we came into His Kingdom would take care of bidness when we need's it to! Should be able to raise the dead, lay hands on the sick and they recover, and do whatever else He say we's can do as easy as it is to drink water. Witout no doubt whatsoever!" Holly's mother nodded and continued to say, "I ain't there yet, but, the want to is in me. Jesus did say that His peoples would do greata works than He did. Uh-huh, so we just gots to keep oura minds thinkin' bout the Word of God alls the time. And speakin' it day and night like it say to do in the book of Joshua." Holly observed the way her beloved mother scratched her head, nodding again as she added, "The Lawd got him now, babygirl. Yep, but I'm sho' He's up there tellin' Jo Jo, how he arrived befo' his time... but, dat little boy's as free as the air 'round us, chile." Holly managed to smile and Cynthia returned one as she stroked her daughter's hair, saying, "He was saved which means his spirit and soul's final destination is glory! Hallelujah! We both knowed he loved Jesus!" Cynthia Reed concluded and began to praise God while one lone tear coursed her cheek with as much momentum as molasses. Holly could also recall how cherished she felt when her mother wrapped her arms around her that subsequent morning, continuing to reassure her that he was in a better place. Heaven. Holly just became aware at that very second that she had joined hands with Ms. King and Jeanne Landers on the Moore case in memory of little Jo Jo Thomas. Well, due to the circumstances she would have done it regardless. But, it was back then in that run-down tenement on Manhattan's Lower Eastside where she discovered her calling. She knew in her heart that God would some day place her in a position to help someone in need. Uphold the law as she did, not wanting to lose another innocent child. Or maybe even a not so inculpable one. Although she was a criminal defense attorney, Holly never took on a case she didn't believe in. If she didn't have full reliance in the alibi given to her, regarding a crime, meaning what she was hearing did not bear witness with her spirit, she refused it, turning down whoever it was without thinking twice. Her mission was to help those who had to protect themselves in self-defense from their assailant. So, because of those convictions, Holly wanted to be there to see Stephen Moore's father get sentenced. She wanted the entire library thrown at him. He wasn't worthy of "the book." At least not at this point. She had cast the care of Leroy Moore's deliverance onto the Lord, knowing that He would do whatever it took to restore the man since she humbled herself and prayed on his behalf. As for the little boy's mother, she gave up all of the rights she had to the child without a fight, breaking down up on the witness stand like she was a little girl herself. Deeply wounded was what Holly saw as Stephen's mother said something about her knowing she wouldn't be able to raise her son on her own. The defense attorney was certain the look she cut Rochelle Moore assisted her with the arrival of that conclusion.

Composing herself, the attorney restacked one pile, slid it to the side of her desk and went on to the next. Maybe Holly's routine wasn't a phobia, something else she would need Jesus to deliver her from. Perhaps it was just a way of proving to herself that she was an attorney with merit. Yes, that was it. This was personal. She just had to believe what God said about Him ordaining her to do what she was doing, not the scoffers. Having heard in the beginning when they first started their practice that it had been nick-named the firm of "Three the Hard Way," after some 1970's Black exploitation flick, made her blood curdle like sour milk. Holly knew it was all a lie. The three attorneys could not have been greater advocates, using their firm to serve people who the world had counted out. First and foremost. And she also knew it would take them a long time to gain the respect they deserved in this particular arena, but all three women were determined to make it. Holly knew with faith in God, all things were possible and although her two partners' are not Christians, they, without giving Him any verbal credit, could not deny the power of the Lord who Holly worshipped on a regular basis as they were partakers of the work she had been born to do. Ever since the law offices of Reed, Benjamin and Mann originated three and a half years ago, they haven't lost a case. Holly scanned the last line of the document before her, grinning. She was pleased. Everything was intact just as Jeanne Landers said. Slipping all of the papers back into their respective files and placing them one on top of the other, the lawyer then put them into her out-box. She would have her assistant, Kelly bring them downstairs to the storage room when she got back from lunch.

Taking a deep breath, the attorney swiveled around in her chair to face the window. She peered up at the sky. The sun had been trying its best to penetrate those stubborn clouds all morning to no avail. Channel sevens weatherman warned the shows viewers of the abnormally cool and dreary weather conditions they would be experiencing tonight. Holly shook her head in annoyance. She wanted to wear something sleeveless out to dinner later that evening. "Thank you for forgiving my attitude, Lord and thank you again that it isn't supposed to rain," the lawyer said this as she adjusted the look on her frowning face. Smiling now, her eyes fell down onto the street, glimpsing at the people walking by. They were all making subtle fashion statements. Some clad in business attire and others less sequestered by what they wore: khaki skirts and pants, linen shirts, sandals. "Most New Yorkers seemed to take advantage of casual Friday", she mused and rose from her chair. Positioning herself in front of the window, her hands rested on the ledge as she continued to look out. While she studied the passersby further, and the cars that had stopped for the light, thoughts of the day she and her two partners' came to view their lavish offices, once they were furnished, crossed her mind. She recalled them all agreeing on how perfect the location was: 71st Street between Lexington and Third Avenues, near Hunter College. The three women climbed the steps of the two-story brownstone, which was a gift from Vanessa and Tracy's parents'. Holly's mother's contribution was a feast that would have satisfied a king. Vanessa turned the key into the door and they eagerly staggered inside. One behind the other like they were on a conga line. The three women glanced around in awe of what had been done. Though the interior designer that Vanessa's mother, Patricia Lawrence hired left none of the space untouched, she still allowed it to have an open, airy type of feel.

Downstairs there was a reception area, decorated in rich earth-toned colors. Hanging above a massive, dark brown leather sofa, accentuated with beige ravioli-shaped pillows, was a portrait of the three attorneys. It was so lifelike, making all three women's mouths hang open in disbelief. "My mother said he'd be able to capture us in an amazing way," Vanessa said, regarding the photographer. "You could say that again," Tracy said as she walked over to the reception desk, hoisting herself up onto it. Holly just nodded while she proceeded to do her survey of the office. Sitting in front of the sofa was an antique walnut wood coffee table with law pamphlets, describing the type of cases they handled on top of it. The chocolate colors helped to bring out the luster of the white-washed hardwood floors and ceilings. To the left of the enormous mahogany reception desk was a conference room closed off via French doors. The kitchenette was right before that and there was a small storage room toward the back of the space, under the stairs. Up the winding staircase was where their offices were. Three tremendous rooms decorated in expensive furnishings as well. Outside of the three offices were work stations for their three secretaries. Each area was large enough to house whatever equipment was needed for the legal assistants to do a superb job for a law firm with the remarkable reputation the young attorneys knew theirs would soon attain. Holly began to smile at the memory of the three of them, giving each other a group hug as they prayed, at Holly's request, for the prosperity of their practice.

Pulling herself away from the window, the attorney walked around her large cherrywood desk, heading for the door. She wanted to see how Tracy's date went last night. Since Holly's break up with her ex-boyfriend, of seven years, Bradford Anderson about six months ago, living vicariously through her colleague's abundant dating life, was the next best thing to watching those movies on Lifetime. "Lord, I promise not to allow anything to enter my ears that I believe will be displeasing to you," Holly whispered, more to remind herself. Opening her office door, she made her way down the hall. As she neared Vanessa's office, which was in between hers and Tracy's, she was taken a bit off guard to find that she was not alone. Courtney, her partner's husband, along with a very handsome man were joining her. Holly smiled politely and kept walking. As she continued down the long hallway, she overheard the dark-skinned man accompanying the couple asked who she was. And, finally after a brief lull, Courtney told him she was Vanessa's other partner. After that, he asked if he'd like to meet her. Not hearing the response, Courtney Benjamin called her back by saying, "I'd like to introduce you to a friend of mine." Her partner's husband was holding his eyeglasses in his hand when Holly returned to the doorway outside of Vanessa's office. He was speaking in his professional voice as he, too, was a practicing lawyer in the city. Holly remained standing in the threshold and the dark-skinned man moved toward her. Flashing a smile, he exclaimed, "Hello, Goldie!" His eyes gazed at her like one would an extravagant item before committing to the costly purchase. Am I supposed to be amused? she wondered. Not really knowing how to interpret his remark, she assumed he was referring to the color of her hair, which had somewhat of a golden hue. Whatever the color, he thought both it and she were gorgeous. He checked out her tastefully fitted ivory-colored single breasted suit. It was cut high enough to be worn without a blouse. Then she watched his eyes as they worked their way down to her beautiful pantyhose free legs then to her brown crocodile pumps. Following the movement of her hand, he managed to catch a quick glimpse of her platinum Rolex watch. It was a congratulatory gift from her best friend, Carmen

Lopez. She gave it to her after the three attorneys started their firm. Once he'd absorbed every piece of clothing she was wearing, his brown eyes found their way back to her hazel ones. Then, as if not satisfied with his first surveillance, Holly patiently looked on as his gaze maneuvered down to her perfect nose and full lips, which were covering beautiful white teeth. But, the one thing his appraising eyes missed, due to the invisible suit-of-armor she'd slipped into that morning, just in case, was the painful past in which the beauty before him hid so well, most of the time. All those young years of unsolicited abuse, is what she had attributed to her insurmountable insecurities, which would have the tendency of sneaking up on her like a cat would a mouse. Without warning or mercy. Holly sensed a gentle reminder from the Holy Spirit, telling her how she should never take off the whole armor of God as a Christian. "Amen," she answered quietly, without even parting her lips. The helmet of salvation, which would block the negative accusations as well as any kind of deception, knowing that through the shed blood of Jesus, she has been delivered from every situation whether spiritual, mental or physical. The breastplate of righteousness, which would guard her heart from despair. The shield of faith, which protects against the fiery darts of the devil. The lies he tells to persuade one to believe the attack on what they felt, saw, heard, tasted or touched wasn't more real than God's Word. Let me check the buckle on my belt of truth right now, Holly told herself, understanding that sometimes the very thing she was standing against, would find a place in her life if she wasn't holding up her shield with one hand and wielding the Sword of the Spirit with the other by speaking in her Heavenly language as well as muttering God's Word, which is incorruptible seed in order to eradicate the opposing situation; or if her helmet was slightly tilted to the left or the right or if one of her shoes of readiness and peace were untied, giving way to worry, another form of fear and if she were leaning more toward that than her stance on the Word of God, she could do exactly what Jesus said not to do. He said, "take no thought, *saying*" and wind up speaking a bunch of doubt and unbelief, allowing the door to open wide for that circumstance that she let concern her to legally enter. Oh, I could go on Holly mused in dismay. Then she heard the Lord say in her spirit, "The verse states that it's the whole armor of God. You're wearing My armor." Holly felt her eyes enlarge as she got the revelation. "When you speak My Word, the enemy will believe it's Me in My armor, but if you speak doubt and unbelief, he'll say that's God's armor, but He's not in there!" Whoa! Holly thought as she was reminded of that very same testimony that Kenneth Copeland shared on his television program. She definitely could not afford to be without any part of her Heavenly Father's spiritual armor, knowing how much she disliked *feeling* a whole lot less than the multitudes. A challenge she'd been trying with all her might to cast onto God like His word instructs, without taking it back. She needed to make it apart of her thought life. "All of my might?" Holly said on the inside. She knew at that moment that it was the Lord's grace that she had to receive and walk in for the Bible says 'apart from *Him* we can do nothing.' "Ok, how much is nothing?" she asked herself, trying to reason for a split second. "Nothing met nothing!" Deep down, Holly knew that mind-set of being worthless was a bold-face lie. She had recently begun speaking God's Word to go against even the tiniest amount of unbelief. So, learning to appreciate the places He has brought her from was high on her list of things to accomplish. Holly was constantly reminding herself to glance back at all the marvelous steps she'd taken with His guidance. And because she had slowly begun to insulate herself with her newfound confidence in God, people would often confuse it for arrogance.

The jingle of Vanessa's bracelets snapped her out of her musings. "Hello, I'm Holly Reed. Pleased to meet you," she finally said, giving his hand a firm shake. "I'm Philip. Philip *Hayes* Williams and, believe me, the pleasure is *all* mine!" Well, Holly thought, what do we have here? Who told him he was James Bond dipped in that yummy stuff Godiva specialized in? She peered at his slightly crooked smile. "Listen!" Philip said, "I don't mean to sound pushy..." He closed his mouth briefly and began grinning again. "Are you busy tonight? I'm havin' a party at my restaurant. Just a little somethin' to welcome the Summer," he continued and licked his lips. Holly found herself smiling a little. She liked the way he spoke. His diction was clear but there was this I-don't-care quality about it. Philip seemed to purposely fail to fully enunciate some words. "You know what? I do have plans," she said. "My best friend is in town and we have dinner reservations." Philip glanced down at Courtney, who smiled faintly and averted his eyes. Then the dark-skinned man turned back toward Holly. "Where? If you don't mind me askin'?" She shook her head no. "Randy's." Philip raised his eyebrows. "Randy's!" He laughed. "Over on 71st between 5th and 6th?" She nodded. "Come on!" he added, "No offense, but my place blows that wannabe establishment out of the water." He started laughing some more. "They can't keep up with what I got goin' on," Philip threw in. This guy really thinks he's something, Holly thought. And looking at him, she was sure he was. Mess couldn't have come in a more tempting package. Holly folded her arms and stifled a grin. "What time does the party start?" "When you show up!" Philip answered without mincing his words. Ooops, and he's corny, too, she confided to herself as she observed the way he was looking at her as if they were the only two in the room. Holly wasn't sure if she liked the way his eyes locked onto to hers, but she kept it tucked neatly on the inside and nodded her head. "Okay. Where's your place located?" Philip looked at Courtney again and then back at her. My *restaurant* is on 55th and Madison. 5-2-3 Madison Avenue; right across the street from the Sony building. You know, ""*Phil's House*"." She could see his chest inflate with pride after giving her the address. Holly nodded again. "Yes, I do know where that is. Red awning, right?" "Right," Philip said, nodding as well, he smiled. She wanted to laugh in the midst of repenting. Holly had known about the hot spot all too well from her secretary who'd frequented the place. She even tried to persuade Holly to come with her several times. In describing it she told her boss when you first walk in there was your usual coat check area, just past that was a bar filled with people laughing, drinking and eyeballing their next prey. The restrooms were downstairs near Philip's office and the dining area was upstairs. Or was it the other way around? Whatever. Holly honestly was not interested in hearing about "Phil's House" during her assistant's description of it. She had no plans on going there. Determined to stay on the narrow path without compromise, the attorney could remember being gracious when listening to Kelly promote Philip's lounge/restaurant even though she had already made up her mind about how the information she was getting would not be retained. Kelly also said there were little romantic booths toward the back, in what seemed to be the darker part of the restaurant. Before that, in the lighter part, there were tables arranged for business groups who wanted to meet away from the confinement of their offices. And music always played. "There's something exciting going on just about every night!" Kelly explained with great enthusiasm. Yes, Holly knew *exactly* where it was, but she thought she'd try putting a little dent in Philip's huge ego. However, it didn't appear to work. "Forgive me for being dishonest, Abba Father," she whispered and cleared her throat. "All right! See you tonight," Holly finally said to Philip who smiled. She waved to everyone and positioned herself to walk away. Glancing at Vanessa before she did, the hazel-eyed attorney wanted her to know how "big of a head" she thought Philip had, but her partner wasn't paying attention. Instead, she caught Courtney's gaze and smiled. Knowing that was a clear sign from the awesome God dwelling on the inside of her, that He was not the one moving her to silently ridicule Philip. Holly took heed and went on about her business.

Chapter Two

Holly and Carmen could hear the music playing from outside as they exited the cab and walked toward "Phil's House" that evening. "I don't want to stay too long," Holly said to her friend. The loud music was already bothering her. "I'm right there with you," Carmen replied, knowing exactly why Holly didn't want to be there for a great length of time. She, herself, didn't desire to be in a nightclublike setting. Though it was June, the gusty winds made it feel as if Autumn was within arms reach. The weather report Holly had heard earlier was accurate. Holding her camel cashmere cardigan closely around her neck to ward off the chill, she then motioned to her friend so that she, too, would increase her pace. It didn't take much coaxing. The Latina woman hurried in front of her friend and pulled open the heavy mahogany door without hesitating. Holly scooted in first. Her hazel eyes instantly began to pan the restaurant to see if it was what she'd envisioned while Kelly described it to her. And it was. Holly continued to search through the large multi-colored group of men and women gathered near the bar as well as the other highly populated areas within the place, finally spotting Philip when her gaze moved upward. "Carmen, there he is at the top of the stairs. Don't stare," she whispered. She grabbed her Latina friend's arm, turning her so they'd be facing one another. "Holly, you know you're wrong. I didn't even get a chance to peek." "Don't concern yourself. He's on his way over." Philip descended the stairs and walked toward them with a charismatic stride that was very intriguing to watch. Holly smiled inside. She liked the fact that his strut had some street attached to it. She couldn't help being attracted to men who had a bit of an edge. Bad boys! She didn't need to be prophesied over to know that this was a major part of her being challenged with believing God for a mate and then waiting for Him to send her the one *He* chose. Holly's sigh went unnoticed as she continued to behold the signature of trouble approach both she and her friend.

Philip had a big smile on his face as he said, "Hello, ladies!" Grinning back a little, Holly replied with a sweet hello along with, "Philip. This is my friend, Carmen Lopez and *Carmen*," Holly paused and raised an eyebrow. She was playfully warning her friend not to do or say something out of the way. "*this* is Philip Williams." He gave Carmen a quick overview and continued to smile at her once their eyes met. "Hi," the Latina woman said. She chose to let his brief summary of her pass. "Thank you for inviting us to your party," Carmen kindly added. Philip told her that she and Holly were very welcome. He also gave her an odd look that she decided once again to completely let go of. Her features were American, is what Philip was thinking. Long, dark, curly hair, green eyes and ivory skin, yet he detected an accent. Hispanic of some kind. "It's really nice to meet you, Carmen," he finally said once he got over wondering why the way she looked and sounded didn't line up to him. "Likewise," she answered, giving Holly, even though delayed, one of those many familiar exchanges which would quickly and lovingly remind her, that she was healed of being that obnoxious person she had become during the period of time in their past when she set Jesus on the shelf, thinking that she was the one who had all the answers. Thank God for His delivering power, Carmen told herself. Holly nodded her head and smiled as if the Holy Spirit reminded her of the Latina's woman's motive. She was making that connection with her eyes, revealing still that she was not the same. "Amen," she whispered to Carmen, "Whom the Son makes free, is free indeed!" Doing a cute little victory dance that only she and Holly were privy to because Philip had turned away from them to greet a patron who had just come in. Carmen agreed with her friend, saying as softly as she could, given the circumstance, "You are going to make me shout a thousand hallelujah's, if you keep talking like that!" The two women laughed. "Ok," Philip said, breaking up their personal celebration. "Come on in. I have a nice spot waiting for the two of you up there." He pointed up the stairs and led the way. Philip brought them to the back of the restaurant but they could still see the bar and the front door from where they were going to be seated. There was a table for five with a tall, slender dark-skinned Black man standing next to it. He was wearing black pants and a white T-shirt emblazoned with the name of the restaurant across the chest. And the smile on his face lit up the area in which he stood. "This is Darryl. He'll get you ladies anything you want," Philip said and glanced down at the door to see who else was coming in. "Hey, Darryl!" both women said in unison as they took their seats. Darryl smiled bigger and turned his pad to a clean sheet. "I'll be right back, Holly," Philip said and headed downstairs again. "Could I get you anything from the bar?" Darryl asked. "We don't drink alcohol, but you can get me a cranberry juice. Thank you," Carmen said, her voice rising above a Rihanna song which was bouncing off the walls and the glasses of the patron's seated at the neighboring tables. "And you?" Darryl asked. He was looking at Holly after he wrote down the Latina woman's beverage order. She got to witness what was revealed to be a battle going on in his mind about them not being alcohol drinkers. "I'll have a hot flavored coffee. Any kind will be fine. Thank you." Carmen waited for Darryl to walk away before she leaned in toward Holly, saying, "Philip is beautiful to look at, but we *know* he's not saved." The hazel-eyed woman knew her friend was correct as his restaurant was a clear indicator of that. The Latina woman took hold of Holly's hand and they both bowed their heads as Carmen prayed, "Father, thank you for already blessing our time together as well as our food and drink, in Jesus' Name. Amen." "Yes, amen," agreed the hazel-eyed woman. Finishing where she left off, Carmen went on to say, "Without Christ in your heart, the only One who can give us true inner beauty, the outer beauty, will fade quicker than..." she snapped her fingers. "that!" Refocusing her full attention on Holly, the Latina woman smiled and added, "Right? Because, I don't have to tell you, when the Lord is living on the inside, He can make someone who the whole world considers "unattractive" become the most stunning person walking the face of the earth. Aesthetically and internally... cause all that kindness and so forth without Him, could be just as fake... So, don't be fooled. We have to do it entirely God's way. You know He doesn't do halves. A little in His Kingdom and a little in the kingdom of darkness. *Oh,* but the devil will certainly do halves!" Shuddering at the notion of what Carmen said, Holly nodded in agreement, "So true." She knew she couldn't get herself involved with Philip because unless, the Lord touched him, bringing him into the Kingdom of God right then and there and miraculously renewed his mind to the Word, and also confirmed that their joining together was His idea, she'd wind up backsliding all over again. Pressing into the chair she sat in, Holly sighed, crossed her long, thin but shapely, cinnamon-colored legs and observed Philip as he strode from table-to-table. She had to admit that she liked the way he handled himself. "Stay mindful," Holly muttered to herself under her breath. Still peering at him as he glided through the restaurant with so much confidence, making everyone he'd come across ignite like fireworks, she took in the way a middle-aged round-faced woman with corn-rowed hair stood up, giving the handsome restaurateur a hug. Philip smiled as he leaned forward, his long arms wrapping around the ladies waist. He was a tall, dark, curly headed man and he had big brown eyes hooded with the longest lashes Holly had ever seen on anyone of the opposite sex. As she began to notice his solid physique, she saw that it was one that would make other men his age be envious with how amazing he looked. "Ooooooo la la!" she whispered to herself.

When Carmen nudged her on the arm, Holly recognized in an instant that her friend was being used by God. She knew perfectly well He heard both her thoughts and what she quietly spoke regarding Philip's fine exterior. His way of warning her not to fall into temptation. The Latina woman was aware of how engrossed her friend was with Philip, simply by the expression on her face.

And, although she couldn't make out what the hazel-eyed woman had said, Carmen did see her mouth move. "What?" Holly asked, seemingly confused as to why she was being steered away from the awaiting darkness. Carmen just said, "Guard your eye gate," and proceeded to pray softly, putting their Heavenly Father in remembrance of one of His many, many promises. God said in His Word that He was well able to keep *them* from falling. The Latina woman humbly included herself in that supplication, realizing that she was suddenly no longer enthralled by the man she was dating. Finally coming to herself like the Prodigal son, Carmen began to acknowledge how the Holy Spirit had been dealing with her regarding her fair-weathered boyfriend ever since she decided to give him a chance and become a couple two months ago. Carmen knew that decision was not God's will for either of their lives, namely because of the way So and So had begun to minimize her value shortly after they got together and she didn't even have sex with him. He would just complain about everything she did, no matter how wonderful and he'd always say one thing and do another still claiming to be a man who knew Jesus better than any other Christian even while he was asking Carmen why she would not sleep with him. So and So was one who believed he had the integrity that astounded the Lord Himself when Carmen would make mention to him on any level about his taking her completely for granted. "The devil is a liar!" she mumbled and heard the Holy Spirit say in her heart, "I said I'm *able* to keep you from falling. I didn't say I *will*. You must continue in Me." The Latina woman almost reached into her pocketbook for her cell phone, wanting to end whatever you would call this thing that she and So and So had before it got any more out of hand than it already was. And, also to wake him up to the truth that he was the one tooting his own horn about having a super-tight relationship with The Lord and Savior and about how impressed to no possible end He was by him. So and So was severely mistaken because whenever you have to announce your own grandeur, you, yourself, don't even believe it! Carmen took a deep breath. No, I'll wait and do this the right way. Face to face, she thought, positive that she, on the contrary, was a mature Christian. Not perfect! She certainly was not a grown-up believer because of some self-proclaimed positioning, or because she'd been following Jesus since she was five years old. Anyone with the slightest bit of wisdom from above would know that long length of time in anything didn't make you an expert and most assuredly when it came to the things of God and His Kingdom. The Lord knows I've jumped off course many times, she thought. Still, while doing it *her* way, deceived as she was, Carmen made sure she kept track of just how far up ahead Jesus was as she stumbled behind Him in her designer shoes. The Latina woman would apply whatever it was she had learned from her Pastor, to every single one of her situations, even the ones that God was not in with the hopes that He would usher her back on His course. However, she wouldn't recommend tempting the Lord like that. Carmen's insight on her spiritual maturity came by the Heavenly Father. He had spoken to her heart just before she met So and So. The Lord was telling her how pleased He was with her for continuing to keep His Word first in what she said and did. He also informed her of the deep and pure heart He'd given her, making room for Him to increase the revelations He desired to give her. The Lord would go further by confirming His delight in her through other brothers or sisters in Christ once she stepped back on the path He had pre-ordained for her to walk on. Shaking her head, Carmen saw so clearly now how this association with So and So was, yet, another distraction, like all the other men from her past were. She glanced over at Holly, who was about to take a sip of her flavored coffee. The Latina woman found her cranberry juice in front of her as well. Unaware of when the waiter placed both drinks on their table, Carmen proceeded to watch her friend as she blew into her cup before tasting the piping-hot hazel-nut beverage. Smiling faintly, the Latina woman was glad that was the flavor their waiter decided on. She was certain it was Holly's favorite, above all the others she had known her to try. The happiness the hazel-nut coffee seemed to bring her friend wasn't the only purpose for her slight grin. It was more for the love Carmen had for her. The second reason for her not to stay with... What's his name? The Latina woman asked herself, causing a laugh to want to rise from within although it really wasn't humorous. Thinking about her previous rocky years with men for a moment, she halted at the seasons where she and Holly were out of touch. The Latina woman almost got choked up as the thoughts of who she used to be became lucid again. She and the hazel-eyed woman met shortly after they both turned ten. The two girls instantly became close, discovering quickly that their friendship was indeed of God. They loved to talk about how He brought them together and how they believed their divine connection was one that would last during their lifetimes on earth as well as all throughout eternity. But, at the tender age of seventeen, right after Carmen Maria Lopez graduated from high school, she started dating a non-believer by the name of Anthony Jacobs. He was an eighteen-year old sophomore from Long Island. They had gone out with each other for six, long years and during that time, she and Holly barely spoke, let alone saw each other. Looking away from her friend, the Latina woman felt the smile fade from her lips while the sensation to cry became stronger. She lowered her eyes toward the glass of cranberry juice in front of her, but that wasn't what she saw as she was still fully conscious of her history. Not more than two months after her split with Anthony, Carmen wound up rushing into another questionable relationship with a man by the name of Donald Sullivan, creating more distance between herself and Holly right after the Lord had so graciously restored their bond during the Latina woman's momentary singleness.

Carmen met Donald while working as a manuscript reader for a literary agent on New York City's upper Westside. He had come up to their offices to have lunch with one of the in-house editor's, whom he'd had a long-time friendship with and the Latina woman remembered how, "She looked at him and he looked at her and they just knew." *"Thought* we *knew!"* Carmen heard herself whisper with a force that said she was not going back to him. She began to reflect on the day Holly phoned her while she and Donald were in the midst of their courtship, inviting her to attend a World Changers Church Conference at Madison Square Garden with her. Pastor Dollar didn't have the church in the Bronx at that time. Looking back, Carmen realized how she had not gone to a mid-week service or any other service when she and Donald had gotten together. The Latina woman perceived now that Holly was on a mission from God to lead her back to Him even though she didn't think, at the time, that she had left Him. She believed this because Donald *called* himself a Christian as well. So, foolishly, Carmen declined her friend's offer. She had already promised to go out on another date with Donald, which turned out to be the one he proposed to her on. The Latina woman knew it wasn't the Lord wanting her to wonder how her life would have turned out had she not become his wife. Or for her to further speculate on what would have happened to her if she'd attended that World Changers Church Conference with Holly instead? Thank God for His goodness and mercy that endures forever! Carmen mused. She began to smile when Ephesians 3:20 entered her mind. The Lord has definitely restored the years of what many who didn't know the God of the Bible would consider to have been a sheer waste. Grinning bigger, the Latina woman saw how He has indeed far surpassed all of her childhood expectations and He wasn't finished. The Blessing keeps on working even when you think you've reached the top! she thought. The Latina woman took into account how Donald was revealed as being an enemy to the call of writing God placed upon her life soon after they began to date. However, still residing in the utter delusion of wanting to do thing's her way then, was the other thing the Lord showed her as the Latina woman thought about how she went on and married him anyway. Carmen had known very early as a girl that she was extremely gifted in the area of storytelling and she had hopes of becoming a New York Times best-selling author all to the glory of her Heavenly Father. And, in His infinite mercy and great faithfulness, He has brought those wonderful visions to pass as her becoming a well-known author, was part of His plan for her before the foundation of the earth. "Excuse me!" said a young Black woman with beautiful brown hair and a bright smile. The Latina woman was pulled out of that reverie. "Yes, how can I help you?" Carmen asked her. The beautiful brown-haired woman glanced at Holly then Carmen. She smiled and made a face that said I'm sorry for interrupting you. "Are you Carmen Lopez, the author of "Love in the Secret Place". I believe that's the title." The Latina woman smiled and nodded her head. "Yes, I'm her." "Oh, wow! I love your books," said the beautiful brown-haired woman as she reached into her purse, pulling out a small pad and a pen. "Could I have your autograph?" Carmen smiled. "Yes, of course," the Latina woman said. She took the pad from the young woman, signed it and gave it back. The young Black woman took the pad from Carmen, looked at it, jumped up and down and waved good-bye to both Carmen and Holly. "That's a Blessing, sis," said the hazel-eyed woman. The Latina woman smiled and nodded her head. "Amen, God is so good." Marveling at that alone for a moment and then at how far the Lord has raised her up, Carmen took in how she's landed at the very top of that prestige's New York Times list five consecutive times in a row! Five the number of Grace. The Latina woman reasoned as she also remembered the days where she had to rest in the Word of God while believing Him for the way of escape from her ex-husband. The Lord had spoken to her spirit about her needing to leave Donald or else the man she defiantly entered into what would appear to be a marriage, was going to kill her if she did not leave him. He would murder her along with the spectacular destiny the Lord had intended for me she surmised. Donald turned out to be completely double-minded. Unstable in all their ways, Carmen mused, the results of such a person, according to the Scripture in the Book of James. So, because her ex-husband so freely allowed fear to take over his entire being, he began to think someone was going to come in and steal her away from him, quicker than he could blink his indigo eyes. Yet, he was the one stepping out on her. While continuing to run hard after those emotions of surmising she'd be taken by another man, Donald asked her to put her writing profession on hold. He used the cliché of his needing her full-time support until he was an established doctor. Carmen agreed even though she didn't have peace with his rational. The Holy Spirit kept telling her it was nothing more than a lie, making her aware in her spirit then that Donald was being unfaithful. But in which way wasn't exactly clear is what she told herself in order to keep doing what she wanted to do, which only drove her deeper into the trappings of his trickery. Once the couple forsook New York City for California, as Donald was born and raised in Los Angeles and always had a tremendous desire to have his own medical practice in Beverly Hills. Carmen's phone calls, letters and visits to both Holly and the Latina woman's whole family, came to an abrupt end. Donald insisted she forget all about where she came from, delete her heritage and Spanish Harlem neighborhood out of her system like it was just some made-up story she decided not to tell. He even used Philippians 3:12-14 to back up his madness. He told her how he needed her to surrender all of herself to him in order for him to be able to release the controversy in his mind. This way, the miraculous healing power of God would no longer be hindered by his concerns over her. It made Carmen's Puerto Rican flag wave like it was in the midst of a fierce wind storm, especially because she hadn't seen Donald crack open a Bible since their wedding day. Therefore, she stayed in their warden/prisoner type union for a few years after his medical profession had finally taken off. Shortly following the couples break-through in that area, they settled down in their newly-purchased home on the sandy beaches of Malibu, overlooking a breathtaking view of the ocean, symbolizing their so-called arrival.

Carmen had spent many a day and night, when Donald was supposedly working, continuing to devour God's Word, occasionally, lifting her eyes from 1 Corinthians 10:13 out of the Amplified Bible, her foundational Scripture for "the great escape" she had been standing in anticipation of. As she meditated on that verse, the Latina woman would stare out at those vast waters almost as if she thought she'd see a sign from the Lord on how He wanted her to approach Donald about her departing their marriage, which was not of Him. Prior to her in-depth immersion of the other verse located in Matthew that she was also rolling over in her mind since it was the one she'd been led to, presenting her with an allowance God would make for any of His children who were seeking Him for a divorce since it was among the list of things mentioned in His Word that He hates. While she studied those two Scriptures line upon line, The Holy Spirit began to be very specific in showing her things to come, mainly in regards to the affair Donald continued to deny he was having. The Lord would tell her to look in the hamper and she'd find Donald's dirty handkerchief's covered in lipstick shades unlike the ones she wore. Or He would tell her to go into her husband's home office and open his desk drawers and there she'd discover love letters to him from his mistress. Carmen was also instructed not to mention any of this to Donald until God permitted her to. She made sure she kept an ear inclined to her Heavenly Father, listening out for her next step. When that day finally came, the Latina woman obediently went to Donald, her moss green eyes gazing into his morose blue ones while she candidly told him that this wasn't how she imagined marriage to him to be. "I really thought this was the Lord's doing, but it wasn't" she said, a tear running down her cheek. "You could say whatever you want. I *know* you're cheating on me. As I told you before when you kept refuting this affair that you're having, that I am like this with God, Papi," Carmen crossed her fingers, signifying how close she was with the Lord. "Look at how crazy you are!" Donald said with sarcasm both in his voice and demeanor. "You're telling me *He* told you that I'm secretly fooling around on you?" She nodded. "I don't have anyone else! I certainly don't need *two* headaches!" he sneered and held up both his index and middle finger's like he was making a similar point to hers. "I'm His child also! Why hasn't He said anything to me?" Donald added and Carmen pulled three of his other woman's love letters out of her back pocket, along with one of his lipstick-stained hanky's, tossing them on their bed. "Those aren't mine!" she exclaimed. She said and did exactly what the Holy Spirit asked her to say and do. Carmen truly felt sorry for Donald when she saw the look of terror wash over his face, but she knew it had nothing at all to do with a feeling. "Thy will be done, not mine, Padre'," is what she quietly said to God at the time. With that, the only thing the broken man before her could do was peer down at his bare feet, indicating that what she spoke, and the evidence she challenged him with, was the truth. Observing her ex-husband- to-be for a brief moment, Carmen, by faith, grabbed hold of the peace that Jesus left her, cleared her throat and said, "Oh, by the way, I beg to differ with you..." She could sense her eyes filling with more tears. "Remember all those bad financial deals you made, much to your own surprise?" Donald looked up at her. "They were supposed to be guaranteed successes, right? And what about the... uh, fifty-something patient's... I believe that's what it was on the last count... Anyway, why do you think they left your practice to go elsewhere for their medical needs without any explanation?" Her ex-husband-to-be just proceeded to stare at her. "He's been speaking to you loud and clear! God's Word states that He resists the proud! The Father didn't bring those loses upon you. They happened because you crossed the spiritual line by continuing to pursue me while the Lord was telling us both that we were not his choice of husband and wife to each other. So... that's how He spoke to you. To *us*! The Scripture tells us that God will not be mocked. We will reap whatever we sow! Good or bad! Of course, the Lord will always love us all, in spite of ourselves. Romans 8: 37-39, Donald! He revealed your dirt to me, simply because I was on His side. I was finally seeking Him with a sincere heart!" Now, receiving some of God's much-needed grace, the Latina woman took a deep breath and gave his arm a pardoning squeeze as she handed him a piece of paper, under the leadership of the Holy Spirit as well, with all of the Scriptures she quoted to him. Carmen moved away from Donald to pack up some of her belongings. She made a final call from their bedroom when she was done. Tapping in the numbers from the business card she'd extracted from her wallet, the Latina woman was also led to place her ex-husband-to-be in the care of a Board-Certified Counselor, who happened to be a Christian. When she hung up, she passed him the information she'd attained, gave him a peck on the cheek as if to seal the forgiveness as well as the mercy she bestowed to him by the grace of God, and quietly exited the home that trepidation built. Grimacing at the sudden recollection of the awful screech that erupted from Donald's inner-most parts as he called, "I want my wife back!" repeatedly from his home office window as it was the only window, facing the side of the house she'd left, the Latina woman was immediately ushered out of her former years by a stirring in her spirit. She was sensing the displeasure of the Lord because she had lingered back there in thought for quite some time and at that moment, He brought Philippians 3:12-14 to her mind. There was no confusion like it was when Donald quoted that Scripture in order to convince her that their literally leaving everything, including family and friend's behind, was the will of God. Carmen knew too much of the truth by now and it was the Holy Spirit telling her to look to the bright future He still has for her. "Amen and amen," she quietly replied with a smile.

"Are we havin' fun over here?" Philip asked, completely bringing the Latina woman back to the here and now. He was shouting over the music. Alicia Keys' sultry voice was floating through the air. Even though he directed the question to both women, his eyes focused on Holly. "The coffee's really good," she said, speaking loudly as well due to the layers of sound. Carmen just smiled and reached for her cranberry juice. "Good. Oh, I almost forgot to tell you, Holly. Vanessa and Courtney said they'd be stopping by." "When?" she asked with a bit of surprise in her response. He looked at his watch. "They called about nine and it's close to ten now." "Here they come," Carmen said. Both Philip and Holly turned toward the door as well to find Vanessa and Courtney almost passing the bar. They appeared to be the ideal couple from the way they were holding on to each other. Arm in arm. You couldn't really tell where one ended and the other began. But, as Holly continued to observe them, the Lord began to reveal how what she was looking at on the outside, wasn't real. Sometimes seeing wasn't believing the hazel-eyed woman reminded herself, knowing that the Christian was to walk by faith and not by site, according to the Scriptures. Vanessa and Courtney's display of closeness was simply a rapidly fading façade as she suspected and now it has been confirmed by the Holy Spirit. Over the years she had discerned something not being right with the couples marriage, but whenever she'd ask Vanessa whether or not everything was okay, the full-figured women would shoot back, "I should be asking you that!" referring to Holly's association with Bradford at the time.

"Court, up here!" Philip called out from the top of the stairs. After spotting him, Vanessa grabbed on to her husband's arm even tighter and he parted the crowd, leading the way. "Hey, guys!" the full-figured woman said while sitting down in a chair next to Holly. "I need a drink!" She exhaled, trying to catch her breath from the stair climb. She reached into her black Prada tote bag, whipping out a compact mirror. The wind had mussed her chestnut-hued shoulder-length hair. "Hello, ladies...," Courtney said to Carmen and Holly then he turned to his wife, replying, "Yeah, so do I," referencing that he, too, needed a drink. Glancing back at the two other women, he cleared his throat and asked "Is that alright with both of you?" Holly saw the way her partners husband looked at her and her Latina friend with overflowing respect while he sat down beside Vanessa, awaiting their answer.

The hazel-eyed woman didn't want Courtney, Vanessa or anyone else seated around her to drink alcoholic beverages so she gave him a little smile, knowing her light was shining bright. "I'd rather you not," she admitted. "But I'm not anyone's final authority,' she added and lowered her gaze. Carmen agreed with her by nodding her head. Courtney cleared his throat again and averted his eyes for a second as well, before quietly saying, "Uh, I'd love a scotch on the rocks, *but* I'm driving so I'll just have one beer." He held up his index finger to Vanessa who twisted her lips. "*One* and that's it!" she demanded. "What am I...?" Philip asked with a grin. He threw up his hands and waited for the couple to acknowledge his presence. Courtney nor Vanessa didn't say anything to him at their arrival. "Ahhh, man. Come on!" Courtney said. He gave Philip a pat on the back while Vanessa threw him a sarcastic kiss as she dropped the pewter-toned looking glass back into her bag, picking up the drink menu afterwards. Philip shook his head at Courtney like he didn't know what the full-figured woman's reaction was about and her husband remained expressionless as if he wasn't a witness to what his wife had done. "Oooooo, I want a nice tall glass of white wine!" Vanessa exclaimed. Although the full-figured woman was speaking aloud, the silent conversation within her was jealous of the evident impact Holly seemed to have on Courtney. She saw the way he looked off when the hazel-eyed woman responded to his wanting a drink inquiry. Philip got the hint on not to pursue anything further concerning Courtney's spouse and said, "Let me find Darryl so he could get you those drinks." He proceeded to walk off toward the kitchen. "So how's everything going, Carmen? You look good," Vanessa said as her gaze left Philip for the menu once again. According to her, there were very few people who deserved her undivided attention. Huh, she should consider herself lucky, *excuse me*, I mean blessed hallelujah, to have me talking to her the full-figured woman thought. If it wasn't *solely* about her, she rarely ever cared. And she never bothered to pretend to be interested, telling herself she wasn't phony like that. Vanessa Benjamin felt secure in being a woman who never bit her tongue. Sometimes her bluntness caused her massive grief, but she wasn't about to change for anyone, was what she'd usually lean on in the midst of a trial. No, pun intended, she told herself as she believed assertiveness was an important tool for a lawyer and independent woman in general, especially when you were married to someone *without* a backbone. She dismissed the resentment she was feeling toward Holly, knowing it was something she had to try and get over before it became lethal. The full-figured woman was convinced that she didn't really want to hurt her hazel-eyed partner physically. She just wanted her to stay out of her personal affairs. Or was she lying to herself about not wanting to bring bodily harm to her beautiful colleague?

Carmen had just gotten finished glancing over at Holly, regarding Vanessa's not making eye contact with her. Choosing to ignore her offensive behavior, the Latina woman quickly brushed it off, finally answering, "All is well." She finished her cranberry juice. Nodding her head in a fashion that looked like she was hoping for more of a negative response, Vanessa set the menu down. She looked over at Holly and gave her a quick, conjured up smile. "Did you ladies eat?" Courtney asked. Holly returned a faint, but sincere grin, which she was able to find in her heart and shook her head no to her partners husband. He nodded and looked at the Latina woman. "So, how do you like living down in Georgia, Carmen?" he asked and started adjusting the tortoiseshell eyeglasses on his face. "It's nice, but a lot slower than what I'm used to. I guess it's what I need for now. I trust God." Courtney nodded his head in agreement. "A friend of mine is moving down there soon..." "How's your new book coming along?" Vanessa asked, cutting off her husband's sentence. Courtney glimpsed Holly, dropping his eyes down toward the bar afterward. "That's nice," Carmen said. She had responded to the back of Courtney's head before, turning toward his rude wife. "It's coming along better and faster than I could have ever imagined. The Lord seems to really be doing a quick work through me with this assignment," she said once she focused on Vanessa. The full-figured woman retorted by rolling her eyes. She didn't feel like hearing *anything* about Jesus! Getting a witness in her spirit to end the conversation at that, Carmen just leaned back in her seat and quietly thanked God for the Fruit of the Spirit, operating on her behalf, which contained self-control. Otherwise, she'd follow right on through with the picture the enemy so subtly shot into her mind of herself going across the table and wrapping her hands around Vanessa's neck.

Holly missed Carmen and Vanessa's transaction because she'd spotted Philip and Darryl approaching the table. "Ah! Some new additions," the waiter said, smiling. "What could I get you both?" He was peering at the couple. "What do you have on tap?" Courtney asked and cleared his throat. Did he really want something from the bar? he asked himself as he glimpsed over at Holly. She wasn't looking at him. Darryl thought for a second, giving him the beer selection: Coors, Coors Lite, Budweiser, Amstel Light and Miller." "Give me a Bud," Courtney said and put his concentration back on Darryl. "He *means* Coors Lite!" Vanessa said, redirecting the waiter while she placed her hand on her husband's stomach, not so discreetly letting him know he was gaining too much weight in that region of his body. Courtney kindly took his wife's hand in his in order to stay in a gentlemen's place. Snatching it away from him, Vanessa told Darryl to bring her a white wine. "Could I have another cranberry juice?" Carmen asked and gave the waiter her empty glass. "Sure. Would you like some more flavored coffee?" Darryl asked, looking at Holly. "Uh, huh?" she said. "Yes. I'll have another cup. Thanks." The hazel-eyed woman got caught noticing the way Courtney had melted in his seat. Quickly straightening his posture, he offered her a brief smile and began to adjust his eyeglasses again. "Where's Tracy? Is she coming? I haven't seen her in such a long time," Carmen said, interrupting the silence among them. "I asked her to come, but she said she had other plans. You know Tracy, her calendar's always booked," Vanessa said, chuckling. Holly drew her brows together. According to Tracy, she had no other obligations tonight. Karl Yearwood, the most recent man she'd inducted into her "Let's see where this goes" agenda, had canceled on her. "But, then again," she thought, her two partners had their own language sometimes.

Holly began to think intensely about Tracy and her steady stream of suitors. The hazel-eyed woman was remembering how her promiscuous partner once told her that she would never just settle into a relationship with a man. She said she had to keep on hunting until she found someone perfect for her. Tracy proceeded to say how she wanted someone who was out-going, generous, romantic, spontaneous, witty and believe it or not, loyal. Both she and Holly had to laugh a little about that last characteristic and with good cause because if the hazel-eyed woman wasn't mistaken, she believes that most of the men Tracy was dating, knew about the other in some way. Tracy asked Holly to try to understand her point about "not wasting her beauty" by using her good looks to get her the absolute best! And for the most part, she has gotten just about every man she'd desired even if it was only for one night. In continuing to reflect on Tracy, the hazel-eyed woman agreed only in part with her. Indeed, her colleague was very pretty. Tracy was average in stature and she wore her soft, fine hair short. She had big brown eyes and a small, pouty mouth, complete with a cute little figure, bringing Holly to the part she didn't agree with. Knowing that it was because of the Spirit of God living on the inside of her, along with His sufficient grace, that brought the hazel-eyed woman to her unchanging conclusion, of it not being right for one to give themselves over to numerous bedding partners. I know that marriage is supposed to be foremost before having intercourse of any kind, Holly reminded herself. Pondering that truth for a moment like she wanted it to sink deep within her heart, the hazel-eyed woman went back to her thoughts of Tracy. She had known her before Vanessa, but Tracy and Vanessa were friends already. She could remember it as though it were an hour ago. Tracy and

Holly were seated next to one another in the cafeteria at Columbia Law School, where they attended. The two young women started quietly talking, of course, about school and some other things like family and where they from over lunch. Tracy comes from an upper-middle class family who resides in Baltimore, Maryland. Her father's an Engineer, her mother's a Principal at the local elementary school and her younger sister, Michelle is studying to become an actress. Holly told her all about her family, too. She was raised by her mother, who, back then was part of house keeping team at Lenox Hill hospital. She's now retired. Holly also told her that she's biracial when Tracy commented on how fabulous her hair was. "My mother's Black and my father was White," the hazel-eyed woman answered, going on to share how her mother brought her up alone as she was their only child. Holly's father died of colon cancer when she was nine years old. "My mother, father and I were new Christian's at the time, especially me," she said, smiling at how young she was when she gave her life to the Lord. "However, the point of me bringing up our spiritual stance," the hazel-eyed woman said to Tracy back then. "Was had we known about all the power God had made available to us, and believed and received it, mom or me would have certainly laid hands on Holly's dad when we heard of his terminal diagnosis or would have made the attempt to raise my father from the dead once his spirit left his body." Completely ignoring the manifestation on Tracy's face during that time, the one saying "and she looks so normal," Holly almost giggled at how her partner didn't even try to mince her opinion of "just how outrageous she considered her to be" in her head, after Holly finished giving her some information on who she was. The hazel-eyed woman's memory of her and Tracy's original encounter became immediately clouded by thoughts of how she and her mother never had any further contact with her father's family once he was deceased. His relatives had a problem with mixing race. And because Holly looked more Black than White with the exception of her hair color and texture, they wrote her off as well. She could hear the words her White grandfather uttered the day of her daddy's funeral for a long time afterward. They'd echoed in her mind like sound would inside of an enormous empty space. Over and over. "You and that *Black* thing you call a little girl, had better get out of our lives after today. Your *kind* just doesn't understand the type of on-going quandary you've caused us. We've lost most of our dear friends because of this absurd marriage. I've told my son how I felt. *Now*, I'm going to tell you, missy!" Cynthia Reed picked up on the way he purposely turned the capital M in missy into a lowercase one, telling her in a very underhanded way that she was nothing to him. Low in every aspect just like he made the first letter of the name he called her without asking permission. Then he continued by saying, "The only thing the both of *you* could ever do for *us* is shine our shoes or clean our houses. You hear me? Lose our number and give us back the Reed family name that we so cherish. I'd give you any amount of money if you're in agreement. Deal? And, if you don't say yes, you won't get one red cent of David's inheritance."

Those were the jarring terms he'd presented to Holly's mother, who in return, left the spirit and began to walk in the flesh, forgetting all about her being a born-again Christian at that moment. Cynthia Reed spat in his wrinkled face and stormed out of the church, holding her crying child tightly by the hand as they both fled together. It wasn't until entering elementary school when Holly realized how prevalent this illness called racism was. Before that she'd thought it was something both she and her mother owned. Their secret. Holly had even shared a few of those disheartening tales with Tracy. Enjoying the hazel-eyed woman's company so much, once she got passed all the laying hands on and raising the dead junk, Tracy thought Vanessa would like her as well. But, the full-figured woman on the other hand, wasn't very cordial to the biracial young woman in the beginning. Holly thought she had done something wrong, but Tracy assured her that she did nothing to provoke Vanessa's cold attitude. "She's like that," Tracy said, waving her hand. She also told Holly that the full-figured woman was very insecure, especially in the company of another pretty woman. She was afraid that Courtney, who was her boyfriend at the time, would be attracted to Holly.

After a few days, Vanessa warmed up, as best she could, toward the hazel-eyed woman because Courtney didn't show any interest, although he was never around them long enough for anyone to truly make that assessment. Whatever the case was, the full-figured woman became more tolerable of Holly. The three women started spending a lot of time together without Courtney. He had become very involved in numerous activities at school, particularly the Black Allied Law Students Association. So during his absence, the ladies would take a break from their studies and go out to a few of the local eatery's, dining on fast food and carbonated beverages. Since Holly refused to step foot into a nightclub, bar or anything that came close to resembling the likes of them, the two other women reluctantly decided to accommodate her as going to such places had become their custom.

The hazel-eyed woman found out that Vanessa, too, came from an upper-middle class background once they exchanged personal data. Her family resides in Philadelphia, Pennsylvania. Her father is the President of a pharmaceutical company not too far from their home, her mother's a housewife and her older brother, Kevin is a dentist. Holly often wondered where she fit in among these two women. If she hadn't received that check from an anonymous person on the very day she graduated from high school in the exact amount needed for her to attend the University she believed God was directing her to, she would have probably wound up finding a full-time job once she'd finished the twelfth grade. Because, back then while in her late teens, she and her mother still did not know how to operate in faith, which is the positive response to what the Father has already done. However, this was not so apparent as they were in the wrong church for many years, keeping them ignorant of the Truth.

Mother and daughter, later learned, once they both became affiliated with World Changers Church New York, how according to His Word, God already completed everything in their lives. They also came to the knowledge almost at the same time, that not everyone who claimed to be called to one of the five-fold ministries was sent by God. This Truth was very clear when they realized how they basically knew nothing about Him or His Word because the spiritual leadership they'd spent many years sitting under, prior to Dr. Creflo Dollar becoming their pastor, was not teaching sound doctrine from the pulpit, placing them in the category of ones who went but were not sent. Thinking back, Holly found herself resting in the goodness of God. "He proved His great faithfulness by still giving her the provision that He'd established for her higher education regardless of her and her mother's Biblical malnutrition. That money didn't come by luck or chance, but by His grace! Holly mused.

Once she entered Columbia University, Barnard College, the hazel-eyed woman worked hard, doing everything she knew to do in the natural to keep her grade point average at a perfect 4.0 while God placed His super upon it, making her efforts supernatural. Holly remembered it all so vividly. Her school work seemed to be easy to her. She recalled the day she was handed her Bachelor of Arts Degree in Political Science, with Honors and later her Juris Doctorate.

"Excuse me, people. I have to go to the ladies room. Where is it?" Carmen asked, interrupting her best friend's reverie. The Latina woman stood up. "Downstairs," Courtney replied. He, too, pulled himself up from his chair. "Thanks. I'll be right back," Carmen said and walked swiftly toward the flight of steps, descending them. "Vee, I'll be right back, too. Let me go check up on Phil," Courtney said and followed Carmen downstairs. Vanessa didn't answer. It seemed to Holly that she couldn't wait to have a few minutes alone with her. The full-figured woman slid over closer to her partner. "Sooo, do you like it here?" she asked. Holly could smell the wine on her colleague's breath. She told her it was okay as it really was not her type of place then she added, "Philip's interesting, too." Vanessa laughed. "That's cute. You'll realize that the man's nothing but talk." She was still chuckling when she took a sip from her glass, eyeing the hazel-eyed woman over the rim. Where's she going with that comment? Holly asked herself. "I'm getting hungry. Let's order when they get back to the table," was what the hazel-eyed woman suggested, sensing in her spirit not to dig any deeper with Vanessa. "I'm actually starving," the full-figured woman said. She saw Carmen emerge at the top of the stairs. "Here comes *your* friend now," she added.

Holly began to smile at the Latina woman once she got closer to their table. "I feel so much better," Carmen said, sitting down. "Where are they?" Vanessa asked. She was looking around for Courtney and Philip. "They just came back inside. They went out there to smoke cigars. I could smell the smoke coming in from outside when I walked passed the bar for the restroom. "Go rescue your hubby from that suffocating atmosphere," she suggested. Taking another sip from her glass, the full-figured woman stood up, moving over to the top of the stairs. Her behind stuck out even further as she positioned herself to get Courtney's attention. Holly and Carmen used their time alone to quietly agree that they'd leave as soon as they were done with dinner. They both glanced at the menu while Vanessa was continuing to lean over the railing with her hands cupping the sides of her mouth, calling out to her husband a second time. He looked up at his wife from the bar and Holly began to observe the way Courtney took a sip of beer. He nodded at her and said something to Philip afterward. They both walked back up the stairs to the three women. "I'm sorry, puddin'," Courtney said. He was about to give Vanessa a kiss on the cheek until she pulled her face away. "Your breath stinks of nasty smoke," she said and took her seat. Courtney stared at her with a sad look on his face before he, too, sat down. "You ladies must be hungry? Has Darryl been takin' good care of you?" Philip asked, breaking the sudden quiet that seemed much too loud. His hands were resting on the back of Holly's chair. She nodded and turned her head to look up at him. Philip smiled as he looked down at her. Then, noticing Darryl, he waved him over. "Is everyone ready to order?" the waiter asked. They all nodded their heads simultaneously. Darryl gazed at Holly so she could start. "I'll have the grilled chicken salad with oil and vinegar, please." She smiled. "I'll have the lamb chops with mixed vegetables and rice. Thank you," Carmen said. "I'll *have* the veal with sautéed broccoli," Vanessa said. She closed the menu and leaned back in her chair and Philip said, "Court, you have to try the new shrimp dish on the menu! *Man,* it'll make you jump up and do the James Brown, brotha. Take my word." The restauranteur sat down across from Holly. Staring at her, he winked his eye, causing her to nervously lower hers. Father, please help me! she said to herself. "All right, I'll give it a shot," Courtney said, closing the menu. "Would you like something?" Darryl asked Philip who was busy smirking at the way Holly's face turned three different shades of crimson. He looked up at the waiter. "Uhhhh, yeah I'll have a club sandwich." Philip handed Darryl all of the menu's while Carmen kicked Holly under the table. It was her indirect way of telling her friend not to fall for his flirting. Holly didn't respond, but she knew the Latina woman was right.

They all sat there eating and enjoying each others company. All with the exception of Vanessa. She must have snapped into one of her moods. Everyone else had a conversation going on. Philip and Courtney were talking about some baseball game while Holly and Carmen still tried their best to catch up with each other without being discourteous. Yet, there was Vanessa, pulling away from everyone. Holly noticed the change in her disposition. It went from total arrogance specifically to anger so she decided to jump in. "How's your veal, Vee?" she asked. Vanessa shrugged, saying, "Good. *But,* they didn't have to be so heavy-handed with the bread crumbs." She cut her eyes over at Philip, who didn't hear or see her. He was caught up in whatever it was Courtney was saying.

Vanessa's mouth was sealed for the rest the evening. Thank you, Jesus! Holly thought quietly, believing that the full-figured woman's silence had some kind of purpose.

"The food was delicious," Carmen said to Philip, "What made you decide to go into the restaurant business?" She was discreetly removing a piece of lamb chop from in between her teeth with her tongue. Philip leaned back in his chair and swallowed the last bit of sandwich he'd been chewing. "Well, you could say it runs in the family." He cleared his throat. "My father owns two McDonald's franchises. And bein' a part of that for many years, he ran one and basically put me in charge of the other..." Philip began to smile and went on to say, "I started really diggin' the industry." "Which one's does your dad own?" Holly asked, quietly. The music was turned down, but she could still hear Whitney Houston's melodic voice drifting around the restaurant, dazzling all who listened. "They're both in Jersey. That's where I'm from." He could see the interest in her eyes. "Oh, where?" Holly asked. Philip grinned. "Hey, is this an interview or somethin'?" Vanessa let out a loud burst of laughter then gasped when she noticed that no one else thought it was *that* funny. "Excuse me," Holly said. She was so embarrassed and knew it showed. Noticing how flustered she had become, he felt bad. "I'm *only* playin'." He leaned up, rested his chin in the palms of his hands and stared into her disconcerted eyes. "I'll tell you everything you want to know if you'd have dinner with me tomorrow night." Everyone at the table was silent. And a few female heads turned in their direction from nearby tables. The quiet came as a surprise given the amount of activity going on. Carmen kicked Holly in the leg under the table again and she tried her best not to look over at her friend, but she couldn't help it. The Latina woman was making a face, signaling for Holly to be careful. Carmen knew Philip was an enemy-set up and Holly knew, too. The hazel-eyed woman gave her friend a reassuring smile in return. Glancing at Courtney, Holly saw how he was grinning at her while Vanessa just stared, waiting for her to answer. Then, looking back at Philip, the hazel-eyed woman said, "You certainly don't waste any time, do you?" He sat straight up and shook his head. "No, I don't. If I like what I see, and believe me, I do *like* what I see, no I don't waste time. Life's too short for game playin'. Soooo?" She took a minute before asking, "What time?" He started to beam at what he'd heard and said, "Let's say 7:00 p.m. Andrew gets into work at 6:30 p.m. He's the manager here on Saturday and Sunday nights." "All right," Holly replied, quietly and began fidgeting with her fingers. She could sense Carmen's displeasure at the choice she'd just made and more importantly she sensed the Holy Sprits displeasure. Looking at her watch, Vanessa said, "Courtney, let's get going since we have to get up early tomorrow." Her eyes made their way around the table and she added while gathering her things, "My parents are in town. They're coming to our house for brunch tomorrow." "I thought they were coming for dinner?" Courtney said. His eyes appeared puzzled behind the glasses. "No, brunch. Let's go!" the full-figured woman said, firmly. She gave her husband a hard, threatening stare. "Relax!" he replied and tried his best to glare back at her. Then shaking his head, Courtney stood up and asked, "Philip, what do we owe for the food, man?" as he dug deep into the pockets of his khaki pants, retrieving a brown leather wallet. "Don't worry about it. I'll have them put it on my tab. Me and the owner go way back. YouknowwhatI'msayin'" Philip teased with a smile. Courtney laughed a little and slapped palms with the darker-skinned man. "Good night, ladies. And it was good to see you again, Carmen. Don't stay away so long next time," Courtney added, giving her shoulder a squeeze. "I won't. It was good seeing you both as well. Enjoy your divine protection on your way home," Carmen said. The full-figured woman blocked the Latina woman's "Christianese" and just waved a quick good-bye to everyone. "Have fun tomorrow night, Holly," was the final word she slipped in. Her face said something else, the hazel-eyed woman thought. "Thanks. I'll see you on Monday," she replied. Philip and Carmen waved as the couple headed away from the table.

Vanessa and Courtney's exit from the restaurant was a direct contradiction to their entrance. They weren't touching and they had not uttered one word until they sat in the car. "My parents are coming for dinner tomorrow night," Vanessa confessed, nonchalantly. Courtney didn't respond right away. He didn't know what to expect from his wife. She always did junk like this. Sometimes it meant something and other times it was just Vanessa being Vanessa. He looked over at her and couldn't help but to shake his head in disgust. "Why did you want to leave the restaurant so quickly then?" he finally asked as he fastened his seat belt. "And why did you tell everyone that they were coming for *brunch*? There was no need to lie, *Vee*!" "I don't know!" she whined and glanced back at the restaurant door. She'd thought she'd heard someone calling her name. Choosing not to ask anymore questions, Courtney started up the car and drove away. "I guess I just wanted to get home so we could be alone," she said, pressing her head back against the headrest. Courtney took his eyes off of the road for a second. Placing his hand on her knee, he was feeling somewhat guilty for getting annoyed at her. "Are you okay, puddin'?" "Yes, Courtney!" she snapped. "I'm fine. Does there have to be something wrong for me to want to spend some time *alone* with my husband?" she added, forcing a smile on her face. "All right, all right. Lean back and relax," he said. Courtney slipped in a CD and she reclined her seat like he suggested, quickly falling asleep to the soothing sound of Luther Vandross.

Courtney and Vanessa have been together for ten years. They dated for four and were married for six. He fell head over heels for her after their first month of dating. She had him in the palm of her hand. And that's exactly where she wanted him. Vanessa found it difficult to be nice and thoroughly irresistible during that period. But she would have crawled from here to the Far East and back to get him to make her his *Mrs*. The S in her middle initial that she never acknowledged stood for Sadie after her grandmother, not stupid. She was nobody's dummy. Knowing that he would be a good husband and father, she gave herself permission to make that sacrifice. And although she couldn't manage to be completely sweet at times, on those occasions where her authentic self would rise up out of the box she so cleverly hid in, it seemed as though Courtney didn't love her any less. At first, he wasn't sure whether or not he was totally ready to marry her because while he did a superb job of covering up the doubts racing through his mind regarding her stubborn and selfish ways that would happen to seep out much more than she was aware, bothered him. But after finding out that she was pregnant, he knew it was the right thing to do. Unfortunately, after they married, she suffered a miscarriage which was extremely difficult for them both to handle. They've been trying to have a baby for six months now, and she's been pressuring him to come with her to be tested. She wanted to hurry up and get to the bottom of why it was taking so long for them to conceive. But, he refused, insisting that there was nothing wrong with either of *them* since she got pregnant once before.

"We better leave, too," Holly said and stood up. "What?! No dessert?!" Philip asked. Carmen and Holly peered at each other and shook their heads. "No. Maybe next time," Holly replied, speaking for the both of them. "Can we have the bill," said the hazel-eyed woman "Yes, how much was our dinner," Carmen said. Philip paused and made a face. "Why would I not charge Court and Vanessa and charge you two?" said the restaurant owner. Both Holly and Carmen smiled and thanked him. "So, you both are sure about dessert? Philip added with a smile, his eyes telling Holly and Carmen that he really wanted them to stay. They were positive. "Ladies, you don't know what you're missin'." Philip babbled on and on as he walked down the stairs first. The two friends smiled a little from behind at his persistence. Carmen waved good-bye to Darryl as they reached the bottom of the stairs in the crowded restaurant. The waiter grinned in return and then he pointed a patron in the direction of the restrooms. Stopping at the door, and turning toward both women, Philip said, "Well, I hope you ladies had a good time. It was nice meeting you, Carmen." He gave her hand a shake. Still holding it, Philip asked, "When do you go back to Georgia?" "Tomorrow morning," she said. "So soon?" he inquired. The Latina woman smiled and told him she'd been in town all week. "I was spending time with my family," she said with a smile. He nodded slowly and said, "Have a safe trip home." "Thank you," Carmen replied. After they released each others hands, he turned to face Holly. She was in the midst of waving good-bye to Darryl, as he headed over toward the bar. "I'll see you tomorrow at 7:00 p.m. sharp, Ms. Lady," Philip said once she looked at him. "7:00 p.m.?" she repeated, nodding her head in agreement. Holly could still feel the conviction in her spirit and she saw Carmen look away from the corner of her eye like it was God's way of confirming the truth she was covering up.

Both women thanked him for the dinner again and walked out.

As the two ladies were about to climb into a cab, Philip came running out of the restaurant, shouting. It looked like he was chasing a thief, Holly thought. "I forgot to get your telephone number and address!" is what he was exclaiming. When the two women stood still, telling the driver to wait, Philip slowed his steps and began walking toward them, his smooth stride back in place. Holly smiled at him and said she'd forgotten to give her information as well. The displeasure in her spirit heightened. Carmen got into the taxi, sliding over to leave room for her friend. "757 Park Avenue apartment 4-B, as in, um, bad boy," she said, giving him her I-know-you're-something-else smile and went on "between 76th and 77th Streets." Philip gave her a crooked grin in return, asking, "And your telephone number?" Holly recited it slowly, watching as he wrote it down on the back of one of his restaurant business cards. "Okay now we're straight," Philip said, smiling again. "Tomorrow at 7:00 p.m., okay?" he added. Holly nodded and joined the Latina woman in the cab. He bent down, waving good-bye to Carmen through the vehicles closed window. She tried to put on her best smile as she peered out at him.

When they pulled off, moving further and further away, Holly glanced back out of the rear window, seeing what had become a tiny male frame, heading back into "Phil's House".

Chapter Three

Carmen retied the string at the waist of her kelly green pajama shorts. She then sank her pale knee into the floral pillows on the window seat in Holly's room as she sat down. Knowing it was time to break the silence that escorted them all the way to the hazel-eyed woman's apartment, Carmen reached up, pulling her long, dark curly hair back into a ponytail. Holly was leaning on her elbows across her king-size bed clad in a white cotton nightgown, her legs hung off the edge. "I know...." They both began to speak the same two words at the exact time. "Oh, I'm sorry. Go ahead," the hazel-eyed woman insisted. Without hesitating, Carmen replied, "Okay," and unfolded her leg in order to position herself so that she would be sitting straight. "You know we don't have to pray about whether or not it was a good idea for you to say yes to Philip's dinner invitation for tomorrow night, right? I don't know about you, but the Lord answered without me having to ask." Holly lowered her eyes, sat up, jerking herself forward. She buried her face in her hands. "Yes, I do know!" is what she finally answered. Her words were coherent but muffled because of the way her mouth was pressing into her palms. "Carmen, I need help!" Holly admitted. She brought her hands down from her face. The Latina woman nodded and said, "Sounds like a job for El Shaddai! Let's go to the throne." She reached for Holly's hands. The two women closed their eyes. "Abba Father," Carmen began to pray. "We know that you are never surprised by anything *or* anyone and we also know that You have *all* the answers because you are God. Your daughter's come boldly before You, in the name of Jesus, like You said we could. We are asking You for direction regarding Philip Williams. Is he part of *Your* will for Holly's life?" Carmen squeezed the hazel-eyed woman's hands so she would pick up where she left off. "Uh, yes, Lord. I don't want to be out of Your perfect will for me ever again. I'm asking you to give me a quick answer, concerning Philip… and our going out tomorrow night, in Jesus' Almighty name. Amen and Amen." Carmen said a hearty amen as well and let go of her friend's hands. Gazing intensely into the Latina woman's eyes, Holly said, "I *know* I shouldn't be going out with him!" She almost made that statement like it was the first time the question of whether or not she were to have any kind of involvement with Philip arose. "Seems like you got the revelation to me," Carmen answered. The hazel-eyed woman forgot to laugh at her friend's humorous way of saying that what she blurted out about how she shouldn't be going out with Philip, was obvious and Holly also failed to mention how the Holy Spirit had already told her as well that the gorgeous restaurateur was not sent by Him the very moment he asked her out. Actually, it was known from the very first moment she'd ever seen Philip, Holly mused. Glancing over at the phone on her nightstand, she asked Carmen, "Do you think he's still at work?" The Latina woman looked at the clock that was sitting on the same table. "I'm sure he is," she replied. "You know what?" Holly quickly spoke as her eyes began to rest on the Bible next to the clock. "I'll let him know when he calls me." Pausing swiftly, Carmen then closed her mouth. The Holy Spirit instantly showed her that her friend was not looking for her input. Holly stood up. "Come into the kitchen. I'll make you a cup of coffee," was what she said.

The hazel-eyed woman poured the French vanilla-flavored grounds along with some water into the designated areas of the coffee maker, turned it on and sat down at the table. Carmen was taking the cups and saucers out of the cabinet, placing them on the counter. During this moment of silence, the Latina woman was also in the midst of listening for the Lord. She didn't want to say anything other than what He wanted her to say. "You said You would be with my mouth and teach me what to say," Carmen muttered under her breath to God. "Did you say something?" Holly asked, her head was tilted to the side in an effort to see her friends face. The Latina woman had her back to her and it was in that instant when she knew exactly what she was to say. Turning toward Holly, Carmen smiled a bit and began to speak. "Are you completely sure you don't want to let Philip know tonight that you won't be having dinner with him tomorrow?" She noticed a look of frustration forming on Holly's face. "Wait! Let me finish," Carmen interjected before her friend could come out with something birthed from her flesh. Reluctantly, the hazel-eyed woman nodded. "You know the story in Luke 16 about the beggar named Lazarus?" Carmen asked and waited for her friend to remember the account she was referring to. The Latina woman settled for Holly's half-hearted shrug of the shoulders and went on. "The verses state that he was covered in soars and dogs would come and lick them..." "I'm sorry, but I really don't know where you're going with this," the hazel-eyed woman interrupted. She was wearing a full face of irritability at this point. Carmen smiled again, bigger this time. Responding in sheer sweetness, the Latina woman said, "Just listen. I trust the Lord that you will get it... Dogs are known to have healing in their saliva, correct?" Pausing Holly said, "Yeah." "Well, this is what Pastor Bill Winston got from that parable. He started out by mentioning the healing contained in dog's saliva then he said "when someone is hurting and are in need of healing, they may attract dogs... People who don't mean them any good." Holly tried not to make a face, but she did. "What does that have to do with Philip?" she asked, squinting from the perplexity in her mind. Carmen was led to wait. She saw the way her friend soon relaxed as the deception she'd been so steeped in was swallowed up by the truth. Holly's eyes got really wide and she lowered her head, saying in a very soft-spoken way, "It would be like it was with Bradford." The Latina woman joined her friend at the table, embracing her. Carmen felt the weight of Holly's head fall upon her shoulder. It became heavier and heavier the harder she cried. "All is well beautiful, chica," the Latina woman whispered and proceeded to worship God in song while her friend's outpour of tears streamed down the arm of the shoulder her head was resting on. "Brand new mercies… Brand new mercies… every morning for me. Brand new mercies O, His mercies are new brand new… every morning for me. Brand new mercies. Brand new mercies every morning for me…" The more Carmen sang, the more Holly wept. The Latina woman believed she heard the Holy Spirit speaking on the inside of her. He was making an exchange, replacing Holly's heart of stone with one made of flesh. It was like He was taking the hazel-eyed woman's tears of pain and giving her greater delight in return. Carmen heard the Scripture "Weeping may endure for a night, But joy comes in the morning," flooding her spirit. Confirmation for what she'd only thought she had perceived, the Latina woman mused. A tear rolled down her own cheek. She started to sing a little louder, rejoicing along with every God-breathed lyric that flowed from her mouth. "Brand new mercies…" Even though Holly was still crying, Carmen was completely saturated in peace. "Father, thank you!" The Latina woman shouted from the heavy place in her heart and once it quieted down, from her release, she knew that everything was all right.

Unbeknownst to both women, they had fallen asleep. Still latching onto each other as their eyes opened, nearly ten minutes later, Holly lifted her head from Carmen's shoulder and the Latina woman brought her arm from around her friend's back. They looked at one another, still surprised at how and when they could have possibly dozed off like that. "It was as if the Lord had a deep sleep come on us…," Carmen said. Holly didn't say anything directly in response to their divine nap other than, "The anointing was very, very strong… Something changed. Can't tell you what, but something definitely changed." "Praise God! That's wonderful!" Carmen replied, knowing that God was further confirming His Word. "I hope so," Holly said and stood up from the table. She was running her fingers through the part of her hair that had been pressed against Carmen's shoulder while she walked over to the coffee maker, turning it off. "You *hope* so?" the Latina woman asked. "Everything God does is good... Do you need me to give you some Scriptures to back that up?" she added. Holly paused for a second before removing her finger from the coffee maker's on/off switch. She turned toward Carmen. "No, I'm familiar with a lot of them," she said. "That doesn't seem good enough," the Latina woman replied. Holly looked her in the eyes and Carmen said, "I'm familiar with a lot of the people who purchase my books. I could even tell you verbatim some of the things they've said about the characters or the characters situations, but that doesn't mean I know them. You must believe that the God of the Bible really exist and then you must become very intimate with Him for yourself. He wants to go deep with His children. This is not a worldly hope that we Christians have, where we're hoping and a wishing that something good is going to happen to us or for us with the chance that it may not. No, Bible hope, which is hope in the risen Lord and Savior, Jesus, is a positive expectation of good always happening regardless of how hopeless looking a circumstance may seem. The Lord will never fail us, Holly. *But*, we, on the other hand, may fail to believe Him, causing us to be disobedient and veer from the truth. That's why someone with nothing but "lip service" who claims they believed, winds up going back to the world." Carmen was peering right back into Holly's eyes. Blinking and averting her gaze, the hazel-eyed woman nodded and asked, "Do you still want coffee?" Carmen wasn't at all satisfied with her friend's answer, but she was led to let it go. "Sure... I'd love a cup," was what she said.

The two women sat at the kitchen table, drinking their coffee in another round of silence. Holly finished hers first. She noticed that Carmen was nearly done as well. "Would you like some more?" she asked her. "No. I'm fine, thanks." Nodding, the hazel-eyed woman said, "So tell me what's going on with you and... I'm sorry... what's his name... again?" Carmen smiled and said, "Trust me. It's not important. Can't be because I keep forgetting it, too." Grinning back, Holly asked, "Well, did he finally agree to attend church with you?"

The Latina woman shook her head no. "Not mentioning him to you since he and I became a "couple" speaks loud. He's still declining to come with me to World Changers Marietta just like he did while we were "friends". I've already told you about his little *modus operandi*. He continues to remind me, as if I have some kind of a mental challenge, that he gets his Bible teaching straight from the "spirit" You should hear some of the foolishness he calls revelation." Holly laughed some and started to bring her coffee cup up to her mouth until she remembered that it was empty. "And, not only that, *my* Bible tells believer's in Hebrews 10:25 'not to forsake the assembling of ourselves together, as is the manner of some...' it should say So and So right there," Carmen added. Laughing a little at her reply, she continued, "Yet, God has given me tremendous insight during the time I've spent with... uh, what's his name... Anyway, He told me last week while I was at my mom's, "To be in love is to be in God." The two women stared at one another, allowing that reality to go deep within. "God is love," Carmen said, quietly. "So, if God didn't bring the couple together..." "It's not love," Holly chimed in, finishing up the Latina woman's sentence. "That's right," Carmen said. Holly nodded and said an almost inaudible amen. "The Lord also revealed to me how So and So, who is a screenplay writer, as I mentioned to you before, only seemed to be interested in me when he was feeling lonely, needed my help with the execution of a scene or was hungry for some authentic Spanish-styled chicken and rice and with God's encouragement and grace, I am no longer willing to be at his disposal unless he steps up correctly." Holly was just about to nod her head in agreement until she saw a look of substantiation wash over Carmen's face. "What is it?" the hazel-eyed woman asked. "For the Holy Spirit to say 'To be in love is to be in God'... He's telling me that So and So, is not in Him." Holly watched as her best friend stood up from the table, said excuse me and marched down the hall for the guest room, mumbling something about forget about face-to-face and how she was going to end this thing right now. The hazel-eyed woman sat still until she heard the door slam close behind Carmen. Rising from the table, Holly placed the cups and saucers into the dishwasher and as she headed down the hall toward her bedroom, the phone on her nightstand began to ring. She hurried inside, answering. "Hello!" "Holly!" "Yes. Who is this?" she asked. "Philip!" He was speaking loudly. "I know it's late, but I just wanted to make sure you both got in safely." Hearing music playing in the background, she knew he was still at work. "Yes, we're fine." She sat down on the side of the bed. It's not a good idea for us to go out with each other. I just rededicated myself to the Lord and I'm waiting for Him to have me appear to the man He's chosen for me; ran through her head, but it never made it out of her mouth. "Good. So, I'll see you tomorrow night," he said. She stuttered, "Okay. Good night, Philip." "Good night and say good night to Carmen for me, too." "I, uh will. Bye!" "Bye!" Holly held the telephone receiver to her mouth for a second then she hung it up. She heard Carmen open the guest room door. "Who was that?" Carmen asked from the other room. "Philip. He wanted to make sure we got in safe." "Oh, that was nice. Did you tell him that you're not going out with him?" Holly took a deep breath, pulling herself to her feet. She walked out of her bedroom and stood in the doorway of the room Carmen was in. "No, I didn't tell him," she said, her voice low. Carmen sat up in the bed. "Why not? Girl, don't waste your time. That man does not look like he's planning to be converted anytime soon." The Latina woman held her hands up. "I know we shouldn't get into this again. We prayed…" "And I got my answer," Holly said. The two friends just stared at each other. "I really feel like a hypocrite," Carmen said. The hazel-eyed woman nodded her head a little. "God has us in the palm of his hand," Holly replied. She smiled a little at her best friend and walked back into her bedroom, closing the door.

Chapter Four

The morning sun streamed through the guest room windows. Holly approached the doorway of the cozy little space, which resembled something out of a Laura Ashley home-furnishing store, and peered at the back of her friend's curly locks. "Are you all packed and ready?" The Latina woman turned to face Holly who was dressed in denim boot cut overalls with a white lycra T-shirt underneath. They smiled at one another. Carmen was wearing a short-sleeved denim shirt with black leggings. "Yep. Looks like I have everything." She zipped up her Louis Vuitton suitcase, hoisted it from the queen-size canopy bed and followed her friend back down the hallway. Holly stepped into the kitchen to make a quick phone call. She asked Peter to hail her good friend a cab. After the kind doorman agreed, she thanked him and hung up.

"It was like old times, having you here," Holly said as they boarded the elevator. "I know, I had a wonderful time. Next time it won't be a year before I come back home." "*Okay,* and you know I won't let you forget." Stepping off the elevator, Holly peered around the regal lobby. She liked calling this place home. The way everything was decorated still amazed her after the three years of living there. Secretly, that's where she'd gotten quite a few of her decorating ideas.

Realizing again at that moment that the vestibule of her beloved building was higher in rank then most of the places she'd lived in as a child, Holly felt herself choking up. She could remember being afraid to walk down such streets as Park Avenue, 5th Avenue and Sutton Place as a youngster. The fear of getting arrested or yelled at simply for being poor often entered her mind when she had to meet her mother for money sometimes so that she'd be able to start dinner before the older woman got home. All those years of cooking never stuck, she mused. Sighing, she opened the door and gestured for Carmen to exit first. The Latina woman shaded her eyes with ebony Donna Karan sunglasses as she walked out of the fourteen-story edifice, turning to face her friend once they were both outside. "Well, here we are." Carmen said. Holly nodded in agreement as she looked over at Peter, knowing that he'd have a cab waiting. The two women headed toward the tall, White, slim uniformed man. Holly thanked him and reached into the small pocket across the chest of the overalls she was wearing to retrieve her money. "You're welcome, Ms. Reed. It was my pleasure." Peter opened the cab door and put the suitcase in the trunk. After he finished, Holly extended her hand. "Here's a little something for you." She was trying to give him a twenty-dollar bill. Peter smiled. "Not necessary," he said, holding up his hands. *"Come on, Peter,"* Holly said. She and the doorman did a little makeshift dance as she tried to stick the money into one of his pockets, finally convincing him. Peter tipped his hat to both women and walked back to the building.

"All right, give me a hug, Ms. Lopez," Holly said, extending her arms. The two women embraced tightly, rocking. They said a quick prayer for the Latina woman to have safe travels. Carmen was the first to pull away. She leaned back and looked at her friend. "When are you coming down to Marietta?" Holly started grinning. "I can't come now. You're in the middle of your book. I don't want to interrupt your fourth bestseller in the making." "Girl, please. This brain never stops conjuring up new ideas. Glory be to God! You won't be interrupting my flow." Holly took a second before she agreed. "Okay, *Lets see.* I'll have some time *in* a few months." "September?" Carmen asked. She held up her hand to the cab driver, indicating that she was coming. Holly nodded. "Okay, I'm holding you to it." "Fine. Call me when you get home." Nodding, Carmen motioned for her friend to hug her again. "I love you," she said. "I love you, too." The Latina woman made a face that said I don't want to preach but. "I know, I know..." is what the hazel-eyed woman said. She knew Carmen was referring to Philip.

Holly's housekeeper, Helen wasn't expected until tomorrow so she decided it would be a good idea to straighten up her apartment. She entered the building and saw that Peter was engaged in a conversation with a young, White woman, who appeared to be about her age. She was wearing jeans, a linen blazer, beige nubuck mules, her pin-straight brunette hair was pulled back into a ponytail and she was carrying the same Prada bag as Vanessa's, only hers was taupe. Holly waved at Peter as she pressed for the elevator and when the doorman smiled, in acknowledgment to her, the White woman turned toward her as well. Holly couldn't help to notice that there was something familiar about her. But what? Was it the sound of her high-pitched voice? Her gaze? She didn't know for sure. Having met so many people in her profession, the woman probably reminded her of an old client or someone who'd presently wanted her representation. Maybe it would come to her, she thought. As the elevator doors were closing, Holly could hear the doorman tell the woman how the building policy stipulated that no one was allowed to move in after nine in the evening on any day of the week, but they'd make an exception, just this once. Holly had known that there were a lot of available apartments. Many of the older residents had moved out of the city in search of living conditions in warmer year-around climates.

Peering around the immaculate apartment with her hands resting on her hips, Holly told herself that Helen may think she's getting fired when she sees how spotless this place is. She'd have to call the older woman and give her the day off with pay.

The telephone rang.

"Hey, girl. Hear you're going out with Philip Williams tonight even though he's not "saved"," said the familiar-mocking voice on the other end of the phone. "Tracy?" "Yeah, it's me. Who else would be calling to harass you like this and criticize you for being a hypocrite?" Holly laughed a little. "Hi! We missed you last night. Carmen was looking forward to seeing you, but Vanessa told us you had other plans." The hazel-eyed attorney spoke with ease. She knew her going out with Philip wasn't going to lead to anything. One date or night out rather, and that would be it, she told herself. "Yeah, Karl and I went to his parents house for dinner. He changed his mind real quick about not seeing me when I told him it was quite all right. I told him I was on my way out the door to meet up with one of my *other* men." Tracy made herself laugh. "Puleaze! Like I have time to wait on him. He's still married anyway." "Yes, he is," Holly said quietly. She knew that she really had no right to correct anyone when she was going down the same road they were on. Holly took a deep breath and she heard Tracy clear her throat. "Let him stay married, too as far as I'm concerned. Knowing my fickle butt, I'll probably be over him in another week or two any ole way!" She lied and chuckled some more. Tracy cleared her throat and thought how she would do anything to make Karl Yearwood love her the way she loved him. She hoped he'd get tired of knowing he wasn't the only man in her dating pool and ask her to marry him once he was divorced. She wanted so badly to be his wife and have his children. Why was it so hard to nab the one you really wanted? It was so difficult for her to gage Karl's feelings for her. He was always so "sometimey" and she didn't have the courage to ask him his thoughts on the two of them. What if he told her *she* wasn't the one? "You know how easily I get bored," she said in keeping with the rest of her untruth. "Then onto some other strong, tantalizing activity I go." Tracy appeared to be a master at going on and on about how she was able to do without Karl. But, inside she hurt like a rotting tooth, wishing she'd figure out a way to influence herself that this was the truth. Fact was scary when you didn't want anyone else *but* the man who seemed as though he could care less about where it was you went and how you got there. However, her persistence would soon pay off. She had hope. Karl would be all hers one of these days, she thought especially since he revealed how he didn't want her to go out with any other man by changing his mind last night. "So where are you guys going tonight?" Tracy asked, holding in a sigh. "I don't know." Holly sat down on the edge of the bed. "When did you speak to Vee? She *is* the one who told you about last night, right?" "Uh-huh. I spoke to her at about nine o'clock this morning." "That's right. She had to get up early to prepare brunch for her parents'." "No. Not brunch. They're coming over for dinner," Tracy said. "Oh, I thought she said..." Holly started to say that Vanessa clearly said they were coming over for brunch. But she realized it wasn't a big deal. Plans do change, she thought. "Philip seems like a real sweetie. I met him once at Vanessa and Courtney's house. He was a real gentleman. Courteous. And wasn't too bad on the eyes, I might add. Wish I could trade eyelashes with him," Tracy said, chuckling. "This way I could stop paying Duane Reades bills on my purchases of eyelashes alone. Fake lashes cost." Holly smiled and shook her head. "Yeah, he is cute, but his not being a Christian is definitely a problem for me," Holly said. "Girl, just take it one day at a time. Who knows maybe he's thinking about giving his life to Jesus," Tracy said. Holly was surprised at her unsaved partners response. Had she not known better, the hazel-eyed woman would have taken that as a sign. "You know I will." "All right, let me let you go." "What are you doing tonight?" Holly asked with a smile. "I might go out with boring John. He's been bugging me all week, doing that 'sweetie, why you doin' me like this?' banter. Oooo, it makes my skin crawl! So, I'll grit my teeth and join him for something that will make me fall asleep." Holly shook her head, trying not to pass judgment. "Okay, well I guess I'll fill you in on Monday about my little adventure with Philip." "You better or else," Tracy teased. "All right, talk to you later." Holly looked at the clock on her nightstand after they'd hung up. It was 12:00 p.m. and her stomach was growling. She decided to make herself a sandwich and take a nap afterward. She wanted to be fully alert with Philip Williams tonight. Walking into her stainless steel and white kitchen, the fact that she was going on a date dominated her. She stood there staring into the refrigerator thinking about her last relationship, which turned out to be a complete disaster. Bradford Anderson, big-time movie producer. He had cheated on her many times, none of which she had any proof of. The only true resource she'd depended on was her female intuition. Holly stood still for a moment, knowing that the Lord had warned her many times. Bradford wasn't right for her. Still she backslid only for Carmen to bust him. "What a blessing", Holly said out loud. Part of her wanted to remain blind to what she'd known to be true. This way she wouldn't be alone because there was no staying with someone who needed to have more than one woman. Holly shook her head at how feeble she used to be and at her convictions regarding Bradford. He never loved her. Make a movie about the look on your face when you ran into Carmen. The Latina woman said "He looked terrified." Holly shook her head again. She was so disappointed with herself. Having gone out with him a few more times after that, she wondered how she could have been so naive. So desperate. She took the sandwich meat and mustard out, placing them on the counter. This time she wouldn't be so dumb and she knew it was time to leave her past behind her. According to the Word of God, she was a new creation. Old things have passed away. She had no intention of settling anymore, she thought as she asked herself what this was she was doing with Philip?

After finishing her lunch, she stood up from the table and walked back into her bedroom for her nap. Holly reached for her Bible to read a little before lying down and the telephone rang again. "Babygirl." "Hi, Mom." "Did Carmen leave?" "Uh-huh, she had an eleven-thirty flight. Is everything okay with you?" "Everything's fine. Praise the Lord for that! I was just callin' to say hello. And to tell you that the furniture finally came." "Oh, good. Are you happy with it?" "Yeah, I love it. Can't believe it. You was right, baby. Quality furniture *does* make a difference even though I hated gettin' rid of my old things. They was like havin' your daddy 'round all the time," Cynthia said, sighing. "But, like you said, this is my new beginnin'

The Lawd sho is doin' a new thing and it's 'bout time that I receive that since yo' daddy's been gone all these years, " The older woman laughed. "I never imagined bein' able to call such a high-class place home before. You made your mama happy. Glory be to God! Wait 'til my friends see these *fine, fine* thangs." Her mother's voice was overwhelmed with splendor. Holly smiled. This was what it was all about, she reminded herself. She loved to take care of her mother. "So, what were you doin', baby?" Cynthia Reed asked, yawning. "I was just about to take a nap." Holly yawned too. "Why you ain't sick, are you?" Her mother's tone was becoming hysterical, getting ready to rebuke whatever it was trying to come on her child. "No, Mom. I'm fine. I have an appointment tonight." Holly's eyes enlarged. She knew a long line of questioning would soon follow. "Oh yeah?" said the older woman, pausing. "Do I know him? Better yet. Do he know the Lawd?" Now Holly would never get off the phone. "No, he's not saved. Um, I just met him yesterday morning." "What! He's not? *Where did you meet him?*" "At my office. No, I didn't pick him up on the street." "Thank goodness 'cause you remember what happened to Wanda Wilson's daughter, Taylor when she went out with that crazy fool she'd only knowed for a hot second? You need to start comin' back to church. Meet yo'self somebody there. The mens are good looking, babygirl and they love the Lawd." "Yes, mom. I know. I'll go with you next Sunday." "Praise God! Well, what was he doin' at your job? He ain't in some kinda trouble. Is he?" *"Noooo,* he's not. He happens to be a friend of Courtney's." Cynthia sucked her teeth. "Courtney okay, but you need yo'self a Godly man." "I know, mom. That's what I want," Holly said. "I know you do, sweetie. How's Vanessa and Courtney doin'?" "They're both fine." "They still workin' on that baby?" "Yes, they are." "Well tell them not to worry theyselves. I still have them on my prayer list," her mother said. "So, tell me 'bout your 'pointment," Cynthia said, changing the subject back to their former topic. "What's his name?" "Philip Williams." "Where's he from?" "Jersey." "Do he live there now?" "No, he lives here in the city." "Where?" "I don't know yet, mom. I guess I'll find all of that out tonight." I'll have your report typed and on your desk first thing tomorrow morning, Holly said to herself. "You goin' out wit him *and* you don't even know where he lives?" "That's correct. The only thing I know is that he's a restaurant owner." "The owner, huh? *Wait* a minute! Don't try throwin' me off. You don't knowd where he lives?" "No. I'm not planning to meet with him anymore after tonight." She could hear her mother let out a sigh of relief. "Well, what has Vanessa and Courtney said 'bout him? I don't like the idea of you goin' out wit him one time. Have you prayed 'bout it?" Holly nodded to herself, knowing the Father had already given her an answer. "Yes, I did. The Lord told me not to go out with him." "And you're still goin'?" Cynthia said. "Chile, you know you goin' against the Lawd by still goin'. You have to trust in Him. Knowd that He knows what's best for you." Holly held her head down. She knew there was no condemnation in Christ Jesus, according to the Word of God. "I know He only wants the best for me, momma. I will not be meeting Philip after tonight like I told you," the younger woman said. "I still don't like how you went against the Lawd like that! You need to ask him for His forgiveness. No, that's okay. I knowd you knowd you's already forgiven It's 'bout havin' a personal relationship with Jesus, babygirl. When you have that, you will not be moved. He'll keep you in all your ways. Start talkin' to Him. Spend time wit Him. He loves you so much." Holly lowered her head again. "I know. I will." The younger woman heard her mother praying quietly in tongues. "I'm gonna go, babygirl. Be careful. I mean mindful." "Of course, I'll be mindful." "What time is he pickin' you up?" "7:00 p.m." "Okay, then, speak to you tomorrow. Oh wait! Where did you say you was goin' again?" *"Mom, I never said."* "I'm sorry, baby." her mother said, her voice soft, not condemning. She believed her daughter would never see Philip again after tonight. "Well, where you goin'?" she added again quickly. "I honestly don't know." "Okay, but *please* be mindful, babygirl. I'll let you go, sweetie. I love you." "I love you, too. *And* I promise to be mindful," Holly said warmly. She could picture her mother's face through the phone as they hung up. Cynthia Reed was not happy.

Holly fell back across the bed and inhaled deeply. She peered up at the ceiling, knowing that the Lord wasn't pleased with her either.

Chapter Five

Smoothing down the fitted jacket of the blue two-piece outfit, Holly gazed at herself several times from the front and then from the back in the full-length mirror once she was dressed. She wondered if the suit she was wearing made her one-hundred and twenty-five pounds appear heavy. She shook her head no. If it did there was nothing she could do. What you see is what you get, she told herself. Philip wasn't for her anyway. When she looked at her watch, she realized that he should be arriving any minute. Then it dawned on her that Carmen hadn't called yet, and it was ten to seven. She decided to give her a ring, thinking that her friend had probably forgotten to call her. As she reached for the receiver, the buzzer sounded. There he is. First she smiled to herself. He was on time. She quickly removed the grin from her lips. "He's not for me," she told herself aloud. Holly decided to call Carmen after she let him in. "Yes, Peter?" "Ms. Reed, there's a Mr. Williams here to see you." The doorman sounded as though he was confirming Philip's name with him as he spoke. "Yes, thank you. I'm expecting him. Please send him up." She ran to the mirror to look at herself again after she'd hung up. Where were her earrings? Holly sighed and hurried over to her dresser, sifting through the Scully & Scully jewelry box. It, sat atop of the mahogany antique. She took out her diamond studs and a pair of pearls. Not knowing which would compliment the ensemble she was wearing more, she held one of each to her ears, gazing back and forth at them. When the doorbell rang, she quickly chose the diamonds. Holly slipped them into her earlobes as she walked toward the front of the apartment. "I'll be right there!" she exclaimed and took a quick peek of herself in the foyer mirror. "Why do I care so much," Holly said to her reflection. She knew she needed more of God's Word. Holly heard a faint "okay" permeate the door just before she opened it. "Hi, Philip." A hint of his cologne found its way up into her nostrils. "Come inside." "How you doin'," he said and strolled in. Philip handed her a dozen of the most beautiful pale-pink roses. They had the longest stems she'd ever seen. Holly thanked him and closed the door. "They're breath-taking." She inhaled a whiff of the lovely bouquet, and he looked her up and down in his usual analytical way. "You look radiant and you smell good, too," Philip said softly. Radiant? She wondered if he consulted with *Webster* before leaving his apartment this evening. He didn't look like the radiant word-using kind of man. Let me behave myself, she told herself. So she thanked him for his compliment. "You have a very nice place here, Holly." "You're just full of nice things to say," she said, smiling. "Please have a seat." Holly motioned toward the living room. "I'll be right back. I need to get a vase." "Sure," he replied. After she had gone, Philip stood in the foyer. He would utilize this time to get a better look at the place. In front of him was a long, dark hallway, leading to her bedroom and bathroom, he'd imagined. To the right was the dining room, large and opulently designed. It had a long mahogany table with six high-back chairs. The seats were covered with expensive fabric. Adjacent to the fine room was the kitchen -- that's where Holly was. From where he stood it was impossible to see inside, but he could hear her going through the cabinets. On the left side of the apartment was the living room. Before entering, Philip peered down at the beautifully polished hardwood floors in the foyer. He then looked at the ivory settee that was next to an antique mahogany end table. It, had an oriental ginger jar sitting on it. He eyed the walls of the impressive entry way. Suspended directly above the stately settee was a huge still-life painting with colors so vibrant it felt as though he'd be able to reach up and take a piece of fruit from the superb arrangement. Philip almost laughed out loud at how tempted he was to do so as he shifted his attention over to the other wall, directly across from the painting. Hanging there was a large brass-framed mirror. He stood there for a moment, admiring his own reflection. After sweeping his fingers through his short mane of curls, every single one of them bouncing back in place, Philip headed into the dimly-lit living room. Inside of this gargantuan room, he saw that she had two ivory and taupe striped sofas with big rolled arms. They, too, had mahogany end tables next to them. On the one closet to the door, there were pictures in gold frames of her family and friends and a Tiffany lamp sat on the other. Gazing over at the mantle, which had a working fire place, he saw that on it sat a huge clock with a golden pendulum, swaying back and forth. The statuesque time piece had crystal candlesticks along its sides, standing straight and still like the guards in front of Buckingham Palace. He then noticed that the walls in this spectacular space had even grander artwork gracing its walls. A beautiful painting of a landscape hung on the wall above the impressive baby grand piano, which was nestled in the corner of the room, near the window. The piano was so shiny he could see the reflection of the painting in it from the fading sunlight trickling in through an opening in the drapes. Philip's eyes were lost in the portrait by *Picabia Le Haneau*. He'd remember seeing it at Christies. Or was it Sotheby's? He'd gone to both places, searching for an anniversary gift for his parents last year. That thing cost $21,000 -- *that* he was certain of as he turned to gaze at something else. Holly sure didn't need a man to take care of her, Philip told himself as he continued to scan the room. He was trying to absorb as much as possible, but he heard her entering the room behind him. So, finally, he took a seat in one of the high-back chairs, facing the entrance. "Philip, could I get you a drink or something?" Holly noticed how he was still looking around. She'd been watching his interrogation of her home the entire time from the kitchen. "No, thank you," he said as he thought, yeah, you could give me a taste of those plump lips, but he quickly added, "We better do this because I made 8:00 reservations." He cleared his throat. His nasty thinking left his mouth parched, causing his booming voice to waver. "Uh, yeah it's getting close," she said, looking over at the clock. Just as she was about to lean down and turn off the lamp, the telephone rang. Smiling, she held up her hand and excused herself. Holly answered the phone in the kitchen, she could see him from where she stood. "Hello!" "Holly, it's Carmen. I didn't think you would be home. I was going to leave you a message on this phone instead of on your cellular phone." Holly smiled, feeling better now that she knew her friend was okay. "We were just about to leave, but I'm glad you made it in okay. What took you so long to call?" "I'm sorry. I ran into a friend of mine and we stopped to get something to eat. Girl, the time just flew." "That was nice. I'm just glad you're all right. Listen, I'm going to run. We have 8:00 reservations." Holly glanced over at Philip, who smiled and waved. "Have fun and call me tomorrow. I want to hear *aaall* about it. I already prayed for everything to go smoothly for you." Her friend was so supportive. Holly played it cool since Philip was staring at her. "Thank you, Carmen. I'll talk to you soon." She hung up. "Are you ready?" she asked, a smile brightening her face as she came back into the living room. He nodded and stood up, gazing back over at the piano. "Do you play?" Philip asked. At first she didn't know what he meant until he gestured in the direction of the baby grand once again. She smiled and shook her head no. "Growing up I loved listening to Stevie Wonder play. The man's so talented. I promised myself that I'd buy a beautiful piano when I got older. I never really wanted to learn how to play, but I thought it would be here just incase someone who knew how to felt like playing me a song. I've accomplished the purchasing part...." She paused, choosing her words carefully. "Do you know how to play?" she asked. "No," he said, wishing that he could. Holly shrugged her shoulders. "A piano and a piece of fine artwork were my two endeavors in life as a child.... and as you can see, I've fulfilled both dreams." She looked and sounded sheepish, humbling to Philip. He gave her a long admirable stare then he smiled, took another quick look around and nodded his head. Holly turned off the lamp and they both walked toward the door. It feels like I'm forgetting something, she thought. Then it occurred to her. It was her pocketbook. She excused herself once again and headed down the dark hallway, leading to her bedroom. After checking himself out in the foyer mirror, Philip sat down on the settee. He could hear her opening and closing her closet, the sliding doors banging together. And as he turned his head in the direction of her room, he could see down the hall leading to it. The light from her bedroom enabled him to see. There was more extraordinary art adorning the linen-colored walls of the narrow space. After admiring what little of the paintings he could see, Philip leaned back in his seat and waited patiently for her return. Not a second had gone by before he saw her bedroom light go off from the corner of his eye and heard her heading down the hall. "Now, I'm ready." She was checking her brown Gucci bamboo-handled pocketbook for her wallet. "Have everything?" he asked and stood up. Holly nodded and opened the door.

Luxury cars were lined up for the valet service in the center of the block in between Spring and Houston Streets in SoHo. The taxi pulled up in front of Louises, the finest French restaurant within the tri-state area. Holly gazed out the window at the elegantly dressed couples and individuals exiting their expensive cars while Philip paid the fair. So this is where it was located, she thought, remembering her intentions to look it up. She had heard so many wonderful things about the place: excellent cuisine, quality service and plush surroundings and here she was about to dine there. The Lord is so beautiful she thought. She had to make sure she stayed focused. Philip was not right for her. God did not want them together.

Holly was so dazed she didn't even realize that Philip had been asking her if she was ready to go inside. "Oh, uh. Sure lets go," she said, stammering on her words. He smiled and exited the cab, climbing out among the swift moving traffic. Looking back over her shoulder, Holly watched Philip as he walked around the taxi to her side, opening the door. He extended his hand to her, helping her out.

Inside of the restaurant, Philip and Holly stood behind two older European women, one fashioned from head to toe in Ferragamo and the other wore a lilac contour suit, her accessories: evening bag and slingback shoes were both silver. "You okay?" Philip asked Holly. He noticed the way she had been studying the two women. "I'm fine," she said with a smile. "Good." They waited their turn in silence as the maitre d' escorted the two women before them to their seats, introducing them to the waiter who would be serving them. "Here he comes," Philip whispered. The tall, olive-colored maître d' had dark hair and a mustache so thick you could hardly see his lips. When they stepped over to where he was, Holly could hear the sensual voice of the late French singer, Edith Pias swaying gently in the air. She was crooning *La Vie En Rose.* "Your name, sir," asked the maître d' as he crossed out, what appeared to be, the names of the European women he just seated. His heavy French accent was barely understandable. "Williams. Philip Williams," he said, looking down at the reservation book. "Ah, *monsieur* Williams. How could I forget." The maître d' clapped his hand on his forehead. "For two, yes? Please come this way I have a lovely table waiting for you and madame over here," he added with a little giggle. Must be a regular, Holly thought. Philip held out his hand so she could go ahead of him as they followed the maître d'. "This is a nice place," she said. Her eyes traveled around the dining area. Everything from the patrons to the fine decor bespoke class. As she began to really focus on the crowd, she could feel an uncomfortable pulling in her stomach. A feeling of not belonging. Displacement was settling in the deepest parts of her body. Parts she didn't even know the names of. But, Holly knew she could not allow any of the smug faces to get the better of her or else she would be a mess all through dinner. Remembering the commitment to herself, Holly straightened her back. She was going to force herself into feeling at home on this "side of town" so she didn't hesitate for one more moment to utilize her ability to shut them out. She knew her deliverance was near. "Stay in the Word," her mother said. "The Lawd's the onlys one who can help you, babygirl. That ole devil is defeated. Just keep walking in yo'victory. The Lawd has blessed you greatly. Made you a wealthy woman. Time to live like one."

"Yeah, it is quite a place, "Philip finally said, pulling out her chair. She smiled at the handsome man accompanying her and thanked him as she slid down into the velvet seat. "This is Rene. He will be your waiter this evening," said the maître d' as he approached the table again with a short, slender man dressed in a white dinner jacket and black trousers. "Bon jour," Rene said. "Bon jour," the couple replied in unison. "It is my first day," explained Rene as if he were asking them to be patient with him. "Bon appetit," said the maître d' as he headed back to the front of the exceptional restaurant. "Could I get you something for starters?" Rene asked. Holly asked Philip to order for her since he'd been there before. "We'll start out *with* the Escargots in garlic sauce and the Artichoke Vinaigrette," Philip said, looking at the menu. Oh, um, Holly. What type of entree would you like?" "I would love a beef dish. Thank you." "And I know from last night that you don't drink," Philip said, looking at Holly. She was surprised. She didn't think he noticed. "No, I don't," she said. "Okay. I'll order the entrees too." Philip was speaking to Rene who nodded and said, "But of course." Rene reopened his pad. "Could I have the Chateubriand and I'll order the Beef Burgundy for the lady. Thank you." "Yes sir, right away." Rene took the menus again and hurried off toward the kitchen. "Man, did you see how he booked away from here?" Philip whispered. And they both laughed. "I don't want you to think I'm holding out on the dessert, Holly. We'll order that later if we have room, okay." She nodded in agreement.

When the dinner arrived, Holly prayed over their meal and Philip tried to charm his way straight to her heart. She felt unbelievably pampered. He'd taken her Escargots out of the shell and fed them to her. He cut the Artichoke's up into tiny pieces and they even sampled each other's entree's. Sure she loved how attentive Philip was being this evening. But she'd have to make certain that she remained on guard. He was not for her, she told herself.

Holly finished her meal and told Philip how wonderful it was. Nodding, he wiped his mouth with a napkin and grinned as though he owned Louises and cooked the devoured food before them himself. "They haven't disappointed me yet," he said. "Would you like some dessert?" Rene asked. He was smiling. He'd overheard Philip's remark. "Why don't we share something? That is -- if you have the room," Holly suggested with a grin. "That's a good idea..." Philip paused, cracking a smile. "Do I have the room? Always." He started rubbing his stomach. Rene was definitely amused by the handsome couple. A chuckle escaped his mouth. "Could we have the peach melba, Rene?" Philip asked. "You are going to share?" Rene confirmed by holding up his index finger. "Yeah, just one," Philip answered. "Would you like a cup of coffee with that?" Philip asked Holly. She nodded her head yes. "Two coffee's too, Rene," Philip said.

Holly swallowed a spoonful of the peach melba when the waiter placed it on the table between Philip and herself, the rich taste of raspberries, kirsch and mint, lingering in her mouth. "Mmm, good," she said with a smile. Philip nodded his head in agreement. His mouth was full of the delicious dessert. "Wow, I can taste a hint of cinnamon in this!" Holly said with surprise. "Shhh," said Rene playfully. "It's the Chef's secret ingredient," he whispered as he carried an order for the couple seated next to them. Holly nodded and smiled and Philip sat there in admiration of the beauty joining him. "Would you like anything else?" Rene asked, passing them again. "No, we're fine," Philip said. He glanced over at Holly, making sure she didn't want anything else. And she concurred. When they finished eating, Philip wasn't ready to call it a night. He was accustomed to being invited up to his date's apartment for part two of the evening. Yes, indeed. *But,* knowing that Holly was different, he didn't expect an invitation from her. Not tonight at least, he told himself, remembering that he definitely had a way with women.

"So are you ready for the interview now, Holly?" A smirk emerged on Philip's face. Holly surveyed his expression before answering. He was only joking. Smiling, she said, "As a matter of fact, I am ready." She moved closer to him, putting her elbows on the table and resting her chin in the palms of her hands. She was giving him the same penetrating stare that he'd given to her last night at his restaurant. And, this made Philip crack up. Not paying him any attention, she just started in with the questioning. "You do know I'm a Christian?" Holly had asked the question as if she'd been suddenly hoisted up from the restaurant and somehow lowered into a courtroom. Confidence clung on the back of each word, like a magnet would a piece of metal. Philip nodded his head, knowing that he was one of the biggest sinners around. "And you know I'm not," he said with a faint smile. Holly stared at him for a second. "I do know that," she said. "So what does this mean?" Philip asked. "You're a big girl," he added. "Yes, with a great big God that I have to continue to please. That I want to please," she said, taking a sip from her coffee cup. "I could respect that," he said, not really sure of what she was saying. "How long have you been a Christian?" Philip asked. Holly relaxed in her seat. "My mother raised me in the Word of God," she said. Philip nodded. "But I left it for a while. I'm happy to say that I am back in it again, trying my best to walk upright before the Lord. I haven't been reading my Bible like I should, but I'm confident that I will get there," she said. Philip didn't know what she was talking about. His family never went to church. Never heard the name of Jesus in their home at all unless somebody was using it in vain. Like a cuss word. His father always told him and his sister that Christians were weak because they were always waiting on God. So he was *trying* his best to be respectful and understanding regarding her religion or whatever it was. "I can't date you, Philip," she said. He coughed as he gazed over at her., His musings came rapidly to an end. "Why not?" he asked. She could tell he was puzzled. Holly knew she would have to explain. She nodded. "I cannot be unequally yoked with an unbeliever." "What does that mean?" Philip asked. "It means I have to be with a Christian man." Philip took a sip of water and told her he understood. "Can we be friends?" he asked. Holly lowered her eyes, knowing she would have to pray on it. "I can't answer you until I discuss it with God." She could feel the Lord's pleasure after she spoke. Philip nodded again. "I understand. Can we at least finish up this evening?" he asked. Holly didn't see anything wrong with it and she wasn't feeling as though the Lord was in disagreement with her decision to get to know Phillip a little more. He was behaving himself. "Sure we can," she said with a smile as she was forgetting that the Lord already answered. "So what part of New Jersey are you from?" Holly asked and Philip started to laugh. "Englewood?" *"And* where do you live now?" He smiled. "Somebody's not wasting any time!" She leaned back, lifting a perfectly-defined eyebrow. "No, I definitely don't. What if this is the last time we see each other. Remember, I haven't prayed about whether we could be friends or not." She tried to stifle a smile, which happened to be stronger than her willpower to do so. The grin on her glowing face would have put the sun to shame. Philip started to laugh really hard again as the word "touche" spilled from him mouth. Then, stopping, he stared at her for a few seconds. A few *uncomfortable* seconds for her. Philip had started feeling something just then. But, it wasn't the usual sexual sensation that he'd feel. This was different. Abnormal for him. He liked the way she smiled and the way her body moved. She did both with such grace. This was a lady sitting across from him, he told himself. There was no denying that. But what he failed to see once again was the rapid demise of Holly's sureness. She began searching her face for remnants of the meal she had just eaten. "Is there something on..." Cutting her own sentence short, she didn't want to draw more attention to herself. Holly grabbed the napkin from her lap, wiping around her mouth. She didn't like feeling insecure. She was believing God for her emotional healing. "No, no," Philip said. He reached across the table for her frantic hand. "There's nothing on you. I'm sorry. I was just admiring how beautiful you are." His compliment had taken her *way* back and her immediate response was to snap at him for provoking an unbearable reminder of her unhappy past. "Stop that will you, Philip." She turned away from him, gazing around the restaurant. She'd heard a burst of laughter erupt from one of the neighboring tables. It felt as though she'd become the focus of everyone's attention. The brunt of all their jokes. But she wasn't. No one was giving them the time of day. Philip put the hand that she'd yanked away back into his. "Come on. I know you probably hear that kind of stuff everyday.... but I couldn't help it." She couldn't help but to react in the defensive way she had. She didn't know him well enough to believe his kind demonstration. Therefore, she wanted to protect herself. Holly used to be the type of woman who hung on the end of every endearing word a man had ever spoken to her. She would become like a child in their hands. "Can't you just say thank you," Philip went on to say not realizing the way his compliment had transformed her back into the little nine year old girl walking across the schoolyard in search of a friend. "I ain't playin' wit no zebra. She *thank* she cute. And I know that ain't even her real hair! Don't her mama know she too young for a weave?" That's what she'd heard one little Black girl tell her friend after she turned to walk in the other direction. "Do you see that little girl right there? My mother said she's a nigger because one drop of Black blood means you are. And she also said that I could never play with her or any other nigger girl or boy, not unless I wanted to be grounded for the rest of my life. I wouldn't want to play with her anyway...... she looks strange." That's what she heard one little White girl say as she turned a rope. Holly had overheard the girl's friends laugh as they all screamed in unison, "Kathleen Parker you're so funny." *Kathleen Parker* was the name that had played over and over in her head as a child for many years after that grief-causing day. Not only had they'd stripped her of her self-esteem, they'd also made her lose something else of great significance. Something dear and precious. Priceless. It was a bracelet that her father had given her. The first *real* gift. The others were toys. It was a keepsake. A treasure. He told her mother to let her wear it at age eight. Those were the amount of years that her parents had been married. Losing that sterling silver trinket, which was inscribed, "*To daddy's little SD*". SD, standing for sugar dumpling, made her sick to her stomach. She had only gotten the chance to wear it every day for a year. And even though she is well aware now that those little girl's were the results of ignorant parenting, she *still* could not rid her mind of the former upbraid and great loss to this very day. "I really didn't mean to upset you," Philip apologized. Holly jumped a little when he hauled her out of her musings. Then, sitting there, she stared across the table at Philip for a few minutes more before finally saying, "I had asked you where you lived now?" Business as usual. Philip smiled and nodded his head slowly. That was his way of letting her know that he was sorry for making her feel uncomfortable. "I live on the Westside. 4-2-1 Westend Avenue. That's between 64th and 65th Streets. Would you like my telephone number?" he asked. Holly held up her finger. "I don't know if the Lord's going to allow me to be your friend. Remember?" Phillip gazed at her with a smile on his face. "I hope He tells you it's okay," was what he said. Holly smiled. "I'm having such a good time," Philip said, "I don't want it to end." He looked serious. No trace of a smile. But, Holly couldn't be fooled by Philip's expression. He wasn't her source. God is. My goodness she thought. "Am I lying to myself? Is God my source?" She shook her head no, knowing that she wasn't living like a Christian. She wasn't going to church regularly. She wasn't speaking to God regularly. "You don't have any more questions," Philip asked because he saw her shake her head no. Holly smiled. "Where are your father's McDonalds franchises?" she asked instead of accommodating his question. Philip paused and just answered. "One's on Edgar Street in East Orange and the others on Hudson Street in Hoboken," "I see. And which one did you run?" She took another sip of coffee. "Wow! She remembered," Philip said. "You have a good memory." He could see a faint smile crossing those... those lips. "A lawyer is supposed to remember the tiniest details." "Touche again," Philip said, staring into her beautiful eyes. "Man, I'm just makin' you wanna jump on a plane to Vegas with me. Will somebody please make me stop," he teased, pretending to search the restaurant for a volunteer. Then he looked back at her, chuckling a little. She smiled, knowing that he wasn't who God had for her. "All kiddin' aside," Philip said, "I am enjoyin' tonight." He examined her expression carefully. He was trying to figure out her unspoken response. The message on her face. What did she think of him so far? Was she as enamored with him as he was with her? He'd dated many women in the forty-three years of his life, but *never* had he found one he'd wanted to really, really get to know. Philip wanted to know what made her happy and he wanted to know all the things she loved. She'd be worth the time. Yeah, Holly was definitely different. Unique in appearance and personality. She was a Christian. Though she tried to come off as hard, Philip could smell her motherly instincts, something he was raised without. Mama could be just as rough as the callouses in the palms of his hands, he told himself as he came back to reality. *Wait* a minute! What was happening here? Were the tables turning? What was softening him up like this? Did she pray and asked her God to convert him? He had no plans on becoming a Christian. He liked the world too much. What did Holly have that was so special? Maybe her God would let her continue to see him or maybe she'd just continue on her own. See him without asking. Philip wanted to grin at the thought but he didn't want Holly to think he was crazy. "Which one did you run?" Holly asked, shaking him out of his reverie. "The one on Hudson Street in Hoboken." She nodded her head slowly. "And your parents?" she asked. "What about them?" Philip asked, confusion in his voice. "Are they still in Englewood?" *"Yes."* He was still wearing the perplexed look on his face. "So their still together?" Holly finally asked. *"Yep,* and very much in love." "That's good. You're blessed," she said. "Are yours still together?" he asked. "No. My father transitioned when I was nine." "Aw, man, I'm sorry, Holly. I didn't know. He died ... that's what you're sayin'?" He gave her hand a gentle squeeze. "Yes, he's in heaven," Holly said with a smile. Philip just nodded his head. He didn't know anything about the Bible and he wasn't even sure if he wanted to know. He hoped she didn't plan on preachin'. "What about your mother? Where does she live?" "She's here in the city. I bought her a condo over on 72nd and York." "That was really sweet of you." "Well, she's all I have. I wanted us to be close to one another." "What about your father's family?" he asked, seeing a sadness wash over her face. "As I said before, my mother is all I have." He knew the deal now. Holly knew she had to find forgiveness in her heart toward her father's family or else God wouldn't forgive her. "Well, I bet the two of you are really tight?" Philip said, regarding her and her mother. Holly nodded. "Very." She took another sip of coffee. "Could I ask you a question?" he asked. She cleared her throat and he could see her shift in her seat. "Sure, what?" Philip started grinning as he revealed his palms. "Don't get mad at me for asking you this." It looked like he was searching for the proper way to ask the question. *"Okay,"* Holly replied. She took a deep breath. What could he want to know that warranted so much calculation? Seeing his mouth fixing itself to spit out whatever it was that he was going to say, she stiffened. "Are you mixed? I mean ma, mu?" he asked uneasily. Philip noticed the way her chest deflated with relief after he had asked his question. "Mulatto. Yes, my father was White and my mother's Black," Holly said. She had to giggle at how uptight she must have appeared. "I guess it wasn't as bad as I thought it was going to be," she added. He had asked the correct way. The evening seemed to be turning into the therapeutic session she had craved for many years but was too fearful to pursue. God was at work, she told herself, knowing how she'd heard he'd use any type of situation to get the glory he deserved. "C'mon, don't slow down on me now. Ask me somethin' else," Philip said. "Um, okay." She sat straight up, but Philip beat her to the next question. "Are you tired?" he asked. He glanced at his watch then took a final sip of coffee, emptying his cup. It was ten fifteen. "No," Holly said. "It's still early," he said, grinning. "So what would you like to do next?" Philip added. Holly smiled. She didn't want to stay out too late with him, but she had to admit that she was enjoying his company as well. "You know what?" she said, "let's go for a carriage ride through the park. My treat." Philip smiled at her innocent enthusiasm. "That sounds like a good idea." He signaled to Rene for the check.

The summer air was warm and humid but the couple was still refreshed from the restaurant's air conditioning. They walked to the corner, the warm breeze whipping them in the face. Philip stood down in the street and motioned for Holly to remain on the curb while he hailed a cab. "There's one," he said, whistling for the on-coming taxi. Philip opened the door, leading Holly in first by placing his hand at the small of her back.

Inside of the hot, sticky vehicle, Holly told the driver where they were going and Philip put his arm behind her, along the back of the car seat. He was trying to get another whiff of her fragrant hair. It had filled the air between them when he held out her chair earlier in the evening at Louises. And besides that, the cab smelled of bad body odor. He could see Holly wrinkling her nose too from the stench as he stared out of her window and for some reason that made him smile.

"How long have you known Vanessa, Courtney and Tracy?" Philip asked when the carriage ride was nearly over. Prior to that, the couple had been discussing Philip's occupation. Holly liked the fact that he was just as passionate and had as much zeal for his work as she had. Bradford, though inexplicably successful for someone with little initiative, had those jealous tendencies when she would express her appreciation of how far she's come professionally. Relaxing in her musings, Holly thought about his question for a minute. "Uh, I've known them," she repeated, "for about eight years." Philip nodded and took a quick glance of their surroundings. Though the tremendous park was dark, there was still quite a bit of activity going on. He could see some people walking and others lounging on the emerald green blanket of grass. "How long have you known Courtney and Vanessa?" Holly asked in return. "Court about six weeks and Vanessa about five." Holly cut her nodding short, thinking six weeks? She wondered why Tracy or Vanessa hadn't mentioned him before. "Yeah, I met Courtney at the racquet club." He started laughing a little and Holly smiled. "We bet on a few games. If he won I had to treat him to dinner and vice versa. And I won, of course." Patting himself on the back, he added, "Sooo, he invited me to his house for dinner. *Cheap!* Don't you think that's cheap!" Philip waved his hand as he really wasn't expecting an answer from Holly. "Anyway, that's when I met Vanessa and Tracy." Holly nodded. "Were they trying to fix you up with her?" Philip shook his head no. "Are you crazy? Court said that woman had more men then the YMCA." They both cracked up. "He wasn't lying," Holly said. She was still giggling a little. "How do you like working with the two of them?" he asked. "We have a great time together and we all have very similar work ethics, which makes it nice." "That's good. Kelly's your secretary, right?" Holly suddenly had a questioning look on her face. "Yeah. Why?" Philip nodded his head. "Because I've seen her at my restaurant a few times with her friends," he explained, noticing the expression on Holly's face. "Yeah, she told me that she's been there before." Philip nodded his head again. "She's there a lot," he said. "I guess she must like the food," Holly said quietly. And he nodded once again. It was almost like he had something more to say on the subject, but he didn't. "Check out that sky," Philip said, looking upward as if he was really interested. Holly leaned her head back and stared at it, too. A moment of silence enveloped the slow-moving carriage. The only sound was that of the horses hoofs trotting along the pavement. Then, turning toward him, she could feel him looking at her. "Okay, were back!" the carriage driver announced, shattering the quiet wall dividing him from them. Philip jumped at the sound of the man's voice. Holly held back a giggle. She saw him wince then try to pretend that he was scratching his head. "How much will that be?" she asked and unsnapped her pocketbook. "That'll be fifty bucks," the carriage driver said, extending his slightly soiled hand. "I got it," Philip said and paid for the ride. "But, I said it was my treat," Holly said, staring at him, who just climbed down from the carriage and looked up at her. She was waiting for an answer, but instead of giving her one, he helped her to the ground, asking, "Where to now?" He made her forget her question. Holly looked at her watch. It was fifteen minutes to eleven. "Maybe I should go home," she said. Philip paused, shrugged and said okay, even though that wasn't what he'd wanted to do. Holly saw the let down in his eyes and remembered what he had said in the restaurant. She did *not* know this man from the guy standing on the corner waiting for the light to change and most importantly, she knew God had already told her Philip was not for her.

In front of her apartment building Philip was staring inside at Peter. "My man is doin' some serious noddin'," he told Holly. The doorman's head jerked as he tried to battle the strong forces of sleep. Holly glanced inside as well and smiled. At this point, she was telling herself that Philip had been a gentlemen the entire night. Not making any passes at her and so on. What harm would it be for her to invite him upstairs for a little while. So, that was exactly what she did. Philip looked at her. Holly could see his mouth forming a smile. "Now this is a treat," he said, grinning broadly, his face lit up brighter than the street light they were standing under.

The scent of roses greeted them at the door when Holly opened it. Walking into the dark apartment behind her, Philip had asked if she would mind him taking off his shoes. Holly clicked on the foyer light and shook her head. "Not at all. Please make yourself comfortable." She slipped hers off as well and walked into the living room, turning on the lamp. Holly faced Philip and asked what he'd like to drink. He was still entering the room. "I have an assortment of hot teas or would you prefer something cold? Water, juice...?"

Clearing his throat, he said, "Orange juice?" even though he could have used a nice cold beer or a glass of wine. She nodded and glanced into his drowsy blood-shot eyes. Peter wasn't the only one playing tug-of-war with sleep, she thought. "Have a seat and I'll be right back," she told him. Holly walked toward the dining room and Philip sat at the end of the sofa closest to the door. He was admiring the pictures on her end table. Just when he was about to pick the one of the older woman up, who Holly had a striking resemblance to, he heard her approaching the space he occupied. "I hope you like pulp," Holly said as she re-entered the room, carrying two wine glasses filled with orange juice. She caught him pulling his hand back from the photo and he realized she had. "Oh, yeah. That's cool. Um, is this your mother?" Philip pointed to the picture of the older woman wearing a brown suit with her hair pulled up on top of her head. Holly nodded. "You look exactly like her except for the hair and complection." "Yeah, I got the hair from my daddy and I got the color of my skin from them both." She directed his attention to her parents wedding picture. Holly's father was holding his bride tightly in his arms. As Holly peered down at the photograph, a few strands of her honey-tinted hair fell against the sides of her face. Philip smiled to himself. He was glad it wasn't a weave. When Holly glanced at him, he motioned for her to sit down beside him by subtlety patting on the sofa. And once she did, they smiled at each other, clinked their glasses together and took a sip of the juice. "This is good," Philip said. He was looking into the glass. "Fresh squeezed?" Philip asked. Holly nodded. "I did it this morning." "So, Ms. Reed, do you have any brothers or sisters?" Philip leaned back, stretching an arm across the top of the sofa. "No. I'm the only child. My mother didn't want children from anyone else. And besides that, she never remarried after my father's death." Leaning forward, Philip set his glass down on the coffee table atop of a coaster. "You don't have to be married to have kids." He's not saved was the first thought that popped into her mind. "My mother's a godly woman," she said. Holly's mind instantly rewound all the days she wanted to place a hand over her mother's mouth, containing some of the things the older woman believed were appropriate to say. She debated on whether or not it was too soon for her to inform her date of her mother's sometimes tactless verbal approach. Cynthia Reed was a traditional woman, sanctified and faithful in the Lord, she thought, reevaluating what she'd said to herself. Nevertheless, the older woman was incredibly spunky. Holly should have added this part of her mother's decorum. But, I won't be seeing him anymore, was her next thought. The hazel-eyed woman was about to share how her mother only went to school up to the third grade. It was a Blessing that she got the house cleaning job at Lenox Hill hospital, the hazel-eyed woman thought. "That was the favor of God, babygirl," said Cynthia Reed when they called to offer her the job. "Oh, mama I'm so happy for you!" ten-year-old Holly said.

The hazel-eyed woman glimpsed Philip's smiling face and decided to go along with Carmen's mother, who told she and her best friend when they were about twenty. "Jew tell *poco* and jew keep *mucho* to jour self." Senora Lopez believed this was one of the reasons she and her husband had been married for forty years. She claimed men didn't like to know too much anyway. Holly sat there staring off in a daze for a moment. This man is not for me.

Philip was still smiling when Holly asked, "Do you have any brothers and sisters?" He nodded. "A younger sister, Brenda. She's married and they have two little people, keeping them very busy. Mark, Jr.'s five and Olivia's three and they live up in Rochester." Holly nodded. "Oh, what does your sister do?" "Brenda works in the home." Holly nodded again and took a sip from her glass. "That's great. I'm sure her family appreciates that." She leaned over and set her glass down next to his. "So, what does her husband do?" "Mark's a Police Captain up there." "*Wow*. Nice." She noticed how Philip looked off into some unknown area, somewhere outside of the room in his mind, after he'd answered her question. Not knowing exactly where or why his mind wandered so far away, Holly peered at him with slight confusion on her face. Philip turned back in her direction. "Not to get off the subject, but do you have anyone special in your life. A man?" Smiling, her facial expression resumed back to the way it was as she shook her head no. "Remember, I'm waiting on the Lord to send me my mate," she said, pointing heavenward. Philip nodded. He hoped she didn't see the look of annoyance on his face. Boy was he tired of hearing her mention "the Lord". "Do you?" she asked. He, too, shook his head no and cleared his throat. He wanted to say that he wouldn't be up in there, but he quickly changed his mind, knowing for sure that that would probably be a lie, given his track record. "How long have you been waiting?" Philip asked. "And have you ever dated a man who wasn't a Christian?" "I haven't been waiting long at all," Holly said. "I just rededicated myself to God. Before that I was with someone for about seven years." "What happened if you don't mind me..." Holly shook her head before he could finish speaking. She took a deep breath. "He cheated on me." Philip couldn't find anything within himself to make him want to reach over to console Holly. If he did, he'd be a liar. "Oh," was what he opted to say. "What about yourself?" she asked him. "Me? Don't really have the time." Holly nodded. She didn't want to go too deep into personal conversation with him. "I was surprised *you* weren't married," Holly said, eyeing Philip. That comment just slipped out of her mouth. "Why 'cause I'ma old man?" She shook her head no. "Who told you that?" Philip shrugged his shoulders. "Society," he said quietly. "Oh, you mean the "elusive theys," Holly said, with a smile. Philip nodded, grinning as well as he replied, "Yeah, them." He smiled. "Well, that wasn't the real reason. I just figured you would be since you are an accomplished businessmen," Holly said. "Oh, yeah? That's why," Philip said, staring into her eyes. "Let's just say I haven't found the right woman... yet." "Okay, let's say that." She nodded and stood up as she thought, how many times have I seen that stare? "Excuse me for a minute. I *have* to get out of this suit." Holly saw the look on Philip's face. "I didn't mean it that way," she said, raising an eyebrow. "Oh," he said, his shoulders vibrating as he laughed. "I'll be right back," she added and stepped over his outstretched legs to get by. Philip reached for his orange juice after she walked passed. He watched her disappear from the dimly-lit room. As he listened to her bare feet make their way down the hall, he shook his head in disgust, mouthing, "Man." Why did he always have to play games? Knowing that he'd failed to mention a couple of things regarding his dating situation, odd for him as it may sound, made him feel lousy. He wouldn't really call it dating though. He hadn't taken anyone out in months. But, his ex-girlfriend, Selma Girard had a way of taking care of his vigorous sex drive. Although she was living with a man, who she claimed she was "nuts" about, she always found the time to give Philip an extremely pleasurable morning, afternoon or evenings worth of loving. "Yeah, she is a "nut"," Philip told himself as he let out a private laugh. As soon as Charles left town on business, she would call, making him an offer he'd be stupid to refuse. She wanted to please him and she always did. Philip grinned, biting down on his bottom lip. She certainly knew how to take care of his business. She would do all the things he liked having done to him. I'm not a bad guy, he told himself. Sliding back on the sofa Philip dangled the half-full glass in his hand. He smiled again at what just came to his mind. When Selma wasn't available there was another woman he was more than able to depend on. But, he sighed, wiping the grin off his face, he'd rather not take that trip right now. Sometimes guilt even had a way of catching up to him. Philip was certain that Holly was going to be his. He just had a way of making women want to be with him, he reminded himself. Gazing up toward the ceiling, Philip wondered just how real her God was.

Holly clicked on her bedroom light, noticing she had a message on her land line as she entered. She checked it before changing her clothes. Her mother's voice bombarded the room, like an old lady would the unsuspecting crook tugging at the other end of her purse. "Hello, baby. Are you there? It's me, mama. The Lawd just spoke to me. He said to give you a call and tell you that He's the living water you're thirsting for. Like I always told you, babygirl, the Lawd loves you. Have faith in Him. He can do anything but fail. I love you. Okay then. I'll talk wit you tomorrow. I thought for sho you'd be home by now. Call me. Bye." Holly stood still for a minute, taking in the word from the Lord. Her eyes found the Bible on her nightstand, focusing on it for a few seconds before they fell to the floor. She'd call her loving mother tomorrow. Holly unbuttoned her suit jacket on her way over to the closet. She hung the navy two-piece up and decided on a T-shirt and a pair of gym shorts. They were who she really was beneath all the glitz and glamour.

Standing in front of her full-length mirror once she'd slipped them on, she nodded at her reflection approvingly. She didn't want to send off the wrong messages. Fast was something she was not. When she entered the living room, she saw Philip leaning his head back against the sofa. Is he sleeping? she wondered. Approaching him quietly, she sat down next to him, tucking her feet beneath her. Feeling her presence beside him, his body jerked then he sat up, wiping what felt like drool from the corner of his mouth. He smiled at Holly, saying, "I thought I was home in my bed." She returned his grin. "Was I gone that long?" she asked. "No. Not at all. I'm just too comfortable here." "This apartment has some nerve," she teased, smiling again as she leaned over, picking up her glass. She took a sip, bringing the glass down from her mouth. Philip leaned over and stole a kiss. Now who asked him to do that? Holly mused, trying not to appear disturbed by his aggressiveness. Philip pulled away and apologized. Holly was speechless for a second but she conjured up enough energy to tell him that it was okay. She felt the old Holly coming back. The backslidden one. Philip extended his arms to embrace her. As he came closer, she could feel the heat from his body and it made her tremble. But, she wasn't afraid or cold. Holly shut her eyes. She had almost forgotten how good it felt to be close to a man. I'm attracted to this man, she told herself, feeling confused.

A few moments had passed before he whispered her name into her ear. Holly cleared her throat, saying, "Yes?" Philip paused for a minute, making her open her eyes. He was staring at her. "You're face and hair are so beautiful." Holly smiled. "I know this is gonna sound weak but ..." "But what?" "It feels like we've been together for years. And I mean that in a good way." Holly pulled herself out of his arms and pressed her back up against the sofa. Philip smiled at her. She returned a grin, her hazel eyes staring into his brown ones. He could see her beginning to relax. Make him leave now, she told herself. Philip started caressing her arm. Holly was still looking at him. "I can't..." She opened and closed her mouth. He leaned forward, kissing her again. They continued to hold each other tightly while their mouths explored one another's. And the next thing Holly knew, she was being carried down the hall leading to her bedroom. She could not resist him. Holly could feel herself getting worked up. Philip approached the bedrooms, noticing that there were two. He glanced at the vision in his arms and she pointed to the one on the left.

Inside, he started kissing her as he placed her down on the bed, which was still unmade from her nap earlier. Philip gave her a sensuous gaze and commenced to undress. Once he finished, he took off her clothes and the two of them did exactly what the Lord was warning her not to do.

When Holly awoke at the early hour of 2:50 a.m., she had a cramp in her neck. She had fallen asleep on top of Philip. In the same position they finished fornicating in. The word the Lord told her mother to give her played in her head. He was the living water she was thirsting for. Holly knew He was telling her not to go against Him once again. He wanted her to turn toward him and He would fill her. Keep her. Holly felt numb. Why was she always looking for Love in all the wrong places? She gazed at Philip. His once tight embrace had become limp across her slender body. Beneath her he snored a peaceful snore, one she did not find annoying. He looked so sweet, she thought, his sensitive appearance did nothing to wipe away the remorse she was starting to feel in regards to the self-control she was not able to exercise earlier. Holly pulled herself up off of him slightly, sliding down onto the bed beside the stranger sharing her usually humble abode. Rubbing at the sore stiffness in her neck, she began studying Philip quietly. The conviction she was feeling nearly choked her. She was acquainting herself with who he was without his knowledge or approval. This would be the last time she'd be doing this until she got married. How could she be such a fool? She gazed at the way his chest rose and fell when he breathed, the way his lips were spread ever so scarcely apart, his hair and the configuration of his right ear, but the thing she focused on most, was the darkness of his skin. She had never been with a man so substantial in color, although every single one of her former boyfriends had been of African-American decent. Holding her arm next to his, she compared their complexions. Both hues were unique but lovely, she told herself as thoughts of the way Philip had greatly appreciated her features yesterday flooded her mind. During dinner she recalled the way he paused, taking her completely in and then once again while he sat on the sofa in her living room. He had called her face and hair beautiful. The naturally straight golden main she used to try to destroy. She wanted to make it less like the Caucasian hair she had inherited from her unforgettable father. Why would she want to demolish the lineage of a man she loved so dearly? The part of him that was so distinct in her? She knew it was time to celebrate her differences, but she had to find the muscle to be able to shove aside the mountain of doubt. She knew she had to start speaking to her situations as God already worked it out. It was faith that moved mountains. Holly suddenly saw herself braiding her hair every night as a young girl and picking it out every morning, hoping to own an afro like the ones ruling the streets of the neighborhood she and her mother inhabited for a little over a decade. Cynthia would tell her it was nothing more freeing than being yourself. "I rather be a *great* original then a cheap copy any ole day. Show'em who you really are and they won't be able to do nothin' else *but* respect you. The Lawd knows what you goin' through. You mo than a conquerer, babygirl. That's what it says in the Word. All you haveta do is believe," the older woman would say as Holly instructed her on how she was to pick out the back of her hair. But Cynthia would not stay quiet while she yanked at the kinks her daughter ignorantly created. "They ain't nothin' but jealous 'cause they know my baby's just as pretty as she wanna be." Holly supposed she'd always carry the guilt for the terrible way she'd roll her eyes at her mother's reflection in the mirror, demanding her to pay attention to what she was doing. Turning over onto her back, Holly started to cry, at those days and the one she was living at that moment. The tears came rolling down the sides of her face, landing on the pillow under her head. Here she was lying beside a man: tall, good-looking and financially secure yet she still felt devastatingly lonely. She needed more God and less of herself. "Lord, let me decrease so that you can increase," she whispered as more tears fell from her eyes.

Chapter Six

Philip walked out of the bathroom yawning and scratching the back of his head, later that morning. He entered Holly's bedroom and stood at the foot of her bed, watching her sleep. She was without a doubt fine as can be, he told himself as a smile crossed his lips. "You got me, baby," slipped out of his mouth unexpectedly as he climbed back into the bed beside her, kissing her bare shoulder. She winced from his moist, tender touch and opened her eyes. "Morning," Philip said, grinning again. Holly stared at him for a second before remembering what she had done. She sinned. "You okay?" he asked, placing his hand on the side of her face. She nodded, knowing that he was referring to the puffiness of her hazel eyes. She had cried most of the night due to the noise she couldn't shut off in her head, telling her she was nothing but a nasty whore. Pastor Dollar always said, "The devil will talk you into sinning against God and then he'll accuse you after you do it." "I'm just really tired," Holly said. "So let me get outta here. I want you to rest up," Philip said. He swung his legs off the side of the bed, standing. "There's no rush," Holly said. Philip glanced back over his shoulder at her as he slipped into his shirt. "Thanks, but I gotta get goin'. They're gonna be lookin' for me at the restaurant in a few." Holly didn't respond. She leaned forward, wrapping the sheet tightly around her naked body. "Do you see my drawers?" Philip asked as he got down on his knees, looking under the bed. "No." Holly said. She got up and quickly put on the shorts and T-shirt she wore last night. "Wait a minute..." Philip pulled the underwear out from under the bed and started to laugh. "What?" Holly asked, peering down at him. "These are yours." Philip tossed the navy thong at Holly. She caught them and her eyes landed on the Bible. Standing up, Philip stepped into his Calvin's and pulled them up. Then he bent down, picking up his pants. "So what are you up to today?" he asked. Holly appeared to be a little stunned at his question. It was almost as if she wasn't expecting him to care. "Um, I was thinking about visiting my mother," she said as she opened the curtains, lifting the blinds. The sun snuck into the apartment from the bottom and sides of the wooden venetians, brightening the room. She wanted him to hurry up and leave all of a sudden. Confusion was seemingly having its way. "Good, good," Philip said, a small part of him wishing he had the same type of relationship with his mother. Holly nodded her head and lowered her eyes before she turned toward the window again, peeking out while Philip continued to dress. She felt nauseous.

She'd make their farewell short and sweet because she knew she could never ever see him again if she wanted to please the Lord and live the life He planned for her.

Moving over near the sink, Holly stared at her reflection in the bathroom mirror seconds after Philip left. She didn't even tell him that she wasn't going to see him again. Why would he call her anyway? The hazel-eyed woman shook her head. It wasn't about Philip Williams, she told herself. It was all about God. Holly's hair was standing on top of her head, looking like a confused knot of threads. Her mind must look like this. The remains of yesterdays makeup somewhat covered her face. She continued to watch herself in the mirror as she thought about a couple of the quotes in some article she had read. "Sometimes people come into your life for a season and sometimes they come into your life for a reason," was the basis of both written pieces. Philip's entry into her world was without a doubt for a reason. Sex. Sin. Holly started to weep. She cried loud, raising her arms heavenward as her head fell back. "Lord, please forgive me," she whaled. Then her head jerked forward, hanging down. Holly could feel her body going limp and she landed on her knees, still sobbing at the top of her lungs. "Father, help me. Help me be who you want me to be," she pleaded.

Making her way over to the toilet, the hazel-eyed woman began to vomit. She cried out to God all morning long.

Chapter Seven

At 2:05 p.m. Holly opened her apartment door. She was heading over to her mother's place. As she stepped out into the quiet hall, she saw that the door of the vacant apartment directly across from hers was opened. She didn't want to appear nosy as she pressed for the elevator so she stared down at the floor until the sound of a familiar voice prompted her to take a peek. It was the woman she'd seen talking to Peter yesterday morning. The same woman she'd thought she'd seen somewhere before. The White woman was standing in the foyer of the empty apartment, talking on a cellular phone. Holly could hear her echoing voice tell the person on the other end that she was having the place painted and how she'd be all settled in about a week. Still listening, Holly jumped when the elevator bell rang, indicating that it had arrived. The sound also caused the White woman to wince. She turned abruptly in Holly's direction, presenting her with a slight smile as their eyes locked. Holly said, "hello" and boarded the elevator. While the doors closed, she forced herself to remember where or how she'd been acquainted with this mysterious woman. Was she an old client as she'd thought before? Well, now that they were neighbors, she'd have some time for the answer to her question to come.

"Wait a minute, Barbara! I think I hear somebody comin' in on me! *Will* you hold on! Yes, I'm gone pray fo' you! Hole on!" Cynthia exclaimed into the phone, her eyes signaling agitation. "*Thank you!*" She huffed and shook her head. Walking out of the kitchen, the older woman's distorted face smoothed out when she saw her daughter. Holly was locking the front door of her mother's apartment. "Hi, babygirl. That Barbara Mathews wouldn't let me put down the phone to save my tail, if I had to," her mother whispered. Holly smiled, giving her a hug. "Well, continue your conversation. I just want to see how the furniture looks," Holly said softly. Nodding her head, Cynthia told her she would only be a minute as she stepped back into the kitchen, lifting the receiver to her ear. "It is my babygirl," Cynthia told her friend. "Yeah, you were right. Maria and her physic friends better watch out. *No, you ain't no prophet*! Now, whatcho want me to pray 'bout?" Holly shook her head at her mother's sarcasm as she turned around to face the sun-lit living room. How did she know her mother would have the chairs and sofa covered in that hideous plastic? Sighing deeply, she couldn't figure out why the older woman failed to see that their days of protecting what little they had were long gone? She could hear her mother hang up the telephone then approach her from behind. "Babygirl, don't it look *fine*?" Cynthia Reed said. Still surveying the room, Holly didn't answer. Her eyes were trying to see what was going on. Where most of the faults were. Knowing that her mother didn't have the gift of interior design, made her not allow her concentration to be broken. Holly frowned at the way things were arranged once she'd taken it all in. Her mother had tables next to tables and chairs next to the sofa without having separated them with something. A lamp, anything. Everything looked as though it were on display at a close-out sale. How could she undo what her mother had done without making her feel bad? "Baby, don't you like it?" her mother asked. Turning to finally face the older woman, Holly smiled as she folded her arms across her chest. "I do. *But* I think we should try it in a few other ways, okay?" she said softly. "Sure, whatever you think. You knowed your mama has no clue when in comes to makin' things look there absolute best. Well, except when it came to my sweet babygirl." The older woman patted her daughter gently on the arm. "Would you like me to fix youa plate? I gotta baked chicken in the oven and some greens and mashed potatoes on the stove." "Sounds good, but let me finish up in here first," Holly said, focusing on what she was going to do.

"Okay. And once you done, I wanna hear all 'bout yo' evenin' out, you hear?" Holly paused and said a quiet,"Okay."

Cynthia had just finished telling her daughter how much better she was at beautifying whatever she touched. Holly thought about the way her mother pronounced the word "beautifying" and she wanted to ask her if she wanted to learn how to speak better while telling the older woman how she, too, could learn to do the same with decorating with God's help as the two women walked into the kitchen. "I'll leave my mother's way of talking in Your Hands," the younger woman quietly said to God like she had done many times before. She took a deep breath and smiled. Every time Holly saw her mother's vibrant kitchen, she got a spark of delight deep within. She was very pleased with the way it turned out. Knowing how much her mother enjoyed cooking, Holly made sure she and the redecorating crew paid special attention to this room. Her eyes danced around the substantial cooking space. The walls were covered with a delicate tea-cup and saucer motif wallpaper and were coordinated to match the curtains. They were silky and ruffled in a creamy ivory color. The older woman was standing at the stove, stirring the collard greens that she had reheated for her daughter. As Holly, who was now starving, waited patiently in the doorway for her to get them the right temperature, her eyes found their way down at the table mats. They, too, matched the curtains and wallpaper. Everything about her mother's kitchen was done in good taste. Now this was the way she'd always envisioned her mother living. The way Holly transformed her mother's living room matched the kitchen as well as every area of her mother's two-bedroom apartment. The entire 1,700 square feet looked absolutely beautiful. The older woman turned toward her daughter, carrying a piping-hot plate of her home cooking. "C'mon and sit down, baby," is what she said as she placed it down on the table atop of the place mat. "So, what did you find out about him?" her mother asked. She pulled one of the oak chairs out from under the table and sat down across from her daughter. Holly began telling her mother everything she'd found out about Philip and his family. She left out the part about her having sex with Philip. And as she spoke, her mother had a look of "oh no" on her face like she knew something about that which her daughter was trying to hide. She'd have to keep praying. There were too many seasons of her having to protect her child so hearing about something like this made her wonder who it was that went up on the line at church few weeks ago to rededicate herself to the Lawd. It felt like a sharp pain was invading her chest. Standing to retrieve the empty plate before Holly, her mother said, "Everything you said made me feel like I was being kicked and punched?" What if she knew everything, Holly mused. How could I be so weak and stupid? the younger woman thought. "Well, when can I meet him?" she asked. Holly stood up and opened the refrigerator, taking a pitcher of iced water out. "You don't have to pray anymore, mom. I'm not going to see him again." The younger woman began to cry. She knew her mother's question was a test. "Don't weep, babygirl." Cynthia hugged her daughter. "Our God is a merciful God," said the older woman as she thought, what in the world really happened between Holly and that man last night? "You wanna tell yo' mama why you cryin'?" Holly shook her head no and pulled away from the older woman. She wiped the tears from her eyes. "I'm just tired I guess," was what she quietly said.

Peering over at the grandfather clock, standing tall in her mother's foyer, Holly realized that two and a half hours had nearly gone by. When the towering time-piece chimed, informing the women that it was now 5:00 p.m, Holly stood up from the sofa, which was now free of plastic, and announced softly to her dozing mother that she was going to leave. Yawning as she stretched her arms and legs, Cynthia lowered her feet off of the brown leather ottoman. Then, suddenly, the older woman jumped up from her seat. She quickly appraised the room once again. "I almost fo'got! My bookclub ladies is comin' over. They should be here any minute!" she said, still looking around. She loved the way everything turned out. "Mom, please be mindful about the way you move!" Holly said. Cynthia nodded. "I will. I will. Baby, I am so glad you changed this place 'round like you did. It feels so much better in here. Comfortable. I never even realized that this stool and chair went together," her mother said, referring to the two pieces she had been resting on. Holly smiled as her "your welcome" was interrupted by the doorbell. She gave her mother a kiss and insisted she let her get it as she waved and made her way toward the front door, opening it. "Hi, Ms. Diane! Oh, hello, Ms. Judy and Ms. Maureen!" The three older women said their "hello's" back to Holly and then Ms. Judy introduced her to the other woman that the hazel-eyed woman didn't know as she let them all in. "This is Cynthia's gorgeous daughter," she said. "I'm Rainy Carmicheal. Nice to meet you, dear." "Ms. Carmicheal, the pleasure is mine," Holly said as she turned toward her mother. "Mom, your bookclub friend's are here ..." "I see'um!" Cynthia said. "Nice to meet you, dear." she added, mimicking Rainy. "Umph, don't letta trick you. Her folks named her Rainy but she more like a storm!" All of the women began to laugh as they came in and sat down. Holly was still standing in front of the door as she needed a good laugh. Ms. Maureen was looking around the apartment. "It looks so beautiful in here, Cynthia," she said. "It really does," Ms. Judy said. She was looking around too. "Yes, Lawd. It does look very beautiful!" Holly's mother said. She nodded toward her daughter. "My Blessin' did it all by haself, wit dat anointin' the Father gifted ha wit." All of the older women glanced over at Holly and smiled. "Ya'll, Barbara asked me to pray for ha!" Cynthia said. She was trying not to giggle. The older women were focused on her now. "I'm onlys tellin' ya'll this so we could all agree!" "I'm not listening to you," Rainy said. She rolled her eyes and crossed her legs as she tossed the book they were all reading down on the coffee table. "Calling me a storm... The Lord told me He named me that because rain makes things grow!" Rainy said, sticking her neck out toward Cynthia, she said, "Grow up, Reed!" and started to giggle. Cynthia waved her hand at her and laughed some more. "Listen! Barbara need the Lawd to tell ha if He want ha here wit us tonight at the bookclub or do He want ha to go out wit dat man from the laundry place where she go? He don't knowed the Lawd but Barbara said he look like he might be on his way to knowin Him." Ms. Judy made a face. "What?!" She waved her hand. "I'm not entertaining no non-sense!" Holly was smiling until she heard Barbara Mathew's dilemma. As Ms. Maureen began to ask questions concerning her prayer request, the hazel-eyed woman opened her mother's front door and quietly left.

A ringing phone welcomed Holly home. Locking her door, she turned on the foyer light and made her way into the kitchen, picking up the receiver. "Hello!" she said, panting as she placed her hand over her throbbing chest. "Hey, it's Philip," said the voice on the other end. "You okay?" Holly sat down at the kitchen table and smiled. He called. "I'm fine. I just got in." "That's right, visitin' your mother." She didn't know if she was surprised, impressed or flattered that he had remembered. But she couldn't be fooled by that. He's not for me. He's not for me. "Yes, that's right," is all she said. "Philip, please hold on for a minute. That's my other line." She said it with a voice that told him that she needed to talk to him about something important. Vanessa could hear the annoyance in her friend's voice when she said hello. Sounds like things didn't work out with Philip last night, she guessed. "I was calling to find out how *your*...date went." "it went." Holly refused to share what had happened with Vanessa. The full-figured woman paused. "What did he do?" Vanessa asked. "I don't want to talk about it, Vee. And, it wasn't a date!" "Okay, but the man was hooked immediately. Courtney said the same thing." Holly felt like she wanted to smile but she didn't. "As a matter of fact, Philip's on the other line." "I'm sorry, go on. We'll talk tomorrow." She clicked back over to him. "Hello." "I'm here." "That was Vanessa." Philip laughed. "What's so funny?" she asked, standing to open the refrigerator. "Was she calling to see how everything went?" She could still hear him laughing a little. Pausing to take a few sips of water, Holly finally said, "Yes, she was." She placed the small bottle back into the refrigerator and sat back down. "Well, what did you tell her?" "That's between me and Vanessa," she teased. "Ooooh! I get it. It's a woman thing." "You catch on pretty fast." Holly paused. I can't see you anymore, she thought. "Do you know if Courtney was home?" Philip asked before Holly could say those words filling her mind. "No, I don't." Just then, Philip's call waiting interrupted them. "Holly, hold on that's my telephone now. You ain't the only popular one." He didn't hear anything as he switched over. "Hello," Philip said. "Are you on the other line?" asked the familiar voice. Rolling his eyes, he said, "Yes, I am! What is it?" "I don't know why you're being so nasty. I never hear you squawk when I ...," said the voice defensively. Sighing, Philip combed his fingers through his hair. "What do I have to do to get you to leave me alone? Tell your man? You have someone good. Why can't you just be satisfied?" The woman on the other line started to laugh loudly. "Yeah, he is good, but nobody and I do mean nobody, knows how to work it better than you, honey. Truthfully, you've become quite addicting. I never realized your ability to....." "Look, I have to go. My girlfriend is holding," he said, cutting her short. Chuckling again, the voice said, "Your girlfriend? Aren't we moving kind of fast?" "I'm gonna hang up!" he threatened. "Okay, wait. Listen! ... I'm home alone," said the voice abruptly. "And?" "*And*, why don't you come over to keep me company? My so-called better half is out of town until tomorrow." Philip was quiet for a moment. He glanced down at the bulge rising in his pants. "I'll see what I could do," he finally said. "But, I'm not makin' you any promises. So if you have other plans, don't break them." Giggling once again, the voice told him she'd be waiting for him. Philip closed his eyes tightly once she'd hung up, taking a few deep breaths. "Um, Holly. I have to go. That was Andrew. He has to leave. Said somethin' about somebody bein' sick. So I have to head over to the restaurant now. Duty calls." "Didn't you hear what I said?" she asked as she was quickly reminded that she never told him that she couldn't see him anymore. "No, what did you say?"

Philip asked. Holly paused, knowing that she never said anything. She just thought it. "Uh, nothing. Let me let you go." "Talk to you later," is what he said and hung up. I got this, he told himself as he rushed out the door for his destination.

After they'd hung up, Holly sat there with her head resting against the wall. Why did she feel trapped?

Chapter Eight

Dressed in a sand Jil Sander suit, Holly lifted her tortoiseshell, Oliver Peoples sunglasses atop her head as she climbed the six steps of the brownstone, smiling to herself. She'd always got an extra surge of energy when she went to work. Though many of her days were tiresome, she never ever regretted the time she'd spent beyond those wooden doors. The thought, alone, of being able to help someone get just treatment, made her working day all the more rewarding. The firm specialized mostly in high-powered cases, but with Holly as a partner, she would not allow Vanessa or Tracy to ever turn down someone less fortunate, if need be. Representing the poor made her feel as though she was doing something deeper than just practicing law. Cynthia Reed once said her child was sent here to do the Lawd's work. So be it, Holly thought. "At least the goodness of the Lord was being revealed through her profession," she muttered under her breath.

As she reached deep into her brown Gucci Jackie O styled bag for her keys, the sun bounced off of the golden sign bearing the lawyers' names. It caused Holly's eyes to squint due to the blinding glare. The attorney opened the walnut door with the glass that allowed you to see in or out, glancing over at the reception desk. Telma was no where in sight, but she could smell the coffee brewing. Hazelnut. Her favorite perk-me-up concoction. Holly walked in, closing and locking the door behind herself.

Heading in further, the white-washed hardwood floors creaked in accordance to her every step. She stopped next to Telma's desk, calling out her name. And, emerging, directly on cue from the kitchen, was the young cafe au lait-colored woman. She was dressed in a white shirt and black pleaded skirt and her long, thick hair was done in a single braid, dangling down the center of her back. As Telma dried her hands with a paper towel she smiled and said, "Good morning, Holly. I was just washing out the coffee cups from Friday's meeting." The attorney returned the smile and thanked her for cleaning up as she proceeded for the stairs. Mounting them, she could hear her secretary, Kelly on the telephone so when Holly reached the top of the landing, she continued to make her way into her office, just waving to her grinning assistant as she passed by.

The sun light spilled through the big picture window in her office. Smiling, though surprised, Holly walked inside. Her eyes were focused on the large amber bouquet of daylilies. They were arranged beautifully in a Waterford vase in the center of her cherrywood desk. Bending over them, she breathed in the delectable scent. The card, signed by P.W., read: "These reminded me of the color of your eyes. I thoroughly enjoyed the time we spent together." Holly was starting to feel giddy. Wait a minute. She told him she couldn't see him anymore. She slipped off her suit jacket, stuck her sunglasses inside of the inner pocket and hung it on a hanger on the back of her door. Oh, no she didn't! After anxiously refastening the second to top button on her shirt that had popped opened, she sat down behind her desk, placing her hand atop of the receiver. She was deciding whether or not she should call to thank him right then and there. No, she thought, pulling her hand away. She'd wait a while, after all it was only 9:15 a.m. and she wasn't his girlfriend. Lord, I want to stay with Philip, she said to herself. Maybe he'd get saved. Come with her to church. If she kept her promise to her mother to go. Help me, Father. Still astonished at his appreciation of her, she slid the bouquet toward the corner of her desk. As she did this, she could hear Kelly hang up the phone and approach her doorway. "Hey, Holly. Would you like some coffee?" her secretary asked as her eyes floated toward the gift her boss had received. Holly was now shuffling through the papers and files she'd lifted from her in-box. She told the young woman that she'd love some. And, before she could look up from the substantial pile, Kelly was crossing the threshold. "Here you go," she said, setting the white cup and saucer down on Holly's desk. "Thanks, Kel." "So, did you like "Phil's House"?" Kelly asked without hesitation. Looking up into the face of her assistant, Holly started to grin. "I did like it. It was just as you described it." Holly reached over, picking up the cup. "Wasn't the food good?" Kelly asked as she continued to stand in the front of her employer's desk. Eagerly shifting her weight back and forth from one foot to the other, she started to ask Holly again. "Delicious," the hazel-eyed woman said. As she took a sip of the nut-flavored coffee, she stared at her secretary through the steam. "The owner's not so bad, either. Did you see him?" Kelly asked. She was out to lunch on Friday when Philip was in the office. Holly took another quick sip before placing the cup back down. "*Yes,* I did see him," she said, clearing her throat. "In fact, Courtney introduced us. You know Vanessa's husband." Kelly's eyes widened. "Of course I know him." "Well, they were in the office on Friday while you were out." "What!" The loud thump caused by Kelly stomping her foot, made Holly jump. She hesitated and nodded. "Yeah, we uh..." "What! What!" Kelly asked. Her eyes growing even wider. "We went out on Saturday night. Philip and I." Holly didn't see her assistant's mouth gradually become a hateful line. She had resumed back to looking through the papers on her desk. "Oh," is what Kelly managed to say, even though it felt as if she'd been kicked in the stomach by Billy Blanks. Her thoughts were going wild. She had wanted Philip Williams for herself. Spending night after night after night alone or with her friends, plotting ways to snatch him up was something she'd done with more determination than she'd ever knew she had. And, now that she'd finally come up with a scheme, the ultimate plan, she wasn't going to just stand around and let this man-stealing "Vanessa L.Williams" wannabe, playing innocent in front of her, turn her mission into some fantasy. Over her dead body she would! Kelly stood there with her lips pressed tightly together. She had to think positive thoughts to prevent herself from saying something inappropriate, as the words *I should kick her skinny ...* raced through her veins like a drunk driver speeding up a rain-slicked highway. Soon she'd have plenty of time to speak her mind, she mused. "That's great, Holly. Ya'll must look cute together," is what the secretary heard herself say. Holly looked up at her and smiled. "So, how did it go?" Kelly asked. She was trying her best not to sound as though she was being too familiar. They were the same age, but Holly was still her employer. "It went really well." "Great." Kelly's eyes wandered back over to the flowers. "I guess he's the one who sent you those?" Beaming stronger than the light trickling in behind her, Holly told her assistant that they did come from him. And as Kelly turned to leave, she was amazed at her own capability to maintain the forced pretense of happiness on her face. Approaching the doorway, she glanced back over her shoulder and lied to Holly once again about her being glad that things worked out. "Well, thank you, Kel. And thanks for enlightening me about his restaurant." "You're welcome. I better get back to work,"she said, pulling the door closed behind her.

Not more than five minutes had passed before Tracy tapped on Holly's door and strolled in. She was holding a cup of coffee in her hand and wearing a smile on her face. "Don't look at me like that. You know why I'm here." Tracy took a seat in one of the burgundy leather chairs opposite her partner's desk. Holly laughed. "I guess a few of my questions have already been answered," Tracy said. She was looking at the flowers. Holly started to laugh some more. "So they are from him?" Tracy asked. Holly nodded. "All right, Ms. Reed. I want details, details and more details,"Tracy said, sweeping her short, well-manicured bangs to the side. Holly giggled again as she watched her partner situate herself. "Enough laughing, honey. *Speak*," Tracy teased and blinked her new eyelash hooded eyes. Sinking back into the cushion frame of her chair, Holly began telling her friend all about her memorable evening while she swiveled back and forth. But, when she came closer to the conclusion of their date, she glanced awkwardly over at Tracy and made her chair become motionless. Holly's eyes were filled with uncertainty. She could feel an uneasiness stirring within. "All right, he walked you home, *and?*" Tracy said. Pausing briefly, Holly said, "*And*, we had a glass of orange juice." She averted her eyes. When Tracy saw the look of embarrassment on her friend's face, she pushed the issue even more. She leaned forward and a few disobedient strands from her bangs followed, covering part of her left eye. "That's it?" Tracy combed them back to the side with her fingers. Holly lowered her head. "Don't look down like that. It's me Tracy. I should be the last person, making you feel bashful. Come on, you're my girl. I'm not gonna call you a ho or something tacky like that. So what happened next?" Sighing, Holly stared across her desk, deep into the eyes of her friend and partner. Then she motioned for her to close the door. "Trace, Philip and I slept together." she whispered after her partner shut it and sat back down. "Are you satisfied now?" she added. Tilting her head, Tracy said, "Am I satisfied? I should be asking you that." "No," Holly said. She wiped the tear that was suddenly falling from her eye. Tracy stood up, set her cup on the credenza and walked around the desk, hugging her partner. "I don't know. Does God forgive you?" is was Tracy said. Holly nodded. "But I have to stop." She swallowed and sighed. "I know you don't want my advice," Tracy said. She smoothed down the back of her skirt and made her way around Holly's desk for the door. "I wouldn't tell Vee if I were you. That woman could create more tension than I had when I was looking for my last period." Tracy smiled, picked up her empty cup off the credenza and headed out the door.

It was 11:10 a.m. when Kelly announced over Holly's intercom that Carmen was on the phone. Detecting something different in her secretary's voice, Holly signed off on a letter she'd been reading and answered. "Hello." "Hi, are you busy?" Inhaling another whiff of the flowers, Holly said, "No. I was just finishing up on a few things." "Well, I won't take up much of your time. I just need to know what happened with you guys before I explode. Did you tell him?" Holly smiled. She was about to take another sip of coffee, but quickly decided against it, knowing that it was probably as cold as ice. "Girl,

I had a great time..." "Uh oh," said the Latina woman. "You didn't tell him that you can't see him anymore..." Their conversation was interrupted by a knock on the door. Excusing herself for a second, Holly covered the mouthpiece of the receiver and told whoever it was to come in. Vanessa opened the door and peeked inside. Holly smiled and motioned for her to enter. "You're on the phone. I'll come back later," the full-figured woman said, glancing at the daylilies. "It's Carmen. I could put her on speaker." Vanessa made a face but she still agreed. She walked in and took a seat. Holly pressed the "hands free" button and hung up the receiver. "Carmen, I have you on speaker now. Vanessa's here. She wants to hear about the date ... I mean, my time out with Philip, too." Carmen stayed quiet as Holly proceeded to tell them all about her evening with Philip without mincing words. "Just tell me one thing," Vanessa said after Holly had finished. "What?" Holly had hesitation in her voice. "Did you use protection? Because between all of us, and this lamp on Holly's desk, I hear that he's got some reputation." Stunned, Holly peered down at the phone. She could hear Carmen make a comment in Spanish. She didn't want to hear anything except that Holly wasn't seeing him anymore. "Holly, how could you?" Carmen asked. Holly stared down at the phone. She knew she wasn't being herself. The full-figured woman gave her a half smile, slapped herself on the knee's, stood up and walked out without saying good-bye. As Holly listened to her heels click down the hall, past her own office and into Tracy's, she picked up the receiver. "Let me go," she said softly to the Latina woman. "Is she gone?" Carmen asked, sounding bothered. "Yes..... she's gone." "I'm so disappointed, Holly. I know I don't have to tell you what I'm thinking right now. Why did you tell Vanessa?" Holly sat there quietly for a moment. "I don't know why I told her," the hazel-eyed woman said. "Okay, let's forget her for a second. I'm concerned about you," Carmen said, the anger leaving her voice. Holly began to explain how she wanted to tell Philip that she couldn't see him anymore, "but I didn't. I like him, Carmen." The Latina woman said something in Spanish again.

"What about God? Isn't He more important?" Holly nodded. "I asked Him to help me." "You have to truly want His help, Holly." "Yes, I know ... but I also accepted the flowers Philip sent me. They're on my desk." "So what! Throw them away and start all over again with the Lord." Holly nodded again. She wasn't going to get rid of the bouquet. "You should've been the lawyer," is what she told her best friend just before they hung up.

Chapter Nine

Holly's head was bent over a file she scanned as the heat from the sun lay across her shoulders. She was going over a possible case that had come in on Friday. A woman by the name of Leslie Stokes called her up claiming that her, as she put it, common-law husband had been physically abusing her and she wanted out of the relationship before she killed him. Holly would have to inform her at their first meeting this afternoon that in New York, as in most states today, there is no such thing as common-law marriage. It pained her, knowing that Ms. Stokes would be crushed. The troubled couple had been living together for twelve years -- ten of them civil, but the last two were unbearable, more than she'd bargained for. She also asked the attorney what she would be entitled to financially. He, was her only source of income, and knowing that he'd refuse to support her willingly, Ms. Stokes had asked Holly to supply her with the most helpful but inexpensive legal advice she could offer. Unfortunately, her answer to this distressed woman was simple. Drumming her pen against the desk, Holly then flung it down, pushing herself back against the chair. Sometimes the law appeared so foggy to her. Almost foreign. Just like London on a dreary night. She let out a long sigh. Now she'd have to tell Ms. Stokes that in the absence of marriage she is left without the support system of a governing body of rules. In other words, according to the law, this woman's plea was useless. She could not look to the state for protection because, without a marriage contract, the state is not involved. Point blank! Turning her seat toward the window, Holly sighed again as she shook her head in dismay. Why do some people get themselves caught up in these type of no-win situations, she thought, glumly. And why did she stick around, letting this man beat on her for two whole years like she had the word everlasting printed across her forehead? Still shaking her head, she spun back around to face her desk, burying her face in the palms of her hands. She let out yet another long sigh. "Who am I?" she mumbled into her hands. She had no right to be in the position to assist anyone out of a terrible relationship when she kept getting herself into them. The sound of Vanessa's secretary's husky voice blaring into her boss' intercom next door forced her to look up. Samantha was alerting Vanessa that Courtney was on the telephone. A few minutes had gone by before Holly heard Vanessa answer. And from the sequence of their conversation, she assumed he was away. She could hear Vanessa asking him how everything was going and what time his flight was scheduled to arrive. Then immediately after that, she heard Vanessa snap violently into the phone, "Do you think I would be asking if I had your itinerary with me? Give me a break, Courtney, please! Yeah, okay. I know you didn't mean it the way it sounded. Well, I'm pretty stressed out myself. All right, all right, let's not argue, honey. Would you like me to pick you up from the airport? Are you sure? Well, then I'll see you at home tonight. Have a safe trip. Bye." Sitting there quietly after the couples' call had come to an end, Holly wondered as she often did, how he could have married someone as unhappy as his wife was. Kelly's somber voice penetrated Holly's intercom before she could think of a rational explanation. The secretary asked her whether or not she would take a call from a Mr. Philip Williams. Glancing down at her watch, Holly was upset to see that it was 12:00 p.m. She'd forgotten to thank him for the flowers. Holly could feel her palms moistening as she told Kelly she'd pick him up in a second. She didn't want him to think she was an ingrate like her partner seated in the office adjacent to hers was. She answered. "Hi, Philip. I've been meaning to call you. These are the most cheerful flowers I've ever seen." "You mean they remind you of yourself, too," he said, smiling. She smiled, too. "Well, I don't know about that, but they made my day. You're so kind." He didn't know what it was about this woman. The sound of her voice alone made him feel like he was a different man. Better than ever before. She took him to a place he'd never visited before. A place he had refused to go many times. He'd always fought it in the past, but this time he was ready and willing to follow her anywhere. "So, tell me, Ms. Holly. Am I too late?" he asked. With a questioning look forming on her face, she said, "Too late for what?" Lord, please don't tell her she'd forgotten something else. "I'm not going to stop seeing you," she said. Philip nodded and smiled. That wasn't what he was talking about, but he was glad. "Thank you. That makes me very happy," he said. Holly abruptly grabbed her mouth almost like she was trying to snatch it off of her face. She could feel a tear streaming down her cheek. She cleared her throat and lowered her hand from her mouth when Philip asked, "Has someone already asked you out to lunch?" He shut his eyes tightly. Although his tone was cavalier, he didn't want to hear the word yes come out of her mouth. "Uh, no and I'm really hungrey," she said with a smile. Philip's eyes sprung open to her response. "Well, I'll take care of that," he said, grinning. Standing up from behind his desk, Philip asked her if she'd like to meet him some place for lunch. "Love to. Why don't we go to........ Randy's?" Holly said. She sucked hard on her bottom lip to keep from cracking up. "And she's funny, too," he said, chuckling. This is not a time for laughter, she thought as thoughts of Jesus entered her mind. She paused. He paid for her stupidity on the cross at Calvary. She cleared her throat again. "I'll meet you there at 1:00 p.m. Is that okay?" "Perfect," was Philip's reply.

At 12:15 p.m. Holly stepped out of her office, heading to meet Philip. She mentioned to Kelly in passing that she'd be back by 2:00 p.m. As her eyes made their way down the small hall, leading to her partners' offices, she saw that they were behind closed doors in Vanessa's office. She turned back to face her assistant, adding, "I have a 2:15p.m. appointment with a woman by the name of Leslie Stokes. I'll let Telma know on my way out. See you later." "I'll be here," said her secretary quietly. She had continued typing all the way through Holly's brief conversation. As she stabbed away at the keyboard, Kelly could feel a quickening in her chest. Pure hate in her heart. Then cutting her eyes in the direction of the stairs, she watched Holly as she descended them. Slut! She listened for the downstairs door to close behind her boss while her hands slowly became two violent fists. Knowing that Holly was on her way to meet *her* man, burned the secretary up. Made her fume. This time she refused to have the man she loved be taken away from her like her last boyfriend, Elliot Dickson had been. She never even saw it heading her way. No indications at all. He just said he needed time to find himself. To figure things out. Claimed he just didn't want to be in a serious relationship anymore. Two weeks later the snake got married to a woman who was light, bright and close to White. Just like Holly. Why did the high-yellow long-haired ones get all the good men? she thought. Didn't these brothers know that the dark sistah's were always better? Kelly lifted a small two-sided mirror from her top right-hand drawer, and peered intensely at her reflection. She studied herself carefully, turning her head from side to side, examining everything. There was nothing wrong, nothing abnormal, nothing she'd have to be ashamed of pertaining to her strong features. *This* was the face of a true sistah. A queen. Wide nose and natural 'fro. Arching her back with the utmost pride, the assistant placed the round looking glass back in the drawer. Evidently, Philip's never had a taste of the real thing. Yes, an authentic woman. She'd have to give him a sample. Soon. Very, very soon. And this time she'd stay abreast of the situation. Like a fly on dog ... you know what, she mused, making herself want to laugh really loud. That's right, she was *not* going to let him get away. First time, shame on them. Second time, shame on you, she reminded herself with a grin.

Holly could see Philip sitting at the bar from the outside of Randy's, which was a small eatery that opened in 1937. The old-school East Side restaurant has decor, staff and menu that have changed little over the decades. When she walked inside Philip looked at her from head to toe as he pulled himself up from the stool. "Hey, sweetness," he said, leaning over to give her a kiss. It seemed as though he'd needed a fix from the way his lips met hers. Like he couldn't wait. He seemed desperate. At this point, Holly wasn't thinking about God. After he moved away, she smiled at the sophisticated-looking hostess standing behind her companion. "Two?" the woman asked, holding up her crimson-nailed fingers. She was grinning at the couple. "Yes," Holly said and they followed her to the table. "Old, but not bad," Philip whispered into the back of Holly's head as he stared around the quiet restaurant. She turned toward him. "I take it you've never been here before?" He shook his head. "Nah!" "So, how did you know that your place 'blew this one out of the water?' Wasn't that what you said while you were trying to pick me up?" Philip laughed. "Ay, that's what a few of my customers keep tellin' me. I can't help it if their partial." He smiled and shrugged his shoulders. Holly returned his contagious grin, shaking her head.

The hostess brought them to the center of the restaurant, where most of the other patrons were seated. Looking around, Holly saw that there were only two waitresses and a bus boy, handling the rather large crowd. She didn't want to be late for her appointment, but at the same time, she didn't want Philip to feel as though she didn't want to be with him. "Lynn, will be with you in a minute," the hostess said. She placed two menus down on the table then pointed to the woman tending their station. "She's really busy today, so please be patient," the hostess added before walking away. When the couple took their seats, Holly's eyes went off in the direction of the freckled-face light-skinned waitress with sandy-colored ponytailed hair. She met her gaze and the woman held up her index finger, indicating that she'd be right over. Holly nodded and started to scan the menu before her just as Philip was doing. "Hi, I'm Lynn. Are you ready to order?" asked the woman. Holly looked at Philip. "Are you?" she asked him. "Um, just a second," Philip said. He was stroking his chin as he continued to peruse the menu. "Would you like something from the bar?" asked the soft-spoken waitress. "This way you'll still have some time to decide," she added. "No, but I will have an iced tea. Thank you," Holly said. "And you, sir?" "I'll have a seltzer," he said. The waitress nodded as she wrote it down on her pad but before the light-skinned woman could walk away, Holly told her that she'd have tuna with lettuce and tomatoes on rye. She could see Philip's face emerging from behind the large menu. "And, I'll have an open turkey sandwich on white bread." "Okay," said the waitress. Once she jotted down their orders, the freckle-faced woman searched the restaurant, seeing whether or not one of the other patrons in her station was trying to get her attention.

Holly handed both menus to her and the woman moved toward the bar. "So, how's your day going so far?" Philip asked. He reached across the table for Holly's hand. "Fine and yours?" "I got a lot done. Andrew had a busy night." Suddenly, he could feel Holly's hand flinch in his. "I thought Andrew had something to take care of. Someone was sick, right?" She glared at him suspiciously. Philip's eyes flashed a little, opening wide at first then going back to their normal state. "Yeah, you're right. *But,* he came back later on." Nodding her head slowly, Holly felt better once his response registered.

"That wasn't so bad," Philip said. He was referring to his lunch. "My mother always said don't knock it until you've tried it," Holly said with a smile. Suddenly the thought of Cynthia Reed crossed her mind. What was her mother going to say about Holly still being with Philip. He leaned back in his seat, wearing a broad grin on his face. "Mine, too." he lied, knowing that his mama always did the opposite. Knocked the heck out of people she felt were beneath her and very rarely did she take to them later. Philip glared across the small table at Holly as she glanced down at her Rolex. "Well, I better be gettin' back to the restaurant," he said, shifting in his seat. There was no way he was gonna let a woman tell him that she was leaving first. Wait a minute. What was he doin'? He had to keep reminding himself that Holly Reed was different. She stared back at him "Oh, uh, yes. I should be getting back to work myself. I have a 2:15pm meeting and it's 2:00pm now." Philip nodded his head as he leaned forward, reaching into his back pocket. He pulled out a brown leather Coach wallet and signaled for the waitress.

Outside among the loud city traffic, the couple could hardly hear themselves say that they'd talk later after giving each other a hug.

As Holly strode quickly down the block, taking peeks at her watch on occasion, Philip stood in front of the restaurant, his arms folded across his broad chest, gazing at her. He watched as the warm breeze blew through her silky hair. Maybe she'd turn back one last time so he'd be able to see that pretty face again. He loved the way her clothing clung to her body, showing off all the right curves. Who would have thought he'd find a woman who deserved him? Deserved his honest lovin'. This lady was beautiful, intelligent and she had a good sense of humor. It felt right. Man, he *should* consider himself to be a lucky brother.

She never looked back so he walked away.

Waiting for the light to change on Park Avenue and 71st Street felt like hours had passed to Holly. The sun was beaming down hard on her and the heat was intolerable. It seemed as though she'd never taken a shower that morning. She didn't smell. She just felt hot and sweaty. Continuing to stand there, she glanced at her watch for what felt like the one-hundredth time. She shook her head. 2:15 p.m. and she still had to make it across this wide street and over to the far end of the next block. She despised tardiness. Why did it always feel as though everything that could possibly go wrong did when you had to get somewhere fast? she mused. Holly could feel the perspiration coursing her skin. She wanted to remove her jacket. But it wouldn't look professional. Besides that, the light was now in her favor.

Holly mounted the last step to the brownstone. As she turned the key in the door, she could see Ms. Stokes sitting on the sofa. She was reading one of the pamphlets found on the coffee table. But because the attorney was later than she planned on being, she'd have to usher her potential client into the conference room as soon as she got inside. Holly was somewhat astonished to see how attractive and nicely dressed the woman was, her voice was deceiving. The attorney was expecting to see someone who cared nothing about the way she looked, someone.... well, she didn't know what she'd expected. But this woman was actually more than attractive. Holly continued to stare at Leslie Stokes through the glass portion of the door for a moment longer. Her shoulder-length ringlets were a reddish brown and her eyes were the color of sparkling emeralds. They appeared greener then Carmen's. Probably because of the color of her skin. It had a magnificent ruddy glow. She was wearing a white ankle-length lycra tank dress, white high-heeled thong sandals and she had a small black leather backpack, resting at her feet. Never in a million years would she be mistaken for someone being abused. But then again, victims came in no particular category. Holly felt as though she'd known that better than anyone. Suffering, was no stranger to her. After all, sometimes contrary to the lawyer's own belief, she, too was still in recovery. She still had her own strength to solidify. "Well, that's in your hands, Lord," she said under her breath.

The loud honking of a car horn snapped the attorney out of her trance. Finally entering the structure, and heading in the woman's direction, Holly's eyes traveled over toward the reception desk. Telma wasn't there. When Ms. Stokes heard someone nearing her, she pulled her head up from the brochure and peered at the lawyer, appraising her from head to toe. It was almost as though she were taking inventory. And once her big green eyes, hooded with long mascaraed lashes, found Holly's hazel ones, she smiled, sticking the legal reading material down inside of her backpack. She lifted it to her lap. The attorney presented her with a grin as well. "Hi, it's a pleasure to meet you. I'm so sorry that I'm late. Please come this way," Holly said. Rising from the sofa, the woman followed the lawyer. As Holly pulled open the mahogany French doors, the sun streaming through the windows hit her in the face. Though it was warm in the meeting room, the heat she felt on her back, generated by the woman's scrutinizing gaze, was no comparison. "Please come inside and make yourself comfortable," said the attorney. The woman walked in and around to the other side of the large oval-shaped mahogany board room table, taking a seat in one of the eight matching high-back chairs. She still had not uttered a word. "Could I get you something to drink before we get started?" Holly asked. She was standing with her back to the doors. As she waited for the woman to answer, she could hear someone stirring about on the outside of the conference room. Telma was probably back at her desk, the lawyer thought. "No, thank you. I'm fine," the woman said softly. "Then, I guess we'll began." Holly, too, sat down at the table, crossing her legs. "So, about our conversation...." The attorney's sentence was cut off by a faint tapping on the door. Holly peered back over her shoulder. It was Telma trying to tell her something. Turning back toward the woman, Holly excused herself and stood up. She walked over, cracking only one door. "Yes," she said to the receptionist. "Sorry to interrupt you, but I just wanted you to know that Ms. Stokes called to cancel her appointment. She and her *fiance* worked things out. Their getting married.... She said that you'll know what she meant." Swallowing hard, Holly stiffened. "Are you all right?" Telma asked, noticing the stunned expression on the lawyer's face. "Um, yes, but who is this sitting...." "My name is Selma Girard," said the woman from behind her. Holly's eyes met Telma's. "Yeah, she's prospecting attorneys to help her and her husband close on a house," the receptionist said. "I told her that you all are criminal defense attorneys, but she still insisted on meeting you." "Oh," is all the lawyer could say. "I was in the bathroom, Holly," Telma whispered, explaining why she'd left the front desk. "Don't worry about it." Holly closed the door, feeling foolish as she turned toward Selma Girard. "I thought you were someone else. You must have thought I was ... well... -- not having asked you a thing about yourself. We're not usually this careless around here. Please forgive me." "You don't need to explain. I understand. It's my fault. I didn't have an appointment," Ms. Girard said with a smile. Sitting back down, Holly began asking her a few questions in regards to the house. "Well, we've all come to an agreement. That's why I'm here. My husband and I need you, if you're willing, to help us with the finishing touches," Ms. Girard said. As the lawyer listened to the woman speak, she realized that a few things didn't make sense. Why didn't Selma Girard and her husband have someone representing them the entire time? "I see. Well, as our receptionist said, we are criminal defense attorneys." Selma nodded and reached down into her backpack I saw that in the pamphlet that took off of the coffee table out there." Holly nodded her head and smiled. "I could probabaly give you the names of some realestate lawyers if you like? I don't know any off the top of my head, but I will ask my partners if they know of any. Where is Mr. Girard? If you don't mind my asking. At this firm we make a point of talking to everyone involved," Holly said. She crossed her legs again. "Of course you do," said Ms. Girard quietly, her eyes investigating the room. "He's out of town until tonight," Selma added. She was now looking across the table at Holly. "I'll inform him of our conversation and give you a call later in the week. Is that okay?" Ms. Girard stood up. Standing too, the attorney told her that she'd be in the office most of the week. Selma's eyebrows rose. "Going on vacation?" she asked. Pausing briefly, Holly said, "Yes, it's long over due. I had just finished participating in a major case a little over a week ago. In fact, all three of us have been working extremely hard for months. My partners just closed on a case they'd been working on. I don't know about them, but I'm burned out." "Well, you look like a good team from the portrait outside above the sofa," Selma Girard said. The lawyer thanked her for the compliment as the woman walked around the table, heading for the doors. "I hope I didn't take up too much of your time, Ms. Reed." Selma Girard gave the attorney a firm hand shake. "How did you know my name?" Holly asked as their hands parted. "I'm sorry. I just thought your names went according to your positions in the portrait," said the woman with a smile as she slipped on her backpack. Holly smiled a little back. "You know, you are the first person who has ever guessed that correctly." Selma Girard shrugged her shoulders. "It makes sense," is what she said, telling a lie. She had seen the hazel-eyed attorney on television during the Moore vs. Moore trial and remembered hearing her name before when Philip told her about the lady who seemed to be stealing his heart. Nodding at the woman's reply, Holly pushed open the doors to the conference room. "I will be in touch with you if I come across the kind of lawyer that you need." "Oh, uh, okay. That sounds great!" Mrs. Girard said.

Nearing Telma's desk after locking the door behind the green-eyed woman, the lawyer said, "I can't believe that happened. They always say that one should never assume." "I still feel so bad. At first I thought she was a friend of yours," the receptionist said. Holly gave Telma an odd look. "What made you think that?" "She asked for you by name." Peering over at the portrait, the attorney then turned back to face Telma and paused. She was obviously consumed with a thought then she smiled at the receptionist, patted the top of her desk twice and started up the stairs without commenting on what she'd just heard.

Samantha was on her way down. "Hey, Holly. Vanessa left for the day." "Is everything all right?" "Oh, she's fine. She just wanted to be at home when Mr. Benjamin got in." "Uh-huh, where did he go?" Holly asked much to her own surprise. Her hunch was right. "He had to fly out to L.A. last minute to meet with a client." "I see." "And she also said it was okay for me to leave early, too." "Good for you. Well, don't let me hold you up. I'll see you tomorrow. Have a good night, Sam," Holly said. The lawyer continued up the stairs and stopped in front of Kelly's desk. "Anything going on?" Holly asked her. Kelly, still typing, said, "No, nothing." She never lifted her head from the computer keys to look at Holly. "That's a relief. Did you get a chance to finish the minutes from Friday's meeting?" the attorney continued not being disturbed by Kelly's attempt to disrespect her.

"Yeah, they're in your in-box," Kelly said quietly. "Thanks." When Holly headed toward her office, she could see Tracy standing at her secretary's desk, dictating a letter as the skinny light-skinned girl typed her employer's words into the computer. "Trace, Ms. Stokes canceled," Holly exclaimed. Turning to face her partner, the short-haired attorney shrugged. "What could you do, Holly? It happens every day. I guess he sang her a song she liked." Holly took a deep breath and nodded her head in agreement.

"What happened in here?" said the attorney from the inside of her office. Holly's tone was sharp. Five of her one dozen daylilies had been snapped at the stems. Getting up, Kelly stood at Holly's doorway, her mouth wide open in shock. "Oh, my God, I must've done that when I slid the vase over. I didn't even realize that the flowers broke off like that. Kelly paused and said, "I'm sorry, Holly." Sighing, the lawyer pulled out the damaged ones, tossing them into the wastepaper basket beside her desk. When she glanced back at the doorway to tell her secretary that it wasn't a problem, she was surprised to see that Kelly was no longer there. She could hear her typing on the computer again. If only that wall dividing the two of them wasn't there, Holly would have seen the sinister grin on her assistant's face. Usually, the dark-skinned woman would have said something more on the matter at hand when she'd caused a mishap. Big or small. But, this time it seemed as though she had absolutely no compunction for what she'd done.

What was going on? Holly thought back to the way her assistant's disposition had changed earlier. Suddenly. Maybe there was something going on in her personal life. Probably had something to do with a man. She'd wait a few days before asking.

Chapter Ten

As the evening descended, clouds drifted across the sky. It was 7:15 p.m. when Holly entered the lobby of her apartment building. Waving to Peter as she passed, she scooted into the waiting elevator. When the doors opened on the 4th floor, she jumped a little. Her new neighbor had frightened her. "Did I scare you?" the White woman asked. She was grinning. "My mind was elsewhere," Holly said, stepping off the elevator. "That makes the two of us," said the woman. "Well, I guess this is the perfect opportunity to introduce ourselves. I've seen you around a couple of times," the woman added. "Yes, I've seen you, too. I'm Holly Reed." "Kitty Wahl. It's a pleasure." The two women shook hands. "Welcome," Holly said. "Well, thank you. This is a lovely building. I'd always admired it." "So, you're from New York?" "Yes, but I moved away to Chicago once I got married." "Oh," Holly said. She didn't remember seeing the woman with a man. Noticing the puzzled look on her new neighbor's face, the White woman said, "I'm divorced now." "I'm sorry." "No, no. Don't be sorry. It was a good thing. My ex is the most difficult man I'd ever known...... well, with the exception of my father. But we won't get into that right now," Kitty said. A forced smile on the White woman's face was quickly erased when her cell phone rang. She stared down at the black object clipped to the waist band of her pants, then looking back up she said, while running her fingers through her hair, getting it out of her face, "I'm working the late shift. Maybe we could get together at either apartment for a chat." Holly nodded, wondering what Kitty did for a living. But she wasn't bold enough to ask. "Excuse me," Kitty said, answering her phone. "I'm on my way," she said into the phone and hung up. "Yes, yes. I'd enjoy that. Have a good night," said the lawyer. As she walked off toward her apartment, Holly glanced back over her shoulder, watching the mysterious, Kitty Wahl as she boarded the elevator. All through their short interaction, Holly tried to figure out where it was they'd met before. Not knowing bothered her more than she'd imagined it would.

Closing the door of her apartment, Holly dropped her keys and sunglasses on the foyer table, tossed her pocketbook on the window seat in her room, along with the suit and silk blouse she was wearing. After today's scorching forecast, there was no way she could have gotten another wear out of either of them without having had them dry cleaned first.

Clad in ivory La Perla underwear, with the matching bra, Holly poured herself a glass of white grape juice and relaxed on the striped sofa in the living room. Tucking her bare feet beneath her, Holly took a long swallow from the glass. Sometimes being alone made her feel wonderfully at peace. Other times she found it hard. But, tonight, it was all right, she began to think about her day. Leslie Stokes in particular came to mind. The attorney shook her head in disbelief. How could they have worked things out in two days? This woman was setting herself up for a disaster. A rude awakening. The man needs help. Maybe Holly would give her a call tomorrow to try talking her out of her new decision or just to let Ms. Stokes know that she'd be there for her incase their relationship had a relapse. Still pondering the thought, the telephone rang. She took another sip, set the half-full glass down on a sterling silver coaster and hurried to answer it. "Hello," she said. "Hey, sweetness," Philip said. Smiling, Holly said hello again. "What were you doin'?" he asked. "Unwinding. I just got in a few minutes ago." "Oh, yeah. I wish I could do the same. I'm still at the restaurant." She could feel the marble counter top against the small of her back. It was cold. "You poor thing," Holly said. She covered her mouth. "I mean, you wealthy thing," she said laughing a little. Philip paused. He had no idea that she was correcting what she said because the Bible states that you will have what you say. Holly cleared her throat. "How much longer will you be there?" she said, sensing his pondering how she corrected herself. "I don't know," Philip said quietly. "The place is packed. These folks don't know how to go home. But, I guess I really shouldn't complain. Life's been good to me. Real good, now that I've met you, Ms. Reed." He couldn't believe he'd just said that. And most of all, meant it. "You're sweet, Philip," she said, taking a seat at the table. Could he really be telling the truth? "Did you make it back on time for your appointment?" he asked. Holly chuckled a little. "She canceled on me. But, I made it back just in time to meet with this other woman." "Oh..." he said, "Let me tell you why I'm callin' before I forget." He cleared his throat. "How would you like to join Brenda, Mark and myself for dinner tomorrow night? They want to go to this little Spanish/Mexican restaurant called Cafe Espanol, down on Bleeker street." "I've heard of it before. The food is delicious there," Holly said. "Yeah, that's what they tell me. So, are you interested?" "I'd love to," she said with a grin. "Good, I'll call you tomorrow at work with the details," Philip said. "Have a good night, baby," he added. "You too."

Holly drained her glass after they'd hung up and decided to take a nice warm bath. She removed a peach-colored towel and bath cloth from the hallway linen closet, and walked into the bathroom, flicking on the light. Setting them both down on the chair beside the tub, she reached into the pale-pink cabinet below the sink, pulling out a tube of White Almond Milk Bath by *Perlier*. It was her absolute favorite. As she poured the creamy liquid into the rapid-flowing water, she watched the bubbles fill the opalescent pool. Then taking off her lacy set, she tested the water with her toes. It was perfect. She eased down into the tub, breathing in the delectable scent, which lingered high up in her nostrils. It was light and soothing. Holly turned off the faucet once the water made it up to her waist. She leaned her head back against the edge of the tub as she began to think about Philip. She smiled to herself. He wants his sister to meet her, she mused in amazement. Never before had a man wanted to introduce her to a member of his family so quickly. She continued to think about the same subject, rewinding it over in her head like one would a song he or she loved. She could hear the way he'd asked. Savoring the excitement in his voice, she closed her eyes. "He must really like me," is what she finally said quietly as a tear trailed slowly down her cheek, splashing into the water. She hoped those tears weren't coming from her Heavenly Father's heart was the next thought that entered her mind.

Chapter Eleven

"I heard the food was disgusting," Vanessa said the next morning. The three attorney's were sitting in the conference room eating breakfast. Holly's eyes fell downward toward the fruit salad before her. "I've gone there once before. And the meal I had was *not* disgusting," Tracy said. "The only thing that bothered me was that the restaurant was on the small side. Tables on top of tables, but as I said before, the food was wonderful," she added. "Yeah, well..." Vanessa said. She picked up a plastic knife and began scrapping a good portion of butter from her plain bagel. Peering across the table, Holly said, "You're a pretty picky eater anyway, Vanessa." "That is not true. I'd try just about anything," Vanessa said defensively. "Oh, yes it is true, Vee. Don't you sit over there telling that lie. You've been picky ever sense I've known you," Tracy said. She chuckled at the expression on Vanessa's face before taking a sip of coffee. "To each his own," Holly said and put a spoonful of fruit salad into her mouth. "Who's going? Just the two of you?" Tracy asked. Holly shook her head no as she took a sip of orange juice. "His sister and her husband," she said. Vanessa tilted her head and made another face. "What? I am in complete shock over this one," is what she said, with a mouth full of bagel. "Why?" Holly asked. She leaned back in the chair, and folded her arms. Vanessa swallowed. "Because I heard him tell Courtney, a number of times, that he would never introduce anyone in his family to a woman....... unless it was serious. I guess he must have changed his mind." Vanessa gazed over at Tracy, who immediately averted her eyes as she stuck a piece of toast covered in grape jelly into her mouth. "Changed his mind, Vee? Does it seem impossible for someone to be serious about me?" Holly asked, feeling somewhat annoyed. She slammed the lid down on top of the plastic container housing the fruit salad, finished her juice and stood up. "No, I don't think it's impossible for someone to want to have a serious relationship with you. *But,* Philip Williams, on the other hand wanting to, does come as a surprise. Why should I hold my tongue on the truth?" "People do change," Tracy said. Her eyes played a quick game of ping pong, shifting back and forth between her two partners. Holly pressed her lips firmly together to keep her from saying something she'd probably wind up apologizing for. Be Christian, she told herself. "For once," Holly heard herself whisper. She took this opportunity to talk about something else. It was useless arguing with Vanessa Benjamin anyway, she thought glumly. The hazel-eyed woman was always baffled at the way Vanessa was during a case. Fair, rational and for the most part, likeable. In her work she'd easily be mistaken for someone with a good heart and mind to match. But, on a personal level, the woman had work to do. Sure, Holly loved her otherwise she'd be working somewhere else. But she had to admit to herself that liking her was another story. Looking at her watch, Holly said, as she thought that she was supposed to love everyone. "As I mentioned to you both earlier, I'm going upstairs to call Ms. Stokes." "Fine," Vanessa said. "When did Selma Girard tell you she'd call? Because I'm taking a few days off myself. The doctor told me to take it easy after our last case," she added, glancing up at Holly. "She just said some time this week. "I told her that we are criminal defense attorney's, remember? So, I told her that I would call her if you two knew of a good realestate lawyer." "Oh, yeah. That's right," said the full-figured woman. "Her husband was out of town, but I trust that she will let him know," Holly said and crossed the room for the doors. Pushing them open, she told her partners she'd see them when they were done. After throwing away the empty cup and remainder of her breakfast in the kitchen garbage pail, Holly mounted the stairs to her office. Passing Kelly's desk, she overheard her say into the telephone receiver, as she typed, that she was going to tell him she loved him. What did she have to lose she went on to say? Holly walked into her office, taking a seat behind her desk. She was right about her assistant having man problems. Holly shook her head, picked up the receiver and tapped in the phone number she'd written down on a yellow Post-it. She swiveled around in her chair and looked out of the window, waiting for Ms. Stokes to answer. The phone rang four times before she picked up. "Hello," said the quiet voice on the other end. "Ms. Stokes, this is Holly Reed. I'm the attorney you had called last Friday...." "I know who you are," Leslie Stokes said, in a why-are-you-calling-me tone. "Could I help you with something, Ms. Reed?" Detecting the irritability in the woman's voice, Holly froze momentarily. "I, uh, wanted you to know that I'd be here when and if you needed me," the lawyer said slowly. "Did you get my message yesterday?" Ms. Stokes asked. "Yes, I did, but...." "Then, I guess it wasn't clear?" "Of course, it was clear." "Don't tell me that the firm is so hard up for money that you'd continue to bug someone even after they've specified that they no longer required your services?" "No, we are not *hard* up for anything. I was just calling to tell you that.... Sometimes women in these type of situations feel alone. Like they have no one to turn to or depend on. Ms. Stokes, I'm telling you he's not going to change. Do you know if he's willing to get help?" Holly paused for a brief moment as she reminded herself in the mind that Jesus is the only answer. She could hear Ms. Stokes suck her teeth. "Please open your eyes," Holly said leaving her thoughts. "What did he do? Give you flowers? Buy you a large diamond that sparkled so vibrantly it blinded you? Listen, if you ever need help, or.... or just want someone to talk to, I'm here as I said before." Holly could feel her joints tightening as she anticipated the woman's reply. An eery hush flooded the line for a second then the attorney winced. Leslie Stokes had begun to laugh bitterly. "Are you finished?" the woman asked. Holly was silent. "Good. Let me tell you something now, Ms. Reed. I don't *need* you! What made you think that I would need you? And who do you think you are? God?" Ms. Stokes said with so much anger in her voice. Turning back to face her desk, the lawyer placed her elbow on the

128

antique, resting her forehead in the palm of her hand. "No, Ms. Stokes." The Scripture "As He is, so are we in this world" came to Holly's mind. "No, I don't think I'm God," Holly said quietly. She was telling her nothing but the truth because she certainly wasn't acting like her Heavenly Father in the relationship part of her life, but Leslie Stokes thought the lawyer was being sarcastic. "Look, Ms. Reed. I'm not in the mood to hear your snide remarks on top of everything else, okay? Don't call my house again!" She went on to say with a heated tone in her voice. Hearing the line go dead, Holly hung up and began massaging her temples. She could feel a headache coming on.

Philip called her at work at 5:30 p.m. with the details like he'd said he would. Asking Holly to meet him at his restaurant in an hour was what he'd suggested so they'd catch a cab and ride downtown together. She thought it was a good idea as well. Checking her watch, she stood up from behind her desk, slinging her pocketbook on her narrow shoulder. She then turned off the lamp and walked out of her office. As she started for the stairs, she could hear Vanessa and Tracy discussing something in the short-haired attorney's office. Doubling back, Holly headed down the hall in the opposite direction. She thought it would be rude to go without saying anything. The three women were the only ones there. Tapping lightly on Tracy's door, while her hand rested on the knob, the hazel-eyed lawyer waited for one of her partners to answer. "Come in," Tracy called. Sticking her head inside, Holly told them that she was leaving. She was a bit surprised to see that Vanessa had been crying. Her eyes were red and puffy. "What's wrong, Vee?" Holly asked, a questioning look on her face. Shaking her head back and forth, Vanessa wiped away a few more hard-to-tame tears as she reached over, snatching a Kleenex from the box atop Tracy's desk. "It's the same old saga," Tracy said. "Court doesn't want to get tested. They had it out a few minutes ago," the short-haired woman added. After blowing her nose and dabbing at her moistened face, Vanessa said, "I don't know what I'm going to do with him. We've had sex every night, and I could still feel symptoms of my period coming on. I know it's going to come, just like it *always* does. I'm due on July 15th. I swear to God I could set a clock by the thing." She was beginning to well up again. Holly could see the tears trembling at the bottom of Vanessa's eyelids. "Vee, you can't get yourself all worked up like this. You still have a couple of weeks before it comes," Holly said. Walking all the way in, she leaned down, giving her sobbing friend a much-needed hug. "That's exactly what I keep telling her. They need a vacation. A little Caribbean get away," Tracy said, imitating a Jamaican accent. All three women smiled. Holly stood up straight, pulling her pocketbook back up on her arm. "Yeah, maybe that would help." She took a peek at her watch. It was time for her to get going. "So, what are you guys doing tonight?" she asked, unconsciously switching the subject. "Probably some more fussin'," Vanessa said and blew her nose again. "Aw, you guys will find a solution," Holly said. "What about you?" she added, looking over at Tracy. Grinning, the short-haired woman said, "I'm going out with Jerome Smith." "Oooooo," Vanessa said. She let out a loud shriek of laughter. "Does this mean we won't see you tomorrow? I thought you'd be around for the whole week to hold down the fort," Holly said, giggling. She extended a high five to Vanessa. Their palms smacked together lightly. "What are you two talking about?" Tracy asked, her eyebrows risen and her mouth hanging open. "You know what we're talking about," Vanessa said. "The last time you went out with the Energizer Bunny, as I recall, you were out of commission for *days*," she added. "I still don't know what you two fools are talking about," Tracy said. She began clearing off her desk. "I'm afraid she's right, Trace. He put a hurtin' on you before, girlfriend. Please be careful," Holly said. She was stifling her urge to laugh, but she managed to add, "None of those agile positions you described to us the last time tonight, okay. Made me sore just hearing about it." Vanessa chuckled enough for the both of them, so much that she began to cough. "Is he meeting you here?" she asked, calming down, but still coughing slightly. When Tracy nodded, the door bell rang. "That must be Killer now," Holly said. She and Vanessa cracked up again. Tracy glared at her partners with squinted eyes. "You know, I don't need enemies with friends like the two of you," she teased and stood up. "Sit back down, girl. I'll let him in on my way out," Holly said. "Thanks, and you have a good time," Tracy said. Vanessa smiled and waved. "The only thing you and Courtney better be doing tonight is making up," Holly said with a wink.

Walking down the winding stairs, Holly could see that it wasn't Jerome Smith who'd rang the bell. It was Courtney. He was shuffling through his briefcase. She passed Telma's desk swiftly, trying to get to the door, knowing he was searching for his keys. Then, as if he'd sensed someone coming, Courtney lifted his head. A smile covered his bronze chiseled face, brightening the graying sky in view behind him. "Hi, Holly. How's it going?" he asked once she'd opened the door. "Good, thank you. Your bride is upstairs," the hazel-eyed woman said. She slid out the way, letting him pass. "I'm sure she's still upset. We had a little fight over the phone." He was straightening the glasses on his face. He and his wife were like night and day, Holly thought as she studied the innocence in his eyes. "She'll be all right," she finally said. "I better not hold you up. I don't want Phil to get mad at me. I just left him.... He, uh, really likes you a great deal. But, I guess you already know that," he said with a partial grin. She smiled back, not knowing what else to say or do. "Well, you have a good night," Holly said, waving as she walked away. "You, too," he said and pulled the door shut. Heading down the brownstone steps, she could hear thunder in the distance, coming from the south and as she reached the ground, she could feel eyes on her back. Just my imagination, she told herself as she hurried up the street. Why would Courtney Benjamin be gazing at her?

Seated at a small table for four in the mid-section of the extremely-dim restaurant, the attractive couple sipped on red non-alcoholic Sangria and snacked on Nachos, dipping them into a spicy Salsa sauce while they waited for the couple joining them to arrive.

Holly's eyes traveled around the very authentic-looking Spanish restaurant, feeling like she'd been transported, in her mind, from New York to Madrid or Acapulco. A Mariachi band would have made the picture complete. "I'm so tired," Philip said, his eyes moving toward the door. Holly was sitting with her back facing it. Every time he took a peek, she'd feel a twinge of uneasiness stirring about in her stomach, the combination of Salsa and Spanish punch not helping. During the day she hadn't even thought once about her meeting his sister, until now. What if Brenda didn't like her? What if she'd influence Philip's decision about her? No, Holly thought, staring at the virile man directly across from her. He was a man who did only what he wanted to do. He appeared to be the pioneer of his own path. Why was that as wrong as her being there with Philip? Wait a minute, she thought and looked around again. Where was Jesus? Holly suddenly remembered what Philip had said. He was tired. "Maybe you need some time off," she finally said. Shrugging his shoulders, he tossed another Nacho into his mouth. "Yeah, well. I'm goin' down to D.C. this weekend for a restauranteur's convention. That'll give me a little reprieve." Holly could feel her eyebrows rising. She tried hard to keep them in place, not wanting him to see the disappointment she was harboring inside. She'd planned on getting to know him better this weekend, would have probably even cooked him dinner. Something she rarely did because she didn't know how to cook. She would have looked up some recipes or perhaps even asked her mother. This would have been the perfect opportunity to utilize that *Sylvia's* Soul Food cookbook she'd been avoiding like it was a contagious disease. Now what would she do on her days off? "Staying up on the industry current events? That's a wise thing to do," she said, taking a sip of the crimson liquid. He gazed across the table at her, smiling. "I try to, but I'm not gonna like being away from you." He closed his big strong hand over her dainty little one. "When exactly do you leave?" she asked and swallowed the lump forming in her throat. "Saturday morning. I'll be back Sunday around eight or nine in the evening."

She just nodded her head. What could she say? Nothing. He wasn't her husband or boyfriend, for that matter. "Man, where are they? I starved myself all day for this," Philip said. It reminded Holly of the reason they were there. She felt that sense of uneasiness rising in the pit of her stomach. Patting his stomach with his free hand, he added, "Gotta watch my weight." Holly started to grin as her mind drifted back to the evening they had sex. He didn't have to watch anything, if her memory served her correctly. Leave all that to me, she thought, quickly pressing her lips together so that the thought would not escape her mouth. Gazing up at the door again, Philip saw Brenda and Mark. They were standing near the bar at the front of the restaurant, their eyes darting around, trying to find them. "Here they are. It's about time," Philip said. He waved his hand to get their attention. Holly latched on tightly to the one covering hers, watching his eyes carefully as they approached. She wanted to see whether or not his expression would change. Was his sister saying something to him behind her back? "What in the world took you two so long? Yellin' at me to be on time," Philip said to his family with a smile. "Brenda and Mark Brennen this is Holly Reed," he said. Peering up at the couple, she smiled. They seemed like good people, Holly told herself. Brenda was dressed in African-inspired clothing while Mark was wearing a pair of jeans and a blue and white striped shirt. "It's nice to meet you both," Holly told them, "I've heard nothing but nice things about you." "Is that so," Brenda mumbled and eyed her brother. "Wonderful meeting you, too," Mark said. He clutched onto his wife's arm, leading her to her seat. Brenda was beside Holly and Mark sat beside Philip.

The evening was progressing well. Holly was finally feeling at ease. The wall of protection had come crumbling down. They all sat around the table, laughing at the stories Philip told in regards to some of the people who'd eaten at his restaurant or who'd just stopped in for a drink. And Mark jumped in periodically, telling outrageous tales about eccentric people he'd come across in his many years as a member of the police force. Though Brenda leaned in toward Holly as if she were liking her company, chuckling with her hand covering her mouth, there was still something out of place, just not right. On occasion, she'd cut her eyes over in Holly's direction. Was she gazing at her or someone else? It wasn't quite clear. Who was it that she'd been giving dirty looks to most of the night? Her eyes hardening, the laugh on her face disappearing when she glanced that way. What was it that disturbed her so? This time when she giggled, it was without a doubt that she was staring at Holly. "These guys are sick, girl," Brenda told her with a nudge in the arm. "It's too late for me, but you could still save yourself. Run for the hills, my sister." the African-garbed woman added. She was still giggling at one of Philip's comments. Holly smiled as she watched the woman beside her pour herself a third full glass of the Sangria from the carafe that had alcohol in it, which was in the center of the table. Holly stuck a final fork-full of yellow rice into her mouth without responding. But, Brenda wanted her to. She wanted to know how serious this golden-haired Black woman was about her brother. With her eyes still planted firmly on Holly's face, Brenda shifted in her direction. "So," she said and paused. She glanced at Philip as she pointed toward the two carafes in the center of the table. "Which ones the one with rum in it?" Philip stared at his sister for a moment. "The one you been drinkin' from, Bren." He gestured toward the Sangria with the rum in it. "That one." Laughing, Brenda picked up the carafe Philip pointed to and poured herself another drink. She was dangling her glass in her hand carelessly as she turned toward Holly again. She was still laughing a little and then a serious look came over her face. "I'm sure you have a few funny experiences to share. Being a lawyer must have its share of humor." For some reason Holly felt like she was being picked on. It was probably Brenda's tone. More schoolyard bully mess she'd have to contend with. "Not really. My partners and I find little humor in most of our cases. Don't get me wrong. I love my job, but I take it very seriously. There's nothing funny about an abused child or a cheating spouse," Holly said easily. Taking a sip from her glass, Brenda turned toward her husband. She gave him a strange look while Philip winked at his date. Then, facing Holly again, a tipsy Brenda said, with a giggle. "You are going to crack up when I tell you this." Her words were loud and slurred and there was a hint of trouble stirring about in her body language. Holly glimpsed at the wineglass in Brenda's hand. It swayed haphazardly each time the woman moved, the Sangria swishing around like an ocean during a fierce storm. "When Mark and I saw you from behind, we nearly died. At least I know I almost did," she said, looking at her husband briefly again. Then she peered at Philip, who stared back at her with watch-what-you-say written in his eyes. She waved her hand as if to say *please* and gazed back at Holly. "I was about to come over here and raise hell. Girl, we all would've met the devil *today* because I thought you were a cracker. I told Mark that I was not *about* to sit down and stare in the face of some White chick for the rest of the night. After all, I'm sure no one wanted to see me throw up all over this place?" Holding up her glass in a toast, Brenda added, "Thanks for keeping it real my dear, sweet, Black-woman-lovin' brother." As she drained the crimson fluid from the glass, it seemed as though a lull had swept over the entire restaurant. Heads had turned. Yes, a lot of people heard. But no one clinked anything together in agreement. Suddenly, the discomfort Holly felt earlier was back, much stronger this time. Her eyes dropped downward at the cluttered table before her, not really focusing on anything in particular. Another painful memory to carry. "Bren, I think it's time for you to go home!" Philip said. Rage was filling his eyes. "Mark, man, you better get her out of here because if I have to, it's not gonna be pretty." He glared at his embarrassed brother-in-law at his side. Sighing, Mark stood up, putting his hand around his wife's arm. "If you don't get off of me, I'm going to punch the boldness out of you. Say I won't!" Brenda said through gritted teeth. "I didn't say anything wrong. The only thing I did was celebrate my gratitude. I don't want no White trash in our family. Since when have you become so righteous, Philip?" There's nothing righteous about her attitude, Holly thought, knowing the truth. "You know, Bren. Your mouth is bigger than I ever imagined it was," Philip continued. "You don't know this woman from a can of paint. How in the world do you know what she is or where she's from? Huh? I oughta reach across this table and strangle you. And if you don't walk your drunk you-know-what outta here now, I might just do it for you!" Philip said, his lips pressed tightly together, his index finger pointed at his sister's face. "Come on, Phil. Calm down," Mark said, holding up his hands. "Yeah, calm down," Brenda said. "You act like she is *White*." She sucked her teeth. "Part of me is," Holly said. She was staring at Brenda, while her eyes were lunging over at her Philip's. "What?" was what she said to him. "That's right. What difference does it make? Didn't you like her before you knew?" Philip asked. He was shaking his head in disgust. Staring up at her husband, Brenda shook her head as well. Then, she looked back at Philip. "It does makes a big difference to me. And I'm sure it will to mommy and daddy, too. I knew something was up. black hair could never be that straight. I don't care how "good" it is. Philip, you ain't nothin' but a sell-out. All these beautiful sisters out there in all shades. You could've got yourself a beautiful sienna-colored queen.... but I guess it fits the bill. Successful business man like you...." Brenda glared at Holly then back at her brother, adding, "well, your package is complete. Congratulations." She stood up without saying anything further and stormed out. So she was the one Brenda had been examining. Holding back her tears, Holly glanced back down, this time at her hand in her lap -- it was trembling. She waited to hear what would be said next. "Listen, guys. I'm sorry. She just had a little too much to drink. Here. Dinner's on me," Mark said. He was hovering over the seated couple with an American Express card in his hand. "That's okay, man. Go on with your wife. I got it," Philip said quietly. "All right, then um. Next time it's on me," Mark said nervously. "Uh, Holly. It was a pleasure, um, meeting you," he added and hurried out. Still looking downward, Holly whispered, "Yeah, a real pleasure." as a tear finally coursed her flustered cheek. Closing his eyes for a moment to find the right words, Philip then stood up, sitting down next to the woman he was starting to fall in love with. He wiped her face with the cotton cloth from his lap. "Baby, I just don't know what to say. I've never seen my sister like that before. I never even knew she felt that way. I don't come from that type of family." "Evidently, she thinks you do. You heard what she said about your parents," Holly said, her blurry eyes glancing around the restaurant. Thank God! No one was watching now. The curtain had come down. "Well, she's wrong. They're not bigots. They're good, solid people. Just like you, baby," Philip said, pulling her into his arms. He was trying to soak up some of the hurt he'd witnessed for the first time in her eyes. He couldn't tell her the truth.

The couple sprinted out of the taxi when it pulled up in front of Holly's apartment building later on that night. She, shielding her head with her pale-blue suit jacket, could feel the rain drops landing on her bare arms. And Philip, with nothing to cover himself with, stooped down and hurried in behind her. Neither of them were prepared for the unexpected down-pour, slicking the city streets. The muddy clouds overhead had opened up in full force.

At her apartment door, Philip apologized once again for his sister's turbulent behavior while dabbing his face dry with a white monogrammed handkerchief that he pulled out of his pocket. Looking up at him, Holly gave him a faint smile. She knew from the way he came to her defense that he'd never deliberately put her in a situation like that. That gave her a sense of security. "When I get home tonight, I'm gonna call her up and give her a piece of my mind," he said, stuffing the linen cloth back into his pants pocket. "They're stayin' at my parents house for a couple of days. I have never seen Brenda act like that before. Like I told you, she's usually sweet as can be to whoever she meets. I'm tellin' you the girl's trippin'." Eyeing Holly, Philip began rubbing the back of his neck uneasily. She took a deep breath and folded her jacket over her arm. "No, she's not going crazy. She was just voicing her opinion. And she's entitled." "Yeah, but...." "Philip, please," she said, holding up her hand. "Brenda just didn't like what she saw. That's all to it. This is not a mystery." "Yeah well, I'm still surprised. I see things every day that I don't like, but I either keep it to myself or tell someone in private." "That's you and your way of handling it. She did it her way." Staring down at the new woman in his life, Philip marveled in the way she kept her composer. To him Holly was the epitome of class, something he now knew his sister didn't have. "Baby, I'm just glad you're okay. Thank you for understandin' and takin' this so lightly," Philip said. He held on to both of her arms gently. She could feel the heat from his grasp penetrating her slender limbs, reaching her soul. "It's taken me years of practice to get to this place and I'm still searching. My mother always told me that everything happens for a reason. I have a feeling she's right," Holly said. She thought about what she just said. God is purposeful. What was He saying regarding all of this? With Philip's expression looking like he truly didn't know what was going on in Holly's mind, he pulled her into his arms, giving her a kiss. Then, once their lips disengaged, he held her close to him while he asked whether she was busy on Friday. Holly had been resting her head against his chest, listening to the subtle beat of his heart. "No, I'm not," she said softly. "Good, because I'd love to see you before I leave." She had forgotten that part, the part about him going away. Easing out of his delicate clutch, she told him that she'd like that, too. "So, I'll see you some time in the evening, okay?" "Okay." "Well, sweetness. It's gettin' late." He looked at his watch. "Here, let me get you an umbrella," she said. Reaching into her pocketbook, she pulled out her keys and turned them into the door. Philip stood behind her, gazing at her from head to toe, like he did most of the time. He was still shocked at the way he felt about this woman. But, then again, he's human, too, was what he reasoned.

It was 11:15 p.m. when Holly finally climbed into the bed, and she knew that Carmen didn't stop writing until midnight. "I hope I'm not disturbing you, but I needed to talk," she told her friend once she answered the phone. Holly could hear Spanish music playing in the background and although she could not decipher the lyrics, she was able to feel the passion behind them. "Didn't I tell you before, and let this be the last time. You are much more important than the books I write?" The Latina woman said, her voice calm and caring. Holly smiled. She knew that she was valued by her friend, but somehow hearing it, made her feel that much more reassured. "Yes, you did tell me that." "So, what could I do for you?" As her head lay against the headboard, Holly stared up at the ceiling. She was trying to will back the tears that threatened to fall. "I met Philip's sister tonight," she said quietly. She spoke carefully, hoping that her friend missed the unsteadiness in her voice, the rattle in her words. "And, it didn't go well," Carmen said with confidence. Holly's sadness must not have gone undetected. "She didn't like me," she said to the Latina woman. "What happened?" Carmen asked. "She didn't like the idea of him dating someone interracial. She called him a sell-out. She said I was his trophy in a roundabout way. It hurt so much," Holly said as she began to cry. Deep sobs penetrated the line. "I'm sorry, honey. What did Philip do?" Carmen was led to be compassionate. Wiping her eyes with the back of her hands, Holly told her everything that he'd said and did. "All right... good. I'm glad to hear that he did the right thing." "Yeah, but his...." "Holly, forget about his sister. This is not about her, Philip or you," Carmen paused. "It's about Jesus, sweetie. He is making this thing so plain." Still wiping away the last of her tears, Holly took a few deep breaths. "Girl, what would I do without you?" she said, sniffling. "What do I do?" Holly asked, her voice low. Carmen had driven down this bumpy road with her more times than they'd both care to remember within their twenty something years of friendship and never once had she let her friend down. "Just be honest. He is not God's choice for you."

Turning off the lamp beside her bed, then sliding down underneath the white eyelet spread, Holly sank her head into the pillow. As she lay there quietly, listening to the rain tap against the window, she knew that everything was going to be okay. God would bring her though this, too. "Lord, I don't know how, but it's finished," she said quietly.

Chapter Twelve

Rain was still puckering the puddles on the streets below. As Holly sat in her office gazing through the big picture window, past her reflection, she saw that it was also very quiet outside. Just a few passer-byers, balancing umbrellas, briefcases and Starbucks coffee's, making their way to work or to wherever it was they were going. Sure, she had a lot of work to do. Things she wanted to have done before she'd taken her four-day weekend. But, for some reason she couldn't function, couldn't think about the files and papers spread out atop her desk. Her mind was still on yesterdays incident with Philip's sister. Turning her head in the direction of the phone, she wondered whether or not she should call him. She couldn't sleep last night. Lying in the bed, listless, she stared at the shadows on the wall, wondering how his phone call to Brenda went. Would she ever reconsider her feelings? Would she ever call to apologize? Blame it on the Sangria? A hard day with the children? Anything? Anything would suffice right now, Holly thought as she sighed. Why was she always willing to settle? "Philip is not God's choice for me!" she said angrily through her teeth. Why am I putting myself through this when I know better, she told herself. Slamming her hand down on top of the desk, her mind changed quickly. Who cares if she doesn't like me. I've done nothing wrong! I will not change who I am for no one. No one! "Lord, You are my Beloved and I am Yours!" she said looking up toward the ceiling. Her explosive confession was broken by a knock on the door. "Holly, it's me Tracy. Can I come in?" Peering at the brass knob as it turned, and feeling her chest rise and fall with fury, Holly told her it was okay to enter while she tried arduously to sedate herself. "I just wanted to say good morning," Tracy said. Then she nodded toward her partners secretarys desk. "Where's Kelly?" Shrugging her shoulders, Holly said she hadn't heard from her, her heart still feeling heavy, not yet at bay. But, she prayed within that it didn't show. "I'm going to have a little talk with her today. She hasn't been herself." The short-haired attorney agreed. "I don't mean to change the subject, but how did last night go?" Tracy asked with one hand resting on her hip. This was the moment Holly dreaded. Maybe the subject would change soon. At least she hoped it would. "The food was wonderful just as you said." Holly lowered her head and began sifting through the files on her desk. "Good. And what did you think of his sister?" "She was all right," Holly said as she thought I'm not lying. Brenda was just that because her attitude had absolutely nothing to do with me, the hazel-eyed attorney told herself. After all, she didn't feel like hearing herself complain about something she should have been used to by now. God hated murmuring and complaining anyway. But, did anyone ever get used to not knowing where they fit in? Or to hearing derogatory remarks? "I'm glad," Tracy said as she heard Vanessa walking up behind her. "Hey, how did it go?" asked the full-figured woman, standing in the doorway. "She said it went well," Tracy said. She turned to face Vanessa. "Good," was her reply. "So, did you and your husband make up?" Holly asked. She leaned forward, folding her hands on the desk. "We almost broke the bed," Vanessa whispered then laughed. Her partners chuckled, too. "Oh, listen, guys. I've decided to give Court a surprise birthday party on Saturday, July 17th. That'll be two weeks from this coming weekend. Clear your calendars because I don't want to hear anything about either of you not being able to attend," Vanessa said, making a face. "Could I invite Philip.... If he's available?" Holly asked softly. So soft that she had to think about whether or not it was her who said it. I need help, she thought as she heard Vanessa say, "Well, since he is a friend of Court's I won't say no." Was she teasing? Tracy started to giggle, ridding the office of the sudden quiet. "I guess that's as close to yes as I'm going to get," Holly said. She just let Vanessa's sarcasm go in one ear and out the other.

Who's side am I on, was what she was thinking since she was doing the same thing to God. Suddenly she could hear Kelly shuffling around at her desk. "She's here," Holly whispered, nodding toward the door. Tracy peered at Vanessa. "All right, lets get to work, Vee,"she said and whispered, "I'll tell you later." She'd seen the puzzled look creeping up on the full-figured woman's face. "Okay, but one more thing," Vanessa said. "Did Ms. Girard ever call back?" Holly shrugged her shoulders and shook her head no. "I told her that I would call her if we knew of a good realestate attorney." "I hear you. I was just asking," she said as she and Tracy left Holly's office for theirs.

Getting up and walking around her desk to the door, Holly asked Kelly to step inside for a moment. The dark-skinned woman lifted her fingers from the keyboard and followed her boss into her office. "Close the door behind you," Holly said, sitting back down. Taking a seat in one of the chairs opposite her employer's desk after shutting the door, Kelly asked what was up. "My sentiments exactly. That's why I called you in." Staring down at the fallen daylilly petals on the floor, the secretary didn't answer. "You know I would not be intruding on your privacy if it wasn't affecting your work," Holly said sincerely. "It's not as bad as it seems," Kelly finally said, her eyes now gazing into her employer's. "Could we still talk about it?" Holly asked. Glimpsing down at Holly's neatly folded hands made the secretary feel uptight. She was disgusted every time she'd imagine Holly rubbing on *her* Elliot. Elliot? Well in a way he did remind her of him. But, of course, she'd meant Philip. Ugh! Have they made love yet? she wondered. "It's just that I have to find some place to stay until my super has my apartment painted," Kelly said. Holly couldn't believe her ears. Was she hearing her correctly? Kelly had been discombobulated for days, making huge mistakes on letters, mailing the wrong information to clients. All because of a paint job? Trying hard not to show how infantile she deemed her response to be, Holly nodded. "I understand. Well, if you like you'd be more than welcome to stay with me until it's done," she said, knowing that Kelly's family was down in North Carolina. Smiling, the secretary told her that she'd like that a lot and how much she appreciated her asking. "I really hate to impose, but my friends don't have the room." "No, no. It is not an imposition. Not at all," Holly said with a grin. Glaring across the desk at her boss, Kelly could feel the words 'she's dumber than I thought' burning in her throat, the pain almost as bad as the sensation she felt across her throbbing knuckles. After seeing the date her boss had with Philip jotted down in Holly's *Fendi* agenda, which simply read: "Dinner with Philip and his sister at 7:30 p.m. tonight" The other day really made her see red. Made her so mad just like she was when she'd find herself pounding on the walls in her apartment. And having to keep it all bottled up inside until she got home, made the situation worse. The secretary reflected walking into her studio apartment yesterday evening, mindlessly dropping everything she was holding in the middle of the tiny spaces floor, searching for something she'd be able to take her frustrations out on. The walls became her release. She pounded on them and pounded on them for minutes maybe even hours. Who was watching the clock? Not me, Kelly heard rise on the inside of her. But today the repercussions could not be measured from her attacking those paper-thin walls. They weren't really. They were more like cement. Had she not paid close attention to herself, she'd be screaming her head off in agony this very second. The pain, so intense, she thought she was going to pass out. Kelly almost smiled, thinking about the saying "no pain, no gain." She must be on the right track. She began massaging the backs of her hands discreetly. "When will they be painting, Kel?" "Oh, uh, he said tomorrow and Friday. I'll be out of your way by Saturday morning." "Out of my way? Please. You won't be in my way. In fact, I'm going to enjoy having the company." Kelly grinned, covering up her wicked thoughts. Furrowing her eyebrows, Holly said, "Why didn't you ask me sooner? Where were you planning to stay had I not offered my apartment to you?" Her questions made the secretary wince. "I would've stayed with my friend Liz. Even though she didn't have the room. We would've made it work somehow. I'm sure it would've been tight over there, but beggars can't be choosy." "I could imagine. Well, tomorrow night I'm going to have myself a roommate. How exciting," Holly said. Real exciting, Kelly thought. Everything was going according to plan. "Thanks again," the secretary said. She bent down, picking up the petals off of the floor. "These are ready to go bye, bye," she said, referring to the remaining flowers. From the tone of her voice it sounded, at first, to the attorney that she could have been talking about something or someone. But, why would she be?

Chapter Thirteen

Three perfectly seasoned Salmon steaks sizzled with round slices of Bermuda onion and a combination of red and green peppers in a non-stick Faberware skillet. Steam worked its way toward the ceiling as Cynthia Reed checked the rice and fresh broccoli simmering in sauce pans on the stoves two back eyes.

Holly was sitting at the kitchen table, flipping through the latest issue of *Essence* magazine. She'd just finished setting her mother's dining room table. When Cynthia had heard that her daughter's secretary would be spending two nights over in what she called "the foodless apartment" she immediately invited Holly to have dinner over at her place on both Thursday and Friday nights. Only accepting the Thursday night offer, Holly told her mother that she was expecting to see Philip on Friday evening. Did that really matter to Cynthia Reed? Of course not, especially because he wasn't who God had for her babygirl. In fact, she tried to persuade her daughter to have him join them as well with hopes that she would be able to convince them to do things the right way. God's way. But Holly wasn't quite ready for her mother to get involved with whatever it was she was doing with Philip. Not pushing her daughter any further, the older woman decided to give in and wallow in the time she was spending with her beloved child right now. Holly sat at the table, watching the smile on her mother's face while she scurried about as if she were preparing a feast for an entire nation. She was holding her palms up, going over in her head, everything that she had planned to serve. "I baked a apple pie for dessert, baby," she told Holly for the third time. "Wonderful, Mom. I can't wait to taste it," her daughter said in somewhat of a rehearsed-sounding tone and closed the magazine, sliding it to the side. As the foyer grandfather clock chimed 6:00 p.m., Holly informed her mother that Kelly should be arriving any minute. "Good, sweetie. Could you turn off the air conditioner and open up some of these windows. I don't want the place to smell like a fish market. Or some nasty woman's unwashed ... " Cynthia said, letting out a hearty laugh. Shaking her head at her mother's humor, Holly pulled herself up and did exactly what was asked of her. She shut the air off in the living room, pushed up the windows and peered at the butterfly-soft flutter of the lace curtains. The two days of rain had lowered the scorching temperatures to a much welcomed seventy-five degrees, making for a delightful night's sleep. The dry breeze felt good blowing across her cheek. Pulling back the dainty fabric, Holly stretched her neck in order to gaze down at the street. She was trying to see whether she could spot Kelly. But it was useless. Her mother lived on the 20th floor. As Holly left the window, making it back toward the kitchen, the buzzer sounded. She could hear her mother start into a panic, shouting spray some air freshener before you let her in. "Mom, calm down. She'll see that you've made Salmon," Holly said as she walked over to the intercom. "Who is it?" she asked. "Holly, it's Kelly," said the dark-skinned woman's voice through the small box on the wall. "She's on her way up," Holly said, now standing in the doorway of the kitchen. "Do you need help?" she added. Her mother was dishing the rice out of the silver sauce pan into a blue and white Tiffany bowl, which matched the beautiful china Holly had laid out on the dining room table. "Not really..... Oh, take the sparklin' cider outta the freezer, sweetie. I bought a few bottles." Grinning at her mother thought "that chile won't be drinkin' no licka in my house!" Cynthia's musings made her think about her daughter as she began to watch Holly take out the sparkling cider and bring it into the dining room, placing it in the middle of the table, next to the centerpiece of sun flowers. The older woman shook her head and mumbled under her breath. "No, my baby ain't out there drinking no licka." Cynthia nodded her head and turned back toward the stove.

Surveying the room one last time, Holly smiled to herself. This was actually her mother's home. How good it felt to hear those words fill her head.

Seated around the mahogany dining table, Cynthia Reed sitting in one of the burnt red wing back chairs, heading the grand table and the two younger women were both at her sides, Holly to her right and Kelly at her left, sitting in two of the four matching high-back chairs, with seat covers that were a tasteful blend of deep crimson, ivory and just a hint of forest green, going superbly with the wallpaper in the lovely room. The three women's empty plates were now pushed aside as they ate their scrumptious dessert and sipped on French Vanilla coffee. "Mrs. Reed, you have certainly made me want to come over again. I don't know the last time I had a meal this good. This really hit the spot," Kelly said, cutting off another slice of pie. Beaming like the crystal chandelier overhead, the older woman laughed. "Where your folks from?" she asked. "A little town call Speed down in North Carolina," Kelly said and took a swig of coffee. "How often do you see 'em?" Cynthia asked. She was leaning back, her arms resting on the arms of the chair. "Twice a year, if I'm lucky," Kelly said. "Umph," said the older woman as she peered over at her daughter. Glancing back at her mother, Holly knew that they were thinking the same thing. How Blessed they were to live so close. The older woman began to ponder Kelly's use of the word "lucky" and she felt herself wanting to correct the dark-skinned woman but she immediately changed her mind. That's what the unsaved did. Instead she asked, "Would you like another cup of coffee?" Cynthia smiled because she could feel the wrinkles of her being slightly bothered leaving her forehead as she eyed Kelly who shook her head. "Um, no. Thank you." The dark-skinned womans mouth was full of pie. She wanted to snap at the old stupid-sounding woman and say, "Don't you see me chewing on this pie you made?" But, those words were swallowed up with the pie as she kept staring at Holly's mother as she turned her unsuspecting focus onto her daughter. "How 'bout you, baby?" the older woman asked, looking at her daughter. "No, I'm fine, too. The pie is delicious, mom," Holly said, eyeing the clock in the china cabinet. It was 7:45 p.m. and Philip hadn't returned her phone call from last night. She'd left him a message on his home machine as soon as she'd stepped foot into her apartment. Maybe he has changed his mind? No, maybe she should try him on his cell phone, but she remembered that she didn't have the number. She never even saw him using a cell phone. She wouldn't be too stunned if he did change his mind about her. Her Heavenly Father is faithful, she told herself as she hid the lie lingering in her mind. She knew she had to stop seeing Philip. This was the truth. Holly managed to sigh without her mother or Kelly noticing. Why did it seem like some great big challenge for her to let this man go? He'd probably found some truth in the way his sister felt, she went on to think. Good. That would be her way out. Noticing the far-away look in her daughter's eyes, Cynthia Reed asked if she was all right. Holly, now focusing, seemed as though she'd almost forgotten where she was. "Oh, yeah. I was just thinking about something. Everything's fine. Will you both excuse me for a minute. I need to make a quick phone call." Holly wiped her hands and mouth with a napkin and got up from the table, tossing the cloth down beside her plate. Feeling sullen, she still could not believe Philip hadn't called her back. He didn't seem like the type of man who'd just run off without saying a word. But, she never quite understood Bradford either. He never seemed like the type of man who would have cheated. Uh, yes he did. Anyway, she thought as she let the obvious just dissipate like she didn't know any better. Holly cleared her throat and began to think. Okay, she'd been at her mother's since noon and had called her apartment to check her messages twice, once at about 1:30 p.m. and the second time at 3:00 p.m. No, it was 3:10 p.m. She remembered glancing at the grandfather clock beforehand. Holly wanted to laugh a little at the truth of her not using her own cell phone.

In the living room, she flopped down on the sofa, tucking her socked feet beneath her as she held the receiver to her ear, listening to her voice on the other end. Once the tape stopped, she pressed in her secret three-number code and waited, her heart beating nervously as she glanced at her cell phone in her hand. Nothing. There were two messages on her home phone. The first one was from Carmen. She was calling to find out how her friend was doing and to hear whether or not Holly had heard anything more on Philip's sister. "Let me be real," the Latina woman added. Her accent sounding stronger for some reason. "Chica, I really don't care about what Philip or his sister has to say. I just want you to submit to God. Forget about him. Make room for your true husband, beloved." Holly smiled to herself regarding the Latina woman's concern. After that message was over, she braced herself just as if Carmen never said a word. She immediately began to smile as she heard. "Hey, sweetness," the familiar voice said. Holly almost screamed with happiness out loud. "I'm sorry I didn't get back to you sooner. I can't even begin to tell you how busy this place has been. The only thing I can say is I cannot wait to see your pretty face tomorrow night. Call me at the restaurant when you get this message." The smile on her face was so extensive it hurt her jaw-line. Why did she always jump to the worst possible conclusion? Better yet, why wasn't she retaining what her mother and Carmen were saying to her regarding Philip. She'd always listen to herself tell Carmen not to worry about finding a man because there was someone out there for her. Holly paused. "The Bible states, "He who finds a wife, finds a good thing and obtains favor from the Lord." Slowly, she placed the receiver on the phone and glanced at her cell phone in her hand. "Whose am I, Lord?" she asked so low she could barely make out what she was saying. You are faithful even when I'm not, Daddy God. Holly picked her mother's telephone receiver back up and dialed information. "Hello, operator. Could you give me the telephone number for ""Phil's House"". It's a restaurant over on... yes, that's right, thank you." As the recording gave her the number, she recited it quietly to herself. And when she dialed it she could feel her stomach fluttering. Philip answered on the first ring. "Hi, its

Holly," she said softly. "I know. Did you get my message?" he asked, the music thumping as it always did in the background. "Yes, I just picked it up." Listening to the sound of her voice, Philip didn't realize until now how much he'd missed hearing it. "So, where did you *pick* your messages up from?" he asked, grinning. "I'm at my mother's. Kelly and I had dinner here." "Kelly? Didn't you take off today?" "Yeah, but I'll, uh, tell you later. It's really not a big deal," she whispered. "Excuse me. I couldn't hear you. I didn't realize you and Kelly were so friendly." "Well." Holly's eyes traveled over toward the living room doorway. She'd thought she'd seen a figure standing there or a shadow on the floor. Telling Philip to hold on for a minute, she listened to see if she could hear her mother and Kelly talking. And once she did, she said," We're not," into the receiver. "Why's she there then?" "Her apartment's being painted." "What?" he asked, catching himself before he'd said something mean and unnecessary. He didn't know why Kelly's flirting irritated him so much. Had it been a couple of weeks ago he would have probably said, "Get it while the gettin' is good." But, ever since he'd laid eyes on Holly things have changed. He's changed. Old age must be creepin' up on him, he reasoned. Naw, what was he talkin' about? He still had some good strokes left in him. "So, I guess she'll be at your apartment tomorrow night," he asked as he thought speaking of a few good strokes. She could hear some tension in his tone, but Holly chose to ignore it just like she was ignoring God. Wasn't it the same thing? "Yes, but I'm sure she's not going to be a problem," she said with some anxiety. She cleared her throat. She heard how anxious she sounded or was it desperation? "We're all adults," Holly said, laughing a little to cover up what the Greater One on the inside of her was still saying. She was about to continue in her delusion by saying something about his sister, but her plan to stay in that place of deceit was silenced by her mother's voice. It was loud and angry. There had to be something wrong. "Philip, I'll call you back!" she said and hung up. Jumping up, she hurried into the dining room. Cynthia Reed was standing up with both hands on her hips. "What's going on in here?" Holly asked. "I was tellin' this chile right here that I'm retired not retarded. I don't play no games. I'll be doggone if somebody's gonna tell me to shut up in my house! *Oh* no! Not in my palace they won't!" "What happened?" Holly asked again. "Go on, tell her!" Cynthia said to Kelly. "You wanted me to shut up! Go on, you tell her! And if my God is my witness you had better tell the truth!" the older woman said with the anger still in her voice. She was waggling her index finger at Kelly. "Because if you don't, I want you to get yo'... You here me! *This* is my home, *sweetheart!*" Cynthia Reed roared. She couldn't manage to calm down. Holly hadn't seen that much anger in her mother's eyes since she was a child. Gazing down at Kelly, who was sitting at the table like she didn't do a thing, she asked her to tell her side of the story. "I don't know what happened," the dark-skined woman lied, shrugging her shoulders calmly. "The only thing I did was ask her...." "*Her?*" Cynthia said, an indignant look on her face. "I mean, Mrs. Reed to excuse me for a second because I thought I heard you call me," Kelly said, her voice quivering now as she tried to appear unmoved. "That's it! Get out! Get out my house! Now! You heard me! *Move!*" "Wait a minute, mom," Holly said, her voice one octave higher. She walked over and stood in between the two feuding women. "What would you say happened?" she asked her mother, sounding less like a daughter and more like an attorney. Rolling up her shirt sleeves, the older woman said, "Like I said! I'm retired not retarded! She didn't say excuse me she *shushed* me! May as well had told me to shut up! Little evil-lookin'.... She was tryin' to listen in on what you was sayin' on the phone. And you know how I feel 'bout a sneak! Can't stand'em!" Cynthia Reed had a huge snarl on her face, her lip turned up, her eyes rolling. Holly turned to face Kelly, who looked as though she was about to cry. "Is this true?" she asked. Although she knew her mother was not a liar, she still had to ask. It was the proper thing to do. The dark-skinned woman lowered her head then lifted it, staring up into Holly's face, the tears trembling in the corners of her eyes. "If that is the truth, I'm sorry," she said, the tears escaping, running down her cheeks. "It's just that I've been under so much pressure lately. I don't know whether I'm going or coming sometimes. And being here, in this beautiful apartment, with the two of you tonight. Well, no offense, but it seems to make matters worse. I miss my family more than ever." Kelly was sniffling as she wiped her face dry with the napkin from her lap. Holly could hear her mother mumble "Oh, Lawd," under her breath. They both felt equally as bad for Kelly. Walking around her daughter, Cynthia Reed placed her hand on the dark-skinned woman's arm, stroking it gently. "Sweetie, don't cry. I'm sorry. Maybe I heard you wrong. These ears don't work as well as they used to even though I knowed I'm healed by His stripes," she said and paused. "Please forgive me." Glimpsing up at the older woman, Kelly managed to bring a smile to her saddened face. She could see Holly smiling a little too from the corner of her eye. Rising from her seat, she embraced both women, holding them tightly. And as they held her back, feeling the warmth filling the room they were in, they, mother and daughter, should have only known that the sudden surge of heat that Kelly was producing wasn't from the appreciation she displayed, but from the hateful thoughts crossing her mind. She still had it. "Look at these two fools," is what she was thinking.

"Kel, follow me. I'll show you your room," Holly said. She locked the door, turned on the foyer light and headed down the hallway, leading to both bedrooms. Kelly walked slowly behind, in complete awe of her employer's surroundings. Even in her dreams of this place she'd never gotten close to the way it looked. As they approached the two adjacent rooms, the dark-skinned woman stretched her neck to take a peek inside of Holly's bedroom. Staring at the large four-poster bed, she imagined Philip lying in there beside her boss, holding her in his arms. Kelly sighed. Her optimistic side knew that her day was rapidly approaching. But her pessimistic side reminded her that she'd have to get rid of the woman in front of her first. Standing in the doorway of the frilly room, glaring at the back of her Holly's head, Kelly sighed again.

Anything worthwhile never ever came easy. "Come on in and make yourself at home," Holly said. She walked over to the closet and drew back the cherrywood sliding doors. "I'll leave you alone so you could put away your things," Holly said, adding, "And I'm going in my room to change into something a little less confining." So what, the secretary thought. She eyed her boss as she walked out of the guest room into hers.

Kelly hung up her clothes and stored her toiletries down in the bathroom cabinet. A place like this must have cost a whole lot of money -- If Holly owned it, Kelly told herself. And even if she didn't, the monthly bills had to be sky high. Too much for a secretary to be able to afford on such a minimum salary. How could she make the kind of money that Holly made? she wondered. But, all of her hopes weren't shattered. One day she'd have just as much, maybe even more than Holly would ever see in her lifetime. Wealthy brother like El... She cut her musings short, stomping her foot. Kelly shook the vision of her ex-boyfriend out of her head. She meant Philip. Yeah, he'd make all of her wishes for a lifestyle such as her bosses possible. She smiled to herself, took off her clothes and put on her pajamas and robe. She thought about going straight to bed before tying the polyester cover up because she didn't have a thing to say to her competition, but then decided it would look too obvious. So after massaging some *African Pride* Castor & Mink Oil onto her scalp and tiny afro as she didn't want the cotton pillowcase to dry out her hair. Kelly headed back down the hallway into the large, bright living room where Holly was. The lawyer was lounging on the sofa clad in a white two-piece set with the matching robe from *Victoria's Secret,* the one her secretary had been saving up to buy. Kelly stared at Holly while she sipped on a cup of Chamomile Citrus tea. "Hey, Kel. Are you all set?" her boss asked. She'd heard the hardwood floors creak as Kelly approached the living room entryway. Holly leaned up, draping her feet over the side of the large stripped sofa. The dark-skinned woman nodded and swallowed hard. She struggled to keep a few unpleasant remarks from slipping out.

"Could I get you something to drink?" Holly asked. She set her cup down on a silver coaster then stood up. "Yeah, um, yes please. I'll have a little of what you're drinking," Kelly said. She walked over and sat down in one of the chairs next to the sofa as she watched Holly disappear briefly, returning with an identical cup to the one she'd been drinking out of. It was filled to the brim with the piping-hot herbal drink. "Here you go," her boss said, handing the cup to her secretary. "Be mindful. It's really hot," Holly said. She sat back down, lifting her feet back up again. As Kelly stole a short swig from the cup, she glared at Holly over the rim. Be mindful, she thought as she wanted to yell. "Really?! I don't see all that smoke coming from the cup!" She just wanted to come right out and ask her how it felt to fool around with someone elses man? But, that wouldn't be *"politically* correct". After all, Miss Thing was still her boss. Peering around the large space they occupied, Kelly reminded herself that they were not in an office. The art on the walls and the fine furnishings were encouraging her to get what was on her chest off even more. Yep, everything was the bomb up in there. Sure, their offices were fly, Kelly mused, but this was beyond all that, this was a place anyone in their right mind would want to call home. Looking back over at Holly, the dark-skinned woman figured if her boss had a few more swigs of that tea, she'd be feeling nice and sleepy enough for her to bring up her sexual rendezvous with Philip without her having to choke, uh, *coax* it out of her. She hoped that stuff she was drinking would relax her like that. The dark-skinned woman took another sip of her tea while part of her was testing it to see if it was something that would make her want to cough up information that she wouldn't have any intention otherwise of sharing. She watched Holly as she slowly brought the cup down from her mouth. Then again, she was too classy to do such a thing. Kelly almost laughed out loud because she'd been surprised many times before by women of a very similar caliber. Just when you'd least expect it, one of these well-mannered chicks would slip up and say something out of character. As Holly brought her cup of tea toward her full lips the words drink up, drink up engulfed Kelly's head.

Bored to death, and twenty minutes into the same conversation, the dark-skinned woman yawned and wondered when Holly would stop talking about work. Work this, work that. She just wanted to tell her to shut up. How could she change the subject without offending Miss Thing, Kelly thought as she twitched around impatiently in her chair. She didn't want to hear her hem and haw over that woman Leslie Stokes. It was clearer than those sparkling candlesticks on Holly's mantle that the situation was still bothering Holly, but she, on the other hand, was bothering Kelly. Annoying the heck out of her. If Leslie Stokes wanted to sit up there and have that man beat her brains out that was her choice. Nobody helped me when I was being knocked around like some worthless bag of trash, Kelly thought. When Holly finally quieted down to take another sip from her teacup, the dark-skinned woman said, "So, how's everything going with what's his name?" Kelly snapped her fingers for effect. "Um, the guy who owns "Phil's House"." Kelly heard and despised the subtle desperation in her voice. But she was going to make Holly talk about him tonight even if it killed her. And it seemed as though she'd brought it up just in time, too. It looked like the lawyer was getting ready to announce that she was going to bed. The dark-skinned woman had seen the way her boss slid her skinny butt to the edge of the sofa and glanced over at the clock on the mantle after she'd drained her cup. "Oh, it's working out nicely," Holly said with a smile. She was stifling a yawn at the same time. What kind of an answer was that? It's *working* out nicely? "Kel, did I give you my schedule for next week?" Here we go again with this work crap. For some reason Kelly was insulted by the way Holly spoke to her. It sounded condescending. Wasn't she able to see passed the employer/employee thing? She'd have to change that! "Is it getting serious?" Kelly asked, cutting Holly off. She crossed her leg. Yeah, say something about that! The dark-skinned woman felt her stomach tighten with the urge to leap up from that chair and go completely off on Holly, but instead she focused on the way the seat and back cushion of the chair she was sitting in. It felt like she was being massaged. It was so comfortable. This was the way she was supposed to be living.

The telephone rang before Holly could answer. "Who could this be at 10:45 p.m.?" she said, excusing herself. Kelly slumped back in her seat and sighed as she watched her answer the phone in the kitchen. "Hello," Holly said into the receiver. "Hey, sweetness. I thought you said you'd call me back. Is everything okay?" Philip asked. "Oh, I'm sorry. Yes, yes, everything's fine," she said. She glanced back over her shoulder into the living room at Kelly, who was now standing up, admiring the pictures on the end table. Little did Holly know, the dark-skinned woman was trying her best to listen to what she was saying. "Are you at home?" Holly asked. "Yeah, I just got in," he said. "Long day, huh?" "As always." "So, tell me, Philip. How did your talk with Brenda go?" Holly asked. He sighed wearily. "Not good. We argued like two dogs over one bone. Bren refuses to budge. She even started up with me again today. But don't you worry about it. I'll take care of her." The silken texture of his voice comforted her. "I can't worry about that," she said, although it was her nature to become distressed over someone not liking her. "Anything else new?" Holly asked quietly. I'm a new creature in Christ Jesus, she thought as the thought of how her old way of thinking was trying to pull her backwards. "Well, Vanessa and Tracy came by for a drink." Holly's brows rose as she refocused on what Philip was saying. She was surprised that her two partners didn't call her to see if she'd like to join them. "Oh," was the only thing she could manage to say at that moment. "I wonder were Courtney was?" she asked afterward. "They said he had to work late. I guess Vanessa was waitin' for him," he said in the midst of a yawn. He began to laugh a little. "She didn't look like she was waitin' on my man though." Waiting for Courtney at "Phil's House"? Holly thought. She remembered Vanessa saying that she was going to take a four-day weekend as well when she'd said good-bye to both of her partners on Wednesday evening. "So, we're still on for tomorrow," Philip said, interrupting her thoughts. "Uh ... Absolutely," she said, bringing a smile to her puzzled face. "Good, good. How's it goin' with your guest?" he asked. "Fine. I'm really enjoying her company," Holly said. But on the inside of the other room Kelly was thinking quite the opposite.

"Have you ever dated a White man before?" Kelly asked once Holly hung up the phone. It was a question she'd always pondered after finding out that Holly was biracial. And, at this point, the dark-skinned woman wanted her boss to go out and find herself one. They'd been discussing the pictures on Holly's end table ever since she'd hung up with Philip. The dark-skinned woman also wanted to know why her boss preferred Black men over White ones. "No, I haven't. And it's not that I prefer Black men over White ones.... I just never ran into a White man I wanted to go out with." "Would you?" "If the right one came along," Holly said quietly. "I only want who and what God has for me," Holly went on to say. She was still very quiet when she spoke. "Uh, Kel, could we finish this some other time?" Holly started laughing a little. "It's midnight and you have to get up at seven." Holly stood up. "I always go to bed late," Kelly said. "Well, you are more than welcomed to stay up, but I'm going to enjoy my sweet sleep. Good night." Holly stood up and walked out. Making a face, the dark-skinned woman reluctantly told her boss that she, too, would be going to bed. Kelly stuck her tongue out at Holly from behind, like a mischievous child, as she pulled herself to her feet.

The next morning, Holly was awake before her alarm sounded. She woke up the way she did on all mornings after she'd been upset by something the night before. This time it was two incidents that had disturbed her. Brenda's still not excepting her being half White and Vanessa and Tracy's exclusion of her. When would she ever fit in? A question that entered her mind too often.

At first she wasn't quite sure if she was really upset about both circumstances. She had stored them in the back of her mind, in the twilight area where worries were almost nothing -- no sleep was lost, because she tried to convince herself that most worries came and passed. "I cast down these vain imaginations and lead them away captive into the obedience of Christ," Holly said with confidence. The scripture rose up in her suddenly.

Holly reached over and turned off the alarm with thoughts of how God said He was a jealous God in His word. "The battle is not mine," she said and nodded her head yes.

Slipping on her robe, she went next door and knocked on the guest room door.

"Kel," she called softly as she stepped inside. There was more than enough time for her secretary to answer.

Today the room was dark and still, Holly thought when she walked inside. On most other day's it was brightly lit and filled with an indescribable life. Holly glimpsed around the space and proceeded toward the bed, calling her secretary's name again. Then she shook her when there was no reply. She could see the dark-skinned woman's eyelids flutter. "Time to get up," she said when Kelly opened her eyes, yawning.

The assistant yanked her body upward, sitting on the bed. She glanced over at the gold clock with the champagne-colored dial, sitting on the nightstand beside the bed she'd slept in. The dark-skinned woman was hoping it was some strange hour so she'd have a good reason to go off on her boss, but she saw that it was exactly the time she needed to get up. "Did you sleep well?" Holly asked.

Kelly nodded. "Yeah, I conked right out," she said. "Good, I'll go put on some coffee while you get yourself together. It's my turn to serve you," Holly said with a smile. As she headed out the door, the secretary made a face, silently mimicking what her boss had just said.

The two women sat at the kitchen table, sipping on hazelnut coffee and nibbling on buttered rye toast. It was the only thing Holly had in the house suitable for breakfast. After Kelly was showered and dressed, in between sips off coffee and bites of rye toast, Holly asked her secretary to make a few phone calls and to type up a letter she'd forgotten to add to the list of things that had to be done in her absence. Nodding and saying okay, the dark-skinned woman reached for another piece of toast from the saucer in the center of the table. It was a subtle reminder to let Holly know that she heard her when she said it was her turn to serve the dark-skinned woman. "Anything else?" Kelly asked as she buttered the crunchy bread. "No, that should be all for now," Holly said. She leaned forward, placed her right elbow on the table, resting her chin in the palm of her hand. "So, who are you going out with tonight?" Holly asked Kelly who felt her head nodding. Okay, maybe she got the hint is what she was thinking. "Liz and her sister Joanna. We'll probably head over to Josephine's. I really like her catfish." Kelly took a bite of toast, cutting her eyes over at her boss. She was waiting to see some sort of reaction. Would she want to know why we're not going to "Phil's House"? the secretary wondered. "I like it, too," Holly said and finished her coffee. Kelly could feel her stomach tighten. She hated that the light-skinned woman had money. She started to feel competitive toward Holly. "Did you ever see Josephine in person?" she asked. Holly nodded yes. That wasn't what she was expecting to hear. "Why don't you come with us?" the dark-skinned woman added after a while. Holly smiled. "No, I can't. I'm having company." The secretary had to concentrate hard on herself. She didn't want her boss to see how excited she'd become. Company? Kelly thought. She'd have to think of something entertaining to do, knowing that it was Philip Holly was referring to.

Holly was down on her hands and knees in the bathroom after Kelly had left. She was wiping up the water that had, according to her secretary must have seeped out from underneath and through the cracks on both sides of the shower curtain. Never before had this happened, Holly thought as she stood up and squeezed the sopping cloth, draining the excess water into the sink. Why didn't Kelly tell her that the bathroom was flooded before they sat down to eat? Holly shook her head in dismay. She then pulled back the shower curtain, slinging the damp rag over the clothing line. The hazel-eyed woman was surprised to see that Kelly didn't use the shower instead she showered in the soaking tub which also had a shower head. The telephone rang. Holly picked it up in her bedroom. "What were you doing?" Vanessa asked when her friend grabbed it on the second ring. "You don't want to know," Holly said regarding the mess she'd been cleaning up. "I'm a little annoyed with you and Trace," she added with a slight grin. "Why? What did we do to you?" "Philip told me that you guys stopped in for a drink last night. Don't tell me the two of you *combined* forgot my number?" Holly sat down on the bed, clicking on the television with the remote control. "You had company. It wouldn't be right to hang out with Kelly anyway." "Well, you still could have called. I don't know why I had to hear it from Philip." "Yeah, you're right, *but* I bet he managed to leave out a few other events from last night," Vanessa chuckled. She didn't give Holly a chance to respond. "Tracy and I were sitting upstairs at a table overlooking the bar because she had wanted to order something to eat. And, girl, the next thing we knew Philip was arguing with some woman down by the door. He had to force her outside because girlfriend was going for his throat. She was furious. I don't know what he did to her, but she was not havin' it." A moment of silence bounced back and forth between lines before Holly realized that it had to of been Brenda. He told her that they'd fought again yesterday. "He mentioned it, Vee," Holly said quietly. She had no idea it had gotten so out of control like that. She didn't want to be the one responsible for causing trouble in their family. She'd have to discuss it with him tonight. "Oh, well. She has some temper," was all Vanessa had said. She was no longer laughing. Suddenly the story wasn't as humorous. It was almost as if she'd called to deliberately upset Holly. "So, what are your plans later?" Vanessa asked. "Philip's coming over tonight." Holly said. She turned to TBN. The "Praise" program was about to come on. He's coming over while Kelly's there?" Vanessa said, giggling. Holly rolled her eyes and paused. "She's going out with her friends tonight." "Oh. Well, let me go. The cleaning lady's at the door," Vanessa said like Holly needed to clean some things up in her life.

Chapter Fourteen

Glancing at the clock on the nightstand in her bedroom, Holly pulled the lavender short-sleeved lycra top over her head and slipped into the jeans she'd purchased earlier at the Gap. Her hair was pulled back into a ponytail. She walked in front of the full-length mirror afterward to examine herself. Once she smoothed out a few wisps of hair that had fallen out of place, Holly was considerably pleased with the way she looked. A sudden knock on her door made her jump. "Come in," she called, knowing that it was Kelly. The dark-skinned woman peeked inside, telling her boss that she was going to take a shower. "I'll use the real shower this time," Kelly said with a subtle smile. The timing couldn't be better, Holly thought. Her secretary's friends would be meeting her downstairs in forty-five minutes and Philip would be there in about twenty. "Here, let me get you a fresh towel. She stepped out into the hallway where Kelly was, opening the linen closet. "Just toss those other towels in the hamper in the bathroom." Holly motioned toward the white quilted box beside the sink. "Thanks," Kelly said as she took the clean towel and wash cloth. She then proceeded to check Holly out. "You look cute," she said to her boss. "What time is your company coming?" "He should be here at eight," Holly said and sashayed down the hall into the living room. Kelly watched her until she was out of view, the smirk on her face spelling trouble.

"Kel, Philip's on his way up!" Holly announced through the bathroom door. He was ten minutes early. Holly could hear the shower running. Not getting a response from her secretary, she wondered if she should knock again. Holly shook her head no. She was sure she heard her and besides Philip was already ringing the bell. As Holly approached the front of the apartment, she quickly stacked the mail she'd carelessly tossed on the foyer table this afternoon into a neat pile. Then she took a rushed peek at herself in the mirror. Having to even out the same wayward strands made her sigh. The bell rang a second time. She opened the door, realizing when she saw him that two days sure made a difference. He looked better than ever. Holly invited Philip Williams inside. He was wearing a black V-neck T-shirt and stone-colored Chino's that looked tailor-made. "Hey, sweetness," he said and leaned down, kissing her on the mouth. Tonight her nostrils picked up the faint scent of Pleasures for men. It was delicious, mingling well with the Allure she'd dabbed on. "You look rested, baby," Philip said. He purposely hung back behind Holly as she entered the living room. He wanted to observe the way she walked. Man! She had to inherit a tight bootie like that from her Black mama, he thought. Then, he threw himself off when he realized he had become upset with his thinking. He was no better than Brenda. Were they raised in a prejudice household? If anything, his mother taught them how to go against their own race. Maybe that's why Bren had a problem with Whites. Shaking his head in disgust, Philip caught up to Holly. "As a matter of fact, I do feel rested," she said, taking a seat on the sofa. He sat down beside her. "What did you do today?" Philip asked. "Some shopping. Food and clothing. So, if you're hungry, I do have something here to eat," she said with a smile. "Then I stopped by my mother's for about an hour. She was holding her book club meeting." Philip nodded, leaning back against the sofa. "Yeah, Oprah influenced my mother's book club. She has one herself," he said. "What are they reading?" Holly asked. He made a face. "I don't know all that!" he laughed. "Why don't you give her a call and ask? She's dyin' to meet you anyway." Philip was grinning, almost every tooth in his head showing as he anticipated her reply. Studying his face for a moment, Holly then lowered her eyes. She had no comment and to hear him use the terminology of his mother dying, when it came to her, made her think about the God she was supposed to be committed to. He's life. The next thought that entered her mind was about Brenda. With the way things were going, she would probably turn their mother against her, too. Philip was just being nice. Wait! Whose side was Holly on? she asked herself when she heard, "Come here." Philip was patting a spot on the sofa closer to him. She smiled, looked up into his eyes and slid over. She had been hanging her head. He grabbed her hand and put it around his neck and she put her other arm there and he grinned at her again and said, "All I've been doin' is thinkin' about you. You're interuptin' my work, Ms. Reed, makin' me slack off." Well, you've entered my mind quite often, too, she thought at the same time that she was thinking look at how the words didn't come out of her mouth. This is God's mouth she reminded herself as the Bible verse where God asked Moses who made his mouth entered her mind. Holly felt Philip's hands on her back then, and he was leaning in toward her, aspiring to press his body into hers. She held back a giggle as she watched him pucker up. The couple kissed for a long time and Holly wondered why she wanted to laugh. Was the joke on her?

She squirmed in his arms, managing to free herself. Holly smiled with a little discomfort forming in her stomach, she glanced back over her shoulder, surveying the doorway. All clear. She could have sworn she'd heard something. But, was that the reason for her sudden discomfort? Then turning back toward her frisky companion, Holly grinned once again at the way he looked. Philip's eyes were still closed tightly and his lips were once again, puckered. He started leaning over in her direction again, pulling her to him. "Wait," she said, pushing him away gently. "Kelly's still here," she added, whispering. Philip's eyes popped open, his mouth now back to normal. "I thought she'd be out partyin' with her friends tonight," he said, letting out an exasperated breath. "She will be soon," Holly said. "When?" Philip leaned back, adjusted himself and stretched his arm across the back of the sofa. "Soon. She's getting ready now," Holly said. She pointed toward the back of the apartment with her chin. Philip looked at her and smiled. But she didn't see him. Her eyes were elsewhere, checking the time. "I missed you so much," he said. Holly could feel his hand stroking her ponytail, twirling it around his fingers. Then she felt him let go, her head jerking a bit from the release. He leaned forward, turning her face in his direction by putting his thumb and forefinger on her chin. "I'm gonna show you exactly how much you were missed when she leaves," he whispered, giving her full lips a peck. Seeing his brows move up and down, she knew he wasn't going to renege, either. Somebody's doing something wrong, she thought, wondering at the same time if he was, too. Holly smiled, took a deep breath and said, "Vanessa told me about the argument you and Brenda had at your restaurant. I'm so sorry. This shouldn't be happening." She had to say it now, get it out on the table before her flesh took over, making her forget her plan to discuss it in the first place. Philip's eyes narrowed with confusion. "What did she tell you? Bren and I didn't argue at my rest...." He paused. Holly watched his mouth open then close. "Oh, last night?" he said, rubbing the back of his neck. "Yeah, I told her that you mentioned it to me," Holly said. "That wasn't my sister. That was just some crazy woman trippin'," he said quietly. "Me and my sister would never resort to violence." Holly nodded. "Man, Vanessa should try to get herself a job down at the *Daily News* or something.'" Philip sucked his teeth, shaking his head in disbelief, adding, "Gossipin' woman." He tried to smile as he leaned back against the sofa, stretching his arm across the back once more. But it didn't work. "I didn't think the two of you would. You know, carry on like that. Especially at your place of business," Holly said, seeing his eyes narrow for the second time, locking on a space just over her shoulder. She was about to say something else, trying to go on as if he weren't staring. Did Holly dare turn her head, follow Philip's eyes? When she saw him blink rapidly a few times, as if he wanted to look somewhere else, or make sure his vision wasn't failing him, she took a chance. As she spun around in the direction of the doorway, Holly's mouth dropped open. She had lost her voice for a moment, not believing what she was seeing. Kelly was standing there naked, drying her hair with a towel, which was covering her face. "Holly, do you have any lotion? I forgot mine," was what the dark-skinned woman was saying. A hush worked its way around the area they were in until Holly broke the silence. "Kelly!" Flipping back the towel with one jolt, the secretary was stunned, motionless as she continued to stand there unclad, her feet appearing to be stuck as her body wiggled, trying to shake them loose. Holly could see her eyes widening with terror, as she covered the top part of her body with the small towel she'd been flailing in her hand, then finally regaining a bit of normalcy to her frantic demeanor, Kelly turned, fleeing down the hall, back where she'd come from all the while suppressing the burst of laugher caught in her throat by covering her mouth with both hands. The towel was resting across her shoulders. How she wanted so desperately to free it, hear it ricochet all through her employer's elegant apartment and land smack dead in Holly's ears. Kelly savored the expression on Philip's face in her mind, bulging eyes, tongue hanging out, as she continued to rush toward the back. He liked what he saw. I know he did, she thought, making it into the guest room and closing the door behind her. When Holly looked at Philip, whose face was buried in his hands, she told him she'd be right back. She wanted to make sure Kelly was all right. Philip did nothing but nod.

"Kelly," Holly called as she tapped on the door. "Come in," the dark-skinned woman said, her voice a whimper. "Are you okay?" her boss asked once she was inside. Kelly was sitting down on the edge of the bed in her bra and panties. She glanced at the two lotion bottles in Holly's hands. "I'm really sorry. That's the way I'm used to walking around after a shower. I like to dry off naturally. I thought it would be okay since.... since we're both women. My entire stay has been nothing but a disaster. First at your mother's now here. I didn't know he was out there," the secretary lied right through her teeth. She had heard her boss loud and clear when she'd warned her earlier of Philip's arrival. Kelly would have come out sooner, but she was having trouble thinking of a way to appear innocent during her incorrigible scheme. And it seemed to work. Holly walked over to the bed, set the two bottles down on the nightstand and placed her hand on Kelly's shoulder. "Don't worry about it. I don't think he saw you," Holly said, knowing that he had. Yeah okay, Kelly thought, looking down at herself. Holly lifted her chin with her index finger, mistaking her secretary's examination of the body she showed off for sorrow. She still wanted to laugh because she was looking her very best, but she managed to maintain her wicked stance. "Look, it's all over with," Holly said and Kelly could feel herself freeze for a moment until her employer went on to say, "I want the sad face to disappear. Do you hear me?" Holly could feel Kelly's head bob up and down on her finger. She smiled and removed it. "Get dressed so you could go out and have a ball. I brought you two types of my favorite lotions." The secretary grinned, too, thanking Holly for her warm hospitality. Could this whole thing get any easier? she mused.

Twenty minutes later the couple heard Kelly's heels clicking down the hall and into the living room. She was all dressed and ready to go, her short afro shining like the sparkle in her eyes. The dark-skinned woman was wearing a white fitted lycra top, black mini skirt and black patent leather over-the-knee boots. "Look at you," Holly said. The secretary blushed. "Kelly Mills this is Philip Williams," Holly said, gazing back and forth at the two of them. Leaning up, but remaining seated, Philip waved and said hello. "Nice to meet you. I want to apologize about what happened before," Kelly said, a wide grin on her face. Philip held up his hands. "Don't bother. I didn't see anything," he said smoothly. You liar, Kelly thought bitterly, the smile disappearing just as easy as it came. She'd seen the way he'd given her a long stare, his eyes closing in on her bare essentials, like he'd never seen female genitalia before. "Uh, she's the one who told me about your restaurant," Holly said, breaking the awkward quiet. "Is that right?" Philip said in a low unenthusiastic voice. "My friends and I have been loyal patrons ever since you opened last year," said the dark-skinned woman. She could've told him the date and time of his grand opening if he wanted her to. Philip nodded and began stroking his chin. "I've seen the three of you there a few times. Back booth on the left, right?" Kelly smiled. She couldn't wait to tell Liz and Joanna that he'd been watching her as well. "Yep, that's our spot. You could see everything from there," she said, her eyes glancing down at the hand Philip just placed on Holly's knee. Each time he squeezed it, it felt as though he was squeezing her heart, breaking it in two. I have to get out of here, Kelly thought, feeling her mouth go dry. The phone rang and Holly knew that it was Peter, telling her that Kelly's two friends were downstairs. She was saved by the bell. "That must be them. Don't bother to answer. I'll go on down," Kelly said. She started backing away while she thought about how she used a word Philip used. Bother. That must mean something, the dark-skinned woman mused as she doesn't really use that word. "All right, Kel. Have a good time," Holly said. It was an interruption to Kelly as she saw how her employer was going to say something else. "There's a spare key inside of the ginger jar on the table in the foyer. I informed Peter earlier that it's okay to let you up tonight without an announcement," Holly said. The secretary nodded, her eyes still focusing on Philip's hand, resting on her employers knee. "See you around," Philip said. He used his free hand to wave, making the dark-skinned woman's pain escalate. "Yeah, see you around," Kelly repeated, for lack of anything else to say. Or, did that mean something, too, she asked herself and turned to leave the living room. The couple listened to the secretary as she fumbled for the key, quickly closing the door behind her. But what they could not hear was all the cursing she'd done on her way to the elevator.

"Alone at last," Philip said, a smirk crossing his lips. Holly grinned. Putting the hand he'd been rubbing her knee with on her neck, Philip then touched her shoulder. His fingertips, hotter then today's one-hundred degree temperature, made Holly arch alittle when they pressed into her back. There was absolutely no way he would be mistaken for an amateur. No, Philip knew all the correct spots to touch. He knew exactly where his hands were supposed to be, how his fingers were supposed to move when he touched her.

Sliding his hands upward, toward the front of her body, he put them on her breasts, and she heard the normal rhythm of his breathing change. Her round breasts filled his hands, warming his palms, making his manhood rise. Holly began to feel uncomfortable with Philip's hands on her like that. It was God's displeasure she was sensing while Philip just wanted to grab the smooth-textured top and rip it straight down the middle, exposing the taut dual he held gently in each hand. Wait, he thought. Tonight he'd take his time. Do it slow, experience every caress and every stroke. But, he couldn't make love to her without taking a shower first. Of course he didn't smell. He just wanted to feel refreshed. He'd been working like a slave all day long, his skin felt sticky. Maybe they'd start out in the bathroom and work their way into the bedroom. Holly had her eyes closed while his hands roamed her upper body. She wondered if her not enjoying it was being revealed to Philip. Holly's tightly shut eyes popped opened as soon as she felt him let go of her breasts and stop touching her all together. She stared at him, now wondering if God had told him to stop touching his daughter like that. Holly began to think as if her Heavenly Father was somewhere around. She was looking forward to seeing just how much she'd been missed by Philip. "Everything okay?" she asked, moistening her lips with her tongue. Holly swallowed hard with sudden thoughts of God going in and out of her mind. She watched as Philip's gaze remained on her lips. *Oooooo,* girl, he thought, catching a glimpse of her tongue as it swept across her top lip first then the bottom one. He stood up and extended his hand. "Baby, I'm gonna need a shower before we do anything. I feel hot and funky," he said, pulling his shirt away from his skin, letting some air flow down in between them. "Is that okay with you?" "That's fine," Holly said. She cleared her throat and put her hand into the one he was offering. She, too, stood up. "I'll get you a towel and wash cloth," she added. As she started to walk away, leave the living room to go down the hall to the linen closet, Philip stopped her, pulling her into his arms. "I want you to join me," he whispered deep into her ear, dampening the lobe with his tongue.

"I'm gonna need some help. I'll wash your back if you wash mine." Nodding her head, Holly swallowed what was now passion in her throat. "Okay?" he asked, smiling. "Yes," she said, her voice breathy. She wasn't trying to be cute or sound sexy. The wind had left her lungs for a minute. It was longer than that, really. "Good," Philip said, grinning some more. He could feel her pushing away again, slowly. This is God's breath, she thought. But, before she could tell Philip that she couldn't do this, he pulled her toward him once more, lifting her up into his arms.

In the bathroom, the warm water steamed up the mirror. Philip had been watching the way Holly's hair, now hanging down, had clung to her slender bare back. Yes Lord, he was liking the view from the front, as she slipped out of her black lacy thong, but he was the type of man who loved every angle of the female body, especially hers. She had nice, even skin he thought just as another thought was presenting itself to his mind. Was he really talking to God in his thoughts as he watched Holly undress? Philip, shaking his head no, went unnoticed. He was focused on the beauty in front of him again. No traces of stretch marks or any other ugly blemishes. Philip followed her into the shower. Then, once inside, he moved closer to her, she opened her arms, allowing him to bend down just low enough for her to wrap her arms around his neck, her legs around his waist. Lifting her as he did before, he placed her up against the wall. The pulsating water flowed fast and hard from the nozzle, into his back. Philip's mouth covered hers. She felt his hands gripping her behind and her legs, his fingers were exploring her body wildly, touching her everywhere. She could tell he wanted her badly, and she wanted him, too. Holly was tempted to cry out with pleasure when he entered her. Philip, winking at her, kissed the tip of her nose and pulled his head back, letting the warm water slip over it, threw his curls, down his face, over him and between them. She combed her fingers into his wet, slippery hair, guiding his face back to hers. Holly kissed him like he'd never been kissed before. Philip wanted to scream like a woman. Holly moaned. And, suddenly the heavy pounding of his pelvis turned into soft, metrical movements of tenderness. Kissing her again, Philip turned her from the wall and into the warmth of the streaming water, holding her tight, tighter until their heated tempo built once more.

Again he kissed her, teasing her lips with his tongue as he moved sensually inside of her, accelerating his pace. Holly unengaging their lips, leaned her head back into the water like he'd done before. Philip smiled. He watched the way the water took hold of her hair, spilling over her face and body. This woman was some kinda sexy, he thought, feeling his juices threatening to let loose. Philip could feel the water sprinkling over his head, pecking at his face. When the couple kissed each other again, roughly, they felt the excess water from Holly's hair squishing between their intertwined bodies. She began rubbing his back, digging her nails into it gently, confirming the pleasure he'd been giving her. "Do it, baby. Come on. That's it.... oh, yeah, that's it," he said, not being able to hold back any longer. Breathing heavily, his chest rising and falling rapidly, Philip asked her whether or not she'd been satisfied, too. Holly felt herself sliding down his mountain of a body, her feet now touching the bottom of the shower floor. She, too, was wiped out. The only thing her mind permitted her to do was nod her head, smile and sweep the hairs sticking to the sides of her face away. Her eyes found Philip's ring finger and there was no ring. She looked up into his eyes as she thought, We are not married. What did I just do?

Holly lay in Philip's arms across her bed, dozing off as he watched TV. The light from the twenty-inch screen was the only thing illuminating the spacious room, giving off a silver hue. Her eyes, though heavy with fatigue, managed to turn in his direction. She'd felt him staring, his breath, replete with a minty scent from the Altoid he'd been sucking. His fresh breath blew through her hair and down the back of her neck. "Go 'head, baby relax," he whispered, his voice soft. "What are you watching?" she asked, her words slurred. Holly pointed toward the TV with her index finger. She was shielding the yawn escaping her mouth with her other hand. Philip could feel her twisting, moving, turning her body so that she'd be facing him. But he didn't want her to. He loved holding her in his arms, loved breathing in the sweet fragrance of her hair. He'd washed it for her in the shower after they'd made love, using the strawberry-scented shampoo that he couldn't get enough of on their first date. He sighed softly, peering at Holly, who was now flat on her back, gazing at him. What was this woman doing to him? he wondered. Was this the feeling his mother described to him as a child, a teenager, a grown man when he'd asked the question, "How do you know when you're in love?" He always wanted to know what it was like. But, he just wasn't sure whether he would be capable of loving a woman with his whole heart. He was having too much of a good time falsifying his feelings to those other women, who, by the way, should *still* consider themselves lucky for the time he had spent with them. He almost laughed as their gullible faces crossed his mind at that moment. "The Holly Reed show," Philip finally said, knowing that it was the television she was referring to. He saw her wince a little at his response. Why'd she do that? He was telling the truth. "You don't believe me, do you?" he asked. "Did I say I didn't?" she asked, conjuring up her courtroom strength. Was she a show to him or better yet, to God? Pulling himself up a bit, Philip leaned on his elbow. "You didn't have to, baby. Your eyes spoke to me," he said, grinning. "It's a bad habit," Holly said. She began fishing around on the bed for the remote control, lowering the volume on the TV. "Sorry," she added. Philip grinned again. "Apology accepted." Although the smile hadn't left his face it didn't seem to mask the concern in his eyes. He couldn't quite figure her out. How did she really feel about him? "Uh, Holly. Do you remember when we discussed our dating situation. I think it was on our first night out," Philip said, knowing for sure that that was when it was. Why did he always have to be the one being chased? Being the chaser might be good for a change, he mused. He could see her take a deep breath before telling him that she remembered. "Well, I.... I, uh, was wonderin' what it was you were lookin' for... in a... in a

173

relationship?" Holly sucked hard on her bottom lip. That was another bad habit. As she pulled herself up, she pressed her back into the headboard. She didn't want to smile. But it was hard not to. Philip Williams wanted her to be his woman, make this official. She grinned anyway, not really knowing why she tried to refrain from doing it. Because she relished the time they shared. He'd done everything he said he would do so far. He's nice, funny and he called her back even though she gave it up on the first night. But, still, she had to think about this commitment possibility. She'd been known to dive into the pool without checking to see if it had water first. Know matter how hard you try, Holly thought, you never fully recover from the fall. She had to be careful. Then, she suddenly thought. No, I have to cast this care like all the rest, unto my Heavenly Father. Holly looked past Philip at the Bible on the nightstand on his side of the bed. Philip sat up, too. He wanted to glance back over his shoulder to see what is was she was staring at, but he didn't for whatever reason. Deep down inside, he knew it was her Bible. "Do you want to give *us* a try?" is what he said instead. "See how things go?" Philip began to stare at the TV after he asked Holly those questions. *I Love Lucy* was on Nick at Nite. It was the episode where a pregnant Lucy and her side-kick, Ethel decide to dress up like men in order to crash a shower Fred had thrown for Ricky. Glancing over at the screen, Holly smiled. She liked this part. The part when Ricky tells his wife how he'd known all along that it was her because he'd never seen a man stick on a mustache with tape before. Holly could see a grin threatening to cross Philip's lips, too, as she put her hand on his knee. His smile was then cut short. Gone completely. Hers was gone completely, too. She was thinking about the two times that the Lord told her not to watch things that weren't speaking His Truth. Holly sighed and Philip thought, this wasn't the way it was supposed to go. He was feeling rejected. She was taking way too long to answer his question. He wasn't happy with her initial reaction. The ecstatic one he'd been used to receiving from the ladies of his past, who swore up and down and around town that he was about to propose.... didn't happen with her like he wanted it to. The ones you don't want throw themselves at you all the time, Philip told himself. They'd leap on him, yelling and screaming I do's, I will's and yes, baby I'm yours, only to be smacked in the face with his telling them how he needed some space. And tonight, after praying most of the day, much to his *own* surprise, on how he hoped Holly would be as excited to be his woman as he would to be her man. The only thing he got was a few minutes of silence and a hand warming his knee. So, this is what a brother gets for trying to do the right thing? She squeezed his knee again for the second time, wanting him to look at her. "Philip, I'd love to." *But*, he thought. "But... let's take it slow. Don't cut your eyes at me like that. I know you're probably saying it's a little too late for that, especially since we've already been physical." Physical? What kind of junk was this? Selma Girard told him he'd get his one day. Was this the day? Philip glared back at the TV for no particular reason, then back at Holly. Wasn't she aware of his muted cry for help? He forced a smile on his disappointed face. "I know where you're comin' from," he said, covering the hand she had on his lap with his. It felt sweaty to her. The poor thing was nervous, Holly thought. There she goes again. "I wouldn't do this any other way," he lied, knowing that he'd marry her tomorrow, if she was willing. But before doing that.... he'd have to muster up some fierce courage. Not in order to get himself to the altar, but to tell her a secret, a secret that would probably make him lose her in a flash. Lifting his hand off of hers, he wrapped his arm around her shoulders, holding her close to him. Man, later for it! Why didn't he just tell her how much he loved her? Weren't those the words every woman wanted to hear? Didn't that make them forgot all the messed up things their man had ever done to them? He was losing his grip.

The telephone rang, startling them.

Holly leaned forward, glancing at the clock on the nightstand, which Philip's body was blocking. 12:15 a.m. This better be good, she told herself, regarding the caller. The couple listened to Holly's soothing voice as it floated out of the answering machine. Suddenly, she felt herself stiffen. Maybe something had happened to her mother, she thought, until Vanessa began to speak after the short beep. "Girl, pick up! I know you're there!" she said, pausing. "All right, I guess you're," she laughed, her voice quieter, less abrasive. "tied up or too out of breath to answer? But, I was sitting here, in my study, trying to plan Courtney's party. I know you think I must be losing it, but I couldn't sleep. My husband's snoring chased me out of the room," she paused again, as if she thought Holly would still pick up. Then, in her usual harsh way, Vanessa said, "Call me tomorrow.... I mean later today! I need your opinion on something!" No good-bye. Just a loud bang from her slamming down her receiver. Philip shook his head in disgust. "She's got a real problem. Court must've been drunk the day he asked her to marry him," Philip said. Holly just waved her hand. "Vanessa Benjamin's bark is bigger than her bite," she said quietly. "What kind of party is she givin' him?" Philip asked. "Oh, birthday," Holly said. "I forgot to tell you." "When is it?" "July 15th, 16th. I can't remember. I have it written down in my agenda." Holly gestured to get up. "Tell me later," he said, holding her at his side. She stared at him, smiling. A slow grinned emerged on his face, too. This was the first time she'd noticed the tiny lines around his eyes. The delicate confirmations of the life he's lived so far. Holly didn't think he was old. To her the forty's meant knowing yourself. Being in the place you wanted to be spiritually and mentally, if you were blessed. She paused and continued to stare at Philip. Was he blessed? "Could I asked you something?" she said softly. "It's sort of personal." Philip nodded. "I have nothing to hide," he said, feeling a pang of guilt erupt in the pit of his stomach. Why'd he lie? "Have you ever been serious about a woman? And if not, what makes you think you'd be ready now? Sorry, I didn't plan on making this a two-part question." She smiled, noticing his Adams apple move up and down. "No," he began cautiously. "I've never met someone who'd made me feel as good as you make me feel, Holly. When I'm around you there's this.... this sense of freedom that I have. Call me corny if you want to, but I feel like I could be myself. And, I dig that. I'm not sayin' that I *need* somebody to do that for me. But, I really like what it is you're doin' to me, baby. That's how I know this is right. There's no other way for me to explain it. I used to think that my mother was to blame for me not ever really carin' "romantically" for a woman. I was wrong." He took a deep breath. "Why would you blame your mother?" she asked with slight puzzlement in her eyes. Philip lowered his head, taking in air, pushing it out again. "It's a long story. A stupid one, really," he said, catching a glimpse of the new expression on Holly's face. She was going to be persistent, force it out of him. The determination in her eyes was that of a lawyer's now. "Come on, tell me. Nothing you say is stupid," she said, earnestly. Where did this woman get these powers from? he wondered. Was that her God doin' this? The urge to say none of your business never entered his mind. Not once. He had heard that God knew everything anyway. "Well, ever since I could remember.... my mother would always say..." Philip paused. He looked just like a little boy to Holly for a moment, the bashful look on his face, the way he began fidgeting with his hands as he peered up at the TV. *The Mary Tyler Moore* Show was up next. "Go on," Holly said, her voice tugging at words buried in a place no woman had ever found. Underneath the hard surface lyed a substance softer than cotton. "She'd always say that... that there wasn't a woman out there in the world good enough for her son." There, he'd said it. Holly placed her hands over his, the ones that couldn't stay still and smiled. "But, every mother must tell her son that." She hated hearing herself say that. How did she know what every mother told their son? Look at this, she thought remember having heard little Jo Jo's mother tell him that no woman would ever want him. Philip looked at her, with what appeared to be welling tears, lying in the bottom of his eyes. Holly was still thinking about little Jo Jo and the way he would look at her the same way. Then, she didn't quite know is this was surprise she felt when she heard Philip finally say, "Yeah, but every son doesn't start to believe it. I did.... until now. Baby, I believed that there wasn't a woman out there, good enough for me." Holly watched in silence as the tears fell down Philip's cheeks. A warmth like no other flooded her entire body.

She paused, swallowed and smiled.

An hour after Philip left, Holly lay back in her bed restless. The room was dark and quiet. As she tossed and turned for a moment, searching for a more relaxing position, she rolled on her side, folding her arm beneath her head and began staring at the moonlight racing across the floor. The curtains blew faintly, making the cast fade in and out. What was she going to do? Did she want more out of Philip? Was she ready to give of herself unselfishly as she'd once done with Bradford? She cleared her throat. That was foolishness. Being unselfish meant doing God's will. What was it about *her* that Philip felt he loved and had to have? She sighed wearily. Did she *really* need to know? Turning on her back, her fingers now laced, resting on her stomach, Holly then realized she had to pee. So she pulled herself up, sat still for a second, peeled the covers back and climbed out of bed. She made her way in the dark toward the bathroom.

Inside she flicked on the light, slid her panties down, her P.J. top up a bit and sat down on the cool toilet seat, all the while thoughts of her conversation with Philip were still stirring in her head.

After relieving her full bladder, Holly turned toward the toilet paper roll, sighing. Where was her house guest raised? she mused, slightly annoyed. It was empty. Kelly had neglected to replenish it. Sighing again, she stood up and reached down into the pale-pink cabinet beneath the sink. Feeling around for a new roll of *Scotties*, she accidentally knocked her secretary's toiletry bag to the floor, each and every one of the contents spilling out. "Oh, no!" Holly said as she shook her head in dismay. She was still a little annoyed. There were items everywhere. Holly quickly wiped herself and washed her hands before cleaning up the mess she'd made.

The dark-skinned woman's bag was cute and practical, Holly told herself as she knelt down, packing everything back into it. She thought she'd carried a lot of unnecessary stuff when she traveled. But, Kelly seemed to beat her, hands down, in that category. There was all kinds of things, and some were even duplicates. Two eyeliner pencils; both black. Two lipsticks in the same shade, two of the same blushes. No, she corrected herself. One was a blush and the other was an eyeshadow. African Pride Castor Oil for the hair. Mmmmm, Holly thought, smelling it. Kelly had Vaseline lip balms, a generic lotion ...... She paused after dropping them into the bag, a strange feeling welling in her stomach. Lotion? The eerie chill running up her spine made the hairs on her arm stand on end. "Didn't she ask me for lotion earlier?" Holly mused out loud, her eyebrows furrowed in deep confusion.

Back in bed, Holly lay on her side once again. This time she didn't see the moonlight rushing across the floor, although her eyes appeared to be taking it all in. The only thing she saw, in her mind, was Kelly's naked body. What was she doing? These were the kind of nights she despised, the nights when she couldn't sleep and when her fears had become magnified. Pondering the subject further, Holly heard her guest coming in. She glanced at the clock. It was 2:25 a.m. Her secretary moved toward the back of the apartment carefully, like a blind person in unfamiliar surroundings. Through her ajar door, Holly watched Kelly quietly as she passed, going into the room next to hers, shutting the door. Holly sighed, she'd discuss her findings with her later on today.

Chapter Fifteen

The next morning, Holly woke to the sun shining like a flashlight in her face. She sat straight up in bed, the sun now lay in slices across her thighs. She felt rested yet some confusion had lingered since she wasn't sure whether she'd dreamt finding lotion in Kelly's toiletry bag last night or worse, it had happened. What was her secretary up to? Holly yawned, stretching her arms above her head. Just as she began to think about how she had not lifted her hands in praise and worship to God in too long of a time, she heard the dark-skinned woman come out of the bathroom, the toilet flushing behind her. Kelly knocked on Holly's bedroom door. "I'm awake, Kel. Come in." Surveying herself quickly, Holly forgot for a moment what she was wearing. My blue pajama top, she told herself as she gazed down at her upper body. She was decent. The dark-skinned woman cracked open the door, sticking her head inside. "I'm about to leave," Kelly told her boss. Holly motioned for her to step all the way in. "Aren't you hungry?" she asked as she hung her feet over the side of the bed. I'm wearing the matching pajama pants, she told herself as she kept her eyes on her secretary. "No, not really," Kelly said, making a face. She was boasting. "We had breakfast at a diner this morning right before I got in," Kelly said, a strange look on her face. Holly nodded and the spirit of discernment revealed that Kelly was looking for a reaction from her boss. The secretary saw the way her boss looked at her. She was thinking didn't she go out to dinner at Josephine's. "Did you have fun?" Holly asked. "Yeah, the place is lively. We saw Savion Glover on the outside signing autographs," Kelly said, smiling faintly. "Oh, did ...," "No, we couldn't get his autograph there were too many people around him," the dark-skinned woman said, answering Holly's question before she could get it out of her mouth. Her boss nodded her head, the lotion thing suddenly entering her mind again. And almost as if she was privy to Holly's thoughts, Kelly said, "I used some more of your lotion this morning. I can't stand the kind I have. I only bought it because it was on sale." Holly could feel her facial expression changing. Something inside of her wanted to commiserate with Kelly, shelter her. Holly opened her mouth but nothing came out. Why would she want to do that when the Spirit of God was warning her? "I left the two bottles on the nightstand in the other room," the secretary added, wondering if her boss knew she wasn't telling the truth. She'd noticed the way her toiletry bag was zipped up completely. That wasn't the way she left it. Miss Thing was spying on her. In the bathroom Kelly had racked her brain, trying to think of a legitimate explanation, an excuse. "Uh, why don't you keep them," Holly said. She felt guilty even though her spirit was sensing the contradiction coming from her head. "I have a few more of the same kind stashed down in the bathroom cabinet." Holly stood up. Why did she always think the worst? This was her head, Holly thought as she was subtly examining her spirit. "I saw them," Kelly said with a smile. "Are you sure you don't want a cup of coffee or tea before you go?" Holly asked with a grin. Sucker! Kelly thought, stifling a laugh. She'd gotten over for the umphteenth time! "No, I'm good. I promised you I'd be out of your way in the morning and I meant it," the secretary said. She walked out of Holly's room back into the one she'd been staying in with accusation still looming in her heart. Holly followed her. "Oh, Kel. You didn't have to make the bed. Helen will be here at some point today." Holly was standing in the doorway of the guest room. "Force of habit I guess. One thing I can't stand is a mess," the secretary told her as she thought, the second thing was a man stealer. Or maybe that was the first thing. She hated to hear Holly mention her housekeeper. But, she was enjoying the way she was making it sound as if the tables had turned. Like she was the boss. "I feel the same way," Holly said. Although she was in agreement with Kelly about not liking a mess, she didn't like that she'd made the bed as if those sheets and blankets she'd slept on and under didn't need to be washed. Something wasn't right about this, she told herself. "Oh, I put your keys back in the ginger jar on the table near the front door," Kelly said with a slight smile. "Thank you," Holly said. She smiled back a little.

After Kelly picked up her overnight bag, which was leaning against the dresser, the two women headed toward the front of the apartment in silence.

Closing and locking the door behind Kelly, Holly decided to return Vanessa's call from earlier that morning. All this drama, she thought as she went into the kitchen, lifting the receiver. "Hello," said the calm, deep voice on the other end. "Hi, Courtney. Is Vee home," Holly asked. She was supporting the receiver with her shoulder as she reached up into the cupboard for a coffee filter and mug. "Holly?" Courtney said, a smile in his voice. "Yes. How's everything going?" she asked. She was pouring water into the coffee machine. "Well. Thank you. What about yourself?" "Oh, I can't complain or let's just say I won't," she said, giggling a little. He chuckled, too. Just then Holly heard Vanessa ask him who it was from the background. "Here's Vee. Take it easy," he said, passing his wife the receiver. "Hello!" Vanessa said, her tone somewhat irritable. "Sorry I didn't get to the phone in time last night," Holly said, pressing the "on" button on the coffee machine. "Liar. I gave you ample opportunity to pick up. I guess your company took precedence," Vanessa teased. Holly paused for a moment. She did lie. Why is what she was asking herself. "What could I say, you caught me," Holly shot back and cleared her throat. She hated strife. But, I'm caught up in it, she thought. "So, Philip was there?" Vanessa asked, snatching Holly out of her musing. "Yes, for a few hours," Holly said. She interrupted the flow of coffee, filling up her mug and placing the pot back down to continue brewing. "Mmmm, a little hit and run action, huh?" Vanessa teased again. "Vee, cut it out!" Holly paused again and sighed. "He had to go away on business," she said, quietly and blew into the coffee cup. She took a slow sip. "Where?"

Vanessa asked. "D.C. Some sort of restauranteur convention." The full-figured woman paused. "Why didn't he take you with him?" "Vee, please. I don't know. We're not joined at the hip, and how do you know if I wanted to go?" Holly asked. "Excuuuse me!" The full-figured woman began to laugh. Holly paused again as she examined the way Vanessa was laughing. It was at her. Holly sighed again and said in a low voice. "I will certainly excuse you. *Now,* what was it that you needed my opinion on?" "Girl, please. I solved that dilemma on my own ten minutes after leaving you the message," Vanessa said. "Good," Holly said. She shrugged her shoulders. "Are your invitations all sent out?" Holly asked. She took another sip from the mug. "Invitations? I've decided to just call people up. I know my mother will probably deny the fact that I'm her child when she finds out, but I can't be bothered. The only thing I care about is the way it turns out," Vanessa whispered. "This man must know something because he keeps walking by the room I'm in," she added, sucking her teeth. "We better go. Sounds like he's getting suspicious," Holly said.

Chapter Sixteen

Eight o'clock that same evening, Holly was sitting on the sofa, feet up, reading Carmen's latest book. They'd spoken about twenty minutes ago. And after hanging up with her friend, she realized how much she'd missed her. So, listening to her words on paper made it feel as though she was close by. The story was about a woman named Maria Sanchez. She was a head-strong Latina, attractive, had a successful art dealership, and she was single and not looking for love. She had been married before and was waiting on God to have the man of her dreams, find her. The man of God that God had for her. Holly's eyes gazed up from where she was reading to what the title of this chapter was. It read: "He who finds a wife, finds a good thing and obtains favor from the Lord." Holly nodded as her eyes lowered to where she had begun reading after turning the page. In this second chapter, Carmen had her lead character, Maria meet Maxwell Chase at a Christian nightclub called; "The Secret Place". This brother was saved for real. Someone your mama and poppa would truly adore if they knew the Lord. Carmen told her that she'd enjoy reading about Maxwell because he grows in love with Maria, the last thing he had planned on as he, too, had just gotten out of a marriage that was not ordained of God. Holly sat there smiling as she delve into his character. '*Chase, as his friend's called him, walked into The Secret Place a few minutes away from midnight. The music was so anointed and the brothers and sisters were all over the dance floor, worshiping God with their every step. It was going to be a good night, he told himself with a grin and glided over to the non-alcoholic bar. After ordering a virgin Apple Martini, he slid up on the stool, swiveling around to face the joyful crowd. And while taking his first sip from the glass, he spotted a beauty seated directly across from him at a table, giggling with her two friend's. It was love at first sight, he thought. He had to find out her name." Chase loved the way she looked it was not just her outward appearance, but for some reason, God was letting him see her inward beauty, too."* Holly laughed out loud when the chapter came to a close. It made her feel the Beauty of God's holiness and she had become excited. Hopeful. Dog-earring the page, she leaned her head back, sinking it into the sofa. Maxwell Chase, oddly enough, reminded her of the kind of man she had believed the Lord for. If she didn't know better, and if the book hadn't been published over a year ago, she would've thought Carmen modeled his character after the type of man she desired. But it wasn't until after her best friend's book was on the shelves of various bookstores, that she had begun to share the desires of her heart with the Latina woman. Holly could recall her friend telling her how Maxwell truly loved Maria from that very night. "Like Christ Loves the church and gave up his life for her," Carmen said with a beautiful smile. But, because of a few circumstances from his past, Maria didn't believe him. She really wasn't believing God, Holly thought. Holly's body jolted forward from that place of rest she was in. She was remembering what Carmen told her about the story. Maria winds up leaving him to remain on her own. Did this mean that Philip Williams was telling the truth? Should she take his confession from last night with more than just a grain of salt? Sighing, Holly pulled herself forward even more. She tossed the book down on the coffee table, staring at the jacket for a moment. Below the beautiful illustration of a Latina woman with her back turned on the man in question, who had his hands extended, grasping for her, read: "Love in The Secret Place." A novel by Carmen M. Lopez. "This maybe fiction," Holly mused aloud, "but Philip Williams, on the other hand, was very much alive. Yet, so unlike Chase." Holly stood up and went into the kitchen to cut herself a piece of the apple pie her mother had brought over that afternoon. Lifting the glass lid on the cake plate and easing the pie from underneath, Holly opened the utensil drawer for a knife and fork. The smell of apples and cinnamon sweetened the air around her. On the inside she felt something so different in her spirit as thoughts of Philip not being saved and therefore, not being the one that her God would have find her, hit her hard. "Help me, Lord," was what she heard herself whisper.

The telephone rang.

She reached up into the cabinet, taking down a saucer. The phone rang a second time. Holly placed everything on the marble countertop and answered. Hearing her say hello brought a smile to Philip's face. Her voice was the only one he wanted to hear. Sure, the convention was informative and he'd been meeting lots of people who'd given him tips on ways to run his restaurant more efficiently, but even with all these folks from all over around, he still felt very alone. Lonely without Holly. He'd just got finish telling her all about the seminar he'd just attended about thirty minutes ago. "I'm glad to hear that your learning so much," Holly said quietly. She picked up the knife and cut herself a piece of pie, placing it on the dish. "Yeah, I'm learning a lot.... I, uh, wish you were down here with me," he said, clearing his throat. He was more stunned to hear himself say that then Holly was. She smiled and told him maybe next time. And the smile left her face. What is wrong with her? "So, what were you doin'? I thought for sure you would've been out somewhere havin' a good time... with.... without me," Philip said. He started rubbing the back of his neck. "Well, Tracy called me this afternoon and asked if I wanted to get together to do something this evening. I didn't feel like going out," Holly said. That wasn't quite the answer he wanted. Philip wanted her to tell him how she couldn't think of being out without him and how she'd been sitting around all day, waiting for his phone call. This lady was in a class all by herself, he told himself in dismay. Was God like that? Somebody he could never figure out? "So, what were you doin'?" he asked again while glancing at his watch. The next seminar started in forty-five minutes. He'd talk to her a little longer, grab something to eat and then make his way back over to the Washington Convention Center. Holly just realized, at that very moment, how ironic it was for Philip to call, especially after thinking that Maxwell Chase was so opposite of him. "I was reading Carmen's latest book. She had sent it to me about a month ago and I thought tonight would be the perfect time to dive into it. She'd asked whether I gotten a chance to start it when she came to visit. I felt bad telling her no," she finally said. "What's the name of it?" he asked, stunned to find out that he was really interested in knowing. He wanted to know everything about Holly Reed. What she liked and didn't like. Was he losing his mind? "Love in The Secret Place," she said and stuck a fork-full of pie into her mouth. "Sounds good," he said. He began to laugh as he rubbed the back of his neck. "Yeah, we all got secret's!" he said. Holly paused and didn't say anything. She was trying not to smack as she chewed. She was also trying not to think about how much Philip was trying to tell her that he loved and missed her. "Listen, baby. Let me go. I'll probably give you another call later. The last seminar finishes at ten-thirty. Will you be home?" Philip asked. He had to play it cool. "I'll be here," she said and found herself trying not to smile.

An hour after Philip's phone call, and two and a half slices of pie into the night, Holly dog-eared the one-hundred and twelfth page of Carmen's intriguing novel. She stood up and carried the book, along with the plate of nibbled on pie into the kitchen. As she tossed the half-eaten apple pastry into the garbage, Holly caught a glimpse of the wilted roses Philip had bought her on their first date. Helen had finally put them to rest. She smiled as he entered her mind. Yes, he is a nice guy, she reminded herself as she placed the plate into the dishwasher. Turning off the kitchen light, Holly headed down the hall to her room, feeling fat from her sugar overindulgence. Just as she got in there, the doorbell rang. She sighed, knowing she wasn't expecting anyone. Who tricked Peter into letting them up without being announced. She set the book down on the dresser next to her jewelry box and walked back toward the front of the apartment, looking through the peephole. Surveying herself quickly once she saw who it was, she opened the door. "Hi," she said softly. "I hope

I'm not disturbing you. I tried to call first, but information said you weren't listed. If it's not a good time, I'll..." "It's fine," Holly said. She grinned and asked her new neighbor, Kitty Wahl to come inside. "Uh, actually. I was coming over to find out if you wanted to come to my place. I have pasta boiling on the stove," she said. "Oh, sure. That's not a problem," Holly said, glancing down at her feet. "Just let me slip on some shoes," she added.

Kitty Wahl's apartment had the same layout as Holly's: four stupendous rooms, an eat-in kitchen and a nice-size spa-like bathroom, but their styles were completely different. The White woman's floors were black and white checkered and nothing was wood. Holly admired her taste from a distance, because she couldn't think of having anything other than traditional furnishings. Eyeing the walls in awe, she studied the two large Hurrell's, facing opposite one another. Both in black and white. On the right was Bette Davis, perched proudly on a faux-fur chaise lounge, cigarette in her hand, a serious look on her face. And on the left, was the glamorous Rita Hayworth, smiling merrily, leaning back on her elbow, taffeta scarf draped daintily around her neck while her wavy tresses cascaded down her back. Holly managed to pull herself out of the brief trance to peer down at the black lacquer console and matching umbrella stand sitting next to it. Then following Kitty further inside after the White woman closed and locked the door, Holly peeked into the dining room. Small track lights lit the unusually designed eating area. She was mistaken about the White woman's apartment having no wood. The diningroom had a long oval-shaped solid alder wood table surrounded by six red-and-white striped Louis XIV chairs, which had come as a visual shock to Holly. To her they clashed way too much with the floors. "Two more Hurrell's?" Holly said out loud accidentally. She had been trying to be discreet as she stood in the doorway, staring at the other two bigger-than-life photographs of Hollywood legends. These pictures were hanging side by side across from four smaller black and white photos in red shiny frames. They were not of celebrities. Kitty turned to face her neighbor. "Yes, I got Bette and Rita as a gift from my boyfriend, Troy. And Marlena and Katie Hepburn came from my best friend, Terry," Kitty said. "House warmings?" Holly asked, still looking at all four pictures in amazement. "Yes, they were." "I read or saw on TV.... I'm not sure which, but supposedly, Hurrell, preferred taking pictures of the stars, or any woman I'd imagine, without having them made up. Absolutely no makeup. Can you believe that? He would draw it on after the photo was developed. I find that fascinating?" Holly glanced over at the White woman then back at all four pictures. "Yes, it is. I never knew that. Huh, we really do learn something new every day," Kitty said. Looking over at her again, Holly smiled. "Why don't you go into the living room and make yourself comfortable," said the White woman. She held out her hand toward the large room at their sides. "Would you like a glass of wine? I'm having one," she added. Gazing at Kitty for a moment, Holly still tried to figure out what it was about her that seemed so familiar, even more so tonight. Maybe it was because Kitty's hair was pulled back into a ponytail, as it was the first time Holly had seen her. "Um, no, thank you. I don't drink alcohol," she said, yanking herself out of her thoughts. "Oh ... okay. How about some water or iced tea?" Kitty asked, the expression on her face clearly hoped she would want something. "Iced tea, please. Thank you," Holly said. She then motioned to her neighbor, informing her that she was going into the living room now. "Yeah, go ahead, I'll be right in. Oh, are you hungry? I made enough pasta for two," Kitty said, backing into the kitchen. "No, thanks," Holly said. If she had only known what I'd been doing before she rang my bell, she mused regarding all the pie she'd eaten. Holly strode into the living room with the question of where she should sit rapidly entering her mind. This area of Kitty's apartment was also oddly fashioned. She had divided the tremendous space into two sitting areas. Across from the mantle, lined with photos in silver frames of all shapes and sizes, sat a long black leather sectional with a round glass table in front of it. On the other side of the room, where Holly's piano was, was a big white fluffy chair, big enough to seat two maybe, even three people comfortably. And stretched out in front of it was a matching ottoman. Next to the chair and enormous foot rest, covering the entire expanse of the wall, was a black unit, complete with a wide flat-screened TV and a state-of-the-art music system. Below that, Holly could see that Kitty had quite an eclectic CD collection. Pavarotti, Patti La Belle and Bonnie Ryatt were the ones recognizable from where she stood. "Let's sit over here so we could set our glasses down on the table," Kitty suggested, as if reading her neighbors mind. Holly didn't even hear her enter the room. She watched Kitty walk over in the direction of the leather sofa, holding a bowl of penne con filetoo di pomodoro in one hand and supporting two glasses; one of red wine and the other was Holly's iced tea. It was also in a wine glass. The steam from the dish billowed upward. "Here, let me help you," Holly said, her hands extended as she followed her new neighbor. "No, that's okay. I'll manage," Kitty said. The two women sat down. "It looks as though you've lived here forever," Holly said. She took her glass out of Kitty's outreached hand. They were both filled to the brim. Kitty shrugged her shoulders and smiled. "Yeah, well it doesn't take me long to get acclimated. I'm used to moving." She took a long sip from her glass, placing it on the table afterward. Holly examined Kitty's profile while she, too, took a swig of iced tea. The White woman's side features did nothing to jog her memory. But there was definitely something about her voice. The high-pitched sound emitted from Kitty's mouth rattled something deep within Holly, unruffled her somehow. But she couldn't decide if it was a good or bad thing. Maybe, if she listened harder, more carefully, she'd remember where it was they'd met. Kitty shifted in her seat, lifted her right leg onto the sofa, bending it slightly at the knee, so she'd be facing Holly. "How long did you live in Chicago?" Holly asked. Kitty had forgotten that she told her that. She rarely spoke about those times, the times with Grant Wahl. "Five lousy years," the White woman said and held up her hand. "Wait a minute I'm not being fair," she chuckled. "It was ..... three lousy years, really. Yeah, that's it." Kitty nodded. "Two of them were...... reasonable. You see my ex-husband was too much like my father in many ways. I think I've already told you that." Kitty sighed then smiled. Chicago, Grant and her father truly belonged in the same compartment. She could almost bet all the money she had in the bank that she'd mentioned the unenlightened old man. "Well, that's probably why you married him. They say we all marry one of our parents, so to speak," Holly said and laughed a little. "I can't believe that I quoted the elusive "theys." Kitty smiled and said, "Yeah, but that was my mistake. His true colors were *unbelievable*. And I'm being kind," Kitty said with a trust-me-kind-of look on her face. The White woman's head was tilted and her left brow was raised. Holly thought about what she'd said to Kitty about everyone marrying someone like their parent. That was before Christ, she told herself as she thought about how she didn't like when people would lump everyone in the same category. Like they knew everyone in the world. "Was he too over protective?" Holly asked as she continued in deep thought. She was thinking about the way her mother was. She could relate. Cynthia Reed was a bit over protective, but she was a good woman. Kitty shook her head back and forth. "No, no, *noooo*," she said, putting emphasis on the final no. She then paused for effect. "Grant was a real... You fill in the blanks. He didn't care about my well being at all. Everything was him, him, him," Kitty said, the bowl in her hand shaking some. Holly didn't know what to say or do. She took a quick sip from her glass. "To tell you the truth I don't know why I put up with him for so long," the White woman said. Holly observed her as she played with the pasta, mixing it around, blending the ingredients together with her fork. "I guess I was used to that way of living," Kitty said. She rested the silver utensil against the side of the bowl. Then looking deep into Holly's eyes, causing her to blink, she said, "For some reason I thought he would change. Hoped is really what it was because my intellectual side knew better. People like that are too set in their ways," Kitty said, letting out another sigh, a long one this time. Although something about her new neighbor made Holly feel a little on edge, like she had to keep up her guard a while longer, there was another part of her that she was beginning to like her a great deal. "But, I've moved on. Troy O'Neil is....." Kitty paused again, this time to find the one word that would tell Holly how wonderful her new companion was. The White woman's eyes drifted off toward the mantle. His photo was amongst the others. "Troy is just super," she finally said, looking back over at Holly, a grin on both of their faces. "He got me saved. Oh, how I wished I would have met him before Grant. But, I guess I had to do it this way so I'd know how much I valued Troy's undying love," the White woman said. She stared down at the bowl in her hands. "He's so Christ like," Kitty said. She smiled and look up into Holly's eyes. Am I Christ like, thought the biracial woman. Did Kitty see Him in her? "How'd you meet him?" Holly asked. Kitty started giggling lightly. "We met during my residency at Beth Israel. We had a little mentor/protégé relationship for a long time. Still do in a way. Boy, has he taught me a lot. Not only about becoming a great doctor. Other things...... like about who I am in Christ." Kitty chuckled somewhat again, a sheepish look in her eyes. "He's all about the important things in life," she went on to say. Holly smiled and took another sip from her glass. "It sounds nice, your relationship." "Oh, it is. He's ten years my senior, but I'd rather have twenty years with him then one day with someone hateful like Grant again. That was another thing Troy taught me. He'd say 'Kitty, God has given us all things richly to enjoy. Believe Him." Holly nodded her head in agreement and smiled. "He sounds like a noble man. He's right. The Word of God does promise that." Kitty paused. She was looking at Holly like she knew her from somewhere, too. But, she said, "He is all of that and more. So, what do you do for a living?" the White woman asked, as if she were tired of talking about herself. Or, was she trying to find out where she knew Holly from as well? Kitty finally tasted the food she'd prepared. The aroma from the fresh tomato, basil and garlic lingered in the air around them. "I'm a lawyer. And what kind of doctor are you?" Holly asked, her eyes dropping down to the cell phone clipped on the waist band of Kitty's jeans. "I'm an Obstetrician. On call like always," the White woman said, giving the tiny black object a pat. "Where?" "Well, I'm affiliated with Lenox Hill, but I share a practice with two other doctors over on 86th between Madison and Park." "My mother used to work at Lenox Hill," Holly said, grinning. "Oh? Was she a doctor?" Kitty asked. She leaned over, picking up her glass. Holly shook her head no. "She was part of housekeeping." The White woman nodded her head and took a sip of wine. "Which firm are you with?" Kitty asked. She took another sip then set the glass back down. "My own. I have two partners. Friends of mine from law school," Holly said as she thought about Kitty's drinking wine. She was still paying attention to the White woman's voice, but nothing was coming to her. "Kitty, did you ever come to the firm of Reed, Benjamin and Mann for representation?" Drawing her brows together, the White woman said no. "Why?" she asked, her food almost finished. "It just feels like we've met before. I guess you remind me of someone else," Holly said. She took a sip of iced tea. "Well, maybe we did meet before. I grew up here in New York. How about you?" Kitty asked. "Uh-huh, the Lower East Side." The White woman smiled, swallowing the last of the penne. "Isn't that something. I grew up in Chelsea. Do you have any brothers or sisters?" Holly shook her head no. "Do you?" "Yep, Rebecca is the middle child and Thomas is the youngest. Maybe you know one of them, if not both." Kitty stood up and walked over to the mantle, where all of the pictures were. She waved Holly over. "Here they are," she said, pointing to a photograph of her siblings. Taking a sip from her glass, Holly smiled. She did that in order to camouflage what she was really thinking. She didn't get it. The picture Kitty pointed to was so ancient. The fading black and white photo, which appeared to be smoothed out, had to be at least ten to fifteen years old. "No, I don't know either of them," Holly finally said, wondering why Kitty had chose to show her this particular picture. She'd keep her mouth shut. Mind your business, the biracial woman told herself. "Do your parents' still live in Chelsea?" Holly added while observing the way the White woman had begun fingering the photo of her siblings. "I'm sorry, what did you say?" Kitty asked, her voice low, sad sounding. "Your parents? Do they still live in Chelsea?" Kitty's eyes locked onto Holly's, just stayed there, as a grief-stricken stare took the place of the new smile that had crossed her lips. She gazed over at the pictures on her mantle then back at Holly again. I must have said something wrong, Holly told herself. What? Did they die? She hoped not. Holly peered at the pictures again, too, trying to find the answer for herself. She was hoping that the Lord would reveal something. She didn't want Kitty to have to rehash the demise of her parents. It made no difference that the White woman had a bad relationship with her father from what Holly gathered. Unconditional love never died. This wasn't a good time. The pain was still too close to the surface for Kitty to discuss it, Holly imagined. Should I change the subject? Still searching the photographs for an answer, she saw that there were no pictures of a couple old enough to be Kitty's mother and father. Why? "No, they don't," Kitty finally said, in a tone that clearly said it was okay to talk about them. "My father inherited quite well from his grand uncle, someone I'd never met. He and my mother live somewhere on Sutton Place now. Their living like big shots, like the people they've always pretended to be." Kitty said, shaking her head in disgust. Then, a grin slowly reappeared on her slender face. Holly stared downward at the glass in her hands once more, just to be doing something. "I'm sorry," was all she could say, guessing that they were no longer in touch. This made her think of her father's family, the family who'd never given her a chance. Holly felt the warmth of Kitty's hand resting on her shoulder. "Please don't be. I'm much happier now," she told her, revealing teeth as she smiled to solidify her words. She had a gap in between the two front ones. Holly had never noticed it before. "So, tell me, Holly, where did you go to school?" Kitty asked. "I went...." "Oh, wait a minute!" the White woman said. She peered down at her cell phone, snatching it off the waist band of her pants. "I don't recognize the number. Pardon me." As Kitty rushed into the kitchen to answer the phone, Holly gazed at the rest of the pictures atop the mantle, the ones her eyes had missed before. She was somewhat astonished to see that her new neighbor's friends were mainly minority, Black in particular. Holly lifted a picture of Kitty sandwiched between two Black women. They were all hugging, cheeks mashed together, grins brighter than the setting sun in the background of the photo. Smiling, Holly could hear Kitty talking. Then glancing at the photo of Troy, Holly smiled again as she read the inscription at the bottom of the sterling silver frame: "To my darling Kitten. I'll love you forever. Abundant Blessings and Shalom, Troy." She could see what the White woman had been talking about. His gray eyes were filled with goodness, his smile a genuine one. Philip suddenly came to her mind then. Did he have the eyes of a decent man? When he looked at her, he did. She had to admit, there was something worthy of her giving him a chance stirring from within. Holly turned to walk back over to the sofa. She listened as Kitty began to speak. "This is doctor Kathleen Parker Wahl," was what she exclaimed into the receiver. Holly froze, dropping her glass to the floor. She had no idea it had fallen or that some of the iced tea had spilled on her shirt in the process. Her body was too numb. *Kathleen Parker?* Holly looked over at her neighbor, whose back was turned, then down at the spillage and shards of glass splattered across the black and white checkered floors. Holly held her stomach, the place where the damp spot was. The reddish liquid? Was it her blood? she wondered. The raspberry tea looked like blood. But it wasn't, she reminded herself even though that name had opened a wound so deep Holly thought she was going to die, transition into heaven, right there in this stranger's apartment. She felt weak like she was going to pass out from the pain engulfing her body. Who would find her? Who would come to her rescue? Protect her? Kathleen Parker was an enemy from her past. That little White girl would not have had it any other way back then. She had to get out of there fast. Run like she did in the schoolyard of P.S. 210 at the age of nine. Holly had to go home and tell her mother that the bully had come back to finish the job, hurt her some more. It was all coming back to her now. Full circle. Holly heard Kitty making her way back over to the area she was dying in. God is here, Holly told herself. "False alarm," the White woman announced and laughed a little. Gazing down at the floor then back up at Holly, Kitty stopped laughing and said, "Oh, you dropped your glass. Don't touch anything. I'll get the broom and a cloth to wipe it up," Kitty didn't notice the change in Holly's eyes. She'd probably mistaken her distressed look for something else. An ooops, did-you-see-what-I-did expression? Maybe that was her interpretation of this whole display. Holly wasn't sure. She didn't really care what Kathleen Parker thought at that moment, the biracial woman was looking for the Hand of God. The only thing concerning her was whether or not she should inform her childhood enemy of her haunting discovery. "Should I?" she whispered to the Lord. Or should she just leave Kitty's apartment, pretending she'd forgotten to do something important at home? Would God have her do such a thing? Before Kathleen Parker turned to head back into the kitchen, she glanced at Holly, now seeing a difference in the way she was standing. She had her hand securing her abdomen, as if she'd suddenly taken ill. The White woman could also see that Holly was covering something up. "Are you all right?" Kathleen Parker a.k.a. Kitty Wahl asked, squinting her eyes as she waited for a response. Looking back at her, Holly didn't behold a grown woman anymore, the woman she was starting to like. She saw that diminutive girl with two tousled ponytails sticking out the sides of her head like devil's horns, clad in red, white and black plaid pants and a white turtle neck sweater, that had been soiled by the baked beans the school's cafeteria had served for lunch that day. The little White girl was standing there laughing as she commenced to jump into a turning rope. She was laughing at the small nondescript girl, who was fleeing in the opposite direction for a third time that week, crying. Holly remembered the way her arms acted like bird's wings while in flight. That was why her bracelet hit the ground without her knowing. She was too busy shouting, trying to get Kathleen Parker to stop calling her those awful names: nigger, strange-looking, and so on. But she didn't. Her tormenting rang in Holly's ears even after she'd gone into the principal's office, begging her to call her mother at work. She had fallen to her knees and begun to pray. Cry out to God. While hysterically speaking to her Heavenly Father, she could still hear that naughty child yelling those declarations by way of Mrs. Nadel's fourth-floor window.

"No, I'm not all right," Holly finally said, both hands at her side now. Kitty peered at the spot on her neighbor's shirt. "Oh, don't worry, that'll come right out." The White woman assumed that the stain was the problem. "I could care less about this old shirt. But you'll be happy to know that I'm finally aware of where it was we met," Holly said, no smile on her face. Her lawyer anointing was in manifestation. Kathleen was grinning enough for the both of them. "Where?" she asked. "I'm just a little surprised that you did not remember," Holly continued, as if Kitty never asked a question. "After all, my name hasn't changed. I was Holly Reed back then, as well. It's funny how your real name came to me instantly." Holly snapped her finger for emphasis. "I guess to you, I wasn't worth the time or day. But then again, you weren't the one running home, sobbing. I cried way too many tears." She paused and swallowed the sadness rising in her throat. "You made me cry so many times. Too many as I said. And, the worst part was that I'd have to see you again the next day," Holly said. She paused again as she sensed the spirit of bitterness rising within her. She recalled not understanding why God didn't deliver her when she wanted Him to back then. He allowed this, she thought and swallowed again. Kathleen stood there with a puzzled look on her face. Who was she trying to trick? "Didn't you attend P.S. 210, Kathleen? Does that help to refresh your memory?" Holly asked harshly, her voice rising slightly. The White woman nodded slowly. She could feel her cheeks flushing. "Yes, that is the elementary school that I attended," Kitty said, appearing to still be uncertain as to why Holly's disposition had suddenly altered. "Well, so did I. Remember me now? I'm the one you weren't allowed to play with." Holly watched the White woman's eyes double in size. "No....." Kathleen Parker said, her hand covering her trembling lips. "My goodness, you're.......?" was what she continued to say, her hand on her chest now. Holly nodded then walked passed Kathleen Parker out the front door. She thought about slamming it, but she closed it quietly, slamming hers across the hall.

Chapter Seventeen

The storage room door was ajar. Law books, files and briefs lay in neat piles on the floor. The tall garbage pail from the kitchen was almost filled to the top with balled up memorandums and other things declared unnecessary to hold on to. "You were right about this place, Kel. We've kept everything from scribbled on Post-its to thank you notes. It was getting entirely too cluttered in here. Vanessa told me that she and Sam would come down tomorrow to straighten out her file cabinets and I guess Tracy and Tina will do the same on Monday," Holly said. She was standing up going through the top drawer of one of her file cabinets while Kelly was behind her on her knees going through the bottom drawer of the other one. The dark-skinned woman glanced down at the tiny protrusion in her blazer pocket, smoothing it down. She couldn't afford to let Holly see what it was yet, until she was good and ready. Even though she should have been good and ready three days ago, everybody had their weak moments, Kelly assured herself. But she'd find the courage today before five o'clock or else Liz and Joanna would either break her neck or tell her to stop wasting their precious time. She could tell that her two accomplices were approaching their "breaking points" on Sunday night. All three women had congregated around a makeshift table in Kelly's East New York, Brooklyn apartment amid the still filthy battered walls, composing a letter to Holly. They had even gone over what Kelly had to say after her boss finished reading it. Liz and Joanna wanted her to convey the hurt she felt when Holly had "backstabbed" her by going out with Philip. Liz instructed her to shed a few tears once the dark-skinned womans sob story had come to a close, insuring Kelly it would "add hype" to the predicament. Kelly looked back over her shoulder and said, "Yeah, Tina mentioned that she should do it today." The dark-skinned woman then stood up, dusting off the knees of her pants. "What time do you have, Kel? I left my watch upstairs so I wouldn't scratch it." Holly's fingers were still roaming the abounding files. Brag on! One of these days I'll have me a Rolex, too, Kelly thought as she said, "Four-thirty five." It was almost time to get out of there. She'd have to whip the news on Holly now.

The doorbell rang. The hazel-eyed attorney leaned her head back, stretching her neck, trying to see who it was, but Telma was blocking her view. The skinny cafe au lait-colored receptionist was already standing at the door with it opened slightly. She asked whoever it was if she could help them. Holly could tell that it was a man because the person's frame was very tall and broad. The large masculine figure spoke softly, his words were barely audible. The lawyer could see Telma nodding as she opened the door wider, letting the handsome gentlemen inside. He stood about six foot two, had a nice build, deep dimples, a rich dark brown complexion and he was dressed very well.

The telephone rang. The attorney continued to observe him through the cracked door while Telma scurried back to her desk to answer it. He began peering down at the coffee table, cocking his head to the right, in order to read one of the pamphlets. Well, if he was in trouble Holly could certainly help him. Stop that!, she told herself, knowing he had to be one of Tracy's latest conquests and besides, she had already told Philip on Sunday night when he'd stopped by after his D.C. trip, that she'd give their relationship a shot. She was his woman now. *But* she wasn't dead or was she? Her spirit wasn't sensing the Spirit of God on the inside of her. Not even in the atmosphere around her, she thought. Holly heard the man cough and clear his throat. Her focus left her brief search for the Lord and settled on thoughts of who he could be. So he was probably the reason why Vanessa told Tracy to have a happy, happy hump day yesterday when the short-haired attorney told them both she had a date tonight. It being Wednesday had nothing to do with it. Vee and her X-rated mind, Holly mused as she heard what sounded like a piece of paper being unfolded behind her and Kelly clearing her throat. At that moment, the lawyer was about to step out of the storage room to ask the good-looking stranger if he needed some assistance, but Telma was already off the phone and heading back over in his direction. The receptionist told him that she'd be right back and turned to walk toward the stairs, no it was the storage room. Lord! This man was here to see her after all. Hurriedly, Holly closed the drawer and slapped her hands together, ridding them of dust.

Telma pushed the door opened slowly, sticking her head inside. First, she looked at Holly, who grinned and widened her eyes as if she were waiting to be told who he was. But the receptionist ignored the eagerness on the attorney's face, turning her attention toward Kelly. The dark-skinned woman stood straight and stiff. Suspicious looking. She was unaware of what was going on and couldn't give two "you-know-what's" about who it was out there. Her mind was on the letter she held tightly in her hand, the one she was now hiding behind her back. The receptionist immediately noticed that her facial expression was not as inviting as Holly's was. Kelly's eyes were shouting, "What the you know what do you want?" If not worse. She gave Telma little respect. "Uh, I'm sorry to bother you both but, Kelly there's a gentlemen out here looking for you." The receptionist spoke softly, stuttering somewhat. She didn't feel welcomed by the dark-skinned secretary. "Who is it?" Kelly asked, her empty hand resting on her hip. She didn't have time for this pion. The business she had to take care of in here with her boss was more important than anything right now. "I didn't ask his name," Telma said, looking at Holly for support. The hazel-eyed woman had reopened the drawer and started going through it once again, finishing up where she'd left off. But she stopped and glared back at Kelly. She didn't like the way she was speaking to Telma. "Why don't you go out there and find out," Holly said, her well-defined brow raised in warning. "From what I could see, you won't be disappointed," she added with a faint smile as she turned back to face the files. Kelly sighed and proceeded out the door, stopping once she saw who it was. Her knees buckled at the sight of the visitor who was sitting down on the sofa perusing a pamphlet. The dark-skinned woman covered her mouth and said, "Oh my goodness. El, is that you?" as her heart pumped faster. When he raised his head, meeting Kelly's gaze, she did a quick rainlike dance, screamed and rushed into his arms, wrapping her long legs around his waist once he stood up. "You came back to me, baby?" she exclaimed and held his face with both hands as she gave him an open-mouthed kiss. After they'd finished expressing how glad they were to see each other, and Kelly's feet were planted firmly on the floor again, he told her that he was back. Inside of the storage room, Holly and Telma glanced at one another and smiled. "What you doin' here, though? Hold up, ain't you still married?" Kelly whispered in her out-of-work diction. "It's a long story. Me and Roxanne separated. She bounced on me." Elliot began to eye Kelly up and down with his head tilted. He smiled and said, "Baby, I know I messed up, bigtime. But ... Will you give me another chance?" As he placed Kelly's hands in his, he peered over at Telma and Holly. The attorney was dragging the large garbage pail back into the kitchen slowly, being careful not to scratch the hardwood floors in the process, and the receptionist was turning off the lights and closing the storage room door. "El, you know I still love you," Kelly said. She forced him to refocus on her with the tone in her voice. "Of course I'll give you another chance." He smiled and eyed Kelly again. "Could we go someplace quiet to talk?" Elliot asked. She grinned at him too and said she'd be right back. Kelly walked into the kitchen where Holly was. "Is it okay for me to leave a few minutes early?" The hazel-eyed attorney was washing her hands in the sink. "Certainly," she said, smiling, "See you tomorrow." Kelly blushed and headed back over to Elliot, forgetting all about the letter she was supposed to give Holly. It didn't matter anymore. Philip Williams was yesterday's bulletin. *He* was the closest thing to the man she really wanted to be with. And here he is in the flesh, the dark-skinned woman thought.

Turning off the faucet, Holly dried her hands with a paper towel, clicked off the light and crossed the reception area for the stairs. She glanced over at the coffee table, noticing that Kelly's friend had left the brochures in disarray. Not wanting to interrupt Telma to ask her to straighten them out because the receptionist was organizing her own desk for the night, Holly decided to do it herself. She headed over to the table. Telma looked up at the attorney and said, "Holly, would you mind picking up whatever that is near your right foot?" She pointed downward at a wrinkled piece of paper sticking out from under the coffee table. Holly bent down, figuring that it was something Kelly had dropped during her reunion. "Thanks, Telma," the lawyer said under her breath as she aligned the paper in order to see what it was. Suddenly, shock took the place of curiosity in Holly's eyes once she began to read the disheartening letter written in Kelly's large penmanship:

Holly,

It was hard for me to tell you what was on my mind verbally, so I figured the best thing to do was write it down. I want you to know, up front, that I have nothing against you because you've been cool to me from the start. But sometimes things happen that are beyond our control. (I'm sure I'm not telling you anything new) I guess I better get to the point because there's nothing funny about what I have to say.

Holly, I'm in love with Philip. I have been from the first day I laid eyes on him. At first I tried to forget all about him when you told me that y'all went out, but if I do that I'll only be hurting myself even more. And, besides that, I could tell that he's into me too. I know you caught the way he couldn't stop looking at my naked body at your apartment when I accidently walked out to where ya'll were.

Last but not least, I'd like to wish you luck because I could tell Philip wants me too every time he looks me in the eyes even when I have my clothes on. So don't get it twisted cause it's on!

May the best woman win!

Kelly Mills

P.S. I hope you don't plan on firing me over this, especially since you are aware of the legal consequences. I DIDN'T DO NOTHING WRONG!

What? This made no sense! The attorney's mouth hung open in disbelief. "All right, Holly. I'm leaving now. I'll see you tomorrow,"

Telma said, making the attorney wince. She'd forgotten all about her. "Okay, uh, get home safe," Holly said, holding the piece of paper close to her chest. She smiled at Telma through the glass window on their front door as the cafe au lait-colored woman locked the door behind herself. She waved once more before descending the steps. Holly then dropped down on the sofa, taking a deep breath. Somehow she couldn't digest what she'd just read, although it explained a lot. Kelly's interest in hearing whatever she could about Philip, her wondering if Holly was falling in love with him. All questions an assistant wouldn't dare ask their boss, especially when the information was never initiated. Leaning forward in her seat, the attorney's arms began to pinch with adrenaline prickles. She was only aware of the paper shaking in her hands. Her mind was still, just producing blank lines. Overhead the floor boards squeaked, Holly jumped, quickly folding and stuffing the piece of paper into her suit coat pocket. It was Samantha and Tina heading out for the night. The attorney pretended that she was still cleaning as the two young women made it around the reception desk to the front door. Why didn't her thoughts go above the second floor of their offices, is what Holly heard in her spirit. "Vanessa wanted to know if you had left for the night," Sam said, her hand resting on the doorknob. "I'm going up in a minute," Holly said, forcing a smile on her flustered face. "Good night, ladies," she added, pulling herself to her feet and mounting the stairs. At the top, she saw Tracy standing in Vanessa's doorway. The short-haired lawyer had transformed her subtle day make up into more of an evening look. She turned, gazing at Holly. "I told Vee you wouldn't leave without saying good-bye, that's something she would do," Tracy said, giggling. "Well, somebody left early," Vanessa said. She was fumbling through her pocketbook for a mirror. "That was Kelly. Some good-looking guy that I'd mistaken as your date, Trace, came to pick her up without her knowing," Holly said, standing next to the short-haired attorney in the doorway. "Was that why she was screaming and carrying on?" Vanessa asked, making a face as she flipped open her press-powder compact. "Proof that she had no home-training." Holly didn't respond to Vanessa's insult. She was thinking about the piece of paper in her pocket again. If it wasn't one thing it was another. But, she'd take care of it tomorrow! Holly sighed. Why didn't she just cast the care unto God? He cares for me, she told herself as she hated the way she felt the distance growing between her and the Lord. It had to be her, she thought, knowing that His Word promised that He would never leave her or forsake her. "So, are you going to see Philip tonight, too? Or, did you have enough of him at lunch?" Vanessa asked while she replenished her Bordeaux lipstick. This had to be the enemy, Holly told herself. She saw the way her full-figured partners question was tossed at her. "I'm not sure," Holly said. Tracy glanced at her watch. "I've got to get out of here. Can you guys believe I have to meet Warren Thompson at the restaurant. This brother must be more than just a pretty face, because ordinarily this meet-me-here business wouldn't fly with me." "Will you listen to her. Since when have you become the lady?" Vanessa asked, chuckling. "Puleaze, Vee. You know how I am! So stop starting trouble. Good-bye!" Tracy said and hurried down the stairs. Holly shook her head and laughed a little. "Are you and Courtney going out tonight?" she asked as she watched Vanessa's chubby fingers comb through her hair. "No, I just don't feel like taking the train home. We took one car this morning which was dumb. He's still working on that big case I told you about a month ago and you know how that goes, so I told him I'd meet him at his office around seven thirty, eight o'clock," Vanessa said. She closed the compact, tossing it back down in her pocketbook. "Why don't you take a cab ride down town with me? We'll drive you home," asked the full-figured woman. "This way we could grab something to eat and catch up. It feels like I haven't spent any real time with you outside of work." Vanessa stood up. Holly paused. She was trying to decide whether or not she was up to spending time *alone* with Vanessa *outside* of work. "Well...... all right, let me give Philip a call first," Holly said and walked into her office. "Of course, we wouldn't want him to worry, now would we?" Vanessa said aloud to herself. Holly didn't hear her.

The forest green awning read "Ellington's". It was a nice little out-of-the-way place on 43rd Street between 9th & 10th Avenues. Inside the jazz music was soothing, but filled with a rhythmic boon, which kept a smile and an upbeat appearance on the faces of the patrons, who were sprinkled around enjoying both their surroundings and the company they were with. The atmosphere was abundant with a down-home New Orleans flavor found sparingly in a lot of the other New York City ragtime dining spots. Holly and Vanessa sat at a booth toward the back of the tranquil establishment, the only minor disturbance was an over-zealous little Black man wearing a shiny burgundy suit with a black equally-as-shiny shirt underneath that had lapels so pointy, giving a brand-new meaning to the phrase, "sharp as a tack." He had an annoying tendency of jumping up out of his seat every now and then to shout some unneeded words of encouragement to the already remarkable band. Holly craned her neck when she heard another undesirable outburst erupt from the other side of the restaurant. The little fella stood up, clapping his hands wildly to the beat as "Go, cat go!" roared from his big snaggle-toothed mouth. She shook her head in disgust and took a sip of the cranberry juice she had been drinking while Vanessa grimaced, shuddering exaggeratedly at the site of the crass individual. The full-figured woman had been nursing a glass of mineral water, explaining to Holly earlier, how she'd been trying to lose some weight so she'd fit into the dress she bought for Courtney's party Saturday. "Did you get a lot of "yes" responses from the people you called to invite?" Holly asked as she swayed to the melodic sounds wafting through the air. "Yeah, I told you and Tracy Tuesday that there will be at least forty attendees," Vanessa exclaimed. "Oh, well, I don't know how you would've expected me to hear you when I was on the phone," Holly shot back, as if her being in the middle of a conversation made a difference. "So, what are you wearing?" the full-figured woman asked, smiling. "I don't know yet. I'm trying not to buy anything new since I have so many outfits and dresses hanging in my closet with the price tags still on them." Nodding her head, Vanessa stared into her friend's eyes as the waiter set an order of chicken stripes along with a large tossed salad down in the center of their table. "Things seem to be going well with you and Philip," the full-figured woman said, easing onto another topic after the waiter left. Holly smiled, nodding her head in agreement. "Yeah, I just want to take it slow…" Holly said as Vanessa cut her off. "You should! Because your God can't be happy with right about now. Philip Williams in not His son!" Holly paused. "My God is pleased with me. As Jesus is, so am I in this world is what the Scripture says," the hazel-eyed woman said softly. "And, I can see some signs of God moving on Philip's behalf." Holly took a sip of her drink. "What do you mean?" Vanessa asked. "I don't know, Vee. It's not clear to me yet," Holly sighed and began to move a little to the music again as she spooned some food onto her plate. Vanessa nodded slowly as she eyed the stripes of chicken. "Do you still love Bradford? I mean, would you ever consider giving him another chance?" Holly gave her full-figured partner a look. "Are you out of your mind? Never. I can't even fathom how you'd be able to bring yourself to ask such an absurd question. You were the one who said I was stupid for giving him a second chance the first time." "I know, but…." "But nothing. I'd slap my own face if I went back to him." Vanessa put some salad on her plate. "I hear you, but…" Holly raised her right hand, palm out. "What did I say? Are you sure they didn't spike that water?" she said, nodding down at the glass in front of Vanessa. "*Yes*, I'm sure … will you let me finish before you cut me off?" the full-figured woman said. She glared passed Holly's shoulder at the booth behind them. There was a Black couple sitting there and the woman had been staring at the two of them since they'd first arrived, Holly didn't notice. And Vanessa didn't want to say anything until the woman's attention was elsewhere. The full-figured attorney couldn't wait for her to look somewhere other than at them because it had occurred to her at that instant that she was the same woman who'd caused a scene at Philip's restaurant the night she and Tracy had thought it was his sister. Was it Brenda coming back to create more ruckus regarding his relationship with Holly? No, this was another wrathful sister on assignment as Holly told both Vanessa and Tracy that Philip's sister would never do that. "All right, I'm listening," Holly said, taking a sip of cranberry juice. She had Vanessa's attention again. "What I'm trying to tell you is, for your own good so don't get mad. I'd been thinking about this since Monday." "What?"asked the hazel-eyed woman. "Remember when you told me that Philip got annoyed when he called you back on Saturday night and you weren't home?" "Yeah, and?" "I don't know about you, but to *me* that could be the start of something ugly." "Vee, what are you talking about?" The full-figured woman let out a long weary sigh as if to say she knew she was speaking English. "What if he turns out to be too possessive? Feel the signs, girl." "He wasn't nasty. The man was disappointed. All he was doing was communicating the way he felt. No harm done. Bradford, on the other hand, was all screwed up in the head. Had it been him down in D.C., he would have caught the next flight out thinking that he'd catch me wrapped up in some other guys arms. That's what happens when you can't trust yourself. His silly self was the one cheating, therefore, his trust for me was minimized. And I wasn't doing anything wrong but loving him. You see, he's ruined it for Philip in a way. I'm not saying that he doesn't have a chance, but it's going to take some serious honesty to allow me to put my entire heart in his hands," Holly said and tasted a piece of chicken. "Uh-huh, you should be leery, because Philip Williams is no angel either. Forget about him not being God's son!" Vanessa said and laughed at her ignorance. "Well, I have faith in God. So, he's innocent until proven guilty." "Girl, please. This is not a trial we're talking about here, but it could very well turn out to be one if you don't be careful. Let's not get it wrong!" Holly glared across the table at her partner and said, "What is it, Vee? Tell me what? You act as though you don't want me to ever be happy. I'm a big girl, big enough to know when to walk away. Yeah, I'll admit that it took me a long time to wake up with Bradford, but I believe that My God won't let me make the same mistake twice. And it's not like Philip and I are getting married, *but* if it came down to that, it would be my choice and my choice alone. "Okay. Where did your God go all of a sudden?" Vanessa shook her head and placed a forkful of salad into her mouth. She was speechless much to her own astonishment. She had absolutely nothing to say. Did she want the hazel-eyed beauty before her to be happy? she wondered as she peered over Holly's shoulder again, looking into the face of the woman at the table behind the one they were seated at. Vanessa persisted to watch as the man with her paid the waitress. They were about to leave. The spying attorney braced herself because although she didn't want the woman to hear her tell Holly who she was, she also wanted to make sure the hazel-eyed attorney got a peek at the trouble-making vixen. The man walked around the woman's chair, draping her jacket over her slender shoulders. She smiled, standing up from the booth. They were heading in the lawyers' direction. Vanessa quickly swallowed the remaining salad in her mouth and shifted in her seat, waiting for them to pass. "Excuse me," the woman said, shocking Vanessa. She was lucky her mouth was empty or else she would've probably choked. Holly placed her glass back down on the table, staring up at the couple. "I thought that was you," the woman added. "Selma Girard?" Holly said, smiling. "Yes, how are you?" she asked and pointed her thumb toward the man accompanying her. "This is my husband-to-be, Charles Richardson. Charles, this is Holly Reed," Selma said. She gazed over at Vanessa as the hazel-eyed woman shook hands with her fiancée. Holly then introduced her partner to the couple, defining who Selma Girard was again. "I remember," Vanessa said. She was about to burst wide open even more so now with wanting to tell Holly what she had known about this woman. "Well, did you guys ever close on the house?" Vanessa asked. Charles appeared to have a questioning look on his face. Now wasn't that interesting? the full-figured woman thought. She cut her eyes over at Holly, wondering if she'd seen the perplexity on Charles' face. "Excuse me?" was what he said and peered at Selma, who had become fidgety at that point. "Oh, uh, yes we did. Thanks for asking," Selma said. She wrapped one arm around her fiancée's arm, patting it with her free hand. It was her way of telling him she'd explain later. "Okay, we'd better run. It was wonderful seeing you again, Holly. Nice to meet you, Vanessa" Selma Girard said, rushing out of the restaurant. She was pulling Charles along. That skinny weasel rolled her eyes at me, Vanessa told herself. Something was definitely up! Once the full-figured attorney saw the couple pull off in their tan Land Crusier, obviously still discussing what had just gone on in the restaurant, she jerked her head to face Holly. Vanessa's hair whipped around, smacking her in the eyes from her vigorous movement. Sweeping it back in place, the full-figured woman stared at her friend. She rested her round elbows on the table and folded her chubby hands. "Now what?" Holly said. She knew Vanessa all too well. "I don't know where to start. If I tell you this you'll just think I'm trying to bash Philip," she told her. "Philip? What about him?" Holly asked. She put a forkful of salad into her mouth, trying to steady herself although her heart had begun to beat rapidly. The hazel-eyed woman saw Vanessa take a deep breath, her large breasts rising and falling. "Selma Girard was the woman Tracy and I saw yelling at Philip last Thursday at his restaurant." Holly paused, the salad slowly sliding down her throat. "Are you sure?" was what she finally asked. Vanessa nodded. "Don't get yourself all worked up until you find out who she is *and* what it is she wants." the full-figured woman told her partner when she saw Holly's hazel eyes harden. Holly looked at her watch. "It's a quarter to eight, let's go up to Courtney's office," was her only reply. The trumpeter was playing "Surrey With a Fringe On Top," a Miles Davis standard as the two ladies paid the waiter and walked out.

Holly was quiet on the ride up to her apartment. She'd seen Courtney glance at her through the rear-view mirror a couple of times, his eyes wondering what was wrong. But she didn't feel like sharing all the confusing thoughts intruding her mind at that time. What she needed was a few uninterrupted moments of solitude in order to map out what her next steps were going to be. She needed to seek God to find out what His next steps were for her, she quickly reminded herself. "Help me, Lord," she muttered under her breath. Holly sighed. Would her Heavenly Father have her face the Philip and Selma Girard situation tonight and Kelly's tomorrow? Holly shook her head no as she lifted her pocketbook onto her lap as Courtney pulled up to the curb in front of her building. All three of their heads leaned forward slightly as the silver BMW came to a complete stop. "Will you be all right going upstairs?" her partners husband asked. Unfastening his seat belt, Courtney turned to face Holly, his right hand resting on his wife's headrest. "Oh, I'll be fine," Holly said, smiling lightly. She peered over at the building. "Peter's right there," she added and thanked them for the ride. "I told you we'd bring you home," Vanessa said as she lowered the air conditioning and folded her arms. Courtney glanced at his wife then back at Holly. "You're welcome," he said. "Have a good night, guys," Holly told them and climbed out of the car, closing the door.

Holly pulled the window down near the piano, straightened out the wind-blown drapes and walked into her bedroom. She noticed that there were three messages before turning on the light. She glanced at her cell phone to see if there were any messages. There weren't any. Philip as well as Holly's mother told her that they had memorized her land line that's why he didn't call her on her cell phone. As the first message played on her home machine: "Hey, sweetness, give me a call at home as soon as you come in. I have good news," Philip said. Holly removed the letter written by Kelly from her blazer pocket, setting it down on the dresser next to the card Kitty Wahl had slipped under her door Monday before she'd gotten home from work. Her neighbor apologized for all she'd done during their younger years then begged Holly to hear her out. She'd listen when she was good and ready, Holly thought. Even though her not going across the hall sooner was probably childish on her part, she didn't care. "I believe I'm being led not to go over there," she said aloud. The second message on the machine was from Cynthia Reed. She wanted her daughter to come with her to Bloomingdale's tomorrow because she needed a pair of shoes to wear with the outfit Holly bought her for her birthday last year. "Sweetie, Barbara Mathews invited me to a dinner dance Saturday night. We'll be praisin' the Lawd. You won't be the only one goin' out. Would you have some time at about one, one thirty. Call me, bye." Holly took a quick peek in her agenda. She was free to go. Walking over to the closet, she slid open the doors, disappearing inside as the final message played: Carmen sounded inordinately excited about a man who'd just moved into her complex. She was telling her friend to call her A.S.A.P. because "this was it!" God had this man find her. "He who finds a wife, finds a good thing and obtains favor from the Lord. It was truly supernatural. The way he looked at me. It was nobody but the Lord, sis!" Carmen was speaking fast. The excitement was so clear. Holly had to chuckle even though her heart was feeling heavy. No matter how down and out she felt, she could always count on God to use Carmen to lift her up from that place of dismay.

Exiting the closet in her underwear, Holly headed into the bathroom to wash her face and brush her teeth. The salad dressing had left a bitter taste in her mouth. Or was it the news she had heard about Selma Girard?

The telephone rang. Philip again, she thought. Holly took two deep breaths and began reciting scripture. "I can do all things through Christ..." She'd only made it to that part of the Bible verse before Philip's vibrant voice droned in her ear from the other end of the receiver. "Did you get my message?" he asked. "Yes, but I just got in a few minutes ago," Holly said. As she sat down on the edge of the bed, she caught a glimpse of her reflection in the full-length mirror. Did she really need to be in this type of situation? she asked herself. Was she happier alone? No, not really, but she wasn't ready to go up against all these women who were vying for Philip's love either.

Who would be the third woman to emerge? "Is everything okay?" he asked, his voice brimming with concern. Holly sighed. "I'm tired," she said, shifting her body away from the mirror. "Busy day?" "No, more like interesting. Tell me, does the name Selma Girard mean anything to you?" Holly asked. Silence flooded the line for a second or two. "She's my ex-girlfriend who won't take "it's over" for an answer. Why?" Philip asked, knowing that the woman had struck again. Holly was quiet for a moment as she thought, so this explains the reason she caused a scene at his restaurant. Selma Girard's not quite finished with him yet. "Well, she came to my office...." "When?" Philip asked vehemently, cutting her short. Holly heard him slam his hand down on something. "A couple of weeks ago. She came in seeking representation. She told me that she needed a lawyer to help her, and her, I don't know, husband or fiancée close on a house. And tonight Vee and I ran into her at Ellington's. She was with a Charles Richardson. Tonight I clearly heard her say he was her fiancée," Holly said calmly. "Yeah, who knows with her. That guy will let her call him whatever she wants to as long as she stays with him, but she'll never be satisfied with Charles. She doesn't love the brother at all. Baby, I'm sorry. I'll handle her. I never wanted to involve you in any of this nonsense. I thought I had taken care of it. And I don't even know how she knew where you worked. She knew your name but that was it," Philip said sincerely. "She must really love you? Am I right? After all, you know that she doesn't love Charles," Holly said quietly. She coughed and cleared her throat. She didn't like the way she sounded. It was very sarcastic. "And you'll never guess who else is in love with you according to this letter I found," she added. She immediately dismissed the way she was coming across. Holly was really amazed at how little these things were affecting her. Hence, the attitude, she told herself. Sure, there was a tiny hint of hurt regarding Kelly. She felt betrayed, but confident that she'd be able to deal with both matters. She felt the Holy Spirit strengthening her. There was a brief lull before Philip said, "Who?" His voice cracked with a strange awkwardness. He sounded jittery, Holly thought. "My secretary, Kelly Mills," Holly said as she set the alarm clock on her nightstand. She was so casual in her announcement, like a woman unfazed, Philip mused as a faint "oh" fell flat from his mouth. He then breathed a sigh of relief and began rubbing his hands together. They had suddenly moistened. Whew! That was close. "She wrote you a letter?" "Yes," was all she said. Holly didn't feel like discussing it right now. "Why don't we change the subject. I'd like to hear your good news." Holly stood up and turned back the bedspread and sheet, sliding under. "Uh, yeah. Brenda says she's sorry. She'd like to get together again, that's if you want to. And my parents wanna be there, too. They wanna see the lady who's making their son a nicer man." Holly could feel her face warming at his kind, yet subtle complement, but she couldn't allow them to interfere with what she had to say. "Could I ask you what brought on the change of heart with Brenda?" Holly asked as she fluffed up her pillow with one hand and sank her head into it. "I don't know. She said she knew what she did was wrong and she was also saying something about two wrongs don't make a right. Like I said. I really don't know, I guess she'll explain when she sees you," Philip said, his mind still on how he'd have to get rid of Selma before he lost Holly. "Tell her that I'd be willing to meet with her again," Holly finally said. Maybe she'd learn something. Or maybe God will just keep showing her what He's already shown her. Holly stifled a sigh and rolled over onto her side.

Chapter Eighteen

The sun shone brilliantly Friday morning and the air was crisp, very low in humidity. Holly liked it better outside. The buoyancy of a July day could not go unnoticed when inside of the law firm a murky cloud seemed to hover, making the air thick, almost suffocating. Well, that's how it always felt to her just before she was about to be involved in a confrontation. The attorney blew on a piping-hot cup of Hawaiian Chocolate Nut coffee before making her first attempt to take a sip. Telma was nice enough to hand her the cup from the kitchen as Holly walked in a few brief moments ago. The receptionist took on the responsibility knowing that Kelly hadn't arrived yet. Holly glanced at her watch. Nine-forty and Kelly hadn't even called. It, however, had become typical behavior for her in the past week or so. But, today the attorney didn't mind. This way she'd have some time to reread the infamous letter for the second time that morning. She did it in order to invoke her courtroom courage, knowing she had to be firm with whatever it was she was going to convey to her assistant. Of course, Holly would never threaten Kelly or tell her to stay away from Philip. Not her style. She just wanted to have a woman-to-woman talk, delineating the man they both had an interest in. After all they were adults, two ladies who just happened to have identical tastes when it came to men. Holly wasn't even certain of how far she wanted to go with what little she and Philip had. For a brief moment she thought about what she'd been thinking about. God wasn't in this, she realized. Lifting her head up away from the letter, toward the door, as Holly further dismissed her full awareness of this whole so-called relationship with Philip was her doing. It wasn't marvelous in her sight, she told herself. Holly peered out into the hallway, listening intently as she heard someone ascending the stairs. It was Kelly. She could tell by the way her secretary dragged her feet lazily across the floor, as if she despised being there these days. The dark-skinned woman exchanged pleasantries with Samantha and Tina as she settled down at her desk. Inside of her office, Holly was a bit incredulous at how perky and personable Kelly seemed today. Ordinarily her assistant wouldn't part her lips to the other two secretary's sharing her space, not unless she had a question pertaining to work. She must've had a remarkable night, Holly thought. The lawyer placed the letter on her desk, pulled herself to her feet and walked over to the doorway of her office, summonsing Kelly to come inside. The dark-skinned woman grinned, a vibrant good morning filtering from her mouth as she stood up, obeying Holly's command. The two women sat down behind closed doors. "Holly, I owe you an apology," Kelly said immediately. She was still smiling as she admired the way the sun clung to her employer's golden hair, forming a halo like glow around her head. Kelly wasn't too shocked. She had always known deep down inside that Holly was innocent. She was able to see Jesus in her. But she had to convince herself otherwise, therefore, she'd have no reason to blame her for Elliot's alienation. Isn't that what everyone did? Take it out on the person nearest and dearest to them? Nobody knew this, including her girls, Liz and Jo, but Holly was like the sister she never had. Her family wasn't there for her both physically or mentally. The only thing concerning those bumpkin's was that little piece of land they owned down south, she thought glumly. And she needed the support, someone to lean on. Even though Liz and Joanna were her friend's, Kelly didn't expect them to be there for her all the time. They had their own worries to contend with and their own men to keep happy. Kelly was grateful she had Holly. She had to admit it to herself. How else would she have gotten through the hurt she endured for losing Elliot Dickson? The dark-skinned woman couldn't help but to continue smiling as her thoughts began to drift off toward the man she'd loved for more than ten years. Huh, El knew what time it was! He came back, she told herself again. And now was as good of a time as any to share her story of their relationship with Holly, who began shifting in her seat. The attorney could feel the puzzlement crossing her face. This wasn't how she'd surmised it to go. It was too easy. "My sentiments exactly," was what she finally said. Meekly, the dark-skinned woman shrugged, like a timid child asking for a piece of candy. "Yeah, I know it was rude of me not to introduce you to Elliot, especially since I used to talk your ears off about him when I first started working here." Kelly grinned some more and added, "He thought I was ashamed of him. Could you imagine? Me, ashamed of him?" She chuckled gently. Holly leaned forward, placing her elbows on the desk and crossing her legs underneath it. How did she know they were riding on two totally different roads, going in opposite directions too, no less. Did this girl really think that I'd call her in here because of her decision not to introduce me to her little boyfriend? Holly asked herself. "Kelly, that's not why I asked you in." "Oh," Kelly said, her eyes dropping downward at the wrinkled piece of paper before Holly. The attorney followed the secretary's gaze, picking up the letter. "This is what I wanted to discuss." Holly placed the note in front of Kelly, who just glared down at it, almost as if she didn't know what it was at first. Then the look she tried to mask found its way to the surface. It turned into something Holly couldn't quite describe..... Was it shock? Sadness? Relief? "So, I guess I didn't lose it outside," the dark-skinned woman muttered as she looked back up at her boss. "No, Kel, you dropped it downstairs in between the coffee table and sofa." Holly slumped back in her seat, laced her fingers across her stomach and added, "I really don't know what to say about it because I don't understand it. The letter is perfectly clear, it's not that. No. I think it's the bitterness of its tone that concerns me." Holly glared across the immense desk with eyes that were demanding a sensible answer. "Did you really think I'd stoop as low as to fight over a man? We are not school girls, Kelly. This whole thing is ridiculous to me." The lawyer could hear the strength backing her words. It made her proud of herself. Pride in Jesus, Holly thought. And she could tell by the look on Kelly's face that she, too, heard it. The dark-skinned womans eyes were telling her that she was sorry without her having to utter a peep. But, Kelly didn't know any better. The hazel-eyed attorney knew that she was speaking her secretary's language. "Holly, this was a mistake." The secretary picked the letter up from the desk and tore it up, tossing the fragments of her thoughtless error into the wastepaper basket beside Holly's desk. "I thought about it and the way I've been treating you all last night while Elliot slept beside me. I don't know what came over me. I never loved Philip and I know I never will. I feel real stupid," Kelly said, her eyes still downward. "Don't feel stupid, Kelly...." The secretary peered up at Holly with tears resting in the bottom of her lids. "But, I do. I took everything out on you because Philip reminded me of Elliot. Don't you think they have similar features?" Kelly asked. She didn't give Holly a chance to respond. "They have the same build, they're both tall and good-looking. I *only* wanted him because he was the closest thing to my man..." Holly observed the way her secretary had become weak-looking as if something she'd eaten upset her stomach. She sat bent over, both elbows on her knees. "Sometimes I think I love him more than I love myself." Kelly began to sob pitifully, a second and third apology spilling from her remorseful lips. "Holly, it's the truth you have to believe that I would never intentionally do something like this. Please -- don't -- be -- mad -- at -- me." The secretarys words were broken up by a sudden case of the hiccups. Holly sighed. She had apprehensions about going on. It wouldn't be necessary anyhow. But, why? Was it because Elliot did resemble Philip a little or better yet, was it because Holly was not supposed to be with Philip Williams? Standing up the attorney walked around the desk, giving the dark-skinned woman a consoling hug. "Come on, relax. Calm down. I understand," was what Holly told her sincerely as she patted her back. And she really did understand. She could recall turning down dating offers because the men asking to take her out had slight features to Bradford, a man she only wished the best for. That's what true Christian's did. She would remind herself when thoughts contrary to that would try to rise within her. The old way of thinking that had her telling herself that "what would come back around to him for his mistreatment of her would be more than his fair share of "getting what he deserved."

Touch not my anointed is what the word promises the righteousness of God in Christ Jesus.

The hazel-eyed attorney sighed.

Holly passed Embassy Wines & Spirits on her way to Bloomingdale's later that day. A reminder. She'd have to pick up three bottles of non-alcoholic Champaign for Courtney. Although, her partners husband drank alcohol on occasion, Holly knew by the Grace of God that she had to stay true to her Heavenly Father and not be a participator in his drinking indulgences. "I know Courtney will love it," Holly told herself under her breath. This would be his birthday gift from both Philip and herself. She was almost positive that Philip would agree with her choice, too. What else could they purchase for a man who had everything his heart desired, anyway? At least that was what the view appeared to be from the outside looking in. And, besides that, Holly had been promising to introduce Vanessa and Courtney to the non-alcoholic drinks as she'd tried them before and enjoyed them. God told me to stop drinking them, she reminded herself. The hazel-eyed woman hoped it would cause them to stop drinking the real thing."

Holly took a deep breath as she could see her mother standing on the outside of the busy department store, her colorful floral dress blowing gently from the warm breeze. Holly could feel it pushing ever so slightly against her own back, causing a few wisps of her hair to flow forward. The older woman had spotted Holly too as soon as she made it to 62nd Street and Lexington Avenue. How she loved seeing her child in that pale-green suit. The way it brought out her unique coloring, that glorious amber hue both her hair and eyes shared, made Cynthia Reed want to shout from anyone of those Manhattan rooftops, that Holly was hers. The older woman surveyed the way others were admiring her babygirl also. Black and White men alike turned their heads, bumping into folks, as they swaggered up the crowded block with their eyes locked on Holly. Cynthia Reed couldn't wait for Julia's eyes to behold the inner and outer beauty her daughter possessed. Yessir, she wanted her to see the outstanding job she'd done all by herself. Well, she thought, knowing that her Father in heaven was right there all along. "You my Help, Lawd," she said and nodded her head. The day I been waitin' on, is finally here, she thought with a grin. "Hey, Mom. I hope you weren't waiting long," the younger woman said. "No, babygirl, I just got here not long 'fore you." The two women embraced, kissing each other on the cheeks.

The designer shoe salon on the 2nd floor was relatively empty. That pleased the older woman. Now she knew for sure they wouldn't be late for their lunch appointment. An appointment her daughter was unaware of. As Cynthia Reed scanned the shoes in the quiet department hurriedly, she also kept a watchful eye on her daughter. Seeing Holly sitting down, legs crossed, going through her agenda made her rush even more. The older woman hoped her daughter had more than just an hour to spare because reunions weren't something you rushed. Cynthia spotted two pairs of shoes she liked so the older woman upset the display by hoisting them from the shelf. She turned and asked the salesmen if she could try them on. As the tall, lanky young man, whose hair resembled Michael Douglases during his role in *Wall Street*, nearly broke his neck toward the back to retrieve her size. Cynthia told a fib, saying she was feeling faint and needed some air. The older woman thought of a way to get her daughter to spend a little more time with her. Sitting down on the sofa beside Holly she said, fanning herself to stay in character for the salesman. "Baby, I'm hungry, are you?" "Somewhat." Holly glanced at her watch. "I guess I could stop for a quick bite. Do you want to go to the Showtime Cafe?" Holly closed her appointment book, slipping it back down inside of her pocketbook. When she peered back up at her mother, awaiting her answer, she wondered why she was giving her such an odd look of disappointment. Cynthia smiled, noticing the way Holly began studying her back. "Well, baby, I thought we'd go to the other restaurant in here. I'm so sick and tired of that Barbara, thinking she's got one up on me. She's always braggin' 'bout how wonderful that place is. I can't remember the name, but, her son and his mean ... I mean, yeah, his wife took her there once or twice and I swear you would've thought she'd done gone to heaven and was promised by the Lawd that she was gettin' through them pearly gates when it was her time," Cynthia said with a chuckle. Her quick burst of laughter was brought on to cover up how bad she felt for holding out on her daughter. "Fo'give me for laughin' so loud, but I told Barbara she ain't gettin' into heaven witout knowing the Father through our Jesus." The older woman waved her hand. I knowed it ain't right fo' me to be laughin' like I said, But..." Holly cut her mother off gently by answering. "That's fine. We can go there to eat."

Le Train Bleu, the finer of the two restaurants in Bloomingdale's, made Holly and her mother feel as though they were about to take a ride on the Orient Express. "I guess Barbara wasn't dressin' up her description of the place. This *is* nice?" Cynthia said, her eyes wandering warily around the mildly-populated establishment. Well, at least that's what Holly thought her mother was doing, admiring the decor. But, what she was really doing was looking for the woman she had promised to meet there at 1:30 p.m. Not a minute later. The silver watch on the older woman's wrist ticked rapidly toward their designated time. When Cynthia glanced back over her shoulder toward the restaurant's entrance, for the second time since they had been seated, she felt a bout of queasiness festering in the pit of her stomach. Here she is, she told herself. Julia still looked good for a woman approaching eighty. The old White woman was tall, skinny and flat-chested. One thing's for sure, Cynthia Reed thought, Julia would never have to worry about saggy breasts. Shoot, me either, the older Black woman thought. The Lawd promised to renew my youth like the eagles. She could feel the large dual resting just above the waist band of her Jockey underwear as she continued to inspect what Julia had on. She was clad in a cream-colored Chanel suit, had a short-strapped quilted purse dangling off her bony shoulder with the matching shoes adorning her narrow feet, both of which bared the same Chanel label and pearly shade. "Who are you staring at like that?" Holly asked, snapping her mother out of her daze. Before Cynthia could turn to face her daughter in order to prepare her for what was about to take place, her eyes met Julia's. The old White woman produced a small smile, a smile only evident across her thin, glossy lips. Those gray eyes didn't bother to budge. But, then again, they had always remained emotionless, as far as Cynthia was concerned. Never ever said a thing! Jesus is the Truth, the Way and the Life. Julia need the Lawd, the older Black woman reminded herself. She knew for sure that the old White woman not having Him was the explanation for the lack of life seen in her eyes. Cynthia watched as Julia thanked the hostess standing next to her and headed over in their direction. "Oh, uh, I'm not starin' at nothin', baby. Listen, I don't want you to be upset. Just remember, sweetie, I did this for you. I just want you to be happy and whole," Cynthia Reed whispered. Her voice was more motherly than Holly could ever remember it being and less obstructed by the way she usually spoke. And, it was more protective as well. The older Black woman's sensing in her heart instructed her to warn her daughter but it was too late. She didn't even know why she had kept it a secret in the first place. I knowed the Lawd's been tellin' me to tell her. "Mom, what are you talking about? I am whole already. That's what the Word says right?" The younger woman asked as the faint scent of Joy made its way up into her nostrils. "Hello," said the prim and proper voice from above the table Holly and her mother shared. Cynthia Reed gazed at her daughter for a second then up at Julia, her surprise guest. "Hi, please have a seat," Cynthia said calmly. She lifted the bag containing her newly-purchased shoes and slid into the adjacent chair, closer to the wall, placing the *Medium Brown* Bloomingdale's shopping bag back down between her right and Julia's left foot. Holly observed this confusing episode through questioning eyes as she waited patiently for an introduction or some kind of purpose for this woman being here. She had to be someone her congenial mother must have ministered to on the bus or in the supermarket, she thought only to appease herself for a while. "Sweetie," Cynthia began gingerly, her eyes resting on the older White woman's face, almost as if she were asking her permission for something. However, Julia had been peering downward, busy spreading the cloth napkin from the table across her gaunt lap. Oh, but she was listening. Because Julia had been waiting for this day to arrive as well, unbeknownst to herself. As she sat there buying time, going over in her mind what she wanted to say, searching diligently for the answers to the questions she had anticipated Holly to have, answers she deserved, memories of herself lying idly, like some zombie, in her bed on many nights, wondering what it would be like to know this young woman before her...... *Wait* a minute! What would she call Holly? What, if anything at all, could she consider this person who she didn't know, seated across from her? This was something Julia had pondered unsuccessfully the moment she left Barnes & Nobles on 53rd and 3rd yesterday at about noon. That's where she and Cynthia had run into each other. Julia practically got down on her hands and knees, in the crowded book store, imploring the older Black woman that she be permitted to meet Holly. And when Cynthia finally agreed, under certain prerequisites, Julia raced home with thoughts of today's engagement never once leaving her mind. But, she hadn't come up with anything. How on earth could she...... would she...... explain to this young woman, the young woman whose face was so close to the one she had conceived it to be, that she had no choice, absolutely no say in the matter?

"This is Mrs. Julia Reed," Cynthia continued, her bottom lip twitching. Was she doing the right thing? She cleared her throat, ordering the White woman at her side to return her gaze. And she did, nodding her head. For a slight second, as Julia's eyes settled on Cynthia's, in a way that made her feel small and meaningless, the older Black woman got that all too familiar feeling once again. The feeling she would encounter when she and David had met his mother for an undisclosed lunch or dinner. The same horrible feeling, which had a way of backsliding her to the days when her Nana, Hatty Mae Banks, her father's mother, the woman who raised her after her parents' sudden death, would say, "Chile, who told you to go on and slap that gunk all up in yo' head. Look like a wet dawg. And you smell like rotten eggs. Blasted chemicals. White folks done made you turn fool. Don't you know we don't need no straight hair to be pretty." The old toothless-snuff-spittin' heifer would go on to say once she had emptied her mouth of the overflowing tobacco juice, "And 'sides that, it gone take a whole lot mo' than that stankin' mess to make any mans 'round here, give you the timea day!" How could Julia have the power to do the same thing with her eyes alone? With a simple glance? No mean-spirited words whatsoever! How was it possible for the old White woman to have the innate ability of making Cynthia feel unattractive and lost at the same time? Displeasing to her Father in Heaven? Struggling with the urge to scream out, "I'm a daughter of God Almighty! That makes me beautiful 'cause He's Beautiful and no one could make me think otherwise!" an affirmation David asked her to say whenever that agonizing feeling would arise. The older Black woman pushed air in and out of her lungs slowly instead, wiping away the haunting retentions of her trying past like one would the unappealing smudges on a mirror or glass-top table. Once they were gone, she said to Holly in a voice not quite her own, "Baby, she your grandmother, your daddy's mama." Cynthia turned toward Holly, who remained speechless for what seemed like hours to the older Black woman. Holly had gone numb. She was unable to speak. All five senses were at a complete standstill, disinclined to be of service, rebelling just as she felt like she had been doing for so long against her Heavenly Father. I've stop going to church, I haven't read the Word in month's … but, I speak it, Holly thought. She didn't know what she was thinking exactly. But, one thing stood out from all the other mixed up contemplation's in her head, the ones passing each other like two trains in the night. It was the fact that this woman before her with the smug face and the casual disposition, had given birth to her father, David Reed, a man so warm and gentle, so full of love. God is Love, Holly told herself as she was pleasantly surprised at the many Bible scriptures that had begun to rise up in her spirit. One of them was: "We walk by Faith, not by sight." How could he have come from the womb of this woman? This aloof individual? She was not the image Holly had perceived when her mother tried her consummate best to fill her up on the stories and information that her late husband had given her regarding his family history. The hazel-eyed woman shook those thoughts off and refocused on the truth. She was to walk by Faith and not by sight! She had to think like God. He looks at the heart of a man or woman. Okay, Holly thought as she remembered how everything appeared to be so positive back then in her young mind. Sure, she could recollect her mother telling her how much she wanted her to feel as close to her White heritage as she was to her Black one. Yes, mom was always conscious of that. "But, remember that the Lawd Jesus Christ is who you really is 'cause He's your Daddy," the older Black woman would quickly say. Cynthia Reed rarely held a grudge. Hurt and despair seemed to roll off her back like perspiration on a hot day. But, somehow all those naive visions of her White grandmother, during her mother's "Reed-data-giving sessions," favoring Aunt Bea, little Oppie Taylors humble relative, have been shattered right there in that restaurant. Lost amidst this public space. Just fusing with the aromas of food and sweet desserts floating aimlessly through the air until they were no more. Holly began to watch Julia Reed for a moment. Why did that happen? The hazel-eyed woman knew to

Walk by Faith and not by sight! But, the Word being brought to her mind was cut off. Why? Help me Jesus, Holly cried out from the secret place in her heart. Although she tried hard not to judge her White grandmother, she realized that she didn't like her. She didn't like what lurked behind her gray eyes, eyes so near to the color of steel. And just as cold as the silver metal, too. She just couldn't like her! Why would she want to like a woman who would have the nerve to reenter her life years later, with the hopes of rekindling a grandmother/granddaughter relationship that had never even existed, when there were so many other opportunities in the past? Phone calls she didn't accept! Letters she didn't answer! Why would she want to like a woman who sat back and allowed the mere question of "what are we going to eat tonight?" invade Holly and her mother's already overwhelmed heads. Not because they had a myriad of choices, but because they had none. So *this* is Julia Reed, her wealthy grandmother, who never once tried to deliver them from hunger. No, instead she chose to sit up in her luxurious apartment overlooking Central Park, conspiring with her wicked husband, Alan on ways to make Holly and her mother more miserable. As if that were achievable? Didn't Alan Reed's hurtful words cause enough harm? And didn't they sustain enough pain when Holly's father was told he was no longer their son, no longer a "Reed" to them after he had gone ahead and married her mother? They disinherited him, cut him off from the family fortune, just because he grew in love with a woman with skin too dark and hair too coarse for their tastes. Knowing from the beginning that Cynthia had no real means of being able to support herself without a trade or conventional skill backing her up, let alone having to raise the child she and her White husband made once David transitioned. All she would've probably needed was a small push in the right direction. Holly's mother was always willing to work and they knew that she wanted to use the gift of cooking that God Graced her with. But, their abandonment didn't stop Cynthia Reed, Holly reminded herself, a smile almost penetrating her lips. Their Heavenly Father manifested many opportunities for her beloved mother. Yes, He is their Source, Holly thought. They have done just fine without Julia and all her millions. She and her mother didn't need this expendable disruption in their lives. Didn't want it! Holly bit down hard on her bottom lip to keep from saying something disrespectful, remembering that her mother had told her just before Julia sat down, that she wanted her to be happy and whole. That unselfish statement is what helped to coat the walls of her throat from all the burning words of discontent stirring about like wildfire. What was Julia Reed's reason for being here today? She would behave for her mother's sake and find out. And, I have to love this woman for God's sake, thought the hazel-eyed woman. "Really?" Holly said in a tone that was polite but distant. She was even a bit surprised at the hearing of the sound of her own voice. "Yes, dear. I am David's mother How do you do?" Julia Reed said, lifting her head. She then extended her frail aged-spotted hand across to her granddaughter, who gave it a weak welcome in return with hers. "I'm not sure yet," Holly said. She was smiling a smile only her mother could identify. Cynthia Reed appeared to have taken a deep breath when she saw the forced grin on her daughter's lips and as she glanced up into Holly's eyes, not seeing their usual light, she realized that this was nothing but a mistake. Julia decided to ignore the young woman's snide remark, complimenting her on how lovely she turned out instead. "The first female attorney in the family. How wonderful!" the old White woman said proudly. Her arrogance aggravated Holly, prolonging her temporary paralysis. The young woman's eyes shifted over toward her mother's, whose lowered, falling downward somewhere toward the table, hiding from her daughter's looming mixed emotions. "I see you've been filled in about me?" Holly said softly, so soft it almost hurt. "Yes, yes, your mother was good enough to inform me of a few marvelous things about you. Oh, dear, your father would have been so proud of you," Julia said, smiling. "Praise God," Holly said. She had a smirk on her face. "This is true," Julia said. She leaned forward, folding her ancient hands atop the table. "So, dear, tell me more about yourself. We have so much catching up to do. And if now isn't a good time, we could start this weekend, perhaps. I'd like to invite you and your mother to my home. But, if it's not a good time, I'm sure your work plate is full, with cases and ....." "Is that why you're here? Are you looking for representation?" Holly asked, intentionally cutting the old White woman short. "*Indeed!*" Julia exclaimed, all of her tucked-away wrinkles showing. Frowning, the old White woman glanced at Cynthia then back at Holly, pausing briefly in order to remove the sudden venom from her tonality. "No, I don't need representation. How silly of me." Julia smiled somewhat, adding, "Surely, you must be wondering why I've asked to see you. Your mother was drastically opposed to the idea at first, not knowing how you'd react. So, I urged her not to tell you, darling. Please don't hold her responsible for...." "Oh, don't *you* worry. The only thing my mother is responsible for is the way I turned out by the Grace of God," Holly said, her voice one octave higher and trembling "Prayer changes things," the hazel-eyed woman declared in a low voice, one that she managed to hide the truth of her not being prayerful behind. Julia Reed nodded again, this time slowly as she turned to examine the faces of the patrons seated at the neighboring table. She knew it would only be a matter of time before one of *them*, Holly or Cynthia, caused a scene. But, what could one do, they couldn't help it, it was part of their origin. Loud. Uncivil. Disagreeable. Kay sa rah sa rah! Good, the young White women weren't listening to their conversation, Julia told herself. They were too engrossed in their interpretation of some television program they both viewed last night. When Julia's gaze refocused on the two Black women she was joining, she began to observed the way they were holding each other's hands now. Cynthia was apparently giving her daughter support. How unusual. Suddenly, Julia's mouth went dry. She needed some water. But there was none on the table. There wasn't even a waiter in site. What kind of asinine place was this? For a moment she wished she had never called this long, overdue family gathering. Wished she had never run into Cynthia. The last thing she wanted to witness was how much Black people loved one another. Alan's theory of them not being able to care, being genetically incompetent in that area, had been dispelled right before her very eyes, her very foolish eyes. Foolish for believing him and her parents and grand parents pure ignorance her entire life. But was she to blame? Of course, she wasn't. It would be preposterous to fault herself. She had never known anyone Black on a personal level growing up in Greenwich, Connecticut. Except Esther and Shirley, the maid and cook. Those two were like sisters, always laughing and singing wonderful songs honoring God, or whomever it was *they* worshiped. She recalled hearing them say Jesus countless times. Ah yes, and then there was Wilber, the driver. Julia could hardly comprehend him sometimes. The poor dear wasn't educated but he was a remarkable man. They were all quite remarkable she decided as she furthered her thoughts on the Blacks of her antiquity. Obedient. Tolerable. Quiet. And how could she possibly forget Thelma; her personal shopper, Lorraine; her housekeeper and cook now, Bebe or is it Dede? Goodness, what is the woman's name? She comes Monday thru Friday, on time, to walk Geoffrey, her furry little baby. Julia would make a point of finding out tomorrow. Sighing, the old White woman began to reflect on the day David brought Cynthia home. She could see her own once youthful face laughing in the parlor mirror, thinking that he had been playing a practical joke on the family. Their son was always guilty of that. He had been a prankster since he was a toddler. But, once they realized that he wasn't teasing, she and Alan went wild, yelling at the young man, telling him he had gone mad. Lost his mind. "You don't marry them, David. They were put here on God's green earth to serve us," Alan told the boy as Julia stood there nodding, stupidly in agreement like some trained seal. My God, the way her husband glared at the Black woman, who was shaking as if she'd been suddenly stricken with some type of nervous disorder at their son's side. His eyes infiltrated with rage and utter hate, "What did you do, put some kind of hex on him? Voo doo? Isn't that what *you* people call it? Well, you had better remove this sinister spell, missy because the last thing in the world that I want is a Black grandchild," is what Alan Reed said. His voice was hotter in anger than the lava in an erupting volcano.

Why did she always refer to her daughter-in-law as the Black woman? Her name is Cynthia Julia and your granddaughter's name is Holly, the old White woman thought. She was chastising herself from within. Was she any better than Alan and all the other teachers of detest she'd been exposed to?

"My dear, you're absolutely right," Julia said, slowly pulling herself out of her saddening reverie. "Cynthia has done a fine job. I guess I should have left well enough alone, but I'm afraid I couldn't. For some reason we were meant to meet. Destined, if you will. Maybe it was something all of us secretively requested. I know I have," Julia continued sincerely. She lowered her eyes for a moment in order to capture the face of her granddaughter in her mind's eye. The old White woman was so pleased with what her money had done. The intellect she helped to cultivate. Sending that generous check on that rainy morning was the best investment she had ever made. It was the least she and Alan could do, although he never knew of their paying for Holly's college education in full.

"I had to suffer as well," Julia said, gazing upward at Holly again. "Of course, my suffering is no comparison to what you and your mother had gone through. But, please give me a chance to set the record straight." Julia proceeded to tell the two women everything Alan Reed had forbade her to do. Even while the waiter took their orders, she told them everything from his prohibiting her search for both Holly and Cynthia to his not allowing her to return their phone calls and letters. And at the end of her very detailed unveiling, amid their barely-eaten plates of food, Holly found herself caught between the opposing resolutions of not knowing whether to reach across the table to hug her White grandmother or to reach across and strangle her. "You see, dear, now that Alan has passed on, *I* would have stopped at nothing to find you, if only to tell you and your mother how sorry I was. Your poor grandfather was always so worried about his reputation in the community and among his colleagues at work." Julia paused, grinning, her dentures whiter than the hair on her head. She was grinning as if knowing this Holly and her mother would become sympathetic, feel sorry for the insurmountable old man. Or, better yet, find it in their hearts to forgive them both. "Even if you're not willing to remain in touch with me, at least I could live, the short time I have left, with some sense of dignity. I was raised a certain way, but I refuse to die in that same dreadful manner," Julia concluded. Dignity? Holly thought. That only came through the Cross. God's Salvation Plan. This had to be the reason for this meeting. Cynthia stared at Julia for a second after she had stopped talking, seeing for the first time ever, a certain glimmer of truth in those gray eyes, a glimmer of hope for the woman she would have liked to back smack too many times for her to count. "Well, the onlys thing I could say is, I'm standin' by whatever choice my daughter make," the older Black woman announced. She pulled her eyes away from Julia's pleading ones in search of Holly's before she was swayed to give into her prematurely. The young hazel-eyed woman also glanced at her mother then down at her watch. They had been sitting there for two and a half hours. Raising her head, Holly peered over at Cynthia again as she thought of the proper way to communicate her decision. During their brief exchange of eye contact, she also wondered how her mother could be so forgiving. Look at Jesus. Yes, she had seen the way her mother's eyes told Julia's that "she understood," but Holly, on the other hand, couldn't find the spirit of forgiveness on the inside of her. She felt so empty. Sighing, Holly knew she would have to get down on her knees and repent later since forgiveness was God's will. "Well, Julia," the young woman began. She was staring at her grandmother now. "Before I tell you what my plans are, I just need to get one thing off my chest. It's been there for as long as I could remember. Holding me back and I let it. Maybe this was the reason for this appointment today, to find some sort of closure, but if it wasn't, I guess I owe God and my father, an apology for altering what may have become," Holly said, swallowing the lump forming in her throat. "But, before going into that, I'd like to first comment about Alan Reed and his trying to save his reputation." Holly watched Julia nod her head slowly. "If those people whom he considered to be his friend's really were, he wouldn't have to worry about what they'd say or think, because from my knowledge true friendship lasts through anything. Therefore, it would be safe to say that your husband, Alan Reed had no friends." The old White woman opened her mouth to reply but Holly continued without allowing her the chance. "Now..... When I was a child my mother and I may not have had the kind of riches you're obviously accustomed to, *but* we had another kind of wealth worth more than all the money in the world. We had God the Father, God the Son and God the Holy Spirit. Wealth beyond measure. We had each other. Hugs, kisses, words of wisdom and encouragement, all things cash couldn't possibly buy. And as I sat here today, listening to your confession, I continued to go way back to the times when my mother and I had very little monetarily. Specifically, to the times when the woman seated next to you would slip a quarter, sometimes a dollar, depending on what she had, under my pillow because I lost a tooth. And after we'd finish laughing about my not waking up during the Tooth Angel's visit, I'd peer into my mother's sullen eyes, knowing without her having to say, that she needed to borrow that silver coin or that crinkled bill, in order to get to work or to purchase something we both needed. At that delicate age, I'd say 'don't worry, mama, you don't have to explain.' Because I really understood. I *knew* she had only done it with the hopes of making our day a little easier. No, excuse me, it was our lives at the time as we were not yet strong in the Faith. *But*, the vision that's still so prevalent in my mind, and I suppose it will always be, was the fact that, no matter how many times I'd convey to this great woman sitting beside you how I understood, I'd always hear her weep, break down and cry seconds later in a part of the apartment, out of my view, because she had to do it, had to take *my* money away..." Inhaling deeply to suppress tears so close to falling, Holly added, "to me those kind of memories are the ones I'd much rather have, the ones which showed me, without my *ever* having to ask, just how much I was loved. They're priceless. Don't get me wrong. I'm sure deep down inside you and your husband meant well. You both did what you knew how to do, but I just cannot bring myself to truly believe that. The Bible talks about how the Truth is so evident because of God Himself. He has told everyone that His existence, is suppressed by wickedness. Although, I'd like to commend you for being here right now. I'm telling you, if we were somewhere in private, I'd probably give you a standing ovation...... but it's just a little too late for me. A little too late for us to try to find what it is *we've* missed out on. If only you were braver back then, willing to stand up for your very own convictions, I'm sure we could have had something quite special. I would have loved to have been able to tell all those children, with big smiles, who were on their way to their grandma and grandpa's house for the weekend, that I, too, was on my way to mine." Holly motioned to the waiter for the check, paid, sent a signal to her mother that she was ready to go, told Julia Reed to, "take good care of yourself. If that's possible without God." The old White woman yelled out "I have cancer and I want to live!" with tears falling from her eyes. Holly and Cynthia paused and looked at each other then back at Julia. "Please pray for me," she said. The older Black woman paused again and then she nodded her head yes as she moved toward the older White woman, laying her hand on the top of her head. "Father, in heaven. The One Who sees and hears everythang. I pray to you, Mighty God in the Name of Jesus Christ Your precious Son, let Julia Reed be healed in that Name that is higher than every other name," Cynthia paused and nodded her head again as she stood up next to Holly. Her eyes met the older White woman's fright-filled ones with her own. She took her hand off of her head and stepped back, beside her daughter. The two women took a deep breath and walked out of that restaurant, leaving Julia seated, with the certainty of them having done the right thing for everyone involved.

Chapter Nineteen

The message from Leslie Stokes, the abused woman who'd decided she no longer required Holly's help, didn't come as a complete surprise to the attorney. She'd expected her to call. Much, much sooner, in fact. Holly sighed as she reached into her pocketbook for her agenda. Usually she did a good job of not mixing business with her personal life, but after today's lunch, she choose to return the woman's phone call on Monday. It would be better for the both of them, Holly reasoned. Ms. Stokes was a little too much for her to have to deal with right then and there and besides that, the lawyer was sure Leslie's mind would more than likely change between now and the end of the weekend anyway. Still and all, doing what she was supposed to do, Holly opened the drawer in front of her, took out a pen and jotted it down in her agenda as a reminder. Calling the confused Ms. Stokes would be the first task on her list of things to do Monday morning.

Just as Holly closed her appointment book, slipping it back down into her handbag, there was a knock at the door. The attorney paused, affixing an "I'm okay smile on her face." Once she was certain that her appearance wasn't a giveaway, echoing the heartache she still felt from declaring herself "grandparentless," she called out, telling whoever it was to come in. Tracy cracked the door, sticking her head inside. "Girl, I was wondering if you were ever coming back! A three-hour lunch? I hope your mother found the ideal pair of shoes." Holly nodded, the conjured up smile still on her face. "Good. Well, I just wanted to know how you and Philip were getting out to Vee's tomorrow?" Holly hadn't even thought of what their means of transportation was going to be. "Trace, I don't know. Maybe Philip and I'll rent a car." "No, why don't you guys come with me and Karl?" Tracy said, her entire body visible in the doorway now. *Karl*? Holly thought. It was a name she hadn't heard in a while. "Oh, so he's the man this weekend, huh?" Tracy chuckled. "Yeah, I guess you could say that, but I don't know how much man he's going to consider himself to be if he finds out about all the men I've been seeing." She glanced over both her shoulders then back at Holly and whispered, her right hand cupping the side of her mouth, "It's that time of the month, and you know I don't play that we-could-still-do-it-anyway stuff." The short-haired lawyer made a face, extending her hand, palm up across the desk to Holly, who smacked it with hers in agreement. The two women giggled for a couple of seconds more about the comment then Tracy asked, "So, what are you buying Court?" "Oh, uh. Three bottles of non-alcoholic Champaign." "Okay, dry but I'm gonna try to understand your flow with your Daddy God. Well, I'm getting him a humidor and an assortment of fine cigars and calling it a day." Tracy waved her hand. "Okay, he does seem to like those things," Holly said quietly. "How does Vee plan on getting him out of the house tomorrow for the surprise?" "She didn't even have to think of anything. Court told her earlier in the week that he had something he needed to take care of Saturday afternoon. You know she was happy, my girl didn't bother to ask him what it was," Tracy said, chuckling. "Well, that's good..." Holly was interrupted by Kelly over the intercom. She was announcing that Philip was on the phone. "All right, we'll pick you guys up at five sharp, okay," Tracy said as she headed out of Holly's office. Nodding in agreement, Holly picked up the receiver. She could feel herself smiling, this time genuinely, for what appeared to be the first time that day, once Philip began to speak after her soft hello. He was telling her how disappointed he was because he'd probably have to work late tonight. "Baby, you don't know how *bad* I wanna see you, but this place is packed," Philip said. A part of her wanted to see him too, wanted to share what had happened during her lunch hours with him. Wasn't that what couples were supposed to do? Discuss the things that brought them pleasure as well as the things that disturbed them? But, then again, the other part of her, the part she had become so used to, just wanted to go home and bury her head under a pillow, separating herself from the world. I'm in it, but I'm not of it, anyway, Holly told herself. "Well, what do you expect when you've been written up as one of the most successful restaurateur's in New York?" she said, trying to sound supportive. But who would be there to hold her hand, Holly thought, adding, ""Phil's House" was right up there with the finest restaurant's according to the article in *Ebony* magazine a couple of months ago, right?" Holly had heard Kelly, in an excited state, telling one of her friend's about the piece over the phone a couple of months ago. "Yeah, it was, wasn't it?" Philip said, grinning. "All right, enough. I want you to be able to fit through the door when you get ready to leave tonight. Has the swelling gone down?" Holly said, chuckling lightly. Philip paused. "Oh, I get it. You're talkin' about my head," he said, grinning once again. "*Right.* So, how late is late?" Holly asked. "Uh, I'm not sure. I'd say about one, two o'clock. Why?" "Well, because I would have waited up, but I can't make any promises I don't intend to keep. I'm exhausted," Holly said, knowing her fatigue was probably more mental than physical. "So what you're sayin' is that you're goin' to sleep *early* on a Friday night?" Philip asked. "Yep. I'm going to take a nice hot bath, curl up on my bed and escape in Carmen's book." "Okay, then. I'll, uh, give you a call later on tonight," Philip said quietly. It wasn't the answer he wanted to hear. Sometimes it felt like he was always the one suggesting that they'd get together, felt like he was always making the first move. Selma and a few others he could name, if asked, would've come down to his restaurant without an invitation. Was that what she was waiting for? Him to say, "Baby, why don't you head over here after work?" Philip twisted his lips, as if to say, "yeah okay." Was this the reason why he loved Holly so much? Because she just didn't do the things he was accustomed to?

She heard the discouragement in his voice, the sudden change in sentiment, but she really was tired. What did he want from her?

"Fine. Talk to you later," was all she finally said before the two of them hung up.

Seven o'clock came quickly that evening. Holly had just crumbled up the final call-back message she'd promised to make that day, tossing it as she'd done the others into the wastepaper basket. At least she was able to resolve someone else's dilemma's. Leaning forward in her chair, the attorney rested her face in the palms of both her hands, sighing. Was this her purpose? To satisfy everyone else, neglecting her own happiness? Letting out another sigh, she pulled her head back, her hands slapping the top of the desk. Sometimes she was just a little too dramatic for her own good. Things were *not* that bad. Look at Leslie Stokes' situation, she told herself. "I have to stop doing this to myself. Lord, help me lean, rely on and trust in You and You alone." Standing up, Holly bent down, picked up her pocketbook, put her agenda inside, turned off the lamp on her desk and walked out of her office.

On her way down the winding staircase, the lawyer was surprised to see Telma still at her desk working. Holly had thought she was there all alone, and if she wasn't, their receptionist would have been the last person she'd expect to find putting in overtime. The cafe au lait-colored woman was good at her job, that went without saying, but she always made a point of leaving it behind as soon as the clock struck five. "You're still here?" the lawyer asked, waving as she rounded the reception desk for the front door. "Yes, I was straightening out my files. Now that the storage room is organized, I felt compelled to make sure my area was too before I left tonight," Telma said, smiling. Holly grinned back. The phone rang and the receptionist answered it. "Have a good weekend, Tel...." The cafe au lait-colored woman held up her hand to the attorney and told the caller to hold on. "It's Ms. Stokes. Will you take it?" Telma asked after pressing the "hold" button. Pausing for a second, Holly glanced at her watch then made a face. She shook her head no. "Please tell her that I'm not available." "Okay. See you

Monday," said the receptionist. Holly waved again and exited the firm.

Brian McKnight's serene voice and song lyrics moved everyone in some form or fashion as the sound drifted through the air, making the afterwork crowd at "Phil's House" party hard. They were embracing Friday like it only came once a year. Seeing their liveliness brought a smile to Holly's face even though her heart was faithfully telling her that she didn't belong there. *Still,* she thought, surpressing the sweet wooing of the Holy Spirit on the inside of her, she was glad she'd changed her mind. And, from Philip's voice earlier on the phone, she was almost certain that he'd be jubilant too regarding her new decision to stop by the restaurant instead of going directly home as she had originally planned. Holly looked around as she weaved slowly through the patrons who were standing near the door, making her way over to the bar. She'd ask one of the bartender's where Philip was since he wasn't upstairs making his rounds yet. "Excuse me," Holly said. She was trying to get the attention of the short, cocoa-colored young woman with a brown mid-back length braid as she squirted water into a glass filled with ice. "Yeah, could I help you with somethin', foxy thang?" asked a raspy voice from behind her. Holly turned to find a little tacky man with Jheri curls trying to meet her steady gaze. His eyes were redder than the Bloody Mary he was cradling in his hand. Glaring down at him with her head pulled back and her nose wrinkled in disgust, Holly slid closer to the bar stool. She'd never smelled breath so bad. And the site of his activated hair, dripping down the sides of his greasy face, made her want to tell him to use the napkin around his glass to wipe it off, but she didn't think it was such a good idea as he appeared to want to cause friction with whoever would entertain him. "No, thank you. I was talking to the bartender," she told him, turning back to face the young woman. She heard him let out a long sigh, his respiration hot on her neck. "Ugh!" Holly moved in further toward the bar, this time waving her hand in front of the young woman's face. She noticed her now. "I know what you mean, foxy thang," dragon breath said, the alcohol and halitosis vying with one another. "They takes *fo'ever* to serve you 'round here. It took me 'bout twenty minutes to get this here drank." He started laughing and Holly held her breath. "So, you see, I understand yo' frustration. I was 'bout to tell that hip cat that be walkin' 'round, you know, smooth dude..... well, well, well, pret-ty thang, looka here. I gots me a idea. You take my drank. I only took me a sip. Here you go." He extended his glass to Holly and she shook her head no. "Why? What's wrong? I ain't got no disease or nothin'," he said, smiling. Lord, his teeth were golder than all the chains around his neck. "I'm sure you don't but she's looking right at me, and I wasn't interested in having a drink," Holly said. She gave him a phony smile and turned her back on him once again. "Can I help you?" the cocoa-colored woman finally asked. She then cut her eyes over at the man who was annoying Holly. He waved his hand, as if to say, "forget you" at the two of them. He swung his head around, Jheri curl juice flying everywhere, as he began searching the restaurant for another victim. Holly ducked out of the way, looking down at her suit, checking it to see if he'd "sprayed" her once he finally slithered away, down to the other end of the bar, grinning in some other woman's disgusted face. "Good," said the bartender as she followed him with her eyes. Holly looked back up at her and smiled. "Could you tell me where I'd be able to find Philip Williams?" The young woman nodded, pointing down the stairs. "He's in his office," she said. "Thanks." As Holly descended the stairs, the sound of music and socializing fading more and more with her every step, she spotted Darryl coming up the stairs, two at a time. "Hello," Holly said to him. He stopped, taking a double look at her. "*Oh*, hey, hi," he said, a grin crossing his lips. "I was trying to remember where I knew you from," Darryl added. Holly smiled. "Uh, I was told Philip was down in his office," she said, nodding toward the closed door at the bottom of the landing. The grin on Darryl's face gradually dispersed, changing into a look of uncertainty. But what was he unsure of? Holly wondered. "Yeah, um, he's in there," said the waiter and continued up the stairs. He glanced back once he got to the top and quickly turned his head. He hurried out of view when he saw Holly staring up at him. Shrugging her shoulders, she walked down, knocking on Philip's office door. "What!" he called out from the other side of it. "This better be good. C'mon in!" he added. His tone was filled with agitation. When Holly opened the door an indescribable feeling took hold of her. What was going on in here? The only thing she could do was peer into Philip's shocked eyes as he stood leaning against his desk with a crying Selma Girard pressing into him, her arms wrapped tightly around his waist, her head resting on his chest. Philip cleared his throat, breaking the uncomfortable silence that was engulfing the room like smoke during a massive fire. But Holly continued to watch him as he pushed his ex-girlfriend aside, sliding his hand down the back of his neck afterward. "Hey, baby," he said quietly. Selma turned to see who he was talking to. Her eyes were puffy and her mascara was smeared. "Well, I guess I surprised you like I wanted to," Holly finally said once the words in her head made sense enough to exit her mouth. "Baby, it's not what you think," Philip said. "It never is," Holly said. He closed his eyes for a second and walked over to her, pulling her inside of his office, shutting the door. "She was just saying good-bye," Philip said, looking at Selma. Her eyes fell to the floor. "Oh, really," Holly said. She folded her arms across her chest, cocking her head to the side. "Yeah. Right, Selma? You heard what I said, tell her. Didn't you stop by to tell me you and Charles were movin' to...." Selma looked up and glanced at Philip then at Holly, nodding her head. "He's telling the truth," she said, wiping under both eyes with the backs of her index fingers. "Charles and I got married yesterday." She held up her left hand, revealing a diamond wedding band. "and he was offered a great job out in Seattle. We'll be leaving tomorrow morning." Holly nodded, dropping her hands to her side. "What about the new house the two of you bought?" she asked, knowing that there really wasn't one. The attorney could see Philip giving Selma a dirty look from the corner of her eye. "What house?" he snapped, remembering just then that Selma had gone to Holly's job to start something. "There isn't a house," Selma said quietly. "I wanted to see what she was like okay, Philip. I wanted to see what kind of woman you would fall in love with. Is that so terrible? Huh?" Selma paused to compose herself. She looked over at Holly and said, "You're a lucky woman." Philip glanced at Holly, wrapping his arm around her shoulders. She didn't know what to say to that except. "I don't believe in luck. I pray the best for you and Charles. He seems like a good man." Holly produced a sincere smile. "Thank you," Selma said. She took a deep breath and looked at Philip. "I hope everything works out for the two of you, too," she said. The couple watched Selma as she removed her black leather backpack from Philip's desktop, slipping it on, her reddish ringlets bouncing as she moved. Selma walked over giving Philip a kiss on the cheek. Holly could feel him pulling her closer to him, assuring her that the woman before them meant nothing at all to him. "Take care of yourself," Philip said to Selma. She nodded, taking another deep breath as she looked at Holly. "Sorry for trying to deceive you at your office. He's all yours." Staring back into Selma's grieving green eyes, Holly only heard the words *"he's all yours"* flooding her mind. Is that what she wanted? she asked herself. For Philip Williams to be all hers?

"Baby, you all right?" Philip asked. He was standing in front of her with both hands grasping her arms, right above the elbows. His brows were furrowed in bewilderment. "Oh.....," she said, climbing out of her daze. "I'm fine," she said, noticing that the heart-broken woman wasn't there anymore. "I'm glad she's gettin' the heck out of here," Philip said, grinning. The telephone on his desk rang, stealing the couples attention. Philip walked around the glass-top desk, answering it on the second ring. Holly could tell that it was his sister from the way he looked at her, nodding his head and smiling. "Yeah, don't worry. I've got it all under control," he said confidently. "I told you before she said she'd see you again. No, Bren she's not like that." Philip said to his sister as he winked at Holly. She smiled in return and took a seat in one of the hunter green leather chairs opposite him. He sat down too. "Yeah, I'll call you with all the info later. All right put her on....... Hey, Olivia. How's my little princess doin'?" Philip threw his head back, laughing real loud. "I'm sorry. I meant my *big* princess. Well, I'm glad you're doin' fine. Yeah, uncle Philip will see you soon. Tell your brother I said hello, 'cause I know he's too cool to get on the phone. That's not nice, Olivia. Don't call Mark jr. a stupid head. Thata girl tell him you're sorry." Philip grinned at Holly, mouthing,"kids" at the same time. "What? No, no, just tell your mother I'll talk to her later. Thank you, sweetgirl. Bye-bye." Philip hung up and said, "I guess you know what that was all about?" Holly nodded and swallowed the way she admired his way of speaking to his niece. It was beautiful to the hazel-eyed woman but that thing she was still sensing on the inside would not let her fully enjoy it. Holly cleared her throat and said, "I've been meaning to tell you that I'd like to invite them all over to my apartment on Sunday, early evening, for dinner. If that's okay with you? I thought I'd persuade my mother to cook, although it wouldn't take much since it's one of her favorite things to do." Philip smiled some more as he sat there for a moment looking her up and down. "I'm sure they'd like that a lot," he told her. He stood up, walking around to where she was seated, kneeling in front of her. "Would four o'clock be good for you?" Holly asked, staring down at him. "That's fine. Even if it wasn't, I would've worked somethin' out for my baby," he said. Holly wanted to smile, but she didn't, adding, "Oh, and I hope you didn't forget about Courtney's surprise party tomorrow night?" When Holly asked her eyes were somewhat wide in anticipation of his response. "No, I did *not* forget." Philip began rubbing her knees. "Good. Tracy offered to take us." "She has a car?" "No. Her boyfriend Karl will be driving." "You mean *one* of her boyfriend's," Philip teased. He looked up into Holly's eyes, smiling. She grinned back as he stood up, moved around behind her and placed his hands on her shoulder's. He could feel some tension so Philip began massaging her slowly, alternating his fingers up to her neck and back down to her shoulder's again. "So, what time does Tracy and her *boyfriend* want us to be ready?" he asked, still rubbing away. Holly couldn't help but giggle, her shoulders vibrating beneath his hands. "What's so funny?" Philip said, still rubbing away. "It tickles," she said, closing her eyes. He smiled, continuing the ritual he'd just made up. "I thought you were laughing about Tracy," Philip said. "No, cut it out. She doesn't owe any of us an explanation. She's not committed to any one of those guys." Holly paused for a second, wondering if she should disclose something humorous about her friend. "Trace is funny. You know what she does?" Holly asked. "What?" "She calls all the guys she dates "honey." This way she never makes the mistake of calling one of them another ones name." Philip laughed on cue. His appreciation of Tracy antics collided perfectly with Holly's. But he wasn't laughing solely because of what the hazel-eyed beauty just told him. Part of it was at the thought of getting rid of Selma Girard, He was doin' real good, he had to admit to himself. He had to give credit where credit was due. He knocked one out the box, now he just had to make the other one follow. Then he'll be all Holly's.

Chapter Twenty

Plandome Manor was a unique kind of Long Island. A treasure all its own. At least it was to Holly. She always enjoyed coming out to the Benjamin residence, enjoyed the breath-taking scenery: large mansions with Olympic-size swimming pools and impeccably manicured lawns, the picturesque golf course, The Whitney boathouse; but most of all she enjoyed passing by the three-hundred-year old Nicoll manor house. It was a magnificent Colonial, currently under new ownership, a few blocks away from Vanessa and Courtney's home which happened to tell a story each and every time she saw it. Today, the tale was filled with an even blend of smiles and tears. As the black Range Rover made its way down the tree-shaded road, the sun hitting it once in a while through a break in the trees, Holly shifted in her seat, keeping the house in clear view a little while longer. As she stared, taking it in fully for the first time, examining everything from the roof to the original shutters on the windows then to the emerald greenery with a few visually-pleasing splashes of color, surrounding it, she stored what she'd known about it in an area of her mind ordinarily used to store the bad experiences she'd encountered. She felt it necessary to share, necessary to make room. Because such history should not be dwelled on, but at the same token, it should never be forgotten. Holly proclaimed the information she learned about this particular haven that she could barely see now, significant. When she thought back to the day Courtney brought to her attention, the glory the splendid structure beheld, she could almost swear she heard the old calamitous Negro spiritual, "Swing high, swing low, sweet chariot" emerging alongside this valuable discernment. A fitting place for the deeply-troubled sound of the mis-treated bondsman. Because when her partners husband said, "Legend has it, that house has an underground railroad which was used to help slaves escape during the Civil War." Holly shuddered so hard that her concern for the rest of Courtney's educational account paled rapidly. She couldn't recollect anything else he'd said. Holly just wanted to ball herself up into a fetal position and cry like she would have as a little girl, falling off into a bottomless sleep afterward. But that was the old Holly. The reformed one, the thirty-three year old one who finally realized she had a "voice" big enough to be heard by the Grace of God, she chose to be strong and fearless just like those wronged field workers of the past. "What's my baby looking at?" Philip asked, clipping short her reverie. As his warm hand squeezed her thigh, bringing her body temperature back to its normal ninety-eight point two degrees, she turned, looking at him, gazing at him as if she'd forgotten where she was. And who she was with. For a while she had. It felt as though she, too, had been running away, fleeing fast and furiously, taking long, quick breaths like they were her last. In the place her mind had taken her to, Holly never ever wanted to look back at the darkness that lay behind so many years before. She would have had to stand in the midst of that great racial divide, being part master and slave, peering down at her feet. One foot would have been bare, dirty and bound with a shackle and the other prettied up and wearing the latest import. Yet they'd be prepared to move in the same direction as the Blacks and Whites today should be doing, searching as if their very lives depended on it. To find a way to make the world a better place. With God, all things are possible, the Holy Spirit reminded her.

Swallowing the ancestral pain, Holly lowered her tense-filled shoulders, leaning back into the soft, safe camel-colored leather seats, smelling again, as she did when she first climbed into it, the newness of Karl's jeep. "The beautiful homes, that's all," was her answer. "That's all," he repeated. And she nodded her head.

The two couples arrived at the Benjamin home a few minutes past seven. The early evening air was still thick and humid as it had been all day. As Holly placed her outreached hand into Philip's so he'd help her down from the vehicle, she glanced across the way at the Portman residence. They were friends of Courtney and Vanessa's. Holly saw that exorbitant cars were lining their immense circular driveway. "Joan and Brett must be having a party, too," she said, looking at Tracy as she, too jumped down from the jeep, but without assistance from Karl. Her tall, broad-shouldered date with the light yellow-toned skin and brown eyes was still on the driver's side stooping down, studying something on the door of his beloved four-wheel-drive. "No, they offered Vee the use of their driveway to throw Court off a little," Tracy said quietly. She then cut her eyes over at Karl, who was the only man she found hard to figure out. Naturally, with her love-them-and-leave-them reputation, Tracy couldn't admit this to anyone else. What would they think? Holly nodded to her friend's answer as she removed Courtney's gift from the jeep, passing the slightly cumbersome package to Philip who placed it under his arm, supporting the bottom half with his hand. Holly had wondered how Vanessa would keep her perceptive husband from suspecting anything once he arrived later. "What time is he expected?" Karl asked. He stood straight up, eyeing his date over the hood of the Range Rover as he engaged its alarm. "Eight o'clock!" Tracy snapped. She rolled her eyes at him and began smoothing down her taupe slip dress; first she did the front then the back, glancing at Karl once again when she was done as she adjusted her tiny evening purse on her wrist and Courtney's present in her arms. Philip chuckled at the episode, knowing that Tracy was upset because Karl didn't help her down. But he found himself doubled over in pain shortly after from Holly swiftly jabbing him in his stomach with her elbow. "Mind your business," she whispered through a slightly cracked mouth. "Should we have parked over there with the rest of the cars?" Karl asked, pointing across the road with his chin. Typically, he was unaware of his dates anger toward him. "No, *honey*. Courtney knows we're coming. Weren't you listening to me yesterday?" Tracy asked, her head tilted as if she was daring him to lie. Smiling, Karl extended his hand to her. He was still oblivious to her other upset. "Of course I was. Have I told you how good you look this evening, boo?" he asked, masterfully changing the subject. "Oh, and Holly you look pretty good, too," he added, tossing her one of his "get over" smiles. But Holly couldn't help but to overlook him while her eyes continued to hold Tracy's credulous ones, waiting to see what kind of answer would follow such an off-the-topic reply. She was hoping that Tracy would put him in his place. Tell him off for the both of them. Holly was tired of all his needless comments and rebuttals about his ex-wife to be or women in general during their drive from the city. As soon as Philip and Holly climbed into his jeep outside of her apartment building, Karl looked at his watch and told them they were late, following that with a, "It must've been hard for you to pull her away from the mirror, man," to Philip, who paid him no attention after seeing the hardness in his girlfriend's eyes. Give it to him, Trace, Holly thought. But, blushing, the short-haired woman fell head first into his trap. Tracy sashayed over to him, taking his hand in hers. She gave Karl a big kiss on the lips. "Yes, you did, honey. You told me that I looked so beautiful as soon as I opened my apartment door," she said and waved Philip and Holly on.

Inside of the large Split-level house overlooking the Manhasset Bay, the two couples stood in the enormous entryway talking to Vanessa, who was clad in a black silk georgette swing dress and black high-heeled strappy sandals, exposing her plump feet and crimson toe nails. Holly liked the way the full-figured womans hair was pulled back into a stylish chignon, giving precedence to the large pair-shaped diamond's glittering in her earlobes. "Those are exquisite, Vee," she told her as she took a closer peek. "Ha! Courtney knows he's got a good woman, girl," Vanessa said, a cocky expression on her face. Holly averted her attention toward Philip who mumbled, "Who told her that?" under his breath. She stifled a smile. "So it looks like just about everyone showed up," Tracy said. She was craning her neck as her eyes scanned the part of the house visible to the five of them. "Just about?" Vanessa said. She made another uncalled for face. "Everyone is here. The others are out back where the party is *supposed* to be." The full-figured woman looked at both couples, telling them that they were late. "You're nearly the last ones to arrive." The four new additions looked around in unison, seeing people chatting, smiling and sipping on white and red wines. Once Holly surveyed most of the guests, who were dressed in semi-formal attire, she realized that there were only a handful of which she didn't know. She could feel herself relaxing. The quickening she felt in her chest when they rang the doorbell had vanished like the heat and stickiness the air conditioning in the house wafted away. She couldn't stand that initial time when others would put on hold what they were doing: laughing, talking, pondering their next topic of conversation, in order to scrutinize the person or persons entering. "Go on in and mingle. You guys are standing over here like this was your first time at my house," Vanessa said. She shooed them down into the sunken living room by waving her chubby hands, palms down. "And the gifts go out back," she added. "Well, it's only my second time here," Karl whispered in Tracy's ear. "You mean your fourth," she said, sucking her teeth and handing him Courtney's present. Karl couldn't get anything right. Holly took Philip's arm, leading him in behind them. And the first group to happen into her range was Courtney's parents. A pleasant pair, who their son was a combination of. They were sitting on the sofa talking to a fair-skinned woman with salt and pepper-hued hair who was about Mr. and Mrs. Benjamin's age. At her left, tucked away in the corner, obscuring a huge photograph of the hostess and her husband on their wedding day was Vanessa's brother, Kevin Lawrence. He was an average-height man with a sienna complexion, deep-set brown eyes, close-cut fade and medium build. Waving at him, Holly glanced at the attractive woman with long, dangling braids and big white teeth accompanying him. She was grinning approvingly and nodding her head to whatever it was he was saying. The two seemed ideal for each other, Holly thought. She was glad for Kevin since he had been looking for someone to love. Nestled on the other side of the spacious room, a wing-back chair and table away from Kevin and his friend, were Vanessa's parents, Walter and Patricia Lawrence. They were a robust twosome filled with a genuine sweetness. Observing them, Holly could hear that Mr. Lawrence was holding a very informative discourse with three younger couples who appeared to be in their mid-to-late thirties. He was telling them another story about the Colonial house that Holly admired down the road. He mentioned something about an attorney, Martin. W. Littleton, whose name had become well known during some proverbial Harry K. Thaw trial to the small assembly. According to what Vanessa's father was saying, he, Harry K. Thaw, had murdered a famous architect, Standford White over a showgirl named Evelyn Nesbitt. Holly found this story almost as mesmerizing as the other one told by his son-in-law. She wanted to go over, as Tracy and Karl did, to listen and ask the knowledgeable Mr. Lawrence questions until she heard the glass doors, leading to the back of the house sliding open. Coming in, along with a melodic sound of a man and woman singing expertly to piano, was Courtney's law firm partner, Bernard Dunn and his lovely wife, Angela. They were both holding drinks. Holly smiled to herself when she saw Angela. She relished the time they spent together. The two woman hardly spoke other than on a special occasion such as the one they were at, but somehow it always seemed as though they remained connected. Not only was Angela a wonderful person: puissant, intelligent, confident and positively positive, she was also interracial. Born to a White mother and Black father. She, too, was finding her place in the world. Holly tried to get Angela's attention by continuing to stare until someone called her name. "How are you, sweetheart? Come here," said Mrs. Anita Benjamin. Turning in the direction of the soft welcoming voice, Holly smiled and she and Philip walked over to the trio. "I'm fine and yourself." The younger woman bent down, kissing Courtney's mother on the cheek. Then she shook his father's hand. "Hey, now, young lady. You forgot my sugar," he teased. Still, he got up, planting a wet kiss on both her cheeks. "I didn't forget about you, Mr. Benjamin," she said, grinning. "I know." He gazed at Holly through glasses similar to the ones his son wore, adding, "You're looking as gorgeous as ever." Holly was wearing a lavender sheath dress with silk shantung pumps in silver and her hair was swept up into an elegant French twist. "Thank you very much," she said. The smile on her face masked her earlier ambivalence about the ensemble she was clad in. "Sweetie, this is Ms. Ernestein Brown," said Mrs. Benjamin, talking to the younger woman. "She's a long-time friend of the family's and she's also Courtney's Godmother." "Oh," was what the hazel-eyed woman managed to say as the thought of this woman being her partners husbands "Godmother" remained in her mind. It was at that moment that she remembered how Courtney's parents were devout Christians. "It's a pleasure to meet you, Ms. Brown," Holly finally said, giving Ernestein Brown's hand a warm shake. "Likewise, darlin'. I would've met you sooner, but unfortunately I couldn't make Vanessa and Courtney's weddin' 'cause I was suddenly attacked with a severe case of influenza," said the fair-skinned woman as she glimpsed Anita Benjamin without turning her head completely toward her. "Nor could I make that big New Year's Eve celebration they had." Ernestein wanted to make sure her friend was listening. Of course Courtney's Godmother was well aware of Anita's being tired of hearing how wrong she thought Vanessa was for her *only* son and child, for that matter, but this was an issue she had intended to bring up as long as she drew breath. She convinced herself that she was being Holy Spirit led. My children knew who and who not to bring home to meet me, Ernestein told herself. Thank God they're led of the Lord, too. And look at how satisfied they are with *our* choices. Shaking her head, she sighed. How many times did she have to tell Anita that a mother's job was never done? Praying without ceasing is the answer, she'd tell her good friend who seemed like she'd be listening each and every time she'd remind her. Lifting herself from her short daze, Ms. Brown continued at Holly with, "But, I'm so glad I *finally* got to meet you today!" When Holly nodded Ernestein Brown began to admire how striking the young woman before her was: eyes and hair just like a Mississippi sunset, she mused. If her youngest boy, Darnell hadn't started courting Rachel, she would have persuaded Holly to fly back down with her so they could be set up. But, she told herself, God assured her that He was the One Who put Darnell and Rachel together. Hmmm, so why does she sense that Holly belonged. "Now who's this?" Courtney's father asked.

He was pointing to Philip with his thumb. "I'ma friend of your sons," Philip said, summonsing Mr. Benjamin's focus. "The one who always beats him at racquet ball?" the older man asked. Philip flashed him his pearly whites and the three older people laughed as he shook their hands in turn. Holly only smiled because she could see Vanessa watching them from the doorway of the living room. They probably weren't working the room fast enough for her. "So, you're the young man whose been giving my boy a run for his money. It takes big money to be a part of that club?" Mr. Benjamin asked. He was still chuckling when he gave Philip a hearty pat on the back. "Yeah, it does and yes, I'm the culprit," he said, smiling. Holly saw him turn too, looking over at Vanessa then back at her husband's parents. Philip must have felt her glare as well, she thought. "Well, it's about time he met his match," Mr. Benjamin said, grinning. He glanced down at his wife then back at the younger couple. "Tell them, Anita. Don't I always say that losing can be good for the spirit? If we won all the time, we'd become bored. Complacent." "Oh, stop that, Richard," Mrs. Benjamin said, her mouth twisted in disbelief. "You only say that when you're the one losing. Courtney got all that ridiculous boasting from your side of the family. Remember," she laughed, "the stink doesn't roam too far from the skunk." Holly had to laugh as well when she saw the way Mrs. Benjamin leaned into Ernestein Brown, both their shoulders bumping into each other's and moving up and down, as they giggled simultaneously at what she'd said to her husband. "Yeah well, you better thank our Heavenly Father that he also inherited '*my side of the families'* legal giftings." Richard Benjamin shot back as he straightened his navy linen suit coat on his shoulders. "Because if we'd left his profession up to you, I don't know what kind of absurd turn it would've taken." Mr. Benjamin took a quick glimpse behind him, grumbling as he looked back at his wife. "That's right, make your boast be in the Lord," she told him not realizing that her husband was looking at her for another reason. "You've already ruined his chances of marrying a woman of God." Holly and Philip exchanged "uh-oh" glances and announced they were going out back. "We want to put Courtney's gift out there with the others," Holly said, nodding down at the superbly wrapped present Philip was holding. "Okay, sweetie. We'll catch up with the two of you later," said Mrs. Benjamin, smiling. "All right, you take care of that jewel, you hear," said Mr. Benjamin to Philip, referring to Holly. "Absolutely," Philip said, grinning. He shook the older gentlemen's hand, sealing the deal. "You see, Anita. That there is a wife," Richard Benjamin emphasized as he sat back down next to his wife. And Ernestein Brown nodded her head in agreement. She would have come out with a bold-faced lie and told Courtney her momma had died all over again before she would have attended a wedding she didn't believe in. Humph, that fat heifer would never hear congratulations come out of her mouth. Vanessa ain't but one way just like Magnolia Street down in Biloxi, Ernestein mused.

Before Holly exited the house for the yard, she skimmed the nice-size throng of people inside, searching for Angela Dunn. There she was, standing up in the entryway chitchatting with her husband and Vanessa. The two womens eyes met at the same time. They both smiled, waving one another over. "Philip," Holly said, tugging on the back of his shirt. He was sliding the glass door open. "Wait a minute. I want to say hello to someone dear to me first." Seeing the grinning woman, with the Brazilian like features Holly was referring to, heading their way, Philip nodded, telling Holly he'd meet her outside. "My arm's getting tired, baby." He wanted to put Courtney's present down. "Okay, go ahead," she said, spinning back around to greet Angela. "Holly, it is always such a thrill to see you!" The two women embraced, rocking in each others arms for a while. "How have you been?" Holly asked as they disengaged. "Great. Everything is just great,"Angela said, shrugging, her even white teeth showing as she formed a smile. "You know, we shouldn't have to wait for Vanessa or Courtney to bring us together. We're grown women." Holly nodded in agreement. "You're one-hundred percent right." "Bernie told me he saw you a little over a week ago," Angela said. "Yes, Vee and I had stopped at Ellington's for a light dinner then we met Courtney up at the office. I'm sorry I didn't call you like I told him I would....." "Don't worry about it, Holly. You know I know that things come up sometimes. Have you seen what Vanessa's done outside?" "No, not yet. I did hear the music." "Oh my goodness, yes. She hired a husband and wife singing team. *Holly,* they sang a song they wrote. It was *so* beautiful." "Really?" "Yes. And the buffet is fabulous. Everything from Beluga to fruit and cheese. She has tables for two and a few for four and more with little votives in the center of them lined up by the water. Courtney is going to be elated over the amount of effort she put into this little shindig." Holly smiled. "So," Angela said. Holly surmised by her body language and facial expression that the next thing out of her mouth wasn't going to be about how outstanding a decorating job Vanessa had supervised. Angela's arms were folded across her chest, she was tapping her right foot against the floor, and the grin on her lips spelled personal question. "Who was that handsome piece of work I saw you with?" she asked. The two women watched as Philip placed the gift, alongside the others, on a long table covered in an ivory linen tablecloth, then walk over to the bar, getting on line. "My, uh, boyfriend, Philip Williams." Angela nodded, stroking her chin with her forefinger and thumb. "Hmmm, that name sounds familiar." Pausing briefly, the two women looked at each other, saying, "racquet ball" at the same time and laughed. "Bernie could not get over the fact that he beat both him and Courtney so badly," Angela said, her voice lowering to a whisper. "Your Philip's got my precious baby going to the New York Health and Racquet Club at least two, three days a week after work, trying to better his game. Don't let either of them know I told you that." Holly grinned. Holding up her right hand, she did the childlike cross your heart hope to die. " I won't, but I'd like to see them play one of these days," she said, still chuckling a little even though she felt a subtle conviction from the Holy Spirit, commanding her not to even play around with death referring to her so-called childlike crossing of her heart hoping to die. "And what are you two giggling about?" asked a boom of a voice. "Must be up to mischief." The two women turned to find Bernard Dunn approaching them with a smile. And as he got closer, Holly thought she felt the hardwood floors shake beneath her feet. Bernard was a massive man, big hands, big feet, and thick neck, with skin as dark as milkless coffee. The stubble framing his upper lip, chin and chiseled jawline only enhanced the richness of his complexion. Holly could recollect Courtney always getting a kick out of describing the alarmed looks on the faces of the opposing attorneys when they'd meet counselor Dunn for the first time. "It was like the smell of defeat filtered up through their tight-buttoned collars," he'd say with a brilliant grin, then, "You would have thought we were all stepping into a boxing ring or onto a football field instead of a courtroom." Holly smiled from the thought of that as Angela's powerhouse of a husband leaned down, kissing her on the cheek. And when he moved back into position, next to his adoring wife, Holly observed the way he settled his seemingly heavy arm around Angela's delicate shoulders while she wrapped hers arms around his waist. Sometimes Holly's investigative training told her that her friend prospect chose to marry a man who was blacker than the nighttime sky just to prove to herself that she had no identity problems. Impossible, Holly mused. She gazed at the elusive, but loving glances Angela and Bernard tossed one another, like they'd just gotten married yesterday, and she had to stop herself from saying impossible once again, this time out loud. Her friend was mixed not mixed up. Holly was the one who'd found it hard to come to the conclusion of who she was sometimes. It had to be because the essence of her face resembled no one elses. Black or White. "We're *all* like snowflakes, babygirl. *Different*, but special in our owns way. That's the way God intended it to be," Holly's mother used to say. Different, although some thought that she looked a lot like her mother except for her sunlike colored features, Holly told herself. She knew now that it was hard for Cynthia Reed to explain the uniqueness found in her daughter's features, especially since her child was produced in the name of love. Adoration was the only thing the older woman saw when she looked into Holly's tearing eyes. "And love has no shame, babygirl. You were born out of a deep, unbreakable love. Your daddy and me were so full of joy. Always, always remember that," her mother said as well on many, many occasions.

"Oh, so I guess it's a secret then?" Bernard said. He was still trying to figure out what it was they found humor in. "No," Angela said, shaking her head. "Holly was just telling me that her boyfriend, Philip...." "Yeah, where is that guy?" Bernard asked, interrupting his wife's explanation. "He owes me a rematch." Holly smiled. "He's on line at the bar." The three of them peered outside at Philip, who was now on his way back inside, cradling a beer in one hand and a glass of cranberry juice in the other. Holly slid the door open for him. "Hey, big B," Philip said, smiling at Bernard Dunn. He passed Holly the cranberry juice, taking a sip of his foam-edged drink at the same time. "What's up?" said Bernard. "Nothin', really, man. Same ole, same ole." "All right, lets cut to the chase. When are we getting together for our long-awaited rematch?" asked Bernard, rubbing his hands together in anticipation. He then glanced down at his wife who had cleared her throat. "Oh, I'm sorry," Bernard said, pulling his spouse closer to him. He wrapped his arm around her shoulders again. "Angela, this is Philip Williams. And Phil, *this* is my loving wife of three years." Bernard planted a kiss on her forehead. "Nice to meet you," Philip and Angela said in unison. "Well?" Bernard asked Philip in reference to his previous question. "I don't know, man. Business in boomin' right about now." "Yeah, but you know what they say about all work and no play? Let's hook up some time next week," Bernard said. "Has he been losin' sleep over this?" Philip teased, looking at Angela. Both she and Holly laughed. Bernard had to crack a smile, too. "Never. Don't flatter yourself," he said.

The telephone rang, silencing the room. Vanessa waved a few people who had continued to talk quiet as she made her way down into the living room for the phone on the mahogany table behind the sofa. "Hi, honey. Where are you?" asked the full-figured woman into the receiver. "No, I don't need anything. Just come straight in. Okay see you in a few minutes." Vanessa hung up. "That was Courtney calling from Shelter Rock road....." "From where?" she heard Philip asked Holly. "Do you mind?" Vanessa asked him, her hands resting on her substantial hips. After giving Philip Williams her best possible "don't mess with me look" she addressed her guests once again, saying, "I'm going to round everyone else up and get them inside." The full-figured woman crossed the room to the glass doors, sliding them open. She signaled the pianist to stop playing and formed a funnel around her mouth with her hands. "I'd like you all to step inside. Courtney should be here momentarily," she announced.

Holly, Philip and the Dunns' decided to find a hiding space in the corner, near Kevin and his friend Pam. The six of them spoke briefly until Vanessa, who was at the big picture window, which faced the front of the house, peeping threw the blinds, gestured that they were making too much noise. She couldn't concentrate was her claim. Shortly after the full-figured woman hushed the room, they all heard the revving engine of Courtney's sky-blue BMW Z3 turning into the driveway. The light from his headlights brushed up against the house before he came to a complete halt. Man! He'd forgotten all about Tracy and Karl saying they were going to stop by. Hitting the steering wheel with his hand, frustrated, Courtney turned off the radio, took a deep breath, got out the car. He slammed the door and set the alarm. As he stood still, eyeing the sleek Range Rover parked beside his wife's midnight- blue Mercedes and the silver BMW he intended on getting rid of, memories of his wanting to buy one just like it once he and Vanessa had their first child, entered his mind. Wasn't that part of the "American Dream"? he asked himself in dismay. Sure, it was. Every suburban family had to own a vehicle big enough to hold the husband, the wife and their two point five kids. Oh, and let's not forget the dog and cat. Sighing, he told himself to disregard that notion as he sniffed back tears so determined to flood out of his eyes like a monsoonal down pour. He really couldn't accept the fact that his plans to expand his family had turned into the "American Nightmare" with a snap of a finger, flashing before his eyes like the slides in a toy view master. Courtney thought, no, he *knew* everything was "all good". After all he and Vanessa had been pregnant once before. But, Dr. Stone said it wasn't that uncommon. "The body tends to transform itself, much to our own disbelief as we start to age, and unfortunately, your change resulted in a low sperm count at the prime of your life." The older distinguished man paused, then, "unless, there wasn't really a pregnancy before. Maybe your wife was mistaken. Well, in any case, there are, however, some options. You and your wife are still young. Think about it. Go home and discuss what we've talked about before with her and call me with your decision at your earliest convenience," was Dr. Daniel Stones closing statement, the shaky pen he held in his hand was his only display of empathy. Courtney sighed. Where was the God of his youth? He made thirty-four years old today. Some gift, he thought. To find out that he couldn't make a baby. Was Vanessa's miscarriage a sign? he asked himself as another painful sigh escaped his lips. Should he have walked away from this debatable marriage back then? Was that his opportunity? Stop thinking like this, man, he warned himself. Why didn't he just take the good doctors' advice and bring Vanessa along with him for support? He'd realized his mistake of keeping this whole testing to himself as soon as he stepped foot inside of the hospital that afternoon. Why did he give the doctors suggestion a second thought in the first place? This way he wouldn't have to tell her himself. It would have been all over with by now. He and his wife would have said their piece, cried together and assured one another that they'd make due. Perhaps even say they'd adopt a "needy" child or two if those "options" that Dr. Stone mentioned didn't prevail. He shook his head, knowing that was *his* idea of a suitable ending. Vanessa's, on the other hand, wouldn't be so easy to conclude. She'd probably just make matters worse by poking out her lips and questioning his manhood. Yeah, his wife could be cruel when she wanted to be. Down right vindictive. Knowing her she'd lunge at his throat while calling him a fagot. It had happened once before. Vanessa never looked at him or respected him as a man from the get go. All she ever saw when she happened upon my face was stability, he told himself. Courtney shook his head again. Yep, her reaction was anyone's guess. Never fully understanding Vanessa's complex ways dampened his hopes of hearing, "Don't worry, honey. We'll make it. We'll find a way because 'together we stand divided we fall.'" Those were her endearing words to him on their honeymoon in that luxurious Paris hotel room overlooking the Seine. Vanessa said he seemed unsure of his decision to marry her. Seemed, he thought, little did she know, he was unsure. But, certain that he was doing the right thing before she lost their baby. Taking another deep breath, Courtney began patting his pockets for his keys. He pulled them out, pausing before mounting the stairs to the house. He couldn't help but to see all the cars over at the Portman place. Brett and Joan had everything, he told himself, his eyes drifting over toward the tri-cycle and dirt bike in front of their neighbor's side door. Courtney almost smiled, surmising that the two boys had abandoned their rides for something much more enticing indoors. A homemade cookie or a piece of chocolate cake. Yeah, that had to be it. Joanie loved to bake. I should go over there and have myself a much-needed drink, he told himself. Maybe it would put him at ease. But, after glancing down at his clothes he realized he wasn't dressed appropriately. How would he look crashing someone's party wearing this? Courtney started up his stairs. At the top, he took another deep breath, this one longer than the rest. What the ..., he thought. The Portman's wouldn't care about his casual appearance (grey *Black Dog* T-shirt he'd purchased on Martha's Vineyard, khaki cargo shorts, white deck sneakers and a tan baseball cap). They were the most sincere and open-minded White folks he'd ever met. The only ones, in fact, who'd had the decency to ring his and Vanessa's doorbell, bearing a coconut cake and a smile, when the Black couple first moved into the exclusive neighborhood. And, although the golf club down the road couldn't specify enough how *honored* they were to have Courtney and Vanessa Benjamin as members, he knew good and well he wouldn't have been able to get in without Brett's help. No one in that family has ever looked at him or his wife with cocked-eyes. He was going to go over there and have himself that drink. Taking all three steps leading down from his house at once, Courtney stuck his keys back down into his pocket, straightened his baseball cap and headed down the driveway for the Portman house.

Back inside, Vanessa could not believe her eyes. "What the....?" she said, the opening in the blinds widening. "What is it, Vanessa?" Joan Portman asked. "He's going over to your house." "Oh no....." "Wait, wait. He stopped." Vanessa let out a sigh of relief. "He's coming back this way," she said, narrowing the space in the blinds again.

Courtney changed his mind. He thought it best to just go home and ask their guests to excuse both him and his wife then he'd ask Vanessa to join him upstairs in their bedroom. Anesthetizing the problem wasn't going to make it go away. He'd fill Vee in on his, well their, depressing news now and face the demons, trying to destroy them head on. No, maybe he'd just slid in, sit down in their circle and participate in whatever conversation they'd been holding. Pretend like nothing was wrong until later. Because knowing Tracy

Mann she'd think he was taking Vee up there for a quickie. Let me just go inside and play it by ear, he told himself.

"All right, everyone get into place. He's climbing the stairs again," Vanessa whispered. Fixing the blinds, she inched away from the window, moving closer to the door. Holly leaned forward gazing through an opening in Pam's braids. She was looking at Courtney's silhouette through the half stain-glass door. Her instincts advised her instantly that there was something wrong with him: the way he paused, fidgeting with the keys in his hands. Skimming the room for his loved ones, Holly began searching their eyes to see whether they, too, had sensed something out of place with the birthday boy. But they were all oblivious. Every single one of their faces brimming with "we can't wait to hear ourselves shout happy birthday or surprise." Holly moved back, shading her vision of Courtney as soon as she heard the key turn into the door. Shutting it behind him quietly, Courtney paused, wondering why he heard no talking, heard no "honey, is that you?" He heard no TV and stereo playing at the same time as they always did when he got home later than Vanessa. She couldn't stand to be alone in a quiet house. Everybody and their grandmother knew that. Courtney crossed the entryway slowly, stopping at the top of the stairs and jumping back from the earth-shattering roar of, *"Surprise!!!!"* arriving from the living room. "Happy birthday, honey," Vanessa said once the great excitement quieted down. She bumped Courtney's parents out of the way, ascending the steps before them to her husband, who appeared to be a bit more than astonished: his eyes darted around the room, his mouth formed an O-shape. He felt humiliated by his prior thoughts. Kissing his wife on the lips, he removed his baseball cap and said, after swallowing the emotion surfacing in his throat. "Vee, you don't know how much this means to me." Now, he breathed, asking himself how could he turn around and tell her that she'll never be the mother she'd been longing to be ever since they'd met? "So, are you as shocked as you appear to be?" Vanessa asked her husband, disrupting his daze. He nodded and she took the cap out of his hand, "Good. Go in and mingle." Courtney pecked her again on the mouth and descended the stairs, sinking down into the sea of grinning faces. "Thanks for coming," he said, shaking hands and exchanging kisses on the cheeks with his guests as he made his way through the path they'd formed. "I had to watch your father every step of the way. He wanted to tell you about today," Anita Benjamin said. She pulled the back of her son's head down with both hands, her fingertips getting lost in the thick of his dark hair as she planted generous wet kisses on his cheeks. "Was it hard, Pop?" Courtney asked his father, who waved his hand. "You should know by now not to listen to your momma," Richard Benjamin said, resisting a smile as he hugged his boy. Courtney laughed, patting his dear old dad on the back. He spotted Ernestein Brown. "Ma Bee, what are you doing here?" he asked, freeing himself from his father's grasp in search of hers. The salt and peppered haired woman extended her arms. "What do you mean by *what am I doing here*?" she asked, mocking her Godson's voice. "I wouldn't miss any of *your* special days, darlin'. You ought to know that by now." They hugged. But, as Ernestein held her Godson close, she knew he had every right to be surprised at her presence. "How's Keith, Darnell and Robin doing?" Courtney asked, unengaging himself from her. "Oh, they're just fabulous. They all wished they could've come, but you know how that goes? Did your mother tell you that Keith and Penney are having a baby?" Courtney shook his head no. It was all he could do since his mind had gone back outside to whimper some more in his previous despair. "That's right your Ma Bee is goin' to be a grandmother. I can't wait." Feeling as though he'd been stabbed in the heart, Courtney stood there quietly, trying to appear happy for her. However, it didn't work. He could feel his eyes becoming watery, his body becoming feeble from the abrupt pain. "Yes, isn't that nice, sweetheart? Your father and I are looking forward to hearing those Blessed words, too, from you and Vanessa, one of these days," Anita said, rubbing her son's back. "Don't rush him," said Richard, because I wouldn't know how to love the baby who fell from that, that...... woman, he thought. Fortunately, Courtney did not have to speak. His parents had begun arguing the why's and why nots of someday becoming grandparents while Ernestein Brown stood in the middle of them like a referee. Courtney eased away, walking through the commending crowd, unconsciously.

The line at the buffet was thinning, but the one at the bar continued to grow. People had scurried over to get a last-minute drink when Vanessa announced, a second ago, that after the next song there were going to be some speeches given in honor of her husband's birthday. Holly and Philip stood up from their table to dance just as the slow melody began. The gentlemen singer closed his eyes and belted out his version of "I'm Only Human" while his wife sat at a small table along the side of the makeshift stage eating lemon chicken and pasta primavera, being extra careful not to spill any of it on her peach beaded halter-top gown. "Excuse us, guys," Holly said to the Benjamins' and the Dunns' as she and Philip sauntered on to the dance floor, finding just enough room in between Vanessa's parents, who were doing a simple two-step and another young couple, who only seemed to be moving their upper bodies while their feet stood rooted, like the roses surrounding them all. Grabbing Holly's right hand with his left, Philip started swaying their arms, in sync, to the rhythmic motion of the singer's voice. Then letting it go, he placed his hand at the small of her back, easing her closer to him. This was his chance to get her undivided attention. Most of the night, although it wasn't her fault, Holly had been yanked and pulled in every other direction, and now, he wanted her to himself. Yeah, he knew his baby was popular, but at this point, he just wanted her to notice *him*, to reassure *him* that she was still his and would always be *his*. Holly hadn't really looked at Philip the way he wished she would have since they'd left her apartment. Courtney Benjamin had become the main attraction throughout the evening. He loved when she stared into his eyes, reaching right down inside of him as if she were performing some kind of secret magic on his heart, tugging at all the right strings. He wanted her to do those kinds of tricks to him forever. Keep him on a natural high, forever. Later he'd bring up the possibility of them getting married. *Whoa!* Philip thought, Mr. and Mrs. Philip Hayes Williams. He had to admit that it sounded pretty good to him.

Smiling, at Philip as they moved easily to the warming sound, Holly followed suit, letting him lead her as he wanted to, for now. She was having fun.

By the time the bar line was no more, and everyone was comfortable and seated, Vanessa stood up on stage adjusting the microphone. She gave a quick, gracious welcome to the party goers and turned the focus over to Courtney's parents, who started out by telling a sweet and uplifting story about the way their son taught himself how to ride a bike once he found out that the boy two doors down from them knew how to and he was nearly "What, Richard? Was it one or two..." Anita Benjamin asked her husband. He filled in the blank quickly, saying, "The boy was a year younger than Courtney." And the older couple smiled down at their son, who smiled back. It was the second smile Holly had witnessed on his face the entire evening. But, despite that brilliant smile he found a way to muster up, something about him appeared to be depressed to her. Troubled, worried, she wasn't sure. "Well, the point of the story is," Anita said to the crowd. "to tell our son how proud we are to be his mom and dad. Sweetheart," she found Courtney's stare once again. "in you we see a strength and integrity which makes you who you are. A leader. A real go getter while always remaining humble." Anita looked at her husband and he glanced down at his shoes so his wife eyed the audience again. "Like our Jesus... We've seen it ever since he was a baby. I'd tell our family and friends 'this boy is going to be a force to reckon with'..... *I did.* And through the years his father and I have chosen to take the back seat. We let the Word of God do exactly what only it can do... Not fail!" Richard raised his head, glaring down at Vanessa. If he'd seen that coming, he would have grabbed the wheel so fast. "We let the Holy Spirit steer the way, *letting* Him steer the way God destined for Courtney." She looked at their son and went on to say, "on countless occasions the Lord through your precious life, sweetheart, has shown us sceneries we, on our own, would have truly missed." Anita gazed at Richard again, placing his hand in hers. Then she looked back down at their son, saying, "And for *that* we give a heartfelt thanks to our Heavenly Father." Together, Richard and Anita said, "We love you, son." Courtney, stifling tears, thanked them by placing his hand on his chest, patting his heart.

Everyone clapped as the senior Benjamins left the stage, Richard in front of Anita, his hands laced behind his back.

Some sniffling and aw's were heard under the breaths of some of the people in attendance as Courtney's parents took their seats.

Then the Lawrences stood up there, saying a few words then the Portmans followed by Ernestein Brown, the Dunns, one thirty-something year-old couple, Shirley and Roger Grant and last but not least Tracy Mann. And after all was spoken and the applause faded to no sound at all, Vanessa sprung up making her way back up to the stage. Lapsing as she gathered her thoughts, she took a noticeable deep breath, licked her lips and smiled nervously when her eyes made contact with her husbands. "Well, as many of you know, I'm not very good at keeping secrets," she began. There was some laughter and some uh-huh's. Holly nodded, smiled and rubbed Philip's knee. He was fidgeting immensely beside her, like a child who wanted out of a stroller. "Stop that you guys, I'm not so bad," Vanessa said, giggling. Then smoothing down her wind-blown dress, she said, "All right, where should I start? Okay...... I think I should just come right out and say it." She cleared her throat, placing both hands on her protruding stomach. "I'd like you all to be the first to know." Vanessa, paused again, looked at Courtney and smiled as if she wanted him to come up there beside her. He just grinned back with his eyebrows furrowed. "that my husband and I are expecting our first child!" First, a simultaneous gasp whisked around, mingling with the air, then a flutter of "congratulations" in all voice types filled the yard. Holly leaned forward, kissing Courtney on the cheek. But his smile wasn't there anymore. His signature radiance had dimmed into a mere flicker of light, like the ones in the votives ornamenting the table tops. What was ailing this man? she wondered as she slid back, resting her hand in Philip's clammy palm. "Are you okay?" Holly asked him, her eyes rising toward the perspiration beads on his forehead. The ones now cascading down the sides of his expressionless face. Nodding, Philip dabbed at the falling sweat with the napkin he had wrapped around his beer mug. "It's so hot out I thought I saw the devil standing on line at the bar," he finally said, grinning. All of a sudden, Holly thought, remembering that he'd told her how good the breeze felt blowing off the water when they first walked outside together. It made her wonder a bit about what was going on with Philip. Holly sighed. Facing the stage again, she managed a smile when she saw the way Vanessa's parents had rushed up there beside their daughter, all three crying tears of joy. Then it occurred to her that Courtney was the missing link. He was still in his seat, hunching forward, his elbows pressing against his knees, his head bent down, his glasses in his hand. He was probably overwhelmed, Holly told herself. "Go on up there beside your wife, daddy," she whispered to the back of his head. Courtney looked over his shoulder at her, holding her warm eyes with his bewildered squinting ones. Then, he turned away, sliding his glasses back on his face and adjusting the thin wires behind his ears. Holly observed the way Courtney stood, real mechanical like, dragging himself up on stage. Why didn't he listen to the beat of his own heart? he asked himself, knowing all along that the marriage he and Vanessa shared was nothing more than a lie. The time has finally arrived for him to decide on the exit he was going to execute, freeing him from this demising institution. Which one, out of all the ways he'd thought up over the years, would bring him the greatest amount of pleasure?

Looking at Vanessa, Courtney knew that what *they* made, was a mistake.

"And when did you find this out?" Tracy Mann asked, peering up at her pregnant friend. "I'd like to know that too," Courtney said in a calm, collect manner. Almost too calm and collect. Vanessa laughed and draped her arm through his. "A few days ago. It was hard holding out on everybody, *trust* me," said the full-figured woman. The audience chuckled. "Come on up here," Vanessa said to her in-laws. Anita was wiping her happy tears away with her husband's handkerchief while he sat there gritting down on his dentures, the fake teeth shifting in his mouth from the pressure. "Richard, don't do this," Anita whispered, urging him to stand as she was now doing. "Pop, you don't have to, really" Courtney said. He motioned for his father to stay put. "It's really not necessary. Ma, you stay there, too." Vanessa cut her eyes at her husband. "You heard me correct," he said, abandoning her offended stare.

"Are you going to find out what you're having?" asked Joan Portman. "Uh, we have to discuss that," Vanessa said half smiling. "So, that's why you've been so health conscious," Holly said, grinning as she added, "In any event, I'd like to say something to the both of you, if you don't mind." She stood up in front of her chair, holding her glass of cranberry juice in the air. The couple in question nodded in unison. "We've known each other for a long time. Right?" They nodded again. "And being a witness to your highs and lows I'd like to tell you both *today* that I hope to have a relationship which fulfills me like yours does you, some day. And, I really hope that "*some day*" is soon." Holly finished with a wink and Brett Portman sprung up, exclaiming, "Here, here!" and everyone with a drink took an agreeable sip. She hopes the "someday" is soon? Philip thought as he lifted his beer mug to his grinning mouth. On stage, Courtney sighed and lowered his head. Where was her God?

It was the beautiful songstresses turn to take center stage while her husband took his break. Crooning Erkah Badu's "Next Lifetime" came naturally to the diva in peach. Below her the floor was filled with couples wrapped in tight embraces, rocking gently to the blues-filled beat. Holly felt a very aroused Philip careening her body along with his, his hands moving about her back in a seductive way. It made her uncomfortable and the title of the song, had her thinking about her Salvation. Being saved made her a new creation in Christ. This was her new life, but was she living it? Through the crowd, she saw Vanessa coaxing Courtney onto the dance floor. He seemed reluctant, still down about something, his head someplace else. She winced a little when he caught her gaze unexpectedly as if he suspected she knew there was something bothering him. The two of them managed a weak smile, his eyes lowering before she could help Vanessa out by waving him over beside herself and Philip. After a few strenuous notes fell effortlessly from the singers glazed-shined lips the song came to an end, but her poetic alto remained forever etched in the minds of the listeners. Everyone applauded peach dresses sensational vocal cords as her husband emerged, standing next to his wife. The two acknowledged one another with a smile, eyed the pianist, who by tickling the ivories, producing another sultry song, a very familiar and romantic one. The soulful collaboration of "Endless Love" was the singing duos best, and final ballad of the evening. Philip and Holly sat down at a table along with Tracy, Karl, Vanessa, Courtney and both their parents', listening to the music-making combination as everyone else got ready to leave. In droves the guests stopped by their table, wishing the birthday boy many more happy and healthy ones. He smiled and thanked them all ever so politely. Like the singers, there was nothing off key in his tone. He was still playing it cool, enjoying the ride as he plotted his marital departure. But just as they took their seats, he already in his, Holly saw Courtney continuously altering his position. He was leaning forward, elbows on knee's, pushing himself back against the chair, his hands folded in his lap as

if he didn't want to be there, like he had somewhere else to go --
urgently. He finally stood after the last person said good-bye, asking
Philip to walk with him over to the bar before they shut it down.
"You want anything?" Philip asked Holly, who said no as she bobbed
her head lightly to the memory-provoking tune. The couple's
rendition of the song had remarkable similarities to the one Luther
Vandross and Mariah Carey had done together. Holly had been
hanging on every lyric, every high and low note and every
enchanting gesture of the calming melody as if the words meant
something more to her. Well, at one time they did. Because *this* was
the song she and Bradford called "theirs." They were supposed to be
"endless lovers." Supposed to make it work no matter how hopeless
the relationship was. Enchanting, Holly thought. How that word was
so perfect a description of what they had. She and Bradford were
indeed living in a fantasy world. Sighing silently, she told herself
how glad she was that their burdening of one another ended,
making her want to laugh at the way the thought came out. But,
funny as it may have sounded in her head, she vowed never to be a
fool for a fine face ever again. If those great big chestnut-colored
eyes, juicy lips and that rock hard body never crossed her path
again, she wouldn't be missing a thing, she told herself. "Baby, you
sure? There's coffee over there, too," Philip said, startling her. She
thought he would have been on his way back, drink in hand by now.
"No, no. You go ahead. I'm fine," she said, a part of her thoughts still
lost in the song as she watched her man leave her side. Philip was a
good guy, she had to admit to herself. But not the one she'd
envisioned herself marrying. She paused, knowing that was the
Holy Spirit who placed the thought into her mind. His Mind, Holly
reminded herself. I belong to God. I am not my own. She paused
again, taking a deep breath.

"You guys were terrific," Vanessa said. She stood up and headed
over to the edge of the stage, shaking the entertainer's hands in turn
when they finished. Hearing Philip and Courtney nearing the table
made Holly look in their direction, catching a glimpse of a familiar-

looking face closing the sliding doors behind himself. Her partners husband, in tuned as he was, followed her glance. He shook his head and inhaled when he saw who it was. "Could you give this to my *wife*?" Courtney asked. He shoved a glass of cranberry juice into Philip's outreached hand and hurried off in the opposite direction, toward the late arrival. Holly could feel herself clenching down on her teeth as she overheard Courtney questioning how this person got in. He'd entered the house as the other guests were leaving. The man explained with his crooked smile, and said, "Happy birthday, bro'," like all was now okay and like his trespassing alibi was supposed to wipe away the disapproval on Courtney's face. "Who is that?" Anita Benjamin asked. Holly forced a smile on her face. She would try to make the best of this personal infringement, even if it killed her. She stiffened as she thought this will not kill me, she told herself. I will live and not die to declare the works of the Lord! "Isn't that Bradford, sweetie?" Patricia Lawrence asked Holly. She didn't answer. Not on purpose. She was just afraid of her own voice at the time. "Uh-huh," Tracy said in her place. She glanced at Holly, shrugging. Glaring over at Vanessa, who said something to annoy Philip as he gave her the drink in his hand, Holly shook her head even though she went unnoticed. The woman loved chaos, she reasoned about the full-figured woman. It was that simple. "Excuse me. I'm going to the ladies room." Holly stood without looking at anyone in particular and walked off toward the house.

"How you doin', Sunshine?" Bradford said, blocking the glass doors so she wouldn't escape him. Holly hadn't seen him since they'd broken up. Didn't want to ever see him again, either. Wasn't that what she just told herself minutes ago? She glared at him, her lips pressed tightly together, her arms folded across her chest as she watched him cover his mouth. "I'm sorry, but I'm so used to calling you that." He chuckled the chuckle she used to find irresistible. Used to, she thought. "Old habits die hard. I don't know what to call you now. I've been saying Sunshine for so long." Bradford was now smiling the smile that *used* to make her day, the smile he *used* to give her when he'd ask whether or not she trusted him. What else was she supposed to say, no? Even though that would have been the truth. "Holly, I had no idea.....," Courtney said. She held up her hand, silencing him. "Holly. You could call me Holly, since it is my name," she said to her ex-boyfriend. He smiled again, broader. "Will you be all right?" Courtney asked her. It took a moment but she nodded and Vanessa's husband slowly disappeared. Holly could see Philip watching her via his reflection in the glass doors. He asked Courtney who that was she was talking to. "I'll give him this later," Bradford said, referring to the gift in his hand. Holly's eyes moved, landing on his sorry-looking face. She began to study him. To her his chestnut-colored eyes appeared to be just a regular brown, setting above bags so dark he looked sick. Tired. Worn-out. He needed a shave, a hair cut, his clothes were disheveled, a mess, and his body was no longer the solid fortress she used to feel protected by. It was more limp and neglected than anything, she thought, checking out his loose-fitting clothes again. What was he doing playing dress up? "So, how's everything going with you? You look the same," he said. Holly smiled, pausing briefly. "Ha, I was just thinking the same thing about your appearance." Love really is blind. No, it's not, she reminded herself. God is love. "I hear you're seeing someone. Some suave brotha. Is that true?" he asked. "Yep! And it feels a little strange." "Why?" Bradford appeared to be waiting for her to say something negative, but he was fooled when she said, "Because I don't have one complaint." Holly gave him a faux smile, flashing a quick show of her teeth and closing her mouth. "Cool... I'm glad. Didn't I tell you when we broke up that you'd find someone who'd treat you like a queen?" "I *beg* your pardon!" Holly caught a hold of herself, lowering her voice. Beg? she thought. David the Psalmist said he never saw the righteous forsaken nor their seed begging bread. Holly sighed. "What you *told* me *was* I'd never find someone who'd accommodate me like *you* did, and how I better be careful because *AIDS* wasn't walking it was running rampant." Bradford smiled, dropping his eyes to the ground and lifting them again, meeting hers. "Well, then," he said. "let's just say I'm glad he's there for you. Oh, and if it'll make you feel any better, I'm still with the same woman your girl Carmen caught me with. *Yeah*, Cherise is a good woman. Sexy as *all* get up." He smiled and added, "She asked me to say hello to you. In fact, the two of you would hit it off..." Holly shook her head and Bradford raised his hands, palms up. "Look, I don't know why you're acting like this," he said, extending one hand to touch her arm. She pushed it away and took a few steps back. "I did you a favor, Sun.... I mean, Holly," "You got that right! ... Wait, no you didn't get it right... God favored me, by getting me out of that death trap that you and I called a relationship!" "Whoa! Whoa! I came here to make peace. Calm the air between us. I'm not a bad guy. There are things about this Bradford you never even met." He placed his hand on his sunken chest. "Well then save the introductions," she said. "C'mon, can't you find it in that sweet heart of yours to give a brother a break?" Holly shook her head no again. "Bradford, being *swift* was never one of your attributes...." "Well, well, well. It's about time you got here!" Vanessa said. She came up behind them, her cranberry juice swishing around in the glass. "Where were you?" the full-figured woman asked Bradford. Holly turned, facing her partner. "Vee, why did you do this? Why did you invite him?" "Wait a minute," Vanessa said, holding up her hand. "I tried to get your opinion. This was the dilemma I had." Holly made a puzzled face and Vanessa's eyes went skyward for a second, rolling. "Remember when I called you the night you didn't pick up because you had *company*," the full-figured woman began. "All I wanted to do was tell you that I had run into Bradford in the city. He's producing a movie." Vanessa's voice paled when she saw Holly looking down, shaking her head. "And, well, my better judgement told me it wouldn't be a problem." Vanessa shrugged. "After all, we're all over twenty-one. Right?" She took a sip of juice while her mischievous eyes rested on her partners over the rim of her glass. Holly paused, taking a deep breath as she glimpsed Philip's reflection through the glass doors. He was still looking on. "Some of us really are!" Holly finally mumbled. She then turned to inform her new boyfriend, along with Tracy and Karl that she was ready to leave. "Wait, Holly ... before you go, I just want you to know that I still don't see your God when I look at you," Bradford said with a slow smile crossing his face. "Remember, how you would ask me if I saw Jesus when I looked at you?" Holly paused, glanced back over her shoulder to see if Philip, Tracy and Karl were coming and they were. She turned back to glare at Bradford. "How silly of me ... Those eyes of yours wouldn't know the Truth if He appeared and stood right next to you." She paused again, noticing how Bradford was still blocking the glass sliding doors of Vanessa and Courtney's house. "Move out of my way," Holly said so she could leave this thing of her past behind once and for all.

Chapter Twenty-One

Holly held her head low when she walked into her apartment building the following morning. With the bright sun at her back, creating a sort of spotlight effect on her plain unmade up face, ponytailed hair and evening clothes from yesterday. She felt awkward having to say hello to Peter, who stood like the gentlemen he was, tipping his hat. "Lovely day, isn't it?" he exclaimed, his voice drawing more unwanted attention to her. "Less humid," Peter added as he sat back down behind the desk. Smiling, she nodded and hurried up the steps for the elevator that some guy was kind enough to hold.

Inside, Holly thanked the tall White man as she instinctively pressed the fourth-floor button, noticing too late that he had already activated it. She cleared her throat, feeling even more uneasy. Holly turned her back on the stranger, who she now recognized as Troy O'Neil, Kathleen Parker's beau. Come to think of it, Holly hadn't seen the woman since that night. Hadn't even considered going across the hall to 'hear her out' as she'd asked her to in her note. Still facing the doors, Holly gazed upward, her eyes glued to the numbers that were igniting as they passed the lower floors. She didn't feel like having Troy O'Neil stare her all in the face, looking the way she did. I'll have to let Philip know that these last-minute "slumber parties" would be few and far between, she thought. Well maybe. Or to compromise she'd let it slide this time since he was so understanding last night when they got to his place. Compromise? she thought. There was no compromising in Christ. Holly took a deep breath. Well, the only thing Philip asked her was if she still had any interest in her former love? God is Love, she told herself. Was He her former love? Has she left her First Love? Holly

275

took another deep breath and found herself shaking her head no. Philip was talking about Bradford Anderson. Holly began to think about how she sarcastically asked him whether or not he was out of his mind? She continued to recollect how Philip smiled and a sigh of relief fell from his smiling lips. Oh, and on the ride home she was amazed that no one uttered a word about what had happened -- not even Karl. He kept his mouth shut with his eyes completely focused on the road. Tracy must have warned him ahead of time, Holly reasoned. Or, better yet, it had to be the goodness of God. The hazel-eyed woman took another deep breath.

Outside on her floor the elevator bell sounded and the doors drew open. She stepped off without looking back. But as Holly crossed the hall to her apartment, she listened for Troy O'Neil's footsteps as he strolled the other way, whistling a tune she immediately recognized. It was "My God is Greater!"

Unlocking her door quickly, Holly slipped inside before Kathleen had a chance to open hers. Her rapid maneuver was also brought on by the fact that she couldn't wait to take off her shoes. Her feet were hurting, throbbing like her heart was from the way the Lord was continuously pursuing her. "I'll go to church next Sunday," she said under her breath.

Holly kicked the silver pumps off in the foyer, went into the kitchen to make some coffee, raised the blinds and cracked the window in the living room and headed into her bedroom to undress for a hot bath.

She had four messages. Holly shook her head at the first one, which was a hang up. The second one was from her mother, asking again, what time she was supposed to come over today. "Baby, your mama danced like it was the last time she'd ever get to cut the rug *last* night. And I'm not even tired or sore. God is so good! My new shoes didn't pinch one bit. Nothin'." Cynthia Reed began to laugh. "Some ole bird asked me if I was a praise dancer." Her robust cackle heightened. "But you and me both know *good and well* it was a pick

up line! I was lifted my arms and movin' them real nice, you know."
The older woman laughed some more like his comment really
tickled her. "I just smiled at'em wit the Love of the Lawd and danced
myself to the other side of that big room!" Her mother continued to
laugh heartily as she told her daughter to call her. Holly checked her
cell phone for a message from her mother. She didn't leave a
message on her cell phone. The next message was from Carmen
who didn't leave her a message on her cell phone either. The Latina
woman was so excited. This morning she was standing right behind
the man she claimed she was going to marry. "Sis, he was at the
front desk in the lobby. I overheard him asking the doorman to hold
all his packages. He's going out of town for a little while. He didn't
even ask my permission. *The nerve.*" She giggled. "Holly, he smelled
soooo good. Padre made that scent just for him," Carmen was quiet
and then she went on to say, "I hope you had a good time at
Courtney's birthday celebration. Call me. Oh, and by the way, I
broke up with So and So. I feel so good about my choice to do that. I
could tell that the Lord is pleased. Call me."

Courtney's birthday celebration, Holly thought. Holly moved in
front of the full-length mirror, twirling her ponytail into a bun as
she waited for the final caller's voice to fill her room. It was Philip
checking to see if she got home okay, then he began telling her how
much he missed her already and how much he couldn't wait to see
her later. He threw her a long kiss and hung up. He didn't leave a
message on her cell phone either. Holly froze for a second, staring at
her reflection. Would she ever grow to love Philip Williams like she
knew he loved her? Holly remained in a frozen state, staring at her
reflection. How could he love her without Christ? The buzzer rang
before she could go deeper into those thoughts.

"Ms. Reed. There's a Mr. Benjamin here to see you. Mr. Courtney
Benjamin," Peter said. Holly stiffened, her eyes dropping down to
her nude body. "Oh, uh, send him up!" she said and hung up the
phone without saying good-bye to the doorman. She rummaged
through her drawers quickly, her fingers lifting and tucking things

back down into them as she searched for something to throw on. She found a short-sleeved bright yellow tunic and a pair of matching leggings. It was a set Carmen had sent to her from California a few years ago. This would have to do, she thought while she smoothed back her hair after cladding herself in the ensemble.

The doorbell rang.

Holly took a quick peek through the peephole. It was almost as though she was making sure her ears had heard correctly. Her partners husband had never come by alone or unexpectedly. She opened the door. When Courtney saw the slight confusion on her face, he began to explain. "I hope I'm not disturbing you," he said, smiling a little. "No. Don't be silly." Holly motioned for him to come in. So he did. "I tried to call you first but when I, uh, got your machine I hung up. I don't like those things." He was smiling more. "And, I didn't have your cell phone number." Holly grinned too as she surveyed what he was wearing: New silver-rimmed eyeglasses, black T-shirt, blue jeans and a really nice pair of black sandals. He had a tan canvas garment bag thrown over his arm. "Going away on another business trip?" she asked softly. He nodded in a way and cleared his throat. "The reason I'm here is to apologize for what had happened last night. I don't know what gets into Vanessa sometimes. Bradford's not my friend so I don't know why she invited him. Frankly, I never liked him." Never liked the way he mistreated you, was what he wanted to add. "I know," she said. "Why don't we get out of the foyer and go in here." Holly gestured toward the living room. Courtney nodded, turned and walked in, his eyes skimming the tremendous sunlit space as if he were looking for something new. He adored Holly's taste. It was so classy, so what he would have liked his home to be. But, Vanessa didn't like the way Holly arranged things, so she said, and she wasn't too enthused over her furniture choices, either even though the appearance of the couples newly renovated home spoke a whole other tune. Courtney sighed. Let it all go, man, just let it go, he told himself, knowing that he wouldn't have to worry about what she liked or disliked anymore. I'm a free man now. Courtney almost said the words out loud until, "Could I get you something to drink or eat?" caught him by surprise. "It's early have you had breakfast?" Holly continued. So thoughtful, he mused as he turned around toward her. "Yes, I did, thanks." But the aroma of fresh-brewed coffee beckoned him. "I'll have a cup of coffee, if you're having one." he said. She smiled. "Please make yourself comfortable."

Courtney watched her as she left the room, kept his eyes on her while she reached up into the kitchen cabinet to retrieve two cups and two saucers. All white. He sighed, walked over to the long striped sofa, resting his garment bag along the back. Now where should he seat himself? Courtney was about to move around to the front of the elegant chair until he was beckoned again. This time by the baby grand behind him. He looked back over his shoulder, peering at the magnificent black instrument, as if he'd never seen the likes of one before. Then he glanced into the kitchen at Holly for a second. She was pouring the coffee now, her head tilted, the bun she made falling in some places. And once the cups were full, she paused, played with her hands and turned, her eyes meeting his. He flinched and she smiled a little. "You take milk and sugar, right?" Courtney nodded and she opened the refrigerator, extracting a quart of *Dellwood* whole milk.

In the living room Courtney relaxed on the piano bench. Flexing his fingers, he tapped the keys lightly, grinning at the sound. Then he closed his mouth and bit down on his bottom lip since what he really wanted to do was shout. Rejoice because he had finally come home.

Man, he hadn't sat down behind one of these since he passed the bar exam. He'd conditioned himself to forget all about the pleasure playing brought him. Why would he deliberately do that to himself, when at one time he thought making music would have become his livelihood? That's right! *He,* Courtney Benjamin, Esq. was supposed to be the next triple threat. The next brother to take the music industry by storm. *And* he would have. No one could ever take away his natural ability, his God-given talent of playing piano, saxophone and trumpet, he thought, telling himself, at the same time, that it was now possible to relive his musical desires. *He* was once called a one-man band. Me! Sure 'nough. It would have been like having Herbie Hancock, John Coltrane and the great one, Mr. Miles Davis himself, all rolled up into one. Courtney began to hit the keys harder. Harder still. Louder, this time. First he did a few bars of the warm up medley Mr. Kent, his old music teacher taught him. Then, he went right into "Ribbon in the Sky," as if he were the owner of the fine tune. Courtney hummed and hummed along to the beat while Holly stood still in the kitchen, balancing both saucers and cups, which were filled to capacity in her hands, like she were walking the tightrope in a circus act. When did he learn to do that? It was the most beautiful sound she'd ever heard. Simply mind-blowing. Holly watched as Courtney closed his eyes and allowed the sound to just come. Flow from his fingers like water from a faucet. The Anointing, Holly told herself. Her heart had forgotten how to beat suddenly as she listened. The music was all that was keeping her alive. The music was all that was holding her up, steadying her feet. It was coming straight from heaven. She could have spied his playing all day. All night. All year long. Forever. She felt her spirit being drawn to it. *Possessed* by it. And the rest of her body followed without any signs of struggle. After all for 'someone to play her a wonderful song' was what she'd been longing for. Today seemed to be that day. Was this God answering that particular prayer? No, He wouldn't use another woman's husband!

At first Courtney didn't hear or see Holly re-enter the room. He'd been imagining himself on stage at Radio City Music Hall, serenading a full house of screaming fans. Young and old alike, who would have given anything just to have him look their way while he played. What would that be like? he wondered, as his eyes suddenly caught sight of a vision. Another presence besides himself and the adoring public, existing only in his mind. Courtney stopped, feeling stupid. "Please don't," Holly said. She was leaning against the back of the sofa, her palms resting atop his garment bag. The cups of coffee sat on the end table closest to the door, smoke billowing upward from them both, fusing then disappearing, who knows where. He looked at her again, staring into those hazel-colored eyes that appeared to be in reverence of him. Had to be in awe of his music, Courtney told himself. Whatever it was, Holly was still gazing at him like he was, like he was........ a man. Feeling somewhat emotional because of his momentary epiphany, he lowered his head and she moved closer to him, settling herself in front of the piano, her elbows resting on it. "I had no idea you played. And so well." Holly was smiling as if she wanted to hear more. Courtney nodded and met her astonished gaze. He saw her blink and bat her eyes. She must have been taken aback by the heinous scratch coursing the left side of his cheek. Courtney knew it was what she saw. Turning his head toward the window he started to say something mundane about the weather being much better than it was yesterday, but decided against it. She was too clever to be distracted. "I could play just about anything," Courtney finally said, his eyes looking at hers, his face still at the window. But as he averted it back toward her, Holly's eyes dropped when she saw herself through his eyeglasses, the question of what happened to him still evident on her face. She shifted her body closer to his right side, choosing not to meddle. It was clear that he was embarrassed enough as it was by the scar. "I have no doubt in my mind that you couldn't, from what I just heard." She looked up into his eyes. "I'm just so surprised Vanessa never mentioned....." "She didn't want me to pursue a career in music," he said abruptly. But I could do whatever I want to do now, was the next thing he wanted to say. Courtney stood up, covered the keys with the piano flap and peered over at the end table. "The coffee smells good," he said with a sad, rehearsed smile washing over his face.

Taking a final sip, Courtney leaned forward on the sofa, cup and saucer in his hands. "Could I put them down?" he asked, nodding toward the coffee table. "Yes, yes," Holly said. She jumped up, taking them from him and setting them down. She had been sitting next to Courtney, her legs tucked beneath her. "So, let's talk a little more about your playing." Holly grinned as she slid back into position. This time she didn't tuck her feet underneath her. She began to feel uncomfortable, remembering that Courtney was Vanessa's husband. "What do you want to know?" he asked and paused for a moment. He liked the fact that someone had an interest in hearing about his second love, the one he'd left out in the cold. Who was his first love, he wondered briefly until Holly spoke. "Well, for starter's. How long *have* you been playing?" "Which instrument?" Holly's mouth opened then closed. "I play the saxophone and the trumpet, too." Courtney leaned back, adjusted his eyeglasses and placed his arm along the back of the sofa. "Let me move this over here." Getting up he put the garment bag down on one of the straight-back chairs, resuming the way he was sitting afterward. "I can't believe I never knew any of this," Holly said, her mind still baffled that he was so melodiously talented. The both of them discussed him for a while. Courtney told her all about how he became so musically inclined and *then* why he went into law. And at the end of the abridged version of his autobiography, Holly felt melancholy. "I couldn't imagine not being able to go after my dreams, especially after being encouraged...." She paused, shaking her head. "You mean to tell me that your father had enrolled you into the pre-college program at the regular *Juilliard* school and then turned around and forced you to become a lawyer because he always wanted to be one?" Not very Christian, Holly thought until she entered her own mind. Who was she to judge on Christianity? The hazel-eyed woman didn't intend to sound so skeptical. Courtney nodded. "Even after knowing how much I loved playing. I made sure I told him every day after class that I wanted to be a musician because I overheard him tell my mother that he was still debating whether or not he'd let me continue. My expression of happiness didn't help in the least. Fell right into deaf ears. He had my future strategically outlined already, way before he called the school. I think he picked up the phone just to pacify my mother. She always believed in my gifts." "And what did she have to say about his taking you out of the program?" "Oh, she had a lot to say. Tried to fight him with every tactic she could think of. One time she told him that dreams should never be deferred. She told him that the Bible said it made the heart sick. And another time she used the silent treatment, which Pop probably enjoyed." Courtney laughed a little and added, "He was never in support of my music. Said all he heard was racket, "stuff that would wake the dead and leave them angrier than they were on the day they dead." "Wow," was all Holly could say to that. She got a revelation of Courtney's music truly having that kind of power if he were to use it for the purpose for which he was created. To raise the dead, to heal the sick to free the captives! Holly swallowed and stayed quiet, knowing that God was speaking to her. "Yep, he refused to put to rest all his years of studying to become a lawyer," Courtney went on to say. "Why didn't he make it?" "My father failed the bar three times. Man, he was and has remained humiliated over it. Because as you know all of his brothers are lawyers. And now, well, so is he by living vicariously through me." Holly nodded and shook her head at the same time. "Then I met Vanessa Lawrence who was determined for us to be the "Attorneys to all mankind." Courtney leaned forward again. Lifting his eyeglasses, he began squeezing the bridge of his nose with his thumb and forefinger. "That's why I think Pop hates her so much........ she reminds him too much of himself," he said quietly. "Thoughtless. What I did..." Courtney chuckled. "was go out there and marry Richard Benjamin in female form." Holly surveyed the way he straightened his new eyeglasses and slid back on the sofa. He then glanced at her, managing to smile. She swallowed what he'd just said hard. "I, uh, like those," she said, referring to his glasses. "Silver-rims are nice," she added. Smiling, Courtney said a quick thank you, told her he'd purchased them that morning and went right into, "So, why did you want to become a lawyer?" Holly wasn't prepared for the question.

She stared at him briefly, wondering if he, too, would laugh like Bradford did when she shared with him her reason for becoming one. No, she thought, this man right here should never be compared to a boy. Holly began. "When my mother and I lived down on the Lower Eastside, there was a little guy who lived directly across the hall from us." She paused to get the choke out of her voice by clearing her throat. "Jo Jo Thomas was his name." She went on to tell Courtney all about the youngster's unfortunate demise. "Man," he said when she got to the part about his father beating him to death for dropping a piece of bread on the floor. "I hope he went down," Courtney said, referring to Mr. Thomas. Holly nodded. "He sure did. And once my mother and I saw it in black and white," she said, the newspaper headlines popping up in her head, "I knew a lawyer was what I was supposed to be. God used that to minister to my heart." Holly smiled at the vision of herself as a small girl, saying, "I'm going to do that to all the bad people in the world! Just like that man did, mama! Just like Randal Epstein, attorney-at-law!" "I read that story and glanced up at the lawyer's eyes that were staring into mine, like a recruiter, said a silent okay, closed the *Daily News* and began my legal quest." Holly wasn't the least bit surprised to see the admiration on Courtney's face when she looked at him. He held her gaze for a while. But what he was really doing was taking sips of each and every one of her words, savoring them then swallowing, as if they were fine wine. Holly refreshed him. Made him feel poised and for once, himself. "You're lucky," Courtney finally said. He looked up at the clock on the mantle. "I better get going. My flight leaves at one o'clock. They always tell you to get to the airport at least a hour and a half before." Courtney and Holly both stood. He grabbed his garment bag and they headed for the door. There, he told her how she'd always been a good friend to him and Vanessa. "I don't know why she'd ever fool around with that, but I don't think any of us would ever be able to figure her out." He didn't know about Holly but he didn't want to try to figure Vanessa out anymore. "Deep down inside I truly believe Vanessa can't even figure her own self out," Holly said, adding, "Sometimes she could be so incredibly wonderful and then there are those other times...." She shrugged, unlocked the door and turned back to find Courtney gazing at her. He wanted to tell her that he was finally leaving his wife. That he was going off to start a brand-new life. But, first and foremost, he would take time out to search long and hard for his old smile, the smile he used to feel inside as well as on his face. Later Holly would wonder why he shook his head like that, for no reason at all. So it seemed. Courtney leaned closer to her, giving her a tight hug. "You're the best," he whispered in her ear.

And then he was gone.

When the elevator doors shut, Holly closed the peephole and made her way down the hall for her bedroom with thoughts of hers and Courtney's conversation still fresh in her mind. Why did she have the feeling he had something else to tell her? He seemed so unhappy in one instant and so happy in another, like a heavy weight had been lifted off his shoulders. It must be disheartening always having to be the "responsible voice" in a relationship, she mused. Iron sharpens Iron is what the scripture's say. It should do just that, work both ways.

Inside her bedroom the phone rang just as she was about to pick her Bible up off of her nightstand.

"I forgot to call you," Holly said aloud as she reached for the receiver, thinking it was her mother. But it wasn't. Instead it was a fast-talking, extremely frantic Tracy. "Slow down, Trace. I can't make out what you're saying," Holly instructed her friend calmly as she made herself comfortable on the window seat. "Okay, wait." Tracy took a few breaths. "What happened?" Holly asked. "Girl, I'm sorry. I'm just in complete shock over this!" Tracy said, starting over. "In shock about what?" A pause, then, "Courtney left Vee." Holly made an incredulous face. "Get out of here. What? He just went away on business..." "Did Vanessa call you?" Tracy asked the question as if it weren't possible for their full-figured friend to phone Holly. No, better yet, it sounded more like Vanessa wasn't *supposed* to. "No, she didn't," Holly said quietly with bewilderment lurking in her eyes. She stood up, looking out the window. And what she saw was Courtney and Peter dragging a bunch of luggage out of the building and placing them into the trunk of a cab. Holly froze, her heart was in her mouth. "So how did you know he was going away?" Tracy asked. "Holly, are you there?"

Not a word.

Holly was steadfast in her observation. She watched as Courtney tipped the doorman and slid into the back seat of the taxi. Where was he going? she wondered, catching herself. She was about to raise the window to ask him. But it was too late. The cab pulled off. She lowered her hand. "Holly!" "Oh, uh. He, he stopped by to apologize for what Vanessa had done, you know, inviting Bradford to his party." Holly stuttered out of confusion. She turned back around, sitting. "Trace, please don't tell me he's leaving her because of that." "It wasn't, but Courtney did tell her it was one of the straws that broke the camel's back." Tracy went on to explain and as she did, Holly sat there quiet and still envisioning the grim scenario play by play.

Courtney walked his parents and Ernestein Brown over to the Portman house. Their car was the only one left in the large driveway besides Brett and Joan's. Everyone else had been long gone. "Everything turned out really nice, sweetheart," Anita said to her son, who managed a brief smile. "Would have been better if that tacky wife of yours did the proper thing and sent out invitations," Courtney's father mumbled real loud. "Calling my house to tell me about my boy's surprise party..." "Oh shut up, Richard," Anita said. She opened her purse and pulled out a set of keys. "I'm driving because you had a little too much to drink, Mister," she added to her staggering husband. He got himself like that right after Vanessa's pregnancy announcement. "Yeah, Pop. Let me pour you into the passenger seat," Courtney teased as he held his old man up. "Or would you prefer to sit up here, Ma Bee?" he asked, peering back at Ernestein Brown. "No, darlin'. I'll be fine right back here," she said, waving her hand. "You go on and get him situated." The salt and peppered haired woman opened the left rear door, getting inside. Anita climbed in too, plopping down in front of the steering wheel. She buckled up and shook her head at the way her husband was squirming and carrying on. "Boy, if you don't unhand me," Richard Benjamin said, his words an intoxicated blemish. Finagling himself free from his sons securing clutches, the older man teetered, his hand finding support on the roof of the automobile before he fell into the passenger seat. Anita Benjamin exclaimed, "ouch" when her husband's unsteady head bumped up against her shoulder and "Umph, umph, umph," was her next remark. "Here put this on," Courtney said, referring to the safety belt. He reached into the car, straightening out his father, who had snatched the restraining device away from him, clamping it across himself in one swift, careless motion. Courtney knew his father was mad at the world over Vanessa's pregnancy as he tried to remind his son that Jesus turned water into wine. He was feeling ashamed by his drunken state. Courtney saw the clear combination of anger and let down on the older man's face from his view on stage. If only he knew the real deal he'd have me and Vanessa drawing up our own divorce papers right now, Courtney told himself. He wasn't really sure why he was holding back on his family, knowing that both his father and Ernestein Brown would rejoice at the news of his wanting a divorce from Vanessa. And his mother would just tell him she wanted whatever it was that made him happy. He knew she would also see that it was the Lord's doing as she would faithfully send him scripture's that didn't hesitate to reveal how this situation between him and Vanessa was not a marriage. Mama was always mindful of doing the right thing, he thought. But now wasn't the time to share his news with her on anyone else. He didn't want to be pitied nor did he want his father to stumble back to the house in his impaired stupor, attacking Vanessa with the bitter "choice words" he'd had tucked away inside of himself since the first time he laid eyes on her. "Lord have mercy on this boy," Richard Benjamin said back then, holding his face in his hands as he sat on the edge of his bed. "Can't you tell when you're being reeled in? See this thing with the eyes of your understanding. What's the Holy Spirit saying to you, son? That girl doesn't *love* you. She *loves* the idea of you." His father stood up and rubbed his eyes, stopping the tears before they'd fall. Then after a long, long sigh, he placed both hands on Courtney's shoulders at first, squeezing them and forcing a smile on his quivering lips. When he found the next sentence in his head, he placed his hands at the sides of his son's face, positioning it so that they'd be eye-to-eye. "Courtney," he began, "Tell me you love this woman and as God is my witness, I will leave you alone. Drop the subject forever... By His Grace." Flinching, the younger man fought with all his might to hold his father's still hopeful stare. Hopeful that his boy would perhaps look away or just flat out tell him no he didn't love Vanessa Lawrence. Instead, breaking down and slipping with a nervous blink, Courtney told an untruth. A lie that haunted him to this day.

"I'll give you a call tomorrow, Sweetheart," Anita said to her son a second time. She was leaning her head forward so that she'd be able to look up into his face from the passenger's side of the car. Courtney cleared his throat and coughed. "Uh, I'll call you guys. I'm going away on, uh, a business trip tomorrow morning," he said. "What? You never said anything...." "I know. I, uh, didn't want to spoil all the fun." Courtney smiled a little at the trio, smacking the hood of the car lightly so they'd get going. He woke his father, who had fallen off into a deep sleep, just that fast. "Sorry, Pop," Courtney said and waved when his mother stuck the key into the ignition. "Drive safely." Anita nodded and backed out carefully while Richard dozed back off, grumbling something incoherent to himself, and in the back seat, Ernestein pressed her hand to her mouth, blowing her Godson a kiss. Catching it, Courtney stuck it in his shorts pocket like he was saving it for a rainy day. Ernestein smiled. But as

Courtney waved again, watching the tan Lincoln Town Car sail away into the twilight, he knew, much to his own chagrin, that the storm wasn't too far in the distance.

What would he do first? Courtney asked himself as he placed his hand on the doorknob of the house. He knew his possibilities were endless since Vanessa already had an attitude with him for leaving her outside with Bradford and her side of the family while he brought his side into the house to better celebrate his birthday. Courtney always wanted to humiliate Bradford. Always wanted him to feel all the hurt he rendered Holly. A few instances came to his mind: Last summer's fourth of July barbecue, for one. Holly's ex made her cry by saying he would leave her if she got fat and sloppy when she sat beside him, taking a bite of a hamburger Courtney just took off the grill. "Eat all you want, Sunshine. But you knew I don't like my women bigger than me." Bradford said in that obnoxious voice of his. Courtney would never forget the sorrow monopolizing Holly's eyes as she glanced around, seeing if anyone else heard the abuse. It wasn't hard to miss it. Bradford's comment was loud and bone-chilling, like the sound of their old lawnmower that morning before it decided that day that it would be its last day of eating grass. Courtney wanted to tell Holly to stay where she was. But she was too fast. Her "Benjamin Burger" was already in the trash. Why didn't I say something right away? Courtney asked himself angrily, knowing that he had more than enough time to show Bradford that he wasn't going to tolerate that type of sophomoric behavior in his home or otherwise. "I don't know where my head was," he said aloud as the next instance surfaced in his mind. The time at Ellington's was one to definitely reminisce. Bradford certainly did not need liquor to prove his immaturity. He got intoxicated and grew testicle's the size of Mighty Joe Young's. Courtney shook his head as the day came back clearer than the one he was living right now. Bradford stood his drunk behind up, eyes rolling all around in his head as he seemed to be flirting with Angela Dunn. Bernie was ten seconds away from committing a cold-blooded murder, until

Courtney stepped in. I should've pretended like I didn't see Big B's fist about to go upside the brother's head, he thought, blowing off steam after he'd inhaled.

Courtney waved his hand hard, like he was pitching a soft ball. Let Vanessa stay mad! It was nice to see her wearing his size ten's for a change. Obviously, his thoughts of Bradford served their purpose, giving him back the backbone he'd lost. Courtney was going to go upstairs and lay each and every one of his had-it-up-to-here cards out on the table and tell Vanessa he'd played the game of fool for the *last* time. He couldn't understand why he wasn't outraged by her having some other man's kid. Wasn't bothered at all about her cheating on him. To him her affair was a blessing. He could not have been more grateful. Hallelujah! God is here is what he found himself wanting to scream. Courtney welcomed the sound of his own laughter when he heard it flowing from a deep place from within. It's been a long time since he'd felt this good.

Inside, Courtney closed the door without locking it. There was no need to since he'd be leaving in a few short minutes. He could hear Vanessa upstairs in the bathroom, water running in the tub. He went and stood in the doorway of the living room, looking around. Nodding his head slowly as his eyes skimmed the space. Courtney knew that one thing was for certain. He was definitely going to miss the house. But with the kind of money he'd made during his successful career, through hard work and wise investments, he would be able to buy two more just like it *if* he wanted to. What for? he asked himself glumly. Did all that *really* matter when you didn't have the right person to come home to? Would he ever find that special someone?

Overhead he heard the water cease from running.

Courtney climbed the stairs two at a time, walking passed his half-naked wife without saying a word. "I hope you had a nice time!" she called from the bathroom with only a touch of upset still left in her voice. "The baby and I are taking a quick bath. We could discuss the evening afterward. Hey, why don't you get in with us?" she added. Vanessa was too busy grinning at her reflection in the mirror over the sink to notice that there was no response. Look at the way you're glowing beautiful, she mused and removed her underwear, settling down into the tub.

Five minutes later Vanessa came stomping into their room wrapped in a towel, the question "what is going on in here!" at the tip of her tongue. Just when I was calming down, she thought, his simpleness turns around and raises my pressure again. She'd shortened her bath when she heard all the banging.

Standing at the door of the French contemporary-decorated room, Vanessa's mouth was open but nothing came out. She was too stunned. Courtney had two large suitcases and a garment bag spread out across the bed, shoving his belongings into them. He never even acknowledged her being there. "Where are you going?" she asked with as much upset in her shocked voice as she could muster. He gave her the benefit of a glance and went back to packing. "Did you hear what I said, Courtney?" Vanessa's voice rose a notch. She was ten seconds away from going off.

No answer from him.

Courtney walked over to the closet, throwing the doors back so hard they hit the wall, chipping away some paint. He didn't mean to do that, but he'd been trying to work himself up, trying to reflect on all the devious things his wife had done to him in order to keep him in this angered state. This would make his exit easier. Guilt-free. Vanessa gasped. Balling her hands into tight, dangerous fists, she moved closer to him. "This time I want an answer or.....!" He dropped the clothing he'd just taken off the hangers, spinning around. Courtney was glaring at her, his nostrils flared and his eyes hitting hers dead on, like a bull would do to the one waving the red cloak during a Spanish bull fight. He saw red all right. Every incident that Vanessa had put him through, all the ones he'd forgiven her for, gathered right there in their bedroom, like dust and cobwebs in a neglected attic. The look on his face alone made her jump back. "Or what, Vee? I know you weren't about to threaten me, now, were you?" With that, she knew her answer should be no, but the fighter in her was unstoppable. "I don't know who you think you are, staring at my face like that!" Vanessa's head was gyrating on her stout neck as she spoke. "Move your hand, Courtney!" He shook his head in disgust. He couldn't stand to hear her say his name anymore. "Don't tell me what to do, Va-nes-sa!" Her eyes grew larger at the way he emphasized her name. It was as though saying it nauseated him, heightening his fury. "Those days are over with." Courtney lowered his pointed finger from her face and turned back around, picking up the two shirts and pairs of slacks he'd dropped. "What are you saying?" she demanded. "Did I stutter?" he said, cutting his eyes at her. "Huh? Huh? Vee, did I?" Courtney rolled his eyes adding, "I thought so!" But when he was about to walk over to the suitcase to put the clothing he was holding into it, Vanessa hauled off, slapping him in the face. Her long crimson-polished nails racked across his cheek. Courtney's head jerked from the impact of the blow and his eyeglasses went crashing to the floor. Dropping the clothes again, he touched the scar, looking at the blood on his fingertips. He then glanced down at his glasses. They were a blur. Raising his eyes in a slow, steady motion, Courtney glared at Vanessa. He wanted to shake her, shake something into her but he didn't know what. Sense? Decency? It didn't matter anymore. Courtney had been divorced for too many years in his head to find an answer. He was weathered and uninterested in being her advocate. He remembered hearing how there was nothing too hard for God. But, he wondered, could He even save Vanessa? That was no longer his problem. When it's over, it's over, he told himself.

"Look at this," was the only thing he could think of to say as he kneeled down, picking up his eyeglasses. The tortoiseshell frames had broken and one of the lenses was cracked. "I don't know how I got myself into this," he said. "Yeah, well. You shouldn't have been in my face like that." Vanessa folded her arms beneath her breasts.

Courtney looked at her, but he couldn't see what her expression was saying. Is that what she thought he meant? "You don't get it do you, Vanessa?" He paused, adding, "I *don't* want to be married to you anymore." Courtney was listless, his words clipped and precise, as if he were talking to someone hard of hearing. Maybe she'd understand better if she read my lips, he told himself. "That's what I'm talking about. *I* have had it *up to here!*" He held his hand horizontally above his head to prove his point. "What do you mean you don't want to be married to me anymore?" Vanessa placed her hands on her hips. "Ooooh, I get it," she said, nodding. "You're just like all those other Black men out there, huh?" She shook her head in disgust. "Running off with your tail between your legs, saying you *can't* cope because your woman is knocked up!" Courtney shook his head no. "Then what's this?" she asked, pointing down at the suitcases, "because I refuse to be a statistic, you hear me?!" Vanessa slapped the front of her thighs and threw her hands up in exasperation. "I'm not like those other men and you know it." Vanessa looked as though she was about to charge at him. "Where's the slut at? I'll kill her!" she screamed. Courtney grabbed her by the shoulders, holding her back. "Vee, there is no one else. I'm not the infidel, you are." She appeared to be puzzled. "Why don't you call Dr. Stone he'll explain everything to you. Take my word. All you have to do is tell him you're having a baby," Courtney said. Vanessa's eyes narrowed. "What does Dr. Stone have to do with any of this?" she asked, her loud voice lowering to a whisper as she backed out of his hold. Courtney turned his back on her, mashing down the top of one over-stuffed suitcase, trying to zip it. "Answer me!" Facing her again, he told her about his challenge. "What!" That can't be true, she thought, he had a smirk on his face and the vein in the side of his neck wasn't sticking out like it usually did when he was upset. "It's not mine, Vee." Vanessa couldn't seem to digest what he was saying. Courtney could see her thinking. "The only way I could make a baby is with some help from a doctor as well as a team of experts." "Wait a minute," she said, placing her fingers on her temples and pressing.

The calmness of his mood perplexed her. Ordinarily he'd scream and yell, get quiet and then an hour or so later he'd bring her one of his apologetic hugs and kisses. She always knew it would only be a matter of time before he said he was sorry and they'd be back to normal, for a little while anyway. But tonight appeared to be different, taking another turn.

"Are you accusing me of having an affair?" "No." Courtney pointed to her stomach with his chin. "I *know* you had one. The evidence is clear, Counselor." He lifted the suitcases to the floor. "You should have seen the look on Dr. Stones face when I told him I got you pregnant before." Courtney searched the room with his eyes to see if there was something he was forgetting while he added, "He turned whiter than that towel you have on. And as he spoke about it still being possible for us to have children *with* some help, he couldn't even look at me." Courtney strolled passed her as if she wasn't standing there wiping tears from her eyes. "Dr. Stone didn't want to stare a sucker in the face."

Vanessa walked out the room a few steps behind him, standing at the top of the stairs. She rewrapped her falling towel and listened to Courtney as he placed a call to a car service. She began to descend the stairs, finding a spot in between the front door and the living room. What could she say to stop him. The tears didn't work this time. And she wasn't about to beg.

He hung up the phone.

Vanessa followed him over to the sofa, sitting down beside him. "Dr. Stone doesn't know what he's talking about, honey," she said, her voice nothing less than a desperate con. "Here feel this. This baby is ours. I know it." She tried to take his hand in hers and guide it toward her stomach, but he pulled away, sliding over. Courtney leaned his head back on the sofa, closing his eyes. Be strong, he warned himself. "Let's go to another doctor. My mother told me about this great doctor down in Phiily....." "Man," he said, opening his eyes and shaking his head in disbelief. "It's all about you, isn't it?" Courtney shook his head again. "I thought you told me that Dr. Stone was the best in his field." He shook his head a third time, shutting his eyes again. Vanessa stared at him for a minute as a single tear fell from her eye right on cue. She tried to lean in toward him and finger the scar she'd made on his cheek, but like before, he pulled away, sitting straight up. "It's no use," Courtney said. "My mind is made up....." He stopped. "I, I would have stayed with you forever, *unhappy*. Making the best out of a terrible situation despite my true feelings. Would you want that?" Vanessa lowered her eyes. She was okay with their set up. A horn honked outside.

Standing up, Courtney peeked out the window through the blinds and grabbed his bags. "You'll be hearing from my lawyer," he said. And the last thing Vanessa heard was the car door slam and pull off. He's not coming back, she told herself. Springing up from the sofa, Vanessa combed her fingers through her hair several times violently, finally yanking the hairpiece from the back of her head and throwing it to the floor. "Forget you, Courtney!" she yelled, holding up her middle finger at the door. "I didn't want your raggedy butt anyway! Forget you and your tired family!" Vanessa began pacing. Back and forth. Back and forth. Again and again like a caged animal. She stopped. Breathing in and out, her chest heaving. She gazed down at herself and started rubbing her stomach. Now, she thought. "Your father's going to have to come through for you, baby," she whispered sweetly, as if she were cradling the unborn child in her arms. "I tried my best to leave him alone, tried to be a good mommy and stay away. But..... I can't." Vanessa paused and her eyes hardened again. "I am not doing this alone. Huh! He wanted me just as much as I wanted him. You play, you pay. That's all to it!" Vanessa marched over to the phone, dialing her child's father and when the machine picked up she slammed down the receiver. She'd let him have his last night of messing around. "But come tomorrow," Vanessa said to the empty room. "This love fest is *over!*"

"Where did he go?" Holly asked Tracy once she'd finished telling her what had happened. "Girl, your guess is as good as mine." "How is Vee?" "Ah, so, so." "Trace, did you know about her sleeping with someone else?" Holly could hear her friend sigh. "Yes," was all she said. Holly shook her head and got up. She moved over to the bed, sitting there. "To be honest with you, I don't know how bad I feel for her. She had a good man. Smart, considerate, kind, always around when she needed him, never ever running the streets and, he was there for others, too....." "Holly, I know," Tracy said. She didn't feel like hearing a sermon. "Look, let me go," Tracy said before the hazel-eyed woman could go on. "I promised Vee that I would go out there for a little while today." "I have plans," Holly said. She couldn't find a place to hide her aloofness.

Chapter Twenty-Two

Lifting her hands to look at them, Holly figured after seeing how prunelike they'd become, it was time for her to get out of the tub. Forty-five minutes was long enough for a good soak. Besides, she thought, her mother was expected soon. And from the way Cynthia rushed her off the phone when the younger woman started telling her about the Benjamins' breakup, Holly knew that soon really meant right now. Her mother always loved hearing juicy details in person. Said it made her feel like she was watching a movie or reading a good book. And that was a big deal for her mother as she had a reading and math tutor for three years. The tutor helped her mother get her high school GED, which gave her the opportunity to have a book club. Holly climbed out the tub and blotted herself dry with a towel. When she was about to drop the dampened cloth to the floor and move in front of the bathroom mirror to brush her teeth and gargle, she heard her mother struggling with the locks. Holly opened the bathroom door when Cynthia Reed finally entered. Who was that she was talking to? Holly wondered. The hazel-eyed woman didn't stick her head out of the bathroom to find out. "Mom will let her know," she said quietly.

"Come in, sweetie. Have a seat in there while I get her,"Cynthia Reed said to the person, who went into the living room before Holly could open the bathroom door. The older woman brought the two hefty bags of groceries she was carrying into the kitchen then made her way down the hall for her daughter's bedroom. "Baby, where you at?" Cynthia called. She stopped, straightening one of the hall pictures on the wall. Holly stuck her head out the cracked bathroom door and when she saw that her mother was about to say something, the younger woman instructed her not to. "Shhh," Holly said, placing a finger at her mouth. "Mom, who's out there?" she whispered. Cynthia smiled. "Oh, baby. It's only your neighbor. Cute little thing from across the hall." The older woman noticed the transformation on her daughter's face. Holly wasn't thrilled. "What is it, babygirl?" Cynthia asked. Holly shook her head. She'd never told her mother that her childhood bully moved into her building. She didn't want her to worry or make her feel as though she had to come to her rescue again. Holly knew it was best. "The chile seem down 'bout somethin'," Cynthia said. She began stroking her daughter's arm. "You go tend to her while I start rollin' in the kitchen, okay baby." Holly managed a nod. "Tell her I'll be right out," she said. Cynthia patted her daughter's arm before letting it go. With a grin, the older woman sashayed back down the hall in the other direction while Holly slipped into her room to put on some clothes.

Twenty-five minutes later, Holly was entering the living room dressed in a pair of boot-cut khaki's and a crisp white shirt that was tied at the waist. Kathleen was sitting on the sofa. She turned her head as her neighbor approached. Their eyes met and the White woman smiled a little. "I won't stay long," Kathleen said, shifting in her seat. "Your mother told me you were expecting company. I had to come over when Troy mentioned seeing you earlier. It took a while to make up my mind, as you can see." The White woman's voice was higher in pitch than usual. Had to be nerves, Holly thought as she moved around the coffee table, taking a seat in one of the straight-back chairs. She crossed her legs. "I recognized Troy, too from the photograph on your mantle," she said. "Yeah, I, uh, described you to him. Plus he said he saw you come in here," Kathleen said. She lowered her eyes. The tension between them made her uneasy. Then, at the same time, the two women glanced toward the kitchen. The gospel tune that Cynthia Reed broke out into seized them. Her strained falsetto made both Holly and Kathleen reflect as they'd done many times before, separately. And from the older woman's choice of words, they also had the feeling she knew exactly what was going on. "Your mother still looks the same," Kathleen said. "Except, she's smiling." She paused, lowering her voice almost as if she were talking to herself. "Not the outraged woman she was when she'd confront my mother and I about the things I'd done and said to you." Holly peered at her. "Well," she said, startling her neighbor a little, "we both have lots to be grateful for." Kathleen nodded as she looked around. "Your apartment is lovely." Thank you was Holly's response, although the materialistic things were not what she was referring to. Their eyes met once again. The White woman sighed and said, emotionally, "I am so sorry for what had happened all those years ago." Kathleen held up her hand when Holly was about to reply. "Oh, I know I can't take away the pain I caused. But, but. I," she said, her hand pressed up against her chest, "was hurting, too." Her eyes were telling the truth. Looking away from Kathleen's teary gaze for a second, Holly met it again. "People always have a way of twisting things, making themselves the victim even when they claim to know the difference between right and wrong." "That's not what I'm doing, Holly. All I'm doing is apologizing for that little lost girl I once was. I'm also asking for another chance. I'm not saying that I want us to become *best* friends, by any means. I just want the opportunity to get to know you better. That's what I've been doing, oh, for fifteen years now." Holly looked perplexed. "I've been surrounding myself with meaningful individuals because I have *so* much to learn. My parents didn't know any better, they did the best with what they knew." Now she wants me to teach her something, Holly thought. Kathleen Parker Wahl sat back, folded her arms beneath her small bust line and dropped her head. She began to take in more of Cynthia Reeds made-up lyrics. "I am a friend," the older Black woman sang slowly. "I'm a friend to the end... Lawd, You said, I'm you friend... to the end." Lifting her head, Kathleen gazed at the pictures on the end table. She leaned closer to them and, said, "May I," regarding the black and white photo of Holly's parents on their wedding day. Kathleen wanted to pick it up. "Sure," Holly said softly. First she looked toward the kitchen because her mother stopped singing.

Then she began to observe the way the White woman studied her parents closely. Kathleen stared at them with a slight smile on her face. But through the smile, Holly detected a subtle bit of envy in her eyes. "Do you have a good relationship with your father?" The White woman asked. "I wish," Holly said, "He transitioned. He's with the Lord." "I'm sorry," Kathleen said sympathetically. "Don't be sorry, sweetie," Cynthia Reed said. She was standing in the living room doorway tying an apron around her waist. "Holly will always, always be my late husband's little SD," the older woman said, grinning at her daughter. She liked seeing her child blush when she told people that. "SD?" Kathleen whispered as she set the picture back down. "*Yeah*, honey," Cynthia said, chuckling. She walked inside, standing next to the mantle, her right hand on her hip. "Mom, please," Holly said, shaking her head in disbelief. "What? This a fabulous story," the older woman said. She waved her hand at her daughter, finding her hip again. "I never understood her shame when it came to her fathers nick name for her," Cynthia said to Kathleen. "Shoot, David loved callin' her that. It's a term of endearment. Means sugar dumpling. He said she was sweet and round just like one." Cynthia Reed gazed over at the photo of herself and the man she would always love, smiling. She was in her own world for a moment, then she sighed, saying, "Well, let me get back in this kitchen. 'Cause I only have a hour and a half to cook up a *thunderstorm*. Might even create a tornado, if I have some left over time." The older woman chuckled some more, waved her hand in the air and headed out. Holly wondered why Kathleen's face had become flushed during her mother's nostalgia. The White woman quickly glimpsed the photo of her neighbor's parents again, standing up. "I'd like to get together sometime this week," Kathleen said the words more like their getting together soon was a must. "If it's okay with you," she added. Holly paused then she nodded her head. "Certainly."

Cynthia told Holly to sit down at the kitchen table and start from the beginning when Kathleen Parker Wahl left. "I hope that chile was all right, but I was in here gettin' a little impatient," the older woman told her daughter. She couldn't wait to hear all about how Courtney left Vanessa. "That's why I came out there when I realized my singin' wasn't scarin' her 'way quick enough," she added, laughing lightly. Even though it wasn't right for Holly to think this way, she was glad her mother had Vanessa's problem to keep her busy. She didn't feel like explaining who Kathleen was. That was the past, she told herself in a way that seemed to mean that she had gotten it. The Lord must be manifesting healing in this area, she thought. "She's fine," the younger woman said quietly. Standing up, Holly took a small bottle of Evian water out of the refrigerator, taking a few quick sips. "I hope these people appreciate my cookin'. I knowed I was led to *lean* in the *bourgeois* direction, you know, since they got all that Mickey D's money and what not," Cynthia said, giggling louder this time. "Well if they don't appreciate it, I guess they don't know what good food is," Holly said. She sat back down. The older woman smiled and told her daughter that she got the recipes from *Gourmet* magazine. "Some of their stuff doesn't even look eatable. It's so pretty. And the portions, *woo-wee! Smaaall.* They probably couldn't even fill the belly's of the little ones. You knowed I made more than the recipes called for. God is a God of abundance." Cynthia glanced over her shoulder, winking at her daughter, who smiled and said, "All right, let me tell you about the Benjamins'."

When Holly finished telling her mother everything from Bradford Anderson's coming to Courtney's birthday celebration without her knowing to Courtney showing up at her apartment that morning without her knowing, wearing new glasses and a fresh scar on his cheek both courtesy of Vanessa, Cynthia Reed gasped and shook her head in disbelief. "I don't understand that woman," she said, her head still going from side to side. "But," she added, waggling her finger in the air, "I always knew she was off. Barely ever smiled. And she had plenty to be smilin' 'bout. What is wrong with people sometimes? I knowed, they need the Lawd! Well! I been prayin' for them a whole lot lately. Now I see why!" "Yes," Holly said, sighing. "That Courtney ain't been nothin' but *good* to her. You hear me?" Cynthia didn't realize she had pounded her fist against the countertop. "Oooch!" "Mom!" The older woman was shaking her hand. "I'm okay, baby," she said and put her hand down at her side. She shook her head again. "He's respectful, he's friendly and responsible. I know he still need the Lawd. He's the only One that can make your life right. I'm prayin' for him, for them both," the older woman continued, suddenly finding herself thinking that *he* was every bit the kind of man she hoped her daughter would meet 'cept she wanted him to be committed to the Lawd. "Where'd he go?" Cynthia asked, regrouping herself. Holly shook her head and shrugged. "I don't know. As I think about it," the younger woman continued, "I could almost swear that he wanted to tell me something this morning, but he didn't. Courtney's not the type to burden others with his problems." Holly's voice was low, sad sounding. Cynthia sighed. "I'm sure he's just some place gettin' his head together. I pray that the Lawd will minister to him real good," she said, trying to smile mainly for her daughter's sake. Holly stood up and told her mother she was going to set the dining room table.

Four o'clock on the dot Peter made his announcement. The William's family had arrived. "My 'hindparts don't look too big in these pants, baby, does it?" Cynthia Reed turned around so her daughter could see. Holly shook her head. "Mom, please. You look so beautiful. Stop looking down at yourself," she said. The older woman glanced down at herself again, nodding her head slowly. Then she gazed at her daughter, who was doing with herself just what she'd asked her mother not to do, looking down at herself. "Sweetie, let me look at you," Cynthia said, her voice soft and gentle. Holly averted her face from the foyer mirror, returning her mother's loving stare. The hazel-eyed womans hair and skin were glowing. But the sparkle in her eyes was dim. What was wrong? "Babygirl, you are the most beautiful thing I'd ever laid eyes on," the older woman began, assuming she was remedying her daughter's problem. "Never ever had I seen someone in all my days who is so beautiful inside and out....." Holly sighed and lowered her eyes. "Mom, I don't know why you think you have to do that." "Do what, baby?" Daughter met mother's gaze again. "Tell me that I'm so beautiful all the time. I already know how much you love me." Cynthia Reed nodded and swallowed the lumps forming in her throat. Okay, she thought, maybe she'd cut down some on the complimenting, but she had to keep telling her. No matter what. The older woman believed it was part of what she was called to do. Lift her precious daughter with words of encouragement.

The doorbell rang.

Holly and her mother gave each other the "It's Showtime!" look and hazel-eyed woman opened the door.

Philip was the first to enter. He pecked Holly on the lips, handed her the same type of pale-pink roses as he'd given her on their first date and strolled into her apartment like he owned it. Walking up to Cynthia Reed, he extended another bouquet to her, only these were white roses. The scent was glorious. "I know Holly doesn't have a sister," Philip began, smiling. "So, you *must* be her mother," he added, his now empty hand still outreached for her to shake. Cynthia blushed as she placed hers in his, breathing in the delectable fragrance of her flowers at the same time. "It's nice to finally meet you," Cynthia said, grinning too. "Mmm, these are beautiful. Thank you," she added. The older woman tried to be subtle as she searched for her daughter's eyes in order to display her approval for the fine specimen of man standing before her, but Holly was in the midst of introducing herself to Philip's mother. That must be a sign, Cynthia told herself. She remembered that this good looking man standing in front of her was not saved. The older woman began to take in Paulette Williams; Philip's mother. She was a well-put together woman, but by no means was she attractive. She had a big forehead with small eyes that she hid well behind tinted designer eyeglasses. They were the kind of bifocal lenses that gave one that tiny bug-eyed look. But her chin-length silver blunted hair set off her nut-brown complection nicely, Cynthia thought as she told herself to focus on the more appealing things about the woman. Those were her own prayers when she caught people staring at her.

"Something smells delicious," Philip said, stealing Cynthia's gaze. "Oh, thank you, baby," she said. Turning, he placed his arm around his mother's shoulder's when she appeared at his side, waiting to be introduced to her son's future mother-in-law, as he called her. The two older women smiled and exchanged pleasantries. But Cynthia Reed's smile was visible more so because she liked seeing the way Philip catered to his mother, honoring her. 'Cause if a man's good to his mama, she mused, he'd be good to his wife. The Word says to honor your mother and father. Cynthia's thought ceased for a moment as she was reminded by the Holy Spirit that it was to honor them unto the Lord. His way of doing things. The older woman found herself saying "Amen!" out loud. She covered her mouth and quickly noticed that no one else seemed to hear her. You so good, Father! Cynthia said to herself with a smile.

Still at the door greeting her guests as they came in, Holly wondered if anyone else could hear the loud beat of her heart. She felt uneasy all of a sudden. Plastering a smile on her face she laughed at some of Donald Williams' brief jokes and asked him if he would be kind enough to set the two bottles of non-alcoholic wine he'd brought her on the kitchen counter. She didn't want them and she knew that it was the Lord's doing. She began to think about how Philip had to be the one to tell his father about them, remembering that she bought the non-alcoholic Champaign for Courtney's birthday from the both of them. Oh, why would she give that to him knowing that the Lord told her not the drink them. He had placed it in her heart that He didn't want her to even indulge in the taste of those things. Holly noticed how her thoughts were now on Courtney. "I cast the care of him onto You Lord because You care for me in the Name of Jesus," she prayed quietly as she refocused on Philip's father. The younger dark-skinned man looked so much like his dad. Holly listened as he told her he'd be glad to put the non-alcoholic wine on her counter. He even offered to take the large bouquet she was holding in there as well. Giving it to him, Holly watched as the older man joined his wife, flowers in one hand, while the bag of non-alcoholic wine was still in the other. He, too, met her mother with a smile. I think I could handle this, Holly thought. Her heart didn't seem to be racing anymore. She turned to say hello back to Mark senior and junior, who was holding his father's hand. Holly could see Brenda from the corner of her eye. The African-garbed woman appeared to be wearing a similar spackled grin. She, too, had to be convincing herself that their second encounter would be better than the first. "I'm glad you guys *wanted* to come," Holly said to Mark senior once he thanked her for having them over. "Aren't you precious," she added to his son, who quickly blurted out, "Uncle Philip said you were gonna be his wife!" The small boy gave Holly a broad grin. He was missing a front tooth. "*Mark jr.!*" Brenda said, swatting the back of his tiny head lightly. "Don't forget your age," she warned and he buried his face in his father's thigh. "Hey," Holly said quietly to Philip's sister when their eyes happened upon one anothers. Brenda gave her a soft hi in return. "I really admire you for allowing me into your home....," the kente-cloth donning woman added. She decided to save the rest of her words for later. Holly just nodded in response as she kneeled down to say hello to Olivia. The angelic-faced child was holding on to her mommy's hand for dear life. "Could I have a kiss?" Holly asked her. Looking sheepish, the little girl peered up at her mother to see if it was okay. Brenda smiled, her head bobbing a yes. So Olivia puckered her lips, planting a sweet kiss on the side of the hazel-eyed woman's face.

Holly didn't particularly care for the view from the kitchen. As she helped her mother transfer the food from the pots onto serving tray's, she observed the way Philip was showing his family around. He was pointing to the photos on the end table and explaining who the people were. Then he walked over to the painting hanging above the piano, waving his parent's over after he'd given Brenda directions to the bathroom. Olivia, still holding her mother's hand, was doing the pee-pee dance as they passed the kitchen for the restroom. His comfort made Holly uncomfortable. Wasn't it clear that she was in this relationship strictly to have herself a good time? Some laughs and someone to keep her company when she wanted it. These were her only criteria. Nothing more. He knew this, she thought. What was she thinking? the hazel-eyed woman asked herself. Or was it the Holy Spirit. The Greater One on the inside of her? The One who God promised would lead and guide her into all Truth? She was thinking the old way. She despised the way it sounded in her head. Her Mind of Christ was faithfully ministering to her. Will you ever listen? she asked herself. She was trying. She had cried out to God so many times and it felt like no real change had taken place in her.

Both Cynthia and Holly had smiled at Brenda and Oliva when they passed, heading down the hall for the bathroom. "She has to be hot in those cloths," the older woman finally whispered to her daughter, referring to Brenda's apparel. "*Mom*." "I know, I know," Cynthia said. "They wear that in Africa, right?" The older woman gazed at her daughter and smiled. "I taught you that, baby. It's not Godly to gossip. But, guess what? I don't think I was gossipin'. It was me noticin'. And, I was concern fo' her." Holly shook her head, glimpsing Philip as he lifted the piano flap, tapping out some undesirable sound that made her want to ask him what it was he was doing. When he looked up from his clueless fingers, smiling in her direction, Holly lowered her gaze and moved toward the dining room door from the kitchen. She was cradling a tray of pasta with butternut squash and spinach and an hours d' oeuvres plater of prosciutto, asian pear, and date canapes with mint. "Help me, Father," she whispered into the quiet space.

Jumping after her plea as she was startled to see Philip standing inside of the dining room when she pushed through the swinging door. He had entered by way of the foyer. "I thought you saw me comin' this way," Philip said, smiling at the way she winced. "Let me get those." He removed the warm tray and cool plater from her hands and asked if he was setting them down in the right place. "Um-hmm," she said. Peering up at Holly as he bent over the table, Philip asked, "You okay?" The hazel-eyed woman started rearranging the cloth napkins, folding them all another way. She could see he was about to ask again. "I'm fine. Just a little pre-occupied." Philip grinned and came up behind her. He wrapped his arms around her waist and kissed the side of her neck. "Don't worry, baby," he said gently. "My folks love you already. So relax." She unraveled his grasp, pivoting to face him. "I'm not worried about them," Holly said. She blinked and lowered her eyes. Philip placed his finger at her chin, lifting her head. "Then what's botherin' you?" he asked, his gaze caring and warm. She couldn't look at him. Holly backed away a little, touching frantically at the table again. "I don't know what it is, really. I have quite a few things on my mind." "All right," Philip said softly. "Let's discuss them, one by one." Glancing in the living room, Holly couldn't see any one from where she was standing. Then she found Philip's eyes and said, "I'll tell you everything later."

"I don't remember the last time I had a meal this good," Mrs. Williams said. "Cynthia, what was the name of these oxtails again?" Paulette added. "Red-sauce braised," Mrs. Reed answered. Nodding, Philip's mother took a final sip of coffee and leaned back in her chair while Cynthia smiled at the unanimous praise her cooking got. It seemed to flow around the dining room table like an ocean breeze. Even the two babies agreed although Brenda and Mark had a rough time getting them to eat the vegetables. "Thank you," Cynthia said, "To God be all the Glory." Both Philip and Brenda eyed Holly at the same time, each wondering whether they were responsible for the look on her face. "Are you as good of a cook as your mother?" Philip's father asked Holly, who shook her head no. "I could barely boil water," she said with a faint smile. "Paulette, meet your new daughter-in-law," the older man said, teasing his wife. He made himself laugh. "Don't listen to him," Mrs. Williams said. "*Personally,* I think I'm a wonder... well, I'm a pretty good......," she added and waved her hand. "He's right my cooking stinks!" Paulette chuckled freely along with everyone else except Holly, whose low laugh seemed contrived. Suddenly, she wanted to be alone. She needed to hear herself think. No, she needed to hear what the Spirit of the Lord was speaking to her. "Baby, could I get you anything?" Philip asked her. She felt his strong hand cover her limp one beneath the table. It was on her lap. Shaking her head no, Holly then followed the precious sound of Olivia's tiny voice. The child was asking her mother for another piece of the apple cheddar bread pudding. "One more and that is it," Brenda said. "You want another one too, Mark jr.," she added. The boy nodded vigorously, smiling wide, the missing tooth revealed once again. "That was good. Unusual but very good," Mark senior said in regards to the gourmet dessert. "I take it you want another piece, too," Brenda said, grinning at her husband. "Sure, if you insist!" he said, provoking another round of laughter. "Cut your father another slice as well," Paulette told her daughter. "No, it's delicious, but I need another piece like I need this extra rim around my waist," Mr. Williams said, chuckling lightly. "You sure, daddy?" Brenda asked, looking at her father. "I'm sure," he said. Holly observed the way Philip's sister stood up cutting three slices of the pudding, placing one at a time down on her family's dishes, a genuine smile on her face as she did it. Yes, Holly thought, she was a kinder, gentler Brenda that late afternoon. What did that mean? she wondered.

Everyone gathered in the living room, some of the adults sipping non-alcoholic wine and champagne while the children sat Indian-style on the floor opposite one another playing a game of Old Maids. "This is a magnificent apartment, Holly. Did you decorate it yourself?" Paulette asked and took a sip from her wineglass. "Yes, I did." "My baby has such good taste. She made my place just as pretty," Cynthia said, proudly. Paulette paused and stared at Cynthia for a moment. Then she said "I was going to ask you if you would want to be a part of my book club, but hearing you, I take it you don't read much." Paulette laughed. "So, what did you say?... Oh, that's right, Holly was able to hook you up, too, so to speak? Philip did tell me that you two live nearby," Holly's mother paused as she thought. This woman bet' not be startin'no trouble. Cynthia chose to nod her head. "We wanted to be close and I got my own book club," she said. Paulette paused, her beady eyes enlarging through her thick glasses. "You do? How nice. We're reading *Becoming* by Michelle Obama. It's excellent so far. So, where did you both live before?" Paulette saw the way Cynthia Reed was going to respond to the book her book club was reading but she just kept talking. "I asked my son but he didn't know," added Paulette Williams. The look on Cynthia Reed's face noticed how Philip's mother was obviously disinterest in hearing what she was going to say. Brenda sprung up, moving over near the children, joining them on the floor. She had seen the way her mother glared at Holly's mother with a viciousness that tried to strike her down. "The Lower East Side," Cynthia said. She noticed the way Philip looked at his mother, warning in his eyes. She don't wanna know me Holly's mother discerned. "The Lower East Side?" Paulette repeated. "Isn't that down by China town?" she added, glancing at her husband, as if she wanted him to get involved. "Yes," Holly said. Mrs. Williams grimaced. "Talk about moving on up," she said, chuckling to camouflage the disapproving face she knew she had made. Shifting her body in the straight-back chair, she crossed her legs. "What's that 'posed to mean?" Cynthia asked. She set her water glass down on the end table next to Philip's fathers, crossing her legs too. Holly's mother was sitting next to Paulette in the other chair, giving her a dirty look. "Oh, don't mind me," Mrs. Williams said with a laugh, "I'm just mimicking the Jefferson's theme song. You both finally got a piece of the pie! You know the words." From the floor, Brenda shook her head in disgust and told her mother that this was the reason she thinks and acts the way she does. "What are you talking about?" Paulette asked, her protruding forehead wrinkled in bewilderment and her beady eyes squinted. Ignoring her, Brenda asked Holly if the kids could play in the guest room? "Of course, they can," she replied in a quiet monotone. Philip's sister collected the cards and told the children to follow her. She returned alone in no time. "Ask me the question again. I know the Jefferson's theme song," she said to her mother as she began to reflect upon an article she read and saved from a 1992 issue of the *New York Times*. Henry Louis Gates Jr., W.E.B. Du Bois Professor of the Humanities at Harvard University wrote the piece entitled "These films." Mr. Gates had been discussing a few movies starring charismatic actor Denzel Washington, calling those films "guiltsploitation." The Professor mentioned something about the thespian betraying his culture in them, arguing that in order to be upper middle class is to alienate from the 'real' black community. The African-garbed woman certainly didn't think the same way about the actor. After all, Mr. Washington was just playing a part in the bigger picture is what she thought. Somebody had to tell these stories. Instead, Brenda had to admit that she felt as though Mr. Gates had been speaking directly to her. No, she thought, she and Philip weren't acting in anybody's film. That professor was indeed telling her shameful childhood story to the public. Putting their life on blast.

Wearing these African clothes never dismissed the truth from my mind, she thought. Never broke free the chains locking her heart. They were just "cover-ups". "Who do you think you are talking to me in that sassy way, young lady?" Paulette said. She uncrossed her legs and peered at her husband for support. "Leave daddy out of this," Brenda said. "Would you like to know the real reason why we're here?" Brenda asked her mother. "What do you mean by *real reason*? Your father and I are here to simply acquaint ourselves with the Reeds'." "Bren," Philip said. He motioned for her to relax. And before Brenda spoke, Mark rose from the sofa, slipping away down the hall to look in on his children. He was well aware of what was next to come. So he wanted to close the bedroom door to insure that his little ones wouldn't hear all the noise he knew would soon transpire. "I'm sorry," Brenda replied to her brother and glared at her mother again. "Wrong. That is *not* why we're here," she said. "I am *simply* sick and tired of you always putting people down! ... *Simply* sick of you thinking you're better then everyone. That is why we're here, mother! Because of *you* I owe Holly an apology," Brenda said. Cynthia looked at her daughter, making a what is she talking about face. Holly never mentioned anything about the incident between Brenda and herself to her mother. She couldn't even remember if she'd told her mother that she'd met Philip's sister before. "Yes, we may have grown up in an exclusive area," Brenda continued. "Philip and I appreciate having gone to the "better" schools. We appreciate meeting all those "high-rollers" as you would call them. We appreciate having eaten at the "finest" restaurants and the fact that we wore "designer" labels all our lives. But, what *I* didn't appreciate and I'm sure I'm still speaking for Philip, too, is that we'd done those things just so we'd be able to hang with the Paul's, the Tyler's and the Winston's of Englewood, New Jersey. Those people never really accepted us. To them we were nothing more than entertainment. Folks they could boss around. I bet you don't recall the time when Philip and I were chased out of one of their homes? First they had the audacity to ask us whether we could teach them how to sing R&B and show them how to tap dance. As if we, being Black, were born knowing how to." Paulette smiled an uneasy smile as her eyes glimpsed Holly's and Cynthia's. "But you didn't hear those complaints coming from your children right, mother? You kept insisting we try to "fit in" when all we wanted to do was find our true roots, find out who we were, learn about our people and make friends with the Smiths and the Browns who unfortunately lived on the "other side of the tracks." That's what you told us, isn't it? Remember those kids, mother, that *you chased* away? You made them feel like we felt when we came home telling you what had happened to us. What goes around, comes around, right?" The African clothes wearing women, turned to look at Holly. "You reap what you sow. Isn't that what the Bible says?" Holly glanced over at Brenda, paused and nodded yes. She wanted to tell her that she'd experienced similar reproaches as a child, but she didn't. Brenda continued, "Gloria Brown and I used to pretend that she was Foxy Brown, the one who Pam Grier played, and I was Christie Love." Brenda took a moment to relish in those times. Her face told them that she was reflecting about her past. She managed a brief faint smile as the memory became clear then she went on. "Together we were going to save her neighborhood. Get rid of all the drug addicts, pimps and whores with the hopes of making it luxurious like ours. This way, I told her, 'my mother would accept you, Glo," Brenda wiped the tears coursing her face with the back of her hand. "Gloria and I obviously couldn't do what we set out to do..... So, she decided to join the prostitutes, since she couldn't beat 'um. She said those other "ladies of the night" were like family to her." Brenda took a deep breath, glanced at Philip then her eyes transfixed on her mother's again. "And do you know how hard my brother took it when you told his best friend, Ronald Smith to get his dirty behind out of our pool and for him to never step foot in your house again? Huh, mother? Did you even notice the horror on Ronald's face when you told him to "go back to the 'hood and run through the fire hydrant sprinklers like everyone else over there was doing?" Paulette Williams sat in stunned silence while Philip's father's eyes fell to the floor. He knew this day would come. His daughter was a time bomb waiting to explode. "Bren, c'mon. That was a long time ago," Philip said, suppressing his own deep-set emotions. He stood up from the sofa and held his weeping sister in his arms. "I know, but.....," Brenda cried, "It still hurts. I don't know who I am sometimes." Holly folded her arms across her chest, comforting herself. She heard the Holy Spirit's still small voice say to her "I'm the Comforter. They are in need of a Lord and a Savior." She felt the tears welling up, blurring her vision. The sound was so sweet. She promised the Lord that she would pray for their salvation. Brenda's confession of not knowing who she was sometimes was one she'd often heard exit her own mouth, Holly thought. Even though she had a personal relationship with God through Christ Jesus, she and Brenda weren't so different after all.

Chapter Twenty-Three

"It was nice of Mark Sr. and Brenda to drop my mother off at her apartment," Holly said to Philip after everyone had left.

The couple was sitting at the dining room table having coffee and more dessert. "I still can't get over Bren," he said. He used the cloth napkin on his lap to wipe his mouth. "That was wild. She went off on my mother. I never knew she felt that way. I thought I was the only one." "Why didn't you ever say anything?" Holly asked. She ate her last piece of pudding and slid the plate to the side. "Not as bold I guess. I'm a laid back kinda guy." Philip smiled, drained his coffee cup and peered over at her. Watching Holly's still pre-occupied state of mind, he told himself that he'd do anything to make her feel his love. He was ready to expose himself. I'm open like I don't know what, he mused. "So," he said. "Is this later enough?" He gave her a little smile. "Pardon me?" Philip grinned more this time. "You told me you'd tell me everything that was on your mind later." Holly took a sip of coffee and leaned back in her chair. She met his steady gaze. "I don't know." She paused, gathered her thoughts and said, "It feels like so much has happened in such a short period of time." Philip nodded in agreement. "First of all," Holly said, "before we go any further into this conversation, I want you to know that I really do enjoy every second we spend together." "But," he said. His mouth was still smiling but his eyes were worried. "Yes, 'but'," she said. "But, I'd like us to slow down the pace....." "Slow down the pace?" Philip said incredulously. "Baby, we've already passed go. I don't understand. What, what? I'm not man enough for you? You wanna see other guys?" Holly shook her head no. Why did they all ask the same type of questions? she wondered. Man enough? What did that mean? "Philip, I just feel as though I don't have much time to hear my own thoughts," she said. "Oh, and I'm in your way?" "No, I didn't say that....." "But," he said sarcastically. "Will you listen to me. I'm only saying that I still need a little time to reclaim myself. I refuse to subject myself to the same degree of pain I felt the last time." Philip gave her that mega-watt smile. "Holly, I'm not here to hurt you, baby or take anything away from you. All I wanna do is love you." He held up his right hand, adding. "I swear." "I know. I know you care, and nobody ever goes into a relationship with the intentions of hurting the other person, but I've been swept off my feet by somebody who did nothing but tell me lies. The joke was on me. And thank goodness I was strong enough to let him go. I mean, thank God!" She paused and said, "Philip, you have to try to see my side." He sighed. "Baby, you're gonna have to stop comparing me to Bradford. Please. 'Cause that brother ain't got a nothin' on me." Holly lowered her eyes. "Talk to me," he said. "I'll be here for you as long as you want me to be, baby. *But* you're gonna have to let me in." Lifting her gaze, she said, "I know you mean well, but the ice is still thawing from around my heart. I'm so numb I can't even tell you that I feel the same way you do for me." "That's okay," he said. "I have plenty of time, and it just means I'm gonna have to work twice as hard to win you over." Holly finally smiled. "Thank you for understanding. I just didn't want either of us to wake up one morning and ask who it is we were sleeping next to. I had asked myself that question when I was with..." Holly caught herself. She was about to bring Bradford up again. Or, did she pause because of how disgusting that sounded to her. Waking up next to this man and that man. What was she doing? I'm somebody's wife! she told herself. Philip was quiet. He wasn't tryin' to fall in love with her like this. Man, what happened? Now he knew what he put Selma Girard and all those other women through. Holly cleared her throat. Did he know what she was thinking? She was able to bring Philip back to the table with the noise she made. He had that far off look in his eyes again. "Philip, Courtney left Vanessa." "What!" he said, jumping up from his seat. "When did this happen?" "Apparently, last night after we'd left."

"Well, well why?" he stuttered. What is he going to think when I tell him this? Holly thought. "She's pregnant and he left her?" Philip furrowed his brows and placed his hands on the back of the chair directly in front of her. "He left because she's havin' a baby?" he asked. She shook her head no. "He left because *she's* having another man's baby." Philip opened and closed his mouth then she saw his Adams apple move up and down as he slowly swallowed. "Whose is it?" he asked and rubbed the back of his neck. Holly shrugged. "I don't know." Philip sat back down. "Now do you understand why I'm so concerned about us?" she asked. "Maybe I'm being foolish," she added with a smile. Philip nodded and started moving his head in a circular motion. He was trying to relieve his neck and shoulders of their sudden stiffness. "Don't worry," Holly said softly. Philip looked at her. "I'm sure Courtney will contact you." She figured that was what his facial expression was saying. Breathing in deeply, Philip asked, "Where'd he go?" "No one seems to know."

The phone rang.

Cynthia Reed was calling to discuss their afternoon. "Mom, could I call you back," Holly said on the phone in the kitchen. Philip appeared in the doorway. "Baby, don't hang up. I'm gonna leave." "Hold on," she said to her mother, covering the receiver. "I'll give you a call tomorrow," he said before she could start asking him questions. Philip gave Holly a kiss on the lips and she watched the back of hm leave her apartment.

Chapter Twenty-Four

The morning sky was cloudy and the air was damp, smelling of rain that subsequent Monday. Holly took her time walking up the quiet block to the law firm. She wasn't anticipating seeing Vanessa. What would she say to her when, still like before, she couldn't find it in herself to sympathize with a woman who would step out on her man. He's her husband! True, her inability to identify with her partners infidelity probably stemmed from what Bradford had done to her, but wrong is wrong, Holly reasoned, no matter who it was. "I don't know, but Courtney is my friend, too," she mumbled to herself, her eyes gazing down at the ground while she walked. That didn't even sound right to her anymore. Could men and women be friends outside of marriage? She believed God gave her a revelation that the answer was no. Well, Holly thought as she pushed that to the back of her mind. Vanessa should have left Courtney first. Holly would have respected her had she done that.

Looking up, she glanced across the street at a man who was walking his tail-wagging West Highland White Terrier. His little fury friend, with the show dog prance was, clearly happy to be outside. She smiled when the owner met her amicable gaze. Then peering ahead at her office building, Holly saw Kelly and Elliot standing at the top of the stairs. Things appeared to be in the couples favor and all the grinning and girl-like capriciousness Kelly displayed last week solidified Holly's assumption. The lovebirds were giving each other a good-bye kiss. How sweet. Holly lowered her eyes and opened the gate. Clearing her throat, Kelly pushed Elliot away and he cleared his throat, too, realizing his girlfriend's boss was there. "Good morning," Holly said with a smile. "How you doin', Ms. Reed," Elliot said. It was evident that Kelly had told him who she was from the assurance in his voice. "I'm fine and yourself?" Holly asked him. "Oh," Elliot said, as if he wasn't expecting a direct response, "I'm good, too." He smiled big. And it was then that Holly saw the likeness Elliot and Philip had in common. She smiled at her secretary and opened the door. "I'll be right up," Kelly told her just before Holly entered the brownstone.

Inside, the hazel-eyed attorney waved at Telma who was on the phone taking a message and when she made it half way up the stairs, the receptionist hung up and said, "Don't forget to return Leslie Stokeses call!" "Thanks, Telma! I have it at the top of my 'things to do' list." Telma nodded and swiveled her chair back around.

Samantha and Tina were already hard at work and Tracy was coming out of the bathroom when Holly reached the top landing. "What are you smiling about?" Holly asked her. But Tracy didn't answer. She walked over to her hazel-eyed partner and extended her left hand. Holly looked down at it, her eyes and mouth widening when she saw the large emerald-cut diamond engagement ring in a platinum setting on her finger. "Wow! ... Karl?" Holly asked. Tracy nodded. "When did this happen?" asked the hazel-eyed woman. "Last night. Don't asked me why I didn't call you. Honey, I was so shocked I couldn't think straight." The two women hugged, letting out squeals of excitement as they went into Holly's office. "Karl, wow, you got him?" Holly said. She turned her desk lamp on and sat down. "Uh-huh. And he said he wants to get married as soon as his divorce is final," Tracy said. She, sat too, and held up her hand, admiring the ring. "He's not as cheap as I thought he was. Three and a half karats is enough to keep me quiet," Tracy chuckled. "It is gorgeous," Holly said, adding, "I don't want to take from your moment, but have you talked to Vee?" Lowering her hand to her lap, Tracy nodded. "Yeah, the day before yesterday. She'll be in." Holly blinked in disbelief and thought back to the time when she and Bradford broke up. I couldn't even get out of bed the next day, she told herself, and Vanessa has the strength to come to work? "Is she okay?" Holly asked. "Uh-huh. You know Vee," Tracy said and stood up. "Yes, I do, but I can't believe she was able to say she'd be at work today. Has she heard from him?" "No," Tracy said. She moved over to the door and said, "I have to return some phone calls." Holly took her agenda out of her pocketbook and set it on the desk. "I have to call Ms. Stokes back." "Oh, she phoned again?" Holly nodded. "Friday as I was walking out the door. I Can't wait to hear what kind of mood she's in this morning." Tracy smiled. "Well, let me know if I could help with anything," she said and left.

Holly took a deep breath and dialed the number. The phone rang four times before an unfamiliar out-of-breath female voice answered. "Hello, may I please speak to Ms. Leslie Stokes." "Who is this?" the woman asked. She was still trying to slow her breathing. "My name is Holly Reed. I'm a friend of Ms. Stokes." The attorney wasn't sure if she should identify herself. The woman on the other end could have been Leslie's fiances sister or mother. "If you're a friend why are you saying her name like that?" the woman asked. "My daughter never mentioned you before," she added. Holly smiled, nodding. "I'm sorry," she said. "I was trying to be discreet. I'm the lawyer....." The woman cut Holly off immediately and began to shout. "Why didn't you help her? Why didn't you help my daughter!" Holly's heart rate quickened. "I will. Is she there?" The woman was crying now. "No. She's gone. She's not here anymore!" "Uh, okay. Where can I reach her then?" Holly asked. "You can't!" she cried. "Leslie's.... oh, my daughter is...... dead! He killed her! Why didn't you help her? She called you on Friday. That was the last time I spoke to her. I never got a chance to tell her how much I loved her!" Holly was stunned. Completely shaken up. She couldn't say a word. Placing her hand over her mouth she leaned forward, dropping the receiver on her desk. She could still hear the woman's painful howls, asking her why? Why? Why didn't she save Leslie from that monster? "Maurice Lemont Carter killed my daughter with his bare hands..." Pulling herself up from the chair, her face moist from an instant cold sweat, Holly felt herself getting dizzy, sick. She rushed into the bathroom, one hand still covering her mouth, the other holding her stomach as she fell to her knees in front of the toilet, vomiting.

Tracy hung up from her call and hurried in behind Holly. She'd heard her partner run by. "Oh, my God. What is it?" she asked as she stroked the back of Holly's head. She was still regurgitating. Finally stopping, Holly brought the back of her right hand to her mouth. Her chest heaved in and out as she balled herself up, resting her head against the cool tiled floor. She was crying so hard she began to hyperventilate. "Oh, sweetie!" Tracy said. She raised her short straight crimson skirt and sat down next to Holly, lifting her head into her arms then onto her lap. "She's dead, Trace," the hazel-eyed attorney said, breathing heavily as tears poured down her face. "Who?" "Le... Leslie Stokes. He killed her! And I could have prevented it." Tracy gasped and covered her own mouth in astonishment. "Oh, my God," she said. "It's my fault!" Holly cried. "I should have taken her call...." "Don't say that. You tried to help her and she didn't want your help before," Tracy said reassuringly. "Don't do this to yourself." Holly sat up, resting her face in her hands. She began to sob some more. "I think Ms. Stokes' mother is still on the phone, Trace. I don't remember saying bye." Holly lowered her hands, breathing in and out slowly. Tracy stood up. "That's right," she coaxed, rubbing Holly's shoulders. "Let it out. Come on, in and out," the short-haired attorney instructed. "I'll be back." Tracy sprinted into Holly's office for the phone.

Curling herself back up on the floor, the hazel-eyed woman could hear someone else's footsteps approaching. It was Kelly, telling by the red loafers the lawyer managed a peek of. The secretary came in, sitting down beside her boss, a glass of water in her hand. She had caught the tail-end of the conversation Holly was involved in with Leslies Stokes' mother and watched her boss run past her, oblivious to her presence. The dark-skinned woman was there to give back this time. It was her chance to show Holly how she, too, could be right toward her.

"Here take a sip," Kelly said. She placed the cool glass to Holly's lips. Sniffing, Holly thanked her. She gazed at the dark-skinned woman through make-up smudged eyes and took the glass, taking a sip of the iced-cold water. "You did try," Kelly told her. "You always do." Holly sniffed back more stubborn tears. Tracy and Kelly were right. She did try and it was time for her to see it. Jesus had taken her guilt and her wrong on the Cross at Calvary. You are free, the hazel-eyed woman heard in her heart.

Tracy asked Kelly to leave she and Holly alone when she came back in with the information she had to pry out of Leslie Stokes' mother. The hazel-eyed attorney was still on the floor, holding her knees. Holly listened in silence as Tracy spoke and watched as she began to wipe away her disgorge with some Fantastik and paper towels she'd gotten from the cabinet beneath the sink. Tracy rolled up her shirt sleeves and went at the mess without making a face. "Maurice Carter came home Friday and apparently pressed the redial button on the phone. He must have known Leslie wanted to leave and had been in contact with someone. Our office machine picked up." Tracy shook her head and sighed. "So, I guess they fought and her death was the outcome." She peered at Holly through the mirror above the sink, adding, "He broke her neck and she died instantly." Holly started to cry again and Tracy continued to speak. But, this time it had nothing to do with the murder or the vomit she'd been cleaning up. She was saying something about knowing when it's not your place to become involved. "I learned that the hard way. Holly, we can't make anyone do what they have no intentions of doing. We could try till we're blue in the face and it doesn't help. Being a lawyer, I sometimes find myself sounding as though I'm the law itself. What I say has to go." Tracy sprayed one more spot, wiped and put the cleanser and paper towels away. She put the toilet seat cover down and sat on top of it, facing Holly. "Certain things are out of our control. Sure, we could blame ourselves, but what good does that do? Make us sick to our stomachs, give us headaches that aspirin can't cure or we wind up with ulcers. We lose our appetites yet people are going to do what they want to do. With or without our consent and support." Holly stared at Tracy, getting the sense that she was talking about something pertaining to herself. But what? Her words had a personal touch that Holly couldn't quite grasp. Maybe she wasn't holding on tight enough. Maybe she didn't want to receive the underlying message. And why not? I'm not anyone's Savior, she thought. His Name is Jesus.

Holly was at her desk talking to her friend, Assistant District Attorney, Jeanne Landers while Tracy sat, facing her. The hazel-eyed lawyer had been giving the prosecutor all the information she had on Ms. Stokes and her murderer. "I know you will, Jeanne. You're the best. Yes, let's get together as soon as possible. I agree. We shouldn't allow our work to dictate our friendship. Okay great. I'll talk to you soon." Holly hung up and sighed. "Now all we have to do is wait," Tracy said. "That's really something how Ms. Stokes boyfriend killed her and then he turned himself into the police," Tracy said. She gave Holly a sympathetic smile. She had heard how difficult it was for her partner to keep from crying during her conversation with Ms. Landers. Looking down at Friday's message from the slain Leslie Stokes, Holly nodded, afraid to trust her voice. She was so mystified over the whole thing, although she warned the victim before of this tragic possibility. "Did her mother tell you that Jeanne was the only person, besides the police that she contacted?" Holly asked. Tracy nodded and the two lawyers averted their eyes toward the ajar door at the same time. The sound of Vanessa Benjamin's voice demanded they did. The full-figured attorney was telling her secretary that she wanted a decaffeinated coffee. "I'm pregnant," she said, although she wasn't explaining her out-of-the-blue request. Because when the secretary sprung up from behind her desk to give Vanessa a congratulatory hug, she stopped her in her tracks like she was directing traffic and asked where Tracy was. "In Holly's office," Samantha said quietly and changed direction, descending the stairs for the kitchen. Vanessa dropped her pocketbook and tote in her office and walked back out. She tapped on Holly's door, entering at the same time. "Hey," she said to her partners, giving Tracy half a smile afterward. "Congratulations. I got your message last night," Vanessa said. Tracy glimpsed Holly, feeling a little bad about the lie she'd told regarding her being too shocked to call anyone about her surprise engagement. But Holly knew that the two of them were closer and had their own secrets together. "I'll take you out to lunch today. I want to hear all about it," Vanessa said. "It's about time Karl snapped out of it. Let me see the ring." Tracy extended her hand. "Hmm, cute. Real cute," was the full-figured attorney's assessment of the more than just cute diamond. Vanessa finally glanced over at Holly who appeared to be waiting her turn.

"I suppose congratulations are in order for you, too," Holly said. She sat straight up and laced her fingers together, knowing that she didn't have a chance to officially congratulate her full-figured partner at Courtney's birthday party. Vanessa placed her hand on her stomach, peering down at it. She nodded. "Yep, and I can't wait to see my baby." "Does the baby's father feel the same way?" Holly asked. Vanessa looked at Tracy then a slow smirk crossed her lips as her eyes met Holly's again. "He has no choice." "You spoke to him?" Tracy asked, breaking the uncomfortable quiet that had crept up. "Uh-huh. Last night and again this morning," Vanessa said. "I wanted to make sure he didn't think he was dreaming. So now that he knows that *this*," she said, pointing to her stomach, "is very real, he knows he's *got* to get his you know what together." Vanessa walked all the way into the hazel-eyed attorneys office, sitting down beside Tracy in the other chair. "Well, at least he sounds like a decent guy," Holly said, hoping she'd find out who he was. "He is. You would like him," Vanessa said, smiling. "It sounds like you've known him for a while," Holly said. Vanessa shrugged. "You could say that," she said. Holly peered down at her hands then back up at Vanessa, saying, "Courtney must have been devastated. Why would you announce your pregnancy at his party, knowing that the baby could very well have been someone elses?" Holly said. Vanessa smirked, shrugging again. "Who would have thought Courtney was sterile? Does that answer your question?" Holly ignored her and said, "Well at least he didn't seem too distraught when he stopped by my apartment yesterday morning." "Why'd he come by there?" Vanessa asked, tilting her head and grimacing. Holly had asked herself that question a few times, too. But now she knew the answer. "To say good-bye," was her honest belief. Vanessa was about to say something else, until, "Oh, uh, Vee," Tracy said, deciding that it was a good time to change the subject. "Remember that woman who'd called Holly a while back saying her boyfriend had been beating on her?" "Yeah. What he do kill her?" Vanessa asked. Holly lowered her head and Tracy nodded. "I'm not surprised," Vanessa said. She looked out into the hall. Samantha was standing there holding a cup in her hand, unsure if it was okay for her to enter. Vanessa waved her in. "You are sure that this is caffeine free, right?" she asked her secretary in a way that would make her want to tell her it was even if it wasn't. "Yes, I'm sure." Samantha set the cup down on Holly's desk and walked back out, closing the door behind her.

"So," Vanessa said, lifting the steaming cup to her mouth. "How did you guys find out about the woman's death?" She blew softly, taking a sip and putting it back down. "Holly returned her phone call and Ms. Stokes mother answered, telling her... the news. She told me he strangled her and called the police on himself. He's probably going to plead temporary insanity," Tracy said, shaking her head in disbelief. Vanessa eyed Holly. She was still looking down. "Why do you seem so bent out of shape over it?" the full-figured attorney asked. "Girl, please. That woman knew what she was up against. The Lord rain's on the just and the unjust, right Holly?" The hazel-eyed woman glared over at Vanessa. "Right! So, this is proof that this terrible situation should have had a good outcome, right?" she asked. "Come on. I thought you were getting better at not taking your work so personally. It's not healthy. What are you going to do ask the D.A. if you could help with this case like you did with the Moore boys?" Vanessa picked up the cup again, taking two more slow sips, awaiting an answer. Holly just sighed and shook her head no.

At 2:00 p.m. Holly tried calling Philip again at the restaurant from her office. He never returned the one she'd placed to him two hours ago, like Darryl told her he said he would. This time one of the bartenders answered, putting Holly on what seemed to be an eternal hold. She sat there patiently, tapping her fingertips atop the desk. Behind her the clouds had finally opened up. The rain was coming down heavily and there was lightening igniting the sky. "Hello," said the bartender when she came back to tell Holly about Philip. "He's talking to the chef. Could I have him call you back?" she asked. "That's okay," Holly said, "I'll try him later." After hanging up the phone, Holly turned, gazing out the window. She saw a couple without an umbrella standing against the doors of one of the brownstones across the street, holding their briefcases close to them, trying to keep themselves and the bags dry. Sighing, Holly wondered if Philip was angry at her because of their conversation yesterday. "He didn't look right when he left," she said to the empty office and spun around to face her desk again. Peering at the files in her in-box, Holly decided not to think about her relationship or anyone elses. She had too much work to do. But when the intercom sounded and Kelly's voice came through with a smile attached, Holly felt her heart lift. Philip, she told herself. "It's Carmen," the secretary said. There was a lull. "Holly, do you want it?" The lawyer cleared her throat and said, "Put her through."

"I tell you I saw the man of God that the Lord told me I'm going to marry and you don't call me back?" Carmen teased. "I'm sorry," Holly said. "When you hear the latest, I'll be forgiven." She removed a file from her in-box, setting it in front of her. "What is it?" Carmen asked with a righteous preparedness in her voice. "How did it go at Courtney's birthday celebration and with Philip's family?" the Latina woman asked. "That's what the latest is all about. Look at our

324

Heavenly Father showing you things to come. Let's just say both situations are something to remember." "Okay, so tell me about Philip's family first. Did his sister start up again?" "No, she was actually well behaved and very transparent. I like her a lot. His mother, on the other hand, took over where she left off." "Really?" "Yes, but … I saw the Hand of God in all of this. He used Brenda to put her in her place." "Good. I know He worked it out?" Holly thought about what Carmen said for a moment. It is finished, she reminded herself. "Yes, He did. So," Holly said, modifying their conversation, "let's talk about this guy, sorry correction, "your husband sayeth the Lord." She didn't think it was a good idea to discuss Courtney with Vanessa sitting on the other side of the wall. The two friends laughed about the 'husband' comment and Carmen went on to tell Holly everything she had found out about the man who she hoped would be hers in manifestation soon.

"He's a doctor?" Holly said. "Give me some time and I will know what kind," Carmen said. "You could only find out but so much from a license plate." They both laughed again. "He must be somethin' for you to resort back to your former P.I. status," Holly said, chuckling lightly for a quick moment. She began to ponder what she just said. "resort back to". Was this Carmen's old way of thinking? Holly thought. "I'm telling you, sis. I heard the wedding march in my head as soon as I saw him. And, then the Holy Spirit gave me a witness in my heart." Holly smiled. "Amen. Just rest in Him. No climbing into his apartment window while doctor whoever is asleep to see whether or not he has a photo out of the woman or women he's dating just so you'd be able to size up 'the competition'," Holly said. "I know," Carmen said, giggling. "Father, help me!" she said with a humorous yet desperate plea in her voice. Holly smiled and told her she'd be praying for her as she peered over at the door. Kelly was signaling her. She had another phone call. Putting Carmen on hold, the lawyer asked who it was. "Philip," Kelly said. Holly nodded and told her friend that she would speak with her soon. Oh, and by the way, congratulations on breaking it off with So and So." Carmen laughed a little at how they couldn't remember her ex-boyfriends name and said "Amen!"

The television set in Holly's bedroom was tuned to HBO. But the Monday-night movie wasn't appealing to her. Then again, she hadn't paid it much attention. Her mind was too focused on how late Philip was. He told her earlier over the phone that he'd be there no later than 7:00 p.m. and the clock was ticking rapidly toward 8:15 p.m. Plopping down on the edge of her bed, dressed in denim shorts and a white DKNY T-shirt, Holly ran her fingers through her hair. She didn't know what was going on with him, but she knew one thing for sure, she wasn't about to call to find out. "I need to be watching Christian television," she said and turned the channel. No more nonsense, she thought as pastor Steven Furtick's voice entered her room by way of the T.V. He was talking about how Jesus "handled it". Holly took a deep breath and nodded her head. "Yes, Lord," she said in a low voice. She could remember literally hunting Bradford down when he'd renege on one of their dates. But she has had enough. Pastor Furtick said it again "It's handled!" Holly nodded again. It was time for her to change. If a man didn't do what he said he was going to do, why should I care? she asked herself. Philip specifically told her he was not angry about her wanting to slow down the pace of their relationship and he also told her how he couldn't wait to see her tonight. "That's what he said," Holly told herself aloud. She was suddenly feeling taken advantage of and lied to. And he had the nerve to sound as though he was smiling, happy to hear her voice. Holly felt cheap? She threw herself back on the bed. Why did she have sex with him on the first date? Or, outside of a marriage covenant? That was the real question. Where was her head that night? And where was her head again the next time she had sex with him? She certainly knew the truth. But, I chose to ignore it, she thought. Was she some kind of whore?

Hearing a car pull up in front of the building, Holly stood up, peeking out the window. Stepping out from the back seat of a taxi, covering her head with a newspaper to ward off the rain, was

Kathleen Parker Wahl. Holly watched her neighbor until she disappeared beneath the buildings navy-blue awning.

Turning off the television, Holly crossed the room to her dresser. She picked up Carmen's book, opening it to the page she'd left off on. That's what she'll do; escape into the lives of her friend's fictional characters. Holly closed the novel and headed toward the front of the apartment. In the kitchen, she opened the refrigerator, picking at some of yesterday's leftovers. She placed the novel down on the counter. Holly removed the remainder of apple cheddar bread pudding, which was wrapped in aluminum foil. She grabbed a fork out of the drawer, tucked the book under her arm and moved into the dining room. When she turned on the light the doorbell rang.

"Is it a good time?" Kathleen asked, looking exhausted, but eager to talk. Holly could tell the White woman had just come home from work. She was still wearing a stethoscope around her neck, her hair was a little messy and her makeup was nearly gone. Nothing left except her mascara. Holly looked back over her shoulder toward the dining room then back at Kathleen. "It's fine. I was just about to have some dessert." "Oh, well bring it over to my place." Holly gazed at her neighbor, squinting. "I'd like you to come to my apartment, Holly. It'll be better for me."

Holly didn't know why it was taking Kathleen so long to change her clothes. She was sitting in the White womans loudly decorated dining room with an empty dessert plate and a piece of balled up aluminum foil in front of her while the Hurrell's suspended on the wall kept her quiet company and the music tiptoeing in from the opposite room delighted her. It was low, but Holly began to sing along to the familiar sound of "Keep Your Eyes Upon Jesus". Finally, she heard Kathleen making her way down the hall. "Sorry, I couldn't remember where I put this," she said. Turning to face her neighbor, Holly stared at the small discolored box Kathleen referred to cradled in her hand. She couldn't tell if the original shade was a light blue or green, it had paled too severely for her to know. "Are you done?" Kathleen asked as she eyed the empty plate. And when Holly nodded the White woman waved her into the living room.

They both sat in the same spots as before, facing the fire place. Kathleen wondered where she'd begin. She wondered how she'd spring her long-awaited surprise on Holly as her gaze held the box tighter than her hands could ever. Holly glanced around the dim room, taking in the hypnotic sound of Billie Holiday. Lady Day's sultry voice entered the room once the last song finished playing. Her neighbor's magnificent stereo system made the late singers lyrics come to life. It couldn't have been any more vibrant had she'd been standing there beside them, crooning her heart out as she always had a wonderful way of doing. "Strange Fruit" was the song she was singing. Pain hung from her words like the lynched bodies did those trees. "I almost forgot how wonderful she was," Holly said in a low almost meditated way. She had been reminded in her spirit about how the Lord taught her not to entertain death. Silently, she prayed that Kitty would get the same revelation. "She's one of my mother's favorite singers," Holly said, not really knowing the reason as Cynthia had stopped listening to secular music quite some time ago. Kathleen finally lifted her head, nodding as her eyes rose up toward the mantle top, searching the rows of pictures for one of her parents, knowing that there wasn't one there. The only memories of George and Sara Parker were those in her head, she reminded herself glumly. Swallowing the lump in her throat, Kathleen eyed Holly. "Surprisingly, my mother loved her, too," she said. "She would tell us that Billie Holiday was.... different. A good different." Holly, much to her own astonishment, was able to mask her bewilderment. "I know I'm acting bizarre to you," Kathleen said, "but don't be alarmed. I'm just waiting to be led on the best way to give this to you." Both women glanced down at the box then back at each other. "No, you don't look... I mean take as much time as you need," Holly said while asking herself what it was that Kathleen had in that worn box to give to her. The White woman breathed in and slid back on the sofa. "I don't know why this feels so difficult," she said. "I should be excited, especially for you." "What? What feels difficult?" Holly asked. The White woman shook her head. "I just want you to know that I learned a valuable lesson the last time you were here. And I learned another one when I was at your apartment yesterday. But the biggest lesson learned for me took place twenty-four years ago. And It took the tears of a child to teach me." She shook the box lightly in a nervous gesture. "Your tears, Holly. That's where this all began. Otherwise you would not have lost this. For year's I had battled racism. I'm not using that as an excuse for my horrendous childhood behavior, but you and I both know it played a major part. Growing up in my home was like living in...." Kathleen laughed a little, adding, "I can't think of anything that bad to compare it to." Pausing the White woman began twirling some loose strands hanging at the side of her face. "Yes." She sighed, letting them go as she went on, "I'm a product of a racist home." The words fell from Kathleen's mouth as if she were admitting to being an alcoholic during an AA meeting. "My parents are bigots, and my siblings chose to stick by their sides rather than break the cycle." She sighed again. "And now they, too, will more than likely raise prejudice children." Holly nodded sympathetically, knowing that Kathleen's admission was difficult for her to convey. "But, I on the other hand, went against their crippling beliefs by leaving my parent's home at the age of eighteen. As soon as I was legal. My sweet heart told me that I had an Abrahamic moment." "You haven't spoken to your parents since then?" Holly asked. She really admired the way her neighbor often referred to the Lord. Kathleen shook her head. "No, I haven't," she said, her voice cracking a bit. "It's tough at times, but remaining their daughter would have been a lot harder for me. I belong to a new family. The family of God." The two women peered down at the box Kathleen had placed between them on the sofa, meeting each other's gaze afterward. "This I believe is yours," the White woman said, smiling faintly. Holly couldn't begin to imagine what it was as she reached for the blue-green box, opening it slowly. She gasped when she lifted the top off, seeing what lay inside. "I don't know what to say," she said, feeling her eyes welling up. "You don't have to say anything," Kathleen said, stifling her own tears. "It belongs to you." Holly removed the delicate trinket, slipping it across her wrist. Flipping it over, she read the inscription, "Daddy's little SD." Her voice was shaky with emotion as a determined tear rolled down her cheek. "You saw this fall off of my arm in the schoolyard?" Kathleen nodded. "And I tried to find you the next day, but the principal told me you were transferred to another school." Holly covered her mouth, keeping the sobs that wanted so desperately to come out in. She couldn't believe that little White girl who had given her such a hard time could have grown up to be so lovely. "I don't know how to thank you," Holly said. "I can't believe you saw this fall off of my wrist that day. Oh, look.... you got the clasp fixed." Holly stared at her new neighbor, who returned an almost identical gaze filled with peace. "How did you, I mean what made you remember having it?" Kathleen smiled. "Your mother, sugar dumpling. And, the Holy Spirit put a witness in my spirit." The two women giggled like they were nine all over again. Then Holly stopped laughing and took a deep breath, her eyes still on her neighbors. "Kathleen, thank you. Thank you so very much. You don't know what this means to me," she said. But, by the Grace of God, Kathleen Parker Wahl knew exactly what it meant.

Chapter Twenty-Five

"Anything?" Cynthia Reed asked her daughter two weeks from the day she'd met Philip Williams and his family. She had done her best to avoid the subject during their quiet dinner. But through the awkward hush, the older woman saw how diligently her child tried to hide the hurt of hers and Philip's breakup. The Lawd only has the best for us, Cynthia told herself. The older woman stood in the living room doorway as she awaited her daughter's remark. Holly hesitated for a moment and said, "Anything?" Holly shook her head no while she peered out the window of her mother's apartment. Cynthia Reed's question was inevitable, the younger woman reasoned as her eyes found their way up toward the sunlit sky. August had truly arrived, Holly thought, spotting a V-shape formation of birds, who were obviously headed south early in preparation for the long winter ahead. "Well, don't you call him no more," Cynthia said as she crossed the room. "The Lawd's showin' you somethin' 'bout him. Take heed to what He's sayin'," Cynthia grunted in disbelief as she flopped down in her leather winged-backed chair, lifting her feet with slippers on atop the matching ottoman in front of her. "I wasn't going to call him?" Holly said. She fixed the curtains and sat down on the sofa. "I knowed you told me that before, but I had to hear myself tell you," Cynthia said, "I'm still yo' moma." Holly leaned her head back, shutting her eyes. And the older woman sighed, thinking, that Philip was just as much a fool as the woman who pushed him out into the delivery room was. "Let's talk about somethin' else," Cynthia said. "Somethin' that ain't tryin' to steal our peace. Okay, baby?" "Fine," Holly said quietly. "Have you met or seen Vanessa's baby's father?" Cynthia asked. Holly shook her head no, staying in the same position: eyes closed, head leaned back. "Well, what she tell you 'bout him?" "Not much." Holly shrugged her shoulders and opened her eyes. She sat straight up. Her mother was shaking her head. "And nobody's heard a peep from Courtney?" she asked. "No. I told you I'd tell you as soon as someone has." "Don't get so touchy," the older woman mumbled, "I'm not the enemy." Leaning forward, Holly rested her elbows on her knees. She peered over at her mother, who was straightening the doilies on the arms of the chair she was in. "I know you're not the enemy, but this conversation is threatening to steal my peace. So, can we please talk about something other than Philip, Vanessa and Courtney?" Holly asked. She was smiling a little. The older woman looked at her daughter. "Yes, baby. We can. One mo' thing, sweetie 'fore we change the subject. I been meanin' to tell you. Philip's family was real pleasant when they drove me home from yo' place. That was God. We discussed how the Holy Spirit led me to make prayer be apart of my book club meetings. The Holy Spirit put it on my heart. Said it would be a good thing fo' us to pray for each other." Holly nodded. "That's great, mom." The two women began to talk about the dinner dance that Barbara Mathews had. Cynthia brought up the gentleman who had used the "you move like a praise dancer" line on her. "I don't knowed why he said that to me," the older woman said then she burst out laughing and raised her hands. "Well, I was holdin' my arms up like this, swayin' them back and forth like this." She was still laughing a little. Holly smiled. "Where's Mr. Freeman from?" she asked her grinning mother. "Chicago," Cynthia said and lowered her arms. "Use to live on Michigan Avenue. I hear it's a lot like Park Avenue." "Yes, it is. But it seems a little cleaner there," Holly said. "Oh, that's right, baby. You flew out there on business last year. I do remember you tellin' me it was nicer. Wow!" "When am I going to meet him?" Holly asked in a way that made her think she sounded like her mother. "Chile, please. I'm not studyin' that ole geezer..." Cynthia paused. "I did pray for him and, baby, you knowed, I believe the Lawd showed me that he is a eagle. He does seem like the real deal and he speaks so good like you." Holly smiled. "What you smilin' at me like that fo'?" the older woman asked, smoothing her hand nervously over one of the doilies. Her daughter grinned some more and said, "Don't be afraid, mom. The Lord may be telling you that Mr. Freeman was sent to you by Him." Holly giggled at the drama in Cynthia Reed's gasped. She, too, had to laugh. The two women continued on their topic for a good hour, giggling like Mr. Freeman was something wonderful that God had revealed. Holly stood up and she continued to giggle as she told her mother that she was leaving. She walked out the older woman's door. In the hallway, she wondered what she was going to do for the rest of that Saturday night. Holly paused, feeling as though the thought of that, suddenly made her forget all about the joy she just experienced on the other side of her mother's door.

Rummaging through her closet, Holly came across a sheath dress in a beautiful coral that she'd never worn. She cut off the price tag and slipped it over her head onto her freshly-bathed and shimmer-moisturized body. If he wasn't going to come to her, she decided to bring herself to him. How dare Philip leave her a message like that? He hasn't seen me in two weeks, she mused, and he's going to act as though there's nothing wrong? She sucked her teeth. "Talking about how much he misses me. We'll see. And I don't care about how busy his night at work is *supposed* to be!" Holly stepped into a pair of beige strappy sandals with a two-inch heel, spritzed on a light-scented perfume, and headed over to "Phil's House" by cab.

Since the traffic was backed up due to a minor accident, the hazel-eyed woman told the driver to let her out on the corner of 56th and Park. "I'll walk the rest of the way," she said and stuck a ten-dollar bill into the taxi drivers hand.

Madison Avenue was active for a Saturday night. Almost as lively as it was during the week. Holly weaved through passersby, craning her neck a bit to see if there was a line outside of "Phil's House". And it was. There were a few groups of twenty-something year old's, some tourists and one couple, who was having a last cigarette before going inside. Holly winced and stopped walking. Karl's black Range Rover was pulling up in front of Philip's restaurant. She couldn't tell if the person in the passenger's seat was Tracy. The tints on the jeeps window were much darker than she recalled. Holly moved up against the wall of a nearby office building. She observed in perplexed silence as she witnessed Philip jumping down from the back seat. He was holding an overnight bag in his hand. Holly saw him say a few words to Karl, the passenger in the back seat of the four-wheel-drive, and turn to walk toward his place of business. He would not have seen Holly if that girl didn't ask him how much longer she and her friends would have to wait for a table. Philip told her he'd find out. Then in one swift motion, he glanced back over his shoulder at the sleek vehicle from which he just departed, waiting for it to take the light. When it did, cruising uptown, Philip lowered his head and turned to meet Holly's hard-to-predict gaze. His first reaction was to present her with his best smile. "And where are you off to, looking and smelling so good?" he asked, kissing her on the cheek. He was really aiming for her lips, but she averted her face. "I decided to pay you a visit. You sounded like you were so miserable on my machine." Philip appeared to sigh. "Good," he said and opened the door. She didn't have to look back at him as she entered first to know that he was examining what she had on and the way her hair was done. "Was Tracy with Karl?" Holly asked. "Yeah. I, uh, ran into them at the racquet club and he offered me a ride. I know it's not that far away, but this brother, *whew*, is tired. I've been workin' like a dog," Philip said as he and Holly mounted the stairs of the highly-populated establishment. "Is that so?" Holly sat down at a table for two, overlooking the bar. Philip nodded. "I need somebody to take care of me. If you know what I mean?" he said, waving over a waiter Holly had never seen. "That could mean a whole lot of things," she said. Philip grinned and his eyes did a devilish dance. "Quincy, get the lady *anything* she wants," he said to the young man and told Holly he'd be right back. She ordered a latte and watched as Philip made his way down to his office. He returned a few minutes later without the overnight bag, made a stop at the bar, whispered something to the hostess, they scanned the reservation book together and Philip walked outside, bringing in the young woman who'd inquired about her wait, along with the small group she was with. He sat them upstairs in the back and joined Holly afterward. "Changing up on me, huh?" Philip said to her, regarding her hot drink. She took a sip and nodded. "Just like you've changed up on me. You're the one who turned the channel on what we had. Was it boring you?" Philip rested his forehead in his hand. What could he say to that? His actions weren't intentional. He had to step back and lay low for a while. Get his thoughts together. Figure out what he was going to do. "Baby, you don't know how much time this place requires. These people expect me to be here. I can't start somethin' and--" He lifted his head and looked at Holly when he heard her sigh. "I work just as hard," she said, "But if I want to do something, I'm going to do it." Philip leaned back, nodding his head. "You're right," he said low, almost to himself. "So did you play racquet ball?" Holly asked switching up on the topic. Philip coughed then cleared his throat. "Yeah, I, uh, um, excuse me," he said, coughing again, "I finally hooked up with Bernard Dunn." A few unsettling seconds of quiet took over the couple's area before Holly said, "Who won?" She could see a faint smile crossing Philip's lips. "He did. But.... it's only because I'm not myself." He lowered his gaze toward the door. And when he saw it wasn't anyone he knew, he found Holly looking at him. "Is there something you'd like to discuss?" she asked, tilting her head. Philip glanced down at the door again then back at Holly. "No," he said, adding, "Did you eat?" Holly peered down at her latte cup. "Yes, I had dinner with my mother." "How's she doin'?" "Good." Philip appeared to take a deep breath as he rose, saying that he was going to get himself a sandwich. Studying him some more, she noticed his smooth way of walking seemed less charismatic, less confident. He really wasn't himself.

Later that evening, at Holly's apartment, both she and Philip lay in her bed sound asleep, their bodies spooned together. Philip's snoring woke him. He cracked opened his eyes, lifted his head above hers to peek at the clock. He pulled himself up and felt Holly move, too. She was changing positions. Philip slid out of bed, yawning as he crossed the room. In the darkness, she watched him leave for the bathroom and smiled at the way his naked body glistened. He had claimed most of the shimmering moisturizer she had on during their hour and a half of heated sex. Holly took a deep breath as the smile left her face. Had her mind become reprobate, she wondered.

Philip came back to find Holly on his side of the bed. "Oh," she said, as if she wasn't aware of being there. But he sat down at the foot of the bed, right below her feet. "Stay there," Philip said and cleared his throat. "I have to go." Holly glanced at the time. "You have to leave at three in the morning?" He nodded and quickly said, "Busy day today. We're doing a bridal shower. First one, may be the last, if it doesn't work out." Philip stood up, picked his underwear up from the floor and slipped them on. Then he grabbed his clothes off the window seat. He pulled on his pants and sat back down at the foot of the bed again to put on his shirt. Sliding into the denim article, Philip could feel Holly's eyes on him. He glimpsed into the full-length mirror. And her reflection proved his feeling to be right. "Baby," he began. "It'll get better, I promise. I wanna be with you just as much as you wanna be with me. Work is just gettin' the best of me...." Holly turned from her side to her back. Philip saw the curvaceous swell of the stark white sheet flatten and watched as she took the pillow she slept on, putting it on top of the one he slept on to raise her head. "I don't believe it's your job," Holly said. Philip could feel his eyes enlarge. "Why can't you be honest? Look," she said, stammering for the correct words, "I don't know if this is what I want either." Philip's heart dropped, thumping in the pit of his stomach. That wasn't what he wanted to hear. "If there's someone else, please, just let me know," Holly said. "I'm a big girl. I could handle it." After all, she wasn't looking for a husband. Just then she heard "He who finds a wife, finds a good thing and obtains favor from the Lord" rise in her spirit. Holly almost sat up. It was like the pages from her Bible on the nightstand had spoken it to her. She paused and peered at Philip. "I will be fine," that was the statement she used when Carmen told her all about her catching Bradford with his other woman. Philip stood up, tucking his shirt down into his pants. She was still watching him from behind as he fixed himself in the mirror. "There's nobody else," he said quietly. He didn't want nobody else. Philip sat down beside her. "Baby, like I said.... It *will* get better. Bear with me for a little while longer, please." Holly didn't say one word. "Could I ask you a question?" he asked. She nodded. Philip's throat felt like it was closing up as the sentence came out his mouth. "How do you really feel about me?" Holly looked at him, almost as if she were checking to make sure he was who she thought he was. Philip Williams sounded like a wounded little boy again. Like he did when he told her about his mother making him believe there wasn't a woman good enough for her son. And because of the countless years his question had eliminated from the forty-some-odd age she knew him to be, Holly almost said she loved him. Almost took him in her arms and held him the way a mother does a child when she calls him or her, her baby. But she drew back, sinking down into the indention in the pillow her head had made. This is not love I'm feeling, she warned herself, closing her mouth to seal in the fib she nearly told. It was called feeling sorry for someone. An Ishmael, not Issac God's promise. "I'm not sure," she said. "I could understand that," he said, "given the circumstance, but like I said, things *will* get better." He'd see to it! Philip looked away briefly in the direction of the window, inhaling as if he were summonsing the air from outside into his tight-feeling lungs. He slid his hand down the back of his neck and turned to face Holly again. She thought from seeing the emotion in his eyes that he would have said one last.... thing. Something. Instead, Philip gave her arm a firm yet tender squeeze, kissed her hand and rose. He exited her room wearing a crooked smile which led Holly Reed to believe their paths would cross again.... soon.

But when he failed to come through with the two promises he'd made to see her the following week, Holly's mind didn't hesitate to change. Seven-thirty Friday evening, she cleared off her desk to start her weekend. Getting up from her seat, she slung her pocketbook on her shoulder and leaned down to turn off the lamp. The phone rang before her fingers pulled the switch. Holly sucked her teeth, answering with a conjured-up perkiness. "Reed, Benjamin & Mann. Can I help you?" she said into the receiver. "Yes, you can," the voice said in a playful manner. Knitting her brows together as she tried to dissect the friendly greeting, Holly stood there waiting for another clue. One didn't come. "Who is this?" the attorney finally asked. The woman giggled and said, "Angela Dunn." Holly's forehead smoothed back out. "*Heeey*, what's going on?" she asked with a big smile. "Nothing much. I was driving by and saw the lights on. Turn around." Cradling the receiver with her chin and shoulder, Holly pivoted to face the window. Angela was sitting in her husband's white convertible mustang, cellular to her ear, smile on her face, hand waving wildly. There were two women joining her. Holly grinned again and waved back. "What are you still doing at the office at this hour on a Friday night? Take a ride with us," Angela said.

When the lawyer got downstairs, the woman with the head full of thick curly blunted hair and high cheekbones who was sitting on the passenger side had climbed into the back seat. Angela introduced them all as Holly got in beside her. "Wilimina Chambray," she said, pointing to the sienna-skinned woman who'd switched seats. "This is Holly Reed, and that's," Angela Dunn said, eyeing the other woman beside Wilimina with the auburn hair and dark skin. "Chloe Johnston. We're all neighbors." "Nice to meet you both," Holly said to the two women. They said they were pleased to meet her in unison. "Before we get started," Angela said to Holly, "I'm going to have to warn you about the two hopeless cases in the back. First of all, they're housewives." Holly and Angela's eyes locked then Mrs. Dunn breathed a heavy "mmm-hmm," continuing with, "who hardly ever get a break from their clingy families, and what's worse, they almost never get to come into the city, simply because they just can't get away from the 'honey where's my clean shirts? Or the 'Did you see my *Batman* lunchbox?' kind of questions, if you get my drift." Wilimina and Chloe laughed when they saw the mock pity on Holly's face. "So, since *their, mmm* let's say off with babysitter's watching their children, and husbands somewhere faraway on a fishing trip, it is my consummate duty as a loyal friend, to show them a good time tonight. And I do mean good time. That's why I ditched the minivan better known as the "wife and mommy mobile" for the lets-see-how-much-trouble-we-could-get-into-without-getting-caught ride." They all cracked up and Holly said, as she continued to laugh about the women behind her, "Where would you ladies like to go?" Chloe held up her hand. "I do not receive anything that Angela just said. I'm a child of the Most High God. Therefore, I am not receiving any thing contrary to what my Heavenly Father calls me or says about me. I am not a hopeless case. I have Hope Himself as my Lord and Savior. His Name is Jesus. The One with the Name above every name." Holly paused and turned around to face forward while Angela proceeded to laugh a little as she said a respectful "Amen!" "Oh, and I am not looking for trouble of any kind," Chloe went on to say. "So, to answer your question, Sis," she said to Holly who paused again and turned around to face the outspoken woman. "Yes?" said the hazel-eyed woman. "Let's go some place with a good atmosphere. It would be nice to see some celebrities, but in a good place. Do you know of any?" I hear Laurence Fishburne's in town," Wilimina said with a smile. "*What?*" exclaimed Chloe. "Why didn't you tell me?" Holly glanced at Angela, who said, "That *was* also part of my promise." Holly smiled. "All right, I know a place. It's not too far from my apartment." Turning to face the front again, Holly strapped on her seat belt and said, "Let's go," With thoughts of how strong in the Lord Chloe was.

Elaine's was known best for being "the celebrity watering hole of the Upper East Side," according to *Zaget's*. Holly had only eaten there once before, with Bradford, who'd frequented the small dining spot. He always did agree with the quote in the New York City restaurant guide. Holly reflected on the days when her former lover would tell her he had lunch there with stars such as Danny Glover and the late Ossie Davis, to name a few. The tables in the cramped eatery were all filled, so the four women sat at the bar. Holly found herself eyeing Chloe to try to discern whether or not sitting at the bar was okay with her. She seemed to be a little uncomfortable from the way she nearly got up when she thought a nearby table was about to be free. Holly made it a point to stay mindful and keep watch for a better place for them all to sit as well.

The first sip of sparkling water with a twist of lime revealed to Holly that she was actually glad it was Friday. The not-too-long-ago-dread she felt that morning as the alarm clock rang loudly in her ear was nearly gone. She paused. "I have to be more grateful," she said under her breath as she took another sip from her glass. Being with Angela and her new acquaintances, made her feel less lonely than she had all week. If her mind was stayed on the Lord, she wouldn't be lonely, she thought. Tina Turner wanted to know, "What Does Love Have to Do With It?" Everything! God is Love, Holly told herself. How could Philip have asked me how I *really* felt about him without bothering to ask himself how he *really* felt about me? Holly mused. This thing that we think we have, is not Love! Huh! Out of sight, out of mind. These were the types of clichés she was learning to live by. But, it was stuff she had already known. And, it wasn't the Truth. "Hold your glass in the air," Angela said, nudging Holly in the arm. "We'll ignore the fact that you've already taken a couple of sips," she teased with a smile. "I'm sorry," Holly said. She lifted her glass, waiting for the toast initiated by Wilimina. "Here's to a girl's night out!" the seinna woman exclaimed, clinking her glass up against the three other women's in turn. As Holly sipped from hers again, she turned, glancing around. There was a group of five getting ready to leave the table behind them. When she faced the three other women again, to ask if they would want to move, she found herself entering a conversation she'd assumed had been sworn off for the evening. The three ladies were engaging in the familiarities of their home life, discussing their children and husbands, comparing the ways in which their spouses handled certain aspects of marriage and fatherhood. "Kenneth always goes to the Bible," Chloe said with a smile. "And I get so encouraged. I thank the Lord at how my precious husband always gives God praise for my being his helpmeet. We come into agreement against the spirit of division when it tries to manifest itself. It's not right for kids to be able to play their parents against one another. Teaches them how to manipulate. Therefore, Kenneth and I have no problem with "training them up in the way they should go," "Uh-huh, I agree," Angela said, "Bernie, is very conscientious when it comes to that. Because the twins would play us like they do basketball. Well, if we we're not mindful!" Chloe, Wilimina and the bartender laughed while Holly smiled and quietly sipped from her glass. The hazel-eyed woman was taking in the way Chloe was allowing God to use her. She was having a positive effect on Angela and Wilimina. "Are you courting someone?" Chloe leaned forward to ask Holly, who nearly choked on her drink. "Are you okay?" Angela asked. She patted Holly's back lightly. "It went down the wrong way." "Yes, are you courting someone, Holly. Oh, I'd love to hear about it. Seems like I married Thomas the day I was born and we had our first child the day after. I love my family dearly, but it could be rough at times. You could easily lose touch of who you are," Wilimina said, "I can't even suck on a mint without one of the kids asking me what's in my mouth." Holly smiled and before she could say anything, Angela said, "Yes, she's involved with a very eye-pleasing brother." She chuckled and raised her hand to slap palms with Holly, but her return was somewhat delayed and on the weak side. "Involved. Does the outside match the inside?" Chloe said. She leaned forward again, eyeing Holly. "Yes, he is handsome," said the hazel-eyed woman, "but Philip and I aren't together anymore." "Since when?" Angela asked, pulling her head back in surprise. "For about a week or so. In fact, we went our separate ways last Saturday. The day Bernie and Philip played racquet ball at the club," Holly said. Angela nodded slowly and took a sip from her glass as Holly rose from her seat. "Are you okay?" Wilimina asked. "I will be as soon as I come back from the ladies room." All three women appeared to be worried. "I forgot to go before I left the office," she added with a smile and they chuckled, nodding their heads simultaneously. Holly turned to walk toward the restroom and Angela slid off her stool, saying she had to go as well.

In the bathroom, the two women exited their adjacent stalls at the same time, moving over to the sinks to wash their hands. Holly could see that Angela wanted to say something when she glanced at her through the mirror. "What's wrong?" she asked. Angela turned off her faucet and reached for a paper towel, drying her hands. She met Holly's gaze. "Something you said out there bothered me." Holly skimmed her previous words quickly in her head as she turned the faucet off. "Whatever it was," she began, "you know I...." Angela nodded. "It wasn't anything you said. It was Philip." Holly dried her hands and tossed the damp paper towel into the garbage pail. "He said something about me to Bernie?" Holly asked. Angela shook her head. "No, he said something about Bernie to *you*." "I don't understand.... The only thing he said was that they played...." "Holly," Angela said, cutting her off. "My husband's been away on business ever since Courtney left Vanessa. He asked Bernie to tie up a few loose ends that he didn't get to on his last trip to L.A. So, unless Philip knows another Bernard Dunn, he lied." Holly raised an eyebrow in astonishment. "I don't know why this comes as a surprise to me. I'm sorry, Angela." "What for? You didn't do anything. And I wouldn't even bother to ask Philip why he did it. You said it was already over. No need to rehash what's been said and done. Some people will do whatever it takes to dig themselves out of a hole. Even if it means pulling someone innocent down into it with them. You're much better off without him. Just like Courtney's probably better off without Vanessa. I saw that one coming a *long, long* time ago." She shook her head in disgust. "How was she able to find the time to have an extramarital affair when she was hawking him all the time. The guilty ones always manage to keep a close watch on the ones doing the right thing. Courtney's a good man. Always has been. He needs to find himself a faithful sister who has his best interest in mind." Angela turned toward the mirror to replenish her lipstick. Holly couldn't agree more. "Between you and I," Angela said, pressing her lips together to even out the red lip color she applied, "he called Bernie a few days ago to check in, but he didn't tell him where he was. It's better that way. But," she sighed, "Bernie really does miss him. I miss him too." Holly nodded and averted her gaze from Angela's reflection to the door. A woman entered with a small boy who was too young to be left unescorted in the men's room. Holly smiled at the child as he peeked at her with one eye, the other was shielded by his mother's hip. Then she acknowledged Angela by saying in a low, truth-filled voice, "I think we all miss him."

When they came back to join Wilimina and Chloe they found them sitting at the table for five next to the bar. "My back was starting to hurt. I hate backless stools," Chloe said. "I was going to suggest we sit here," Holly said as she sat down. Angela sat opposite her. "Don't look now," Wilimina whispered after ordering another round of the different drinks they had been drinking. She had her eyes on the door. "Here comes Allen Payne. Oh my goodness." "Who?" Chloe said, wanting to turn her head around. "You know, Lance from the Cosby Show," Wilimina said. Angela Dunn giggled and said, "Wil, I think you better take those eyeglasses out of your pocketbook because they are not doing you any good in there. That is *not* him." Wilimina opened her bag, snatching out her eyeglasses. She put them on hurriedly and frowned. "Not even close." she said, shaking her head. "I must be drunk off of that new wine, you know, Bible verses, that Chloe's been feeding us." Wilimina began to laugh at herself. And, as if it were something contagious, all three women joined in, finding more humor in the sienna-woman's mistake of identity as the man came closer. Then, suddenly coming out of the state of laughter she had been apart of, Chloe said, "Don't even get it twisted. The "new wine" that I've been feeding you and Angela does not lie and it would not get you drunk. The Word of God is Truth. So, you better check yourself!" Holly refrained from the giddiness that had tried to take hold of her as well and began to gaze over at Chloe, knowing that her well needed to be filled.

The starless sky patterned that of a dark blue blanket, keeping the climate beneath it warm and dry. The threat of late evening showers seemed to go away for another day. Holly lifted her head off the headrest as Angela pulled up in front of her building. Inside, through the partial glass doors, Holly saw a dozing Peter yawn and rub his eyes. "Can you believe I have to use the bathroom again," Angela said to Holly. Sleep had claimed the two women in the back seat. "Well, you were drinking a lot of water after that second glass of wine," Holly said. "Come up," she added, opening the car door. Wilimina and Chloe both opened their eyes at that moment. "It was a pleasure, ladies," Holly told them. "I had fun, too," Chloe said as she stretched her arms above her head. "We have to do this again," Wilimina said, stifling a yawn. "I'd like that," Holly said. She waved and Angela told them she'd be right back down.

Holly was removing her keys from her pocketbook as they stepped off the elevator. She didn't know about Angela, but without fail it always seemed like she had to pee worse when she saw her front door. She knew it was all psychological. "Whoa, I have to go some kind of bad," Angela said, shifting from one foot to the other. "This way," Holly said. She began giving the woman accompanying her directions to the bathroom while she turned the key into the lock. "Okay, okay," Angela said once inside. She dropped her pocketbook on the settee and went storming down the hallway, which much to Holly's surprise was illuminated by the light of the television set in her bedroom. Angela, too busy unbuttoning her pants, didn't notice as she entered the bathroom, closing the door behind her. Holly set her pocketbook down next to Angela's and crossed the faintly-lit apartment for her room. Knowing me these days, she thought, I probably forgot to turn it off this morning. But, in there she was shocked to see Philip lying fast asleep, in his underwear, across her bed. His mouth was wide open, the snoring coming out of it louder than the sound of the TV. Holly stood in the doorway watching him. She was stunned mainly because of the way she felt. Full from the Word that came forth from Chloe most of the night. How did he get in here? she wondered. Peter didn't even say anything even though he was on a call when the two women walked inside of the building. Holly's eyes fell downward toward the trail of brown lace-up shoes and the clothes he'd torn off that were scattered across her floor. She took a deep breath and moved toward the bed, waking him. Philip's eyes cracked open slowly after a few shakes. He glanced at Holly then around the room as if he was trying to assess where he was. "Who let you in?" she asked, taking her hand off his arm. "Ay, baby," he said in a lethargic tone as he rose up on his elbows. "Don't ay baby me. How'd you get into my apartment?" Holly asked. She placed her hand on her hip. Philip didn't answer. He moaned, "What time is it?" instead. "Don't you worry about the time and don't make me ask you again..." Holly was tapping her foot against the floor impatiently. "Aright, aright." He sat up and her foot tapping ceased. Philip slid all the way down to the foot of the bed, opened his legs the way men do, leaned forward, resting his elbows on both knees. He put his face in the palms of his hands and started rubbing his eyes. "Pete let me in," he said and turned to face Holly, adding, "But leave him out of this. I told him you wouldn't mind." "Oh you did, did you? And what made you think I wouldn't mind..." Holly stopped speaking when she heard the bathroom door open and Angela's footsteps coming their way. *"Thank you"* she said, sounding relieved. Holly told Philip she'd finish with him in a minute and met Angela at the bedroom door before she could come in. She caught a quick glimpse of Philip and backed away. "Excuse me, Holly. I didn't know you had company." As the two women went down the hall toward the front of the apartment, Holly could see the look on Angela's face, saying I thought you broke up with him. "The doorman let him in," Holly said. "I'm going to read him like a book once I'm done with that one in the room," she told Angela. "Girl, handle your business," Angela said. She pointed to Holly, adding, "Take care of you. Okay." "I will," the hazel-eyed woman said as she immediately thought. That was her problem. She was trying to take care of herself. Cast your cares upon Me because I care for you, is what the Lord says. The Holy Spirit reminded her how the verse before that one informs that it was the lowest form of humility. To cast my cares upon the Lord ... because He cares for me. "Holly, did you hear me? I want you to come out to have dinner with Bernie, the kids and I when you get the chance." The hazel-eyed woman smiled and gave Angela a hug at the door. "Thank you," is what she said.

When she got back into the bedroom Philip was on her phone checking his messages. "Just make yourself at home," Holly said when he hung up. "Baby, I was just callin' home to make sure there wasn't a crisis at the restaurant. I forgot my cell phone in my office again. I left work early today and came straight here. I was hopin' for a nice, romantic evening alone. Just you and me." Philip walked around the bed over to the side Holly was standing on. He placed his hand gently on her face. "I don't like to see hurt in your eyes," he said. "I'm gonna make it disappear." "How?" she asked. Philip sighed, lowering his hand. He turned toward the TV then back at her. "I know you just took a long weekend about a month ago, but do you think you'd be able to take another one soon?" He sat down on the edge of the bed, guiding her toward his lap. She obeyed his request, sitting there with her arms folded. "What for?" Holly finally asked. "To maybe go somewhere. Let's hit one of the islands. Go down to St. Bart's or we could go to Paris. The weather should be nice around this time, right?" "If I go away to an island, it's going to be longer than a four-day weekend," Holly said. Philip smiled. He could see that she wanted to grin too, but she held it inside. "Aright, let's take it one day at a time. How about startin' off with a nice dinner and some dancin' tomorrow night." Philip started bouncing her playfully on his knees. "I don't know..."she said. He stopped moving and furrowed his brows. "Wait a minute, hear me out before you go breakin' a brotha's heart. I want you to put on the best dress in that closet, make your hair look pretty like it does right now." He kissed her cheek. "And I'm gonna show you the best time you've ever had in your *entire* life. Bet? Are we on? C'mon, baby, say we're on." Holly breathed deeply, glanced at the television then back at him. Best time she's ever had in her entire life? Was she going to die after their date? This wasn't God. The One Who promises that with long life He will satisfy her and show her His Salvation. "Like I said," Holly said to him. "I don't know if this is the right thing for me to do. For *us* to do. Philip, I'm not trusting you right now." And, she definitely wasn't putting her trust in her Heavenly Father who told her to trust God and love people. Holly lowered her eyes and then gazed into Philip's eyes. Although he began to smile at her, she knew in her heart that she wasn't loving Him the way God wanted her to love Him. She knew better than this and she knew that it was sin when you didn't do what you knew to do. "Why? Because I've been workin'? Bustin' my uh butt to make my restaurant a success?" Philip said and stopped smiling. He was still gazing back into her eyes. Holly shook her head. "No, because you lied to me." Philip grimaced. "Lied to you? About what? Baby, I have nothin' to hide..." "About playing racquet ball with Bernard Dunn. Angela told me he's been out of town since Courtney left Vanessa. So what is it that you're covering up?" Philip lowered his eyes and Holly stood up, walked over to her dresser and removed her earrings. "You know what," she said as she crossed the room for the closet. "I don't even want to know why you told me that. You don't owe me anything." Philip looked at her. "If I want you to be my woman I do. To tell you the truth, I don't know why I lied. I felt awkward that day and the way you were lookin' at me didn't help." "Don't make me the bad guy, Philip," Holly said, shaking her head in disbelief. She stripped down to nothing but an ivory thong and slipped into a lavender silk robe, tying it at the waist. "I'm not blamin' you. Listen, can we just start all over? Make this all about you and me." He gestured at the both of them with his hand. "No more lies. Just the straight up honest to God truth for now on." What did he know about God? Holly asked herself as the verse in the book of Romans rose so sweetly in her spirit. It was the one about how some people would hinder the truth by their wickedness when the Lord Himself revealed the truth to them. Philip stood up and walked over to where Holly was. He took her in his arms. "Do you think you're capable of telling the..." Holly cut herself short, peering him in the eyes. She knew what was going to happen next. The chemistry was thick. Her head couldn't think clearly, couldn't think of any of the daily affirmations she'd made up for herself this week: Mondays was; Lord, help me to rest in You. Tuesdays was; I am the righteousness of God in Christ Jesus. Wednesdays was; it's time to walk deeper into my true purpose. Thursdays was; the joy of the Lord in my strength. And this mornings was; My identity is hidden in Christ Jesus.

Holly didn't even remember what the Holy Spirit had just spoken to her as she suddenly realized how Philip had begun kissing her. His lips were tender in some ways hard and forceful in others as he worked his tongue into her mouth, tasting hers. He pulled his head away and his eyes fell to her full mouth. Philip smiled and began to absorb her face. A bigger smile crossed his lips as he moved her backward toward the bed. He sat down, positioning Holly in between his legs. Philip marveled at the way her hair fell forward while she looked down at him. She was his baby, he told himself as he untied her robe. She could see the ecstasy already filling his eyes. She heard him grunt with desire. Holly was breathing fast and hard on top of him. Then carefully, he led her down on the bed beside him. Pulling her body beneath him, he stopped to observe the lady he believed he loved. He saw that the tension had drained from her face. Her eyes were closed and her mouth was slightly parted. The euphoric expression was a clear indication that she was a woman experiencing rapture, the pleasure he was providing. Philip smiled and kissed Holly's forehead while he thought, Who's the man?

Chapter Twenty-Six

Holly rolled over to an empty spot beside her in the bed the following morning. Feeling it with her hand, almost as if she were assuring herself that he was truly gone, she then sat up, clicking the TV on with the remote control. She didn't understand why Philip had to sneak out again, as he'd done the last time, in the wee hours of the night. It was almost like clockwork. He said he had to open for the day manager and had to leave like that because he needed a fresh change of clothes. How naive did he think she was? Doesn't Philip know Whose she is? She belonged to God. Holly took a deep breath. "I'll let it roll off my back for now," she told the room in dismay as she turned the channel in search of a weather report. The hazel-eyed woman glanced over at her Bible. Then, she looked up. Why didn't she speak to the Father? Ask Him what it was she should do regarding all of this. This whatever it was that she was caught up in with Philip. Holly took another deep breath and faced the television. Already seventy-two degrees, according to the temperature displayed in the lower left-hand corner on the screen. And it wasn't quite nine o'clock. New York One's newscaster was just finishing up the New Yorker of the Week segment as Holly climbed out the bed, slipping into the silk lavender robe that had spent the evening on the floor. She went into the kitchen, brewed some coffee, made some soggy French toast, topped it with a little syrup and gobbled it down. After cleaning up the small mess she'd made, she decided to treat herself to a day of beauty. But, before scheduling her appointment at Elizabeth Arden, she'd call to see if her mother wanted to join her. Cynthia Reed answered after two and a half rings. The older woman was breathing heavily, panting as though she'd just swam the English Channel. "Mom, what did I tell you about racing to the phone? If you miss the call, just call whoever it was back." Holly shook her head. She was tired of sounding like she had all the answers. "Babygirl, your timin' is off today," Cynthia whispered into the receiver. "Did I interrupt something?" "Um-hmmm. Remember what we was talkin' 'bout when you was over here last?" "No, uh...." "Mr. Freeman is here. He took me out to dinner last night and while we ate and was havin' a good time, I invited him here for breakfast this mornin'," she chuckled, "I was still tellin' him how much I *enjoyed* myself last night." "Oh, Mom, that's wonderful," Holly said with a smile. "So, you don't think I was pushin' it when I invited him back today? I promise you. He spent the night in the guest room. No hanky panky." Cynthia was whispering. Holly was quiet. She was pondering the way her mother was asking her for advice regarding her actions toward a man. "Speak, chile speak." Holly could hear her mother cover the receiver. "Be right there," the older woman told her guest with a giggle. "Mom, would you like to come with me to Elizabeth Arden's?" the younger woman ask as she didn't have an answer to fill her mother's uncertainty. "Oh, baby I'd love to, but," she said, clearing her throat this time. "Mr. Freeman won't be leavin' 'til tonight. I can't leave him here alone. He checked out of his hotel room already. You go and have yourself a good time. Okay, sweetie?" "I will. Talk to you later. And ..., please tell Mr. Freeman I said hello."

Holly glanced at her watch as she came out of the spa, the famed red door closing and locking behind her. She still had plenty of time before "the date," that in a way would be a deciding factor for her future with Philip. Would she give him the key to her heart? Or would she continue to boomerang him for a little while longer? Throw him away and wait for his return. Holly knew the mixed signals she was sending him weren't mature, but she never set out in search of a constant companion. Not right now. Philip Williams just happened. Fun was the only prerequisite despite the feelings she was gaining for him. Though it wasn't love, she assured herself and then she heard, "I hold the key to your heart" as the scripture, "The Lord holds the heart of the king in His hand like the rivers of water, He turns it in the direction He wants it to go." Holly stood still for a moment and slowly began to walk down the street.

Before heading home, she wound up purchasing a black teddy, just because, and a simple yet stunning black Calvin Klein dress from Barney's, which would look fabulous with the black Manolo Blahnik leather pumps, gathering dust in the closet, she'd only worn once before.

At her apartment, Holly took a quick shower to basically rinse her body of the rich creams they had doused her in at Arden's. She wanted to relax, take it easy so she would be ready for tonight. After all, she couldn't remember the last time she had gone dancing prior to Courtney's party. Philip was nearly ten years her senior so she wasn't about to be the first one to say she was tired or ready to go home. The phone rang.

Holly wrapped herself in a towel and entered her bedroom. "Hello," she said into the receiver as she pulled up the blinds. She also checked to see if there were any voice mails on her cell phone as Vanessa asked, "What are you up to?" "Hey, Vee. Nothing, really. I just got out of the shower." Holly sat down on the window seat, feeling the sun at her back. "Why don't you come out to my house with Tracy today. I'm having Joan Portman and her sister over, too. I was going to throw some shrimp kebabs on the grill and make a salad..." "That sounds like it would be the perfect thing to do on a day like today, but I have a date tonight." Holly could feel herself hesitating a bit because she had virtually told both Tracy and Vanessa all last week at work that she had no intentions of ever seeing Philip again. "Wow! Does the grass ever grow under your feet?" Vanessa teased with a chuckle. "Where did you find the time to meet someone?" "I didn't," Holly said. "I'm going out with Philip." The full-figured woman fell silent, then, "I thought that was over with. What happened to 'he's nothing but a liar. He better go find himself another dummy?'" "I know what I said, but I changed my mind..." "What? You're thinking about taking him seriously?" "I didn't say that. I'm just saying that I have a nice time with him. And he makes me feel like a woman." "He makes you feel like a woman? Well, how did he swindle his way back into your too-forgiving heart?" Holly smiled. Vanessa and her way with words. "He was here when I got home last night and I saw another side of him...." "You gave him keys?" "No. Peter let him in." "I hope he's out of a job." "No, but I asked him never to do that again." "All right, so what did it? What put Philip Williams back on the A-list? I've got to hear this." "We talked, had some fun, talked, had some more fun and talked again." Vanessa was quiet a second time for a brief moment before she said, "Well, if you change your mind, the offer still stands. Tracy's leaving her place at about three." She hung up without saying good-bye. Holly pulled the receiver away from her ear, staring at the mouth piece. She shook her head and placed the phone down into the cradle.

Ten minutes later the phone rang again. Tracy was trying to persuade Holly to spend the day with her and Vanessa. "The summer's almost over and we haven't spent any time outside of work together. Let Philip wonder sometimes. Keep him guessing. I bet he'd call to cancel on you *again* if something better came up." "I know you and Vee mean well, Trace, but I want to go out with him tonight. I can't leave him at a time like this...." "*What's* wrong with him?" "He's just going through a little something. I'm not sure, but I think it has something to do with the restaurant." "Sounds like a set up to me. Remember when Bradford tried to pull the same crap on you? Saying it was work?" "Why would you bring him up?" "I brought him up because you thought he was going to save you. Make you whole. Finish you. When all he did was deplete you, honey. Take away your identity. You barely kept in contact with us, except at work. And look at you doing it again." Holly paused. She heard God using Tracy. Was she looking for another? Someone other than her Lord and Savior Christ Jesus? Holly shook her head no. Certainly she wasn't doing that. She would be going back to church soon. Her mother stopped asking when she would be going back. Holly felt a sudden panic in her heart. She took a deep breath. "Did you take a good look at Bradford at Courtney's party, Trace?" "Yeah. He looked tore-up." "And how do I look?" Not a word. "*Thank you.* A lot could be heard when it's quiet. Your silence just spoke volumes. So, you see, if anything Bradford was a catalyst. I hoped I was used to make him a little better while we were together. I guess that's the reason why he chose to show up at the party, knowing that the majority wouldn't want to see him. So, as I said before, I'm going out with Philip tonight and the next night and the night after that, if I want to, and I'll see you and Vanessa on Monday. Have a wonderful time at the barbecue and give Joan Portman my regards." Holly caught a glimpse of her reflection in the full-length mirror after she put the phone back on her nightstand. She needed help and no one could help her except God.

Holly had some time to sit down in her living room and relax for at least another forty minutes longer before getting fully dressed. She'd already taken a nice, long bubble bath, set her hair with hot rollers, moisturized her body and made up her face beautifully, except for her lips. She would do them after she finished the lemon water she poured. Just a taste, she told herself. It was half a glass. She needed something refreshing to drink. The hazel-eyed woman had been asking herself what it was she was looking for from Philip. What it was she expected him to supply? But no answer came. Was it because deep down inside she knew he wasn't the one? A smile suddenly crossed her lips. The man certainly knew how to make her knees buckle. God, does he have power behind his punch. The thought alone made her quake. Holly took a sip from the glass, the grin fading from her face. She needed more than that. Holly began to think about the way she had said "God". She shook her head. "I wasn't talking to Him," she said quietly. Glancing down into her glass, Holly finished the sour drink all at once.

The phone rang.

The hazel-eyed woman answered it in the kitchen. "I was just callin' to see how my baby was," Philip said with a smile. "She's doing fine," Holly said as she washed the empty glass. "I can't wait to see you," he said. She smiled. "It sounds busy." "Yeah, the usual crowd, then some. I'm behind the bar helpin' with the drinks." "Really?" Holly said with a light laugh. "Yep, and I don't know what I'm doin'. But I'm doin' a pretty good job playin' it off. Hold on, baby…. Okay, you want a slow gin fiz? Comin' right up. Am I pourin' it slow enough for you?" Philip teased, laughing with the patron. He began speaking into the receiver again. "So, listen, baby. I'll be there around seven, seven thirty, okay? I made reservations at the Rainbow Room. I figured we'll check it out up there then head over to, I don't know, let's play it by ear. Maybe go somewhere where we could really *get down*." "I'd like that." "All right, let me go," he whispered, "'Cause some dude just asked me to make a Cosmopolitan for his lady. Whatever that is," he said with a laugh. "I know how to make it," Philip lied, talking to the guy in front of him. "Bye," Holly said.

Philip handed the receiver to Ki Ki, the hostess, who was putting money into the cash register so she would hang it up. Then glancing back at the man with the Cosmopolitan request, Philip excused himself for a second, walked down to the other end of the bar, taking one of the bartenders to the side. He wanted to know how to make the drink. "Here turn this way so he can't see what we're talkin' about. I'm gonna show the brother that I know what I'm doin'. He's down there mouthin' off to his woman," Philip told the bartender in regards to the agitated patron. He kept one eye on his employee as she gave him careful instructions and one eye on everything else going on around him. Back at the other end of the bar, the phone rang. Philip observed as Darryl answered, continuing to nod his head respectfully as the bartender finished up. While Philip repeated the drink recipe back: "Absolut Citron, cointreau, cranberry juice, fresh lime juice, shaken in a martini shaker over ice and served in a martini glass," he could see that the waiter was being given a hard time by the caller. It had to be for me again, Philip told himself glumly. And then Darryl proved him to be correct. The dark-skinned waiter turned toward his boss, covering the mouth piece of the receiver. Philip thanked the bartender for her help and swaggered in Darryl's direction. "It's you know who," the waiter whispered to his boss. "What should I say this time?" Philip pondered the question. "Say I'll be there in a minute," the restauranteur said, adding as he pivoted to face the man waiting, "Right after I make this gentlemen's lady friend the best Cosmo she's ever tasted." The annoyed patron patted the stool in front of him. He wanted the date he was trying to impress to sit down. "Could I pour you another one?" Philip asked him, noticing his beer mug was empty. "Finish that first," the man instructed, nodding at the drink Philip was making. "Sure thing," the restauranteur told him and eyed the woman the man was with. She grinned, batting her eyes at Philip. He smiled back until Darryl appeared at his side, telling him that the person on the phone was getting angry. "I could hear the yelling over the music," the waiter said. But Philip didn't budge any faster. He laid two napkins on the bar, topping them with a Cosmopolitan and clean iced-cold mug filled with beer. "This is on the house," he told the couple and reached for the phone. Philip started talking through clenched teeth almost instantaneously. It was clear that the caller had tried him several times to no avail. "Yeah, so. They gave me the messages. *All* five of them! I don't know who you think you're raisin' your voice at. I'll hang up. I've done it before. What! Say I won't!" Philip turned his back on the public, blocking the stares from the people at the bar. "If that's what you need to do, do it! Don't threaten me. No, I can't. I've got things to do tonight. None of your business, that's what. Oh, you don't have anything hangin' over my head. I'ma grown man. Whatever! Like I said, do what you got to do.... What! Where?" Philip shook his head and looked at his watch. "I'll think about it," he told the caller and slammed the phone down.

Holly stared at herself in the full-length mirror in her bedroom. In the clingy, black dress, with her hair just so, she'd done a good job of working on her outside. But, her inside was another matter. She had no peace. Glancing at the clock on her nightstand, she saw that Philip would be arriving in twenty minutes with his face wearing a big smile, signaling hope. Oh, sure, she thought. They would go out and have an amazing time, come back to her apartment, and complete the evening with sex that seemed to get better each and every time they got together. And then, she mused on. Then Philip would ask her to move their relationship to the next level. Marriage. He brought it up again last night and she heard the Spirit of God say into her heart. It's not marriage if it's not of Him. How would she get out of answering the question this time? Holly breathed. That powerful revelation was enough to send her into a guilt trip. Was she a bad person for leading him on? Jesus took my guilt, she remembered. But, she still felt like an all around bad person now as Tracy Mann emerged in her mind. Look at the way you spoke to her earlier, Holly. All she and Vanessa wanted to do was spend time with me, she mused. "And I had to get nasty." She'd leave her partner an amusing message on her voicemail. She may need to laugh once she gets home from Vanessa's house. Holly sat down on the edge of her bed while the phone rang. She furrowed her brows. "Trace, what are you doing home?" "Holly? Oh, uh, Vee changed her mind and decided to come into the city. Joan and her sister had to cancel anyway." "Why didn't you guys call me. I would've come over there. Is Vee still there?" "Yep, she's stretched out on my sofa, watching some boring television program." Holly laughed a little. "So what are the two of you going to do later on tonight?" "Nothing, really. Uh, the baby's father said he'd stop by," Tracy said and sneezed. "God Bless you. He lives in the city?" "Yeah, uh, hold on. Is that the doorbell?" Tracy asked Vanessa, who Holly could hear say "Yes, and what about it?" "I can't believe you, Vee. You are not a guest in my home." Tracy called the full-figured woman a lazy bum and started speaking to Holly again. "She's not going to get it. Let me see who it is and I'll talk to you later."

Holly hung up with a smile. Everything was still the same. She was glad that she called Tracy.

The hazel-eyed woman stood there staring into the mirror hanging over her dresser. She was becoming impatient. She'd already switched earrings three times. And at this point, none of them seemed like the right pair. She sighed and peered at the clock on the nightstand. Where was he? And how much more time should she give him? Philip was nearly fifty minutes late and he hadn't called.

The phone rang. .

"I'm fine and yourself?" Holly said with surprise in her eyes. "Good, thank you. I've been meaning to call you," said Paulette Williams. "My son," she laughed lightly. "All he does is talk about you. But, of course, I don't have to tell you this. We women know when we've captured a man's heart." The older woman laughed lightly again. "Yes, my husband and I do believe you will be the *one* to win him over and become his wife." At least the Williams' family hoped she'd be, considering. Holly wanted to tell her that the only thing Philip would be winning if he didn't show up soon, was what they call out in the streets: a beatdown. "So have you seen him lately? I know he's been busy with the restaurant," the older woman said, stumbling slightly on her words. Paulette made a face, knowing she didn't sound convincing. "As a matter of fact, I saw him last night. And I was supposed to see him again tonight, but I haven't heard from him yet." "Oh, you will. I'm sure he's on his way. Philip always had a reputation of being tardy." Paulette laughed lightly once more. For some reason Holly was getting the impression that the older woman was calling for her son. "Oh, uh, listen, sweetheart, I have to go now. My husband and I are having a late dinner with Brenda, Mark and the children. They should be here any minute. It's Olivia's birthday. They spent the day at Great

Adventures. So, you kids have a great time. Please ask Philip to give me a call when he gets an opportunity." "I will." "My husband says hello." "Hi..." The line went dead.

Thirty minutes came slithering in like some old desert snake. Holly turned the dining room light off as she exited it, slipped her shoes off and carried them into her bedroom, tossing them back in the closet. She didn't know what to think or feel because she had become indifferent. Numb. Philip's well-being was no longer an issue to her since she'd already exhausted herself with every vision of Philip's being laid up in one of the New York City hospitals as she sat in the dining room, drinking a glass of water. Someone would have called her by now. Maybe, she told herself, not knowing how common, common sense was in his family. Sure, it was possible for her to try to contact him, but she didn't know how she'd react to his being perfectly fine. Was this a horrible self-confession? she wondered, feeling manipulated. Perhaps it was, but still, she didn't care. She was just about to re-write the scene and make herself the heroine. Philip Williams was no longer the star. It was all about Holly's agenda now. "I'm a daughter of The King." What a revelation, she thought, hoping that she'd be able to sustain her newfound attitude.

Well, it worked for a few more minutes. Twenty to be exact.

There was a faint vein on Holly's left temple that could go virtually undetected. But, right now, one didn't need to stare too hard to see it. She stood in front of the bathroom sink, washing her hands after flushing the toilet. In and out, she breathed, trying to calm herself down as she walked out, hoping that the feeling she felt in her chest would somehow be left behind.

Holly lifted the phone receiver to her ear, thought about what she was about to do for a second, and slammed it back down into the cradle so hard she nearly broke the nail on her index finger. Shaking her hand and head in unison, she wanted to scream as loud as she possibly could. But, she could not calculate whether the pain engulfing her finger was the catalyst for the eruption surfacing in her throat, or the frustration caused by the man in her life, who was making a fool out of her again. As she sat there, fully clad in her beautiful black designer dress on the window seat in her bedroom with the telephone beside her, waiting like a desperate schoolgirl to be asked to the prom by the boy of her dreams. Deep down inside she knew where this doormat mentality was coming from. She had come face-to-face with her ailing self many times. Holly felt like she ran into her old nature like you would an old friend who kept reminding you of where you came from. The vision of her former self was so difficult to digest although it was necessary for her to take a long, critical look in order to prune off the trouble areas and move forward. "Your Will be done, Lord," she whispered. Why can't I just rest in You, Father? All this self effort was wearing on her.

Holly appeared surprised when the word, "*Ring!*" exited her mouth with such force, blending with the atmosphere surrounding her. The sound of her voice was still at a whisper. It did not match the anger she felt invading her body. This was why she was alarmed, she thought. To think of it, the entire setting unfortunately, failed to match the promise she had made to herself less than a year ago. She wasn't supposed to be going through this. Not again. How had she been caught up in yet another dead-end relationship? She didn't find it necessary to chronicle the previous so-called-love she'd lost. After all, she was an intelligent woman as far as she was concerned. "Why am I acting like I don't have a God who is full of grace?" Holly asked the quiet room, her voice more amplified this time, coordinating well with the question she had asked. She would sit there and believe for a manifestation of the Lord's peace that surpassed all understanding for ten more minutes. And, if Philip didn't call by then, she was going to take off that brand-new dress, put on a T-shirt and R.S.V.P. yes to the invitation her king-sized bed was sending her. The kind offering was for her to rest her weary head upon the fluffy pillows lying on it. Holly began rubbing her temples, trying to rid herself of the immense tension she was starting to feel alongside the anger and letdown she was experiencing. Ceasing from massaging herself, she let out a laugh. "This was supposed to be, as he promised, an evening I would not forget! Philip may have forgot about me, but I know you will never leave me or forsake me, Father!"

More than twenty minutes had passed. She stood up, slamming the phone down on her nightstand. She started to pace back and forth. She was shaking her head in disbelief. "Baby, *you* don't know how much you mean to me! Tomorrow I'm gonna prove my love to you! Wait and see! Just you wait and see!" She was shouting everything he'd said to her last night. The more she spoke the louder the words became, her voice quivering with the deepest emotion. "He begged and he pleaded to get me to say yes to this date! Lord, I almost broke it off! I almost did it! I am a fool for going against myself this way! I went against You, Father! I've been sinning against You! I really do deserve this slap in the face for believing in that no-good..." She paused, releasing a pain-filled sigh. "Holly, it's about time you wake up and realize that *they* are all the same." The hazel-eyed woman spoke those words as if she had just been struck by a revelation. Was that God speaking to her? Holly was infuriated, livid more at herself then she was with Philip. She knew she should have questioned his honor at least a month prior to this evening. She marched over to her closet to undress while she continued to yell at the top of her lungs. Tears coursed her cheeks relentlessly. "If this guy thinks he has another chance with me after this, he better for-get it! I am not playing this time! Ooooh, no! Philip, you are finished! Fii-nn-ished! F-i-n-i-s-h-e-d!!! Poor Selma Girard. Huh! Poor me," she paused. "I'm not poor. I'm Blessed," she said quietly. "I have news for you Philip *Hayes* Williams! Tonight... you have been officially dismissed... *I'd rather be by myself.*"

She stormed into the bathroom to wash her face.

Holly had been lying down in bed with the covers pulled up to her chin for about two and a half hours. She had dozed off a number of times, her droopy eyes often checking the clock. She had a feeling Philip was still going to call, with the same lousy excuse, no less, *but* he would call. Leaning up slightly, she grabbed the remote control off of the nightstand and clicked on the television. The light from the large screen casted a silver glow throughout the substantial sized room. Holly unconsciously turned the channels over and over, passing by the one she was aiming for as thoughts of how she needed to read her Bible entered her mind. Once she finally focused to find her desired HBO station, the telephone rang. She took a deep breath, mumbling, "Lord, *please* help him," as she pulled herself up, kicking back the covers to reach for the receiver. "Hello, *hello!*" Holly repeated. The second one was a few octaves higher than the first. The line was obstructed with static. "It's me," said the masculine voice. "Me, who?" She knew good and well the voice on the other end belonged to Philip, but she thought by pretending she didn't know who he was she would some how hurt him the same way he's hurt her. She could hear him quietly sigh before answering. "Me, Philip. I'm at a pay phone. I forgot my cell at the restaurant...again." Holly bit down on her bottom lip to keep from smiling. She had to become stronger. "Can I help you?" "I hope so." He discharged a quick, nervous laugh. "Okay, okay. Let's stop playing games and get straight to the point. Where were you?" She propped her pillow up against the headboard, falling into it. "Well, if you let me explain. Maybe you'd understand!" Rolling her eyes, she thought, let him explain once again. He was saying it like it was the first time he had to. "All right, Philip. Go right on ahead." He cleared his throat and tapped at the phone, as if that would rid it of some static interference. "I was involved in what turned out to be a very long, drawn out meeting. Wait a minute let me finish," he said, hearing that Holly was about to cut him off. "Darryl and KiKi, the hostess haven't been gettin' along." And the NAACP Award goes to... Holly shook her head in disgust as she asked herself, couldn't he even have the decency to come up with more of am innovative excuse? At least he was consistent. She had to give him that much. "Yeah and?"

she finally said. "*And* I was wondering.... *Actually*, I was more like hopin' that we could still get together tonight?" Holly stifled another smile. "But, *it's,*" she said, glancing at the clock on her nightstand, "1:00 in the morning." "Is that a problem?" She wanted so desperately to have the courage to say, "Yes, as a matter of fact, it is a problem because you were dismissed two and a half hours ago...." But he won again for the last time, she secretly promised God by way of her heart as she turned off the television. Hurrying out of the bed, she patted the wall for the light switch, clicking it on. Holly pulled off her T-shirt as she moved toward the dressing area in search for something sexy to put on. "Now," she sighed, ignoring how stupid she felt. "Where is that red teddy?" No forget it. She didn't like the way it hung. It made her look disproportionate. "All right, where's the black one I just bought? He will lose his mind when he sees this little piece of nothin' on me." She was scrambling through her lingerie drawer as fast as she could to find it. And once she did, she slipped it on and waited anxiously for Philip to come.

It felt like she was having an open vision, sitting there on the edge of the bed so Holly stood up, moving in front of the full-length mirror. She sighed, knowing that she was ignoring the Spirit of God again. Studying herself, she shook her head with dissatisfaction although she looked very beautiful. Unhappiness hit her like a brick as she heard the Lord say that she was giving herself away to a man that wasn't her husband. Why did she feel the need to have to compromise in such a humiliating way? The inner strength she worked tenaciously to foster through the Word of God a few months ago, had become an even greater laugh than the ones she'd give Jamie Foxx while viewing reruns of his sitcom. Holly realized she was about to throw all that time she had set aside prior to meeting Philip. She wanted to allow God to minister to her through the Bible. She was missing that woman who seemed to be progressing so nicely until she stuck the *open* sign in the window, letting Philip in. Holly managed to withstand the rising tears as she spoke to her reflection. "Philip, you better be ready to do some serious making up because next time... I might not be..." She hesitated, correcting herself. "*won't* be so dumb." The buzzer sounded as soon as her sentence was completed. She walked over to the phone, drew some breath into her lungs and answered. "Yes, Peter?" "Good evening, Ms Reed. I mean good morning. Uh, sorry." "That's okay. Can I help you?" "Uh, yes Mr. Williams is here." "Please send him up. Thank you." "Sure, Ms. Reed right away." Holly took a few more deep breaths as she slowly headed toward the front of the apartment. She was trying to figure out what she was going to say to him this time because the only thing the Lord wanted her to tell him, was that she could not see him anymore. She heard the elevator doors draw open and Philip approach her apartment. Holly turned on the light as he rang the bell a second time. "Just a second!" she exclaimed and checked her hair in the foyer mirror.

Philip looked exhausted standing there in the confines of the dimly-lit hall. His eyes were blood-shot and his curly hair appeared to be uncombed. He had probably been running his fingers through it most of the night, Holly told herself. "Hi, come in." She was relieved when her voice didn't crack. He gave her a quick overview as he glided inside. Holly closed and locked the door. When she turned to face Philip Williams, her eyes fell down to his mouth. He was moistening his lips with his tongue, revealing his teeth as he smiled. He was returning her stare. "Hey," Holly said quietly and folded her arms across her chest. Philip pulled her to him, giving her a kiss. She could smell liquor on his breath and wondered what it was he had on his mind. Leaning back, he gazed at her, grinning again. He began shaking his head approvingly. "You look like somebody yanked you off the cover of *Essence* magazine." Holly didn't speak. "Is this sexy thing all for me?" He was still admiring her silky garment as she gave him a nod in response to his question. Philip took her by the hands and led her over to the settee. He positioned Holly between his legs, taking a seat. She stared down at him, watching as he lowered his head. She observed how clean his hair was cut at the nape of his neck. Philip saw the way she blinked, flinching too in a way, when he lifted his head, meeting her gaze with a swift jerk of his head. She smiled back at him as he caressed her hands. What was it he had to say? she wondered. But nothing came out of his mouth. Holly could feel that there was something wrong in the air. She backed away a bit in anticipation of what he was going to do next. Then it happened. Philip sighed and stood up. He gave Holly an open-mouth kissed. She could feel his hands undressing her, removing the slinky teddy slowly. First he slid the straps across her shoulders and down her arms, stopping at her elbows because Holly was holding him around the waist, kissing him back. Philip relished the sensation of her bare breasts touching his chest, although his shirt prevented him from experiencing true pleasure. Holly pulled away from his mouth, disengaging their lips. "Let's go into the bedroom," she said, her voice breathy with exhilaration. He shook his head, reclaimed her lips and removed her hands from his waist. Before Holly could close her eyes to concentrate on the excellent way he kissed, she found herself standing before Philip in the nude. She suddenly heard the elevator bell sound, the doors open and Kathleen Parker Wahl exit in an abundance of laughter. The male voice mingling with hers must have belonged to Troy O'Neil. The happy couple's cheerful exchanges disappeared behind a closed door after Kitty's beau let out a joyful "Hallelujah!". Philip let Holly go to undress himself. She stood still, meditating on how Troy gave God the highest praise.

Once Philip was naked too, he sat back down on the settee, bringing her toward him. Holly glimpsed the gleaming vitality of his maleness. She could feel Philip's hands roving, probing the small of her back as he brought her down atop him. He began tasting her with his tongue. Holly shut her eyes, as she expertly ignored the displeasing smell of the alcohol from Philip's tongue. He was smothering the once sweet scent which covered her silky skin. She held back her head when she felt Philip's finger entering her female parts. He moaned with contentment as he delighted in the wetness he found there. "Come here, baby," he whispered seductively and inserted his manhood inside of her. Philip grabbed the back of her head, lifting it, he pulled her toward him, kissing her lips roughly as his passion for her heightened. Holly could feel him pressing up against her lips, nibbling at them erotically with his teeth. He moved his body beneath hers until she broke away from his mouth, screaming with satisfaction. Holding on to him tightly, Holly wrapped her arms around his neck. The noise the small, elegant bench made sliding across the wooden floors, due to their movement, alarmed her in one way and excited her in another. And seconds later she released the enjoyment from within. Philip breathed deeply, smiling like a man who'd just completed a task well done.

Holly knew Philip was awake as he lay beside her in the bed on his back. He had fallen fast asleep fifteen minutes after their sexapade, but his deep doze didn't last long. He was too preoccupied about something. He had something troubling on his mind. She could tell. It was all in his breathing. Sighs followed by rapid intakes of air. But she wasn't going to ask again. She had already inquired twice. "Nothing. You go on to sleep," was what he said with an unwelcoming insistence contained in each word.

When the sun lifted its optimistic head at 6:15 that Sunday morning, Holly sat up, hanging her feet off the side of the bed while Philip continued to lay quietly on his side now, his eyelids fluttering, leading her to believe once again, he really was awake. Holly glanced back at him a second time and stood up, closing the blinds. The room became dim. She crossed it, walked out into the hallway, and eased the door shut behind her.

Inside, Philip finally opened his eyes.

Holly wondered if her nose was being bias. The aroma from the omelette's she'd prepared for herself and her possum-playing lover smelled appealing. Not as appealing as Helen's, however, but very appealing for something she had made on her own. She smiled, tossing the egg shells into to the garbage pail. If Cynthia Reed knew this, she wouldn't be able to find someone to brag to quick enough, Holly thought as she heard her bedroom door open and Philip move into the bathroom. He used the toilet without closing the door. She shook her head in disgust. She didn't feel like listening to that. And, besides that, they weren't that close. They were still getting familiar with each other. Is that what you called this, Holly thought, shutting out the possibility of an answer as she exclaimed, "I made breakfast!" "Smells good," he told her in a quiet, unenthusiastic tone. "Be right there." Philip observed himself in the mirror while he washed and dried his hands. Man, he looked bad, but not as bad as he felt. And being hungover had nothing to do with it. He wished he hadn't tried to drink his problems away. Why did he go to that bar last night in the first place? He was acting like a man who hated himself, gulping those doggone shots down, one after the other, like somebody told him booze was being banned the next day. In a way he did hate himself because of the mess he had gotten himself into. After blowing off some steam with a deep exhale, Philip went into the kitchen. The way Holly set the table: fancy china, linen napkins complete with the Sunday news, made Philip feel like smiling, but for some reason he couldn't. Smiling didn't fit the program right now, he mused. "Have a seat," Holly said as she pulled out the chair opposite his. "Oh, would you like some toast?" she asked, rising from her seat. "No, baby. This is just fine." She nodded and sat back down. As Philip cut into his omelette, it seemed as though he was only pretending to find interest in an article in the newspaper. Holly leaned forward, turning the paper right-side up for him. He cleared his throat, thanked her and stuffed a fork-full of egg, ham and cheddar cheese into his mouth. "Tastes good," he mumbled, chewing and peering at the newspaper page at the same time. Holly smiled. "The coffee should be ready soon," she said, turning around to check on the pot. Philip didn't say anything. He ate his food and eyed the same short article until his plate was empty. Holly stood up and poured coffee into their cups. "Was that enough?" she asked him, nodding down at his plate. "Uh, yeah. Thanks," he said. Philip picked up the paper, leaned back in his chair and crossed his legs. "Oh, I forgot to tell you," Holly said, "Guess who called me last night?" Philip paused and said, "Who, baby?" He never looked up at her, but he smiled a little and added, "With this headache, I can't guess anything right now," Holly noticed the way he still did not take his eyes off of the paper. "Can I pray for you?" Holly asked. She saw a bit of surprise on Philip's face even though he looked at her this time. She was a little surprised herself. "Uh, I have Tylenol in the bathroom cabinet...," Holly changed her offer with some uneasiness in her voice. She was about to exit the kitchen for the bathroom but Philip held up his hand. "Don't worry about it," he said. "Who called?" He brought his hand slowly up to his mouth in a fist form as he cleared his throat, still not looking at Holly yet she could see the desire to know in the expression on his face. "Oh, your mother." Philip's steady gaze, shifted to the other page as he said, "Oh, yeah." Holly watched him as she put the Mr. Coffee pot back. She leaned against the countertop with her arms folded beneath her chest. She saw Philip glimpse her from the corner of his eyes and wince a little when he noticed how she was studying him. "What's wrong with you?" she asked. "And please don't tell me nothing," It took Philip a few seconds to finally look up from the paper at Holly. "Huh?" he asked. "I know there's something wrong. What's on your mind, Philip?" "This article," he said, trying to smile. "No, there was something bothering you before the article. Let's go back to last night." Philip looked down at the paper then at the table. He folded the newspaper and set it next to his plate, sighing as his reluctant eyes met Holly's. "Do you have any of that non-alcoholic wine around?" Holly paused and shook her head no. "The Lord doesn't want me drinking it," she said in a low voice. Philip paused, too and nodded his head. "Is it okay if I shower first," he asked. "Then we'll talk. I promise."

Philip sat on the toilet, lid down, holding his face in the palms of his hands. The seat was cool against his skin as he wasn't wearing anything. He shook his head and sighed. The seat on this bowl was less cold then Holly was going to think he was after he told her what was on his mind. Why did he have to jack this thing up? Something like this could only happen to him. Philip's hands came down from his face, slapping into his knees. He wanted to yell as he began to pump his fist in anger, yanking himself up from the toilet. Standing in front of the sink now, he couldn't look at his own reflection for the fear of recognizing the shame in his eyes. What did his mother say from the phone in the bar last night when he'd asked her to give Holly a distracting call? Holly better be lucky she has his heart? Philip thought. Was that it? He shook his head again, at his mother's words of so-called encouragement. Deceit and betrayal were Paulette Williams' favorite way to waste a day. *Man*, what did his mother know? He learned half his street hustle from her anyway. Philip shook his head once again, turning on the faucet. A woman like his baby wouldn't want to hear that kind of noise. She wouldn't go for no B.S. like that! B.S., he thought remembering that his mother told him and Brenda that it meant "Business Strategy" when they were kid's. Philip's hands came hammering down on the sink basin. The fiery rising in him like a flame on a dynamite wick, quick and steady. It made him bold enough to take on his glare in the mirror and much to his surprise, he had begun to cry hard and heavily like a man who knew defeat was only seconds away. The tears rolled down his cheeks, under his chin, dropping into the sink and blending with the water rushing down the drain. He had no other choice but to tell the truth. Wiping at his eyes with the backs of his hands, Philip turned on the shower, stepping inside. The gushing water felt like an offensive slap in the face to him, although he never had one before. He had successfully managed to escape the onset of the countless swings he witnessed coming swiftly at his face. Selma Girard had swung at him many times. She even went as far as holding her hand in the air like she was waiting for some annoying fly to land in the perfect spot so she would definitely get it. Philip pulled his head back, away from the harsh running water, letting it flow down the front of his body. Holly was courageous enough to swing at him, too. He could picture her beating on him like she was a seasoned fighter. But, he told himself, if she did get indignant, it was only a sign that she loved him. Why else would she trip? Philip grinned a little as he suds himself up. Two, three days, his baby would be back to her old self, letting him love her like he's been. Hey, come to think of it, he wasn't really worried.

Holly was putting the clean dishes up in the cabinet when Philip entered the kitchen. He still didn't feel comfortable returning her gaze, even though he'd come to the realization that she would forgive him no matter what. "All set?" she asked as she closed the cabinet door. Philip shrugged. "I don't know about that," he said with a crooked smile, "I wasn't about to put those same funky drawers back on. So, uh, the Big Bad Wolf has to be loose, til I get home, if you know what I'm sayin'" If Philip wasn't holding his head down, he would have seen the smile on Holly's face as she shook her head in disbelief at what he had said. The hazel-eyed woman felt the grin leaving her mouth as she wondered if that was who he was in his entirety? A Big Bad Wolf who has come into her life. God's sheep's life to destroy her. "Before we talk, I have to dust the top of the piano," Holly said with a slight stutter. "Helen called last week, saying she wouldn't be here today. Her son and his wife had a baby girl." Philip followed her into the living room and sat down on the sofa. As Holly wiped down the piano and the other tables, Philip must have changed the way he was sitting at least six times: crossing and uncrossing his legs, resting his foot on his knee. She heard him clear his throat. Then he stood up, facing her. He took a deep breath, his chest rising and falling as he compressed his lips. Holly peered at him with her head tilted. "Baby, could you finish that later?" Philip asked. He took another deep breath. "I can't wait." "Yeah.... sure. I just have....," she said softly, the dust cloth in her hand pointing toward another powdery surface. Philip shook his head. "No, c'mon. Let's do this now. I really can't wait." Holly nodded her head, folded the cloth and set it on the end table next to the lamp. She walked over to him, her hands smoothing the front of her robe. The couple sat down beside each other on the sofa. "Let's see," Philip said, scratching the top of his head, "where do I began." Holly watched as the hand Philip was using to scratch his head went to the back of his neck, rubbing it. And she saw the way his Adams apple moved up and down at the same time. She had thought it before. But, now, it was safe for her to conclude that these subconscious, simultaneous gestures occurred when he was nervous. "Why don't you start from the beginning," Holly said. "That's the problem," he said. "I don't really know how to." Holly fell silent. She didn't know what to think. "Maybe I could help you. Is it the restaurant?" the hazel-eyed woman asked. Philip paused. Then he shook his head no. He wished it was that simple. Looking at Holly, Philip got lost in her eyes for a little while. "Girl," he said, "You don't know how much you mean to me." She smiled inside, but on the outside her facial expression was full of concern. "Remember when I told you, on our first date, how I beat Courtney in racquet ball?" he asked. This time Holly revealed the hidden smile. It was nice to hear Courtney's name. At that moment she wondered how he was doing. Was he happy? "Yes, I do," she said. "And do you remember when I called him cheap because he invited me to his house for dinner when the bet was for the loser to take the winner out to dinner?" Holly nodded and chuckled lightly. Philip never realized, until now, how much he liked the sound of her laugh. If she gave him one more chance, he would never take anything about her for granted. "What about it. He had you come to his house, right?" she asked, breaking his brief reverie. First Philip lowered his eyes, staring at his trembling hands, then he closed them, his Adams apple doing a solo as he swallowed. Philip's eyes reopened. "Well.... let's just say I got a bigger prize than me and Courtney bargained for." Holly's brows furrowed and she tucked that smile that Philip also realized he liked away. "Did he also take you out and you forgot to tell me?" she asked, her mouth opening again to say something else. She closed it when Philip shook his head no. "No, no, nah," he said and sniffed. He began rubbing his nose briskly. Then he cleared his throat and paused. "Vanessa gave me dessert the following night and a few more times after that." I know he's not talking about cake and ice cream, Holly told herself. She sighed and leaned back. "The kind of dessert her *husband* wouldn't approve of?" Holly asked quietly. "Is that what you're saying, Philip?" He paused again and nodded. "Yup." Letting out an incredulous, short laugh, Holly shook her head in disbelief. "You and Vee had sex?!" She slid to the edge of the sofa, gazing at Philip. He nodded yes as she turned away. Everything was becoming clear. There wasn't a spec of dust *anywhere* in that apartment as far as she was concerned. If there was some, it didn't matter any more. "But she doesn't mean *nothin'* to me, baby," he said, placing his hand on top of hers. Holly pushed it away. "They never do after you get what you want!" she said loudly. "Explain something to me, Philip." Her eyes were squinted in bewilderment, "What do you men do? Take a secret course that women aren't privy to? How to get over on a woman?" Philip wanted to grin because that mess sounded funny. But, if that was the deal, didn't she know he'd be the instructor? "No, I..." "No," she said, holding up her hand in his face. "Do you? Is there a class only for men that we don't know about? Bradford said the same *exact* thing when he got caught and the man who I dated before him said the same thing, too. Verbatim! But they're still with those women that they said they cared nothing about." Holly shook her head, letting out another incredulous laugh. "Silly me. That must be part of the course." She glared at Philip. "So, why now? What possessed you to tell me this now?" she asked with disgust. The more she thought about what he just said the sicker she became. Why didn't Vanessa tell her? Holly and Carmen would never *think* about sleeping with the same man. Real friends didn't do that! Oh, but then again, the Still Small Voice on the inside that she often ignored, always told her Vanessa Benjamin wasn't a true friend. The Lord reminded her that friendship was a covenant like marriage. Vanessa took every opportunity to throw the fact that their offices used to be *her* parents' former home in Holly's face whenever she wanted to have something done her way or just to get on the hazel-eyed attorney's last nerve. And it didn't make a difference where they were: courtroom, office, out to lunch, in front of prospective clients. Sure, Holly hadn't heard her say it since the Stephen Moore case, but Vanessa had said it enough for it to be forever etched in her mind. "I told you because I love you and you deserve to know if you're gonna be my wife." "Your what?" Holly looked at Philip as though he had three eyes. "My wife, baby. I was hopin' you would support me through this." "Through what, Philip? All those hearts you've already broken by yourself and you're asking me to support you? Vee isn't even giving you a second thought. How does that make you feel?" Holly saw his hand reach back and massage his neck again. This time it did a solo. "Baby, you don't understand what I'm sayin'," he said, his eyes welling up with tears. Now his Adams apple moved. Holly breathed, giving him a blank stare. "Clarify it for me then," she said without thinking. Philip closed his eyes once more, crying. And Holly sat there looking at him. She watched the way his face contorted into a pain-stricken "ugly cry". Sobbing deeply, Philip said through short, desperate breathes, "That's my.... That's my baby Vanessa's carryin'. I'm the father. She had me do a DNA test!" Holly gasped, her hand pressing up against her mouth. He could tell she was clueless at that point. She was so shocked as if she never even thought about the possibility of Vanessa's baby being his. Somehow part of him wanted her to say she had already known. Say it was not a problem. Holly stood up, holding her robe closed with both hands, like she had caught a sudden chill. "Get out!" she said through clenched teeth. Philip looked up at her. She was holding her jaws so tight her face resembled an exotic mask. "Did you hear me?!" Holly asked, pointing toward the front door. She pictured him walking into Tracy's apartment last night and Vanessa telling him that their short-haired friend just hung up with her. She could picture Philip spending time with the mother of his child. While I sat around, wondering where he was, Holly thought. She shook her head, knowing that she had been made a complete fool of.

So, this was what had inspired Tracy's speech that day in the office bathroom? She was talking about herself. She was trying to tell Holly that she didn't agree with what was going on, but Vanessa just wasn't going to hear it. You still went along with this whole thing, Trace, Holly mused as she glared at Philip, saying, "I don't want any part of this!" He sat there staring up at her with eyes that were emptying out the stubborn ache in his heart. "Before I go, baby," he said, "can I ask you one last question?" Holly paused as tears began to stream down her cheeks. "What is it?" "Do you hate me?" She paused again and said, "No. I feel sorry for you." Holly felt the emotion looming within her. "This is why...." she said, stopping her words and thinking the rest. This is why Vanessa never had anything nice to say about you, she mused, staring into Philip's tear-filled eyes as he stood up. She wanted you for herself. Isn't that the way this story was destined to go! Holly swallowed as she heard her voice yelling at her on the inside. "My shoes?" he said. "They're waiting for you at the front door where you left them." Holly was leading the way. "Slip them on and slip out of my life," she said, her voice weary. Philip sat down on the settee, easing his feet into the black nubuck lace-ups. As he tied the first one, he said, "I'm gonna respect your wishes by leavin' here today, but I want you to know, I'm not givin' up. I love you, Holly. Vanessa was threatening me. She said she was gonna tell you. That's why I was leavin' here in the wee hours of the night. She hated us spendin' the night together." She folded her arms. The hazel-eyed woman was protecting herself. "Love?" she said, shaking her head. "The only love you know, is for yourself. Because, if you really loved me, it would've made you tell me about this sooner..." Holly shook her head. "God is Love and He would never treat me like I'm nothing when He told me that I'm His beloved in Whom He's well pleased." Philip lowered his eyes and tied the other lace. He knew she was playing a game she wanted him to win. Barry Whites song was true, he told himself. "Oh, He's pleased with you? I thought you Christian's didn't have sex when you weren't married?" Philip lifted his head up from his shoe after he finished tying it. He looked at Holly with a look on his face that she didn't like. "See that, Ms. Reed. I wanted to make a honest woman out of you." He twisted his lips like she wasn't who he thought she was. Like she was even more nothing now. Holly just stared at him. She felt dirty and for a second it felt like she deserved to feel that way after all she's done in the face of her God. "I know how I feel," Philip said, "How you gonna tell me about love? And, I didn't tell you because I was afraid this would happen." Holly shrugged, holding her hands up like she didn't care, as Philip stood up, straightening his pants legs. "I told her to get rid of it," he said while viewing himself in the foyer mirror. Holly grimaced, shaking her head. "You are something else. How would you make an honest woman out of me? You're not God, Philip." He was still looking at himself in the mirror when he said, "I guess there's no hope for you if He can't get you to stop screwin'... up. You need to dust that Bible in your room off so you could finally read it." Holly sucked her teeth. "Hurry up and get out! I've got things to do. My Heavenly Father has a godly man that He has ordained for me. He will find this good thing in God's perfect timing," she told him as she walked over to the front door. "How does somebody like me get to know that God who's pleased with somebody like you?" Philip asked the question sarcastically. Holly stared at him and said, "Go ask Vanessa!" He stared at her with a hardness in his eyes, surprising her with a smile. "Uh, uh, uh. Don't you go judgin'. I heard it say's in that Bible of yours over there collectin' dust on that table in your room ..." He paused to hold back the laugh, but it came out anyway. "Don't it say that the truth will make you free?" Holly paused. "Yes, it does. So go on. Be free! Because the Truth is, we don't belong together!" she said. Philip started to laugh again with that same hardness looming in his eyes. "You gonna be all alone again," he said. "I'll never be alone. I have God the Father, God the Son and God the Holy Spirit with me all the time," Holly told him, like that was a stupid comment that he made. Philip checked his pockets for his wallet and keys. He glanced down the hall to her bedroom, nodded his head, and turned toward the woman who proved his mother wrong. Holly Reed would always be good enough for him, he told himself. Philip left before the eager tears burning the corners of his eyes exposed again that he was without any uncertainty experiencing a real blow to the heart for the very first time. Out in the hallway, he turned to face Holly. "I had big plans for us," he said. She shook her head no and held up her hand. "Do you really want to know, my God?" she asked, knowing that the Lord was telling her to give Philip the opportunity to be His. Holly saw his eyes widen with some kind of hope, but it wasn't the kind she knew from the Bible. The dark-skinned man's hope was; maybe it could work. She shook her head no. "We are not for each other," she told him. Philip paused and his eyes fell to the floor. He nodded his head. "Yeah, what do I have to lose." Lifting his head, he said with a hateful look on his face. "How do I go to ... your Father in heaven?" He smiled arrogantly. "Pardon me, not the one who died. I'm talkin' about God." Holly paused. "I know who you're talking about!" She shook her head in disgust and took a deep breath. At that moment, just when she was thinking how she had forgotten the prayer of Salvation, the Holy Spirit had it enter her mind. "Repeat after me," she said. Philip nodded, wiped his mouth and took a deep breath, too. "Okay." Holly was still finding it hard to be obedient to the Lord as she continued to set her eyes on yet another situation which was standing in front of her. "Dear Jesus," she began and Philip repeated what she said. He hoped this prayer as he prayed it would truly bring him out of the hell that he had called home way too long and into the light of this glorious Gospel of the Lord Jesus Christ like he had heard some preacher talking about on T.V. one night when he didn't have anything else to watch. "I believe in You," Holly continued with Philip following her words seemingly somewhere from a distance. "I believe You are the Son of God, that You died for my sins, and that you were buried and rose again as it says in the Bible. I'm sorry for the things ... I've done that hurt You. Forgive me of all my sins. Come into my heart, take charge of my life and make me the way You want me to be. With Your ever present help, … I renounce all my sinful ways. Cleanse … my heart with Your precious blood. Write … my name in Your Book of Life. I … confess You now as my Lord and Savior... Fill me with Your Holy Spirit... Thank You, Jesus! In Jesus' Name … Amen. After they prayed, Holly glared at Philip's closed eyes and she shut the door with him standing there.

Inside of her apartment, the hazel-eyed woman tried to comfort her stomach, her body bent over as if she were in agony. She was, but it was the pain of yet another betrayal by the man who told her he loved her and by the business partner she thought she was also able to consider a friend. More than that, she was overflowing with such a guilt that she had never known. She felt so convicted. She had to find the place of rest, knowing that God would not be condemning her. It was for her good, too, she told herself. Making it into the kitchen with tears pouring from her eyes, Holly reached for the phone, dialing Vanessa's home number. When she got her machine, she took a deep breath before the long beep. "All I want to ask is why? Why would you do this to me, but more than that, why would you do it to Courtney? Why couldn't you just tell us both the truth? Well, Vanessa... Philip is all yours now... if *he's* willing. He may not be the same person the next time you see him. It's my prayer that God's perfect Will be done in your lives in the Name of Jesus." Holly hung up and called her mother. She told Cynthia everything before hello came out of the older woman's mouth and the only thing her mother said was, "I'm on my way over to you, babygirl."

Chapter Twenty-Seven

Cynthia Reed administered one last prayer before she stuck the key into her daughters' door. Vanessa wasn't Holly's friend. She ain't nothin'. I know vengeance is yours dear Lord, the older woman thought. "Thank you fo' forgivin' me, Father." She ain't nothin' 'cause she don't have you, Lord." Entering Holly's apartment, Cynthia called her child. She said another quick prayer as she didn't want to see her babygirl all tore up. 'Course, it would be hard seein' Holly's pretty face all somber, Cynthia admitted to herself. She knew that they could tell each other just about anything. The older woman was led to say another prayer. The Holy Spirit placed it on her heart as she took a step further into her daughter's place. "Father, thank you that Holly is forgivin' too. I knowed we makes our share of mistakes. I ask that you put her on the path that you made for her, Lawd. That straight and narrow path that smooth, bright by the light of your Word in the Name of Jesus! Cynthia didn't bother to holler the young woman's name. She headed down that hall and opened Holly's bedroom door without any further hesitation, because she had to do what she had to do. She heard the Spirit of God tell her to rest in the authority He gave her and He would back her up.

There she was. The child was sitting at her window peering out. The curtains were pulled back and her bare feet were tucked beneath her too-tiny-for-Cynthia's-liking hindparts. Holly jumped, looking at her mother. She stood up and extended her arms. The older woman noticed a bracelet dangling from Holly's wrist. "Mom." The younger woman shook her head as she walked over, hugging her mother around the neck, her head resting against the older woman's shoulder, which seemed, at that moment, to be built for such a thing like support and comfort for her babygirl. "I'm here now, sweetie. Everything is gonna be okay. The Lawd already worked this whole thing out." Cynthia Reed examined Holly once the younger woman stepped back. She didn't look good. "Are you sure you done wit this man?" she asked. Holly made a face. "I've never been more sure?" she said, "The cross before me, the world behind me... No turning back. Like the songwriter wrote," Holly said it with a newfound strength. Cynthia nodded and glanced around the room. The bed was unmade, there was an ankle-length black dress with a split that looked like it nearly ended under the armpit, thrown across the window seat and there was a, what seemed to be, black lingerie on the floor, near the closet. "Did he do more than what you told me on the phone?" the older woman asked. She was peering into her daughters' eyes. Holly shook her head no and said, "I consented to the sex. What you see in here ... I permitted, but it's over for good." Cynthia didn't respond so fast because in her day, women were in a sense, taught to give a man, no matter how many times he had done them wrong, chance after chance after chance. Like he owned you, she thought. But, her late husband David was different. 'Cause God gave him to me the older woman thought. "Good," Cynthia said. "To be honest with you," Holly said as she retied her robe, "I'm not as disappointed in him as I am in Vanessa. I know I shouldn't be disappointed at all. If I were leaning and relying on the Lord, I wouldn't be." "I knowed, baby. Courtney would *laugh* if he found this out!" Cynthia said, throwing her head back, like she was aiming for God's ears. The older woman pulled her head forward and covered her mouth with her hand as she eyed her daughter. Holly lowered her eyes. She didn't discern her mother's sudden reaction and she wasn't going to try to figure it out. Before the older woman got there, Holly had asked the Father to Grace her more. She was so tired of trying to figure things out. The older woman quickly realized that her daughter didn't see her holding back what she knew, so she said, "Paul don't belong to you and if him and Vanessa walked they stubborn's butts into the Kingdom of

God like I knowed the Lawd's been wantin' them to, they would probably find out that they don't even belong to each other... Well they might." Cynthia smoothed the fly-away hairs down on Holly's head. "My baby," she said, smiling with emotion consuming her eyes and throat. "Mom," the younger woman said, "his name is Philip." The older woman waved her hand. "Paul, Peter, Philip. Same thang when they ain't nothin' to you. I knowed it was somethin' from the Bible. C'mon, let me make you some lunch. 'Cause you's too thin, baby." Holly smiled a little and the bracelet on her arm caught her mother's attention again. "Where'd you get this, sweetie," she asked. The younger woman gazed into Cynthia's eyes before she lifted her arm, looking at the bracelet. "My neighbor, Kitty found this for me," Holly said. She smiled and peered at her mother. "Let me see this," the older woman said. She reached for her daughter's wrist, lifting it up to get a good look at the delicate little thing. The younger woman saw how her mother jerked her body when she read the inscription. Cynthia covered her mouth and a tear immediately coursed her cheek. She continued to cover her opened mouth with her hand as she continued to weep. Holly wanted to cry too, but she couldn't. She had done too much crying already and the Lord placed such a peace in her heart when He told her to put the bracelet her daddy gave her on. At first, she thought she was hearing things because she didn't think it would fit. "She found it in the schoolyard when we were kids," Holly said. "And, she was led to add some links to it... God is so wonderful." Cynthia lowered her hand from her mouth as the tears kept falling. "You knowed who she was as a chile?" she asked her daughter as her eyes left the bracelet for Holly's. The younger woman paused and nodded her head. "I wasn't friendly with her. I tried to be, but she was one of the bullies. The one who called me a nigger." Cynthia made a face and yanked her head back, "What!" Holly lifted her hand. "It's over. Her parents had such a bad influence on her back then, but God has restored what was a terrible situation. He made it good." The older woman smiled and nodded her head as she lifted her daughter's wrist again to look at the bracelet her late husband bought her. "He always had the best taste," she said and gazed at Holly. "You got that from him, baby. C'mon let me find you somethin' good to eat." The older woman watched her daughter walk over to the jewelry box on her dresser. She removed the bracelet and put it inside of it, slowly closing the lid.

Although the aromatic-scent of the food Cynthia Reed prepared brought Holly back to her childhood roots, the younger woman only wanted a cup of flavored tea. "You want peppermint or Raspberry wit this?" Cynthia asked, her hand fumbling up in the cabinet, grabbing at the other box to read it, "Looks like Sleepy Time or Strawberry." "It is Sleepy Time," Holly said from the living room sofa. "I'll take peppermint." "Okay," the older woman said. She removed the spicy-smelling tea bag from the box and stuck it down into the cup of hot water. "You want it in there?" she asked her daughter, who nodded and leaned her head back against the plush pillows. Cynthia added two packettes of Splenda and brought it to her child.

Sliding forward, Holly took the steaming cup from her mother's hand. She blew into it and took a sip. The older woman sat down beside her, stroking her back. Holly set the cup down on the end table nearest to her and laid in her mother's arms. She sighed, asking, "When will I get it right?" "Soon, baby, soon. God knowed what He doin'. Trust Him." Holly sighed. "Why did He allow all this to happen to me?" "Babygirl, it happenin' 'cause you 'pose to be goin' in another direction. A better one. The one God been tellin' you to go in." The older woman smiled as she gazed down at her child. "Why won't I listen to Him?" Holly asked. "I feel so all alone, even with you holding me." "That what it is. You need to trust and believe that the Father is with you all the time. Said He would never leave you or forsake you. His Spirit is in you, baby," the older woman said, placing her hand on the side of Holly's face. "I know He is, but I don't understand." "Whatcho don't understand?" "Why I keep falling for the same type of guys." Cynthia Reed nodded, her bosom rising and falling as she inhaled deeply. "If they ain't got they minds renewed to the Word of God, it's gonna be all wrong." Holly sat straight up and looked at her mother. "That's me. I need to renew my mind to God's Word." Cynthia nodded her head. "Amen!" The older woman began to gaze at her beautiful daughter and then she said, "When I had you I nearly hit the ceilin' 'cause I was so full a joy. Your daddy laughed at the way I carried on. I had to have myself a little girl. A boy would've been fine, too since it was your father who helped me make him. And, above that, it was God who would've given him to me and David. *But*," she said, pausing as if she'd gone back to that day, "when I saw your tiny face staring up into mine, in a way... I saw myself. Me. And I told myself, I may've even said this to yo' daddy," the older woman laughed and became quiet momentarily. "I knowed I told the Lawd in prayer. 'Cause it felt like He was sayin' it to me." Swallowing she continued. "Anyway, what I told myself was, whenever I give this Blessin' in my arms a Bible verse, a warm, cozy smile or even a few words of wisdom, it would be a way of lovin' me." Holly started to cry. She heard the voice of God speaking through her mother to her. "If that is the way you see it," the younger woman said, her words strained from trying to hold back more tears, "you must love yourself unconditionally, too. Because that's the way you love me, Mom. I wish I could be surrounded with more people like you." Cynthia waved her hand, knowing that Holly was referring to Vanessa. "That child ain't nothin' but a cooter," she told her daughter, who gave her a puzzling light laugh. "A cooter? What's that?" Holly asked. "A cooter is something ugly I think." The confidence in Cynthia's voice had gone. "Who told you that?" Holly asked. The older woman fell silent as a sad look crossed her face. "My grandmama, Hattie May Banks." The younger woman was gazing into her mother's eyes while she asked, "Was it something she made up? You did tell me she was challenging." Cynthia looked down at the coffee table and nodded. "It was what she made up for me," she said. Holly could feel her mouth drop open. "Why would she say such an awful thing?" she asked. The older woman shrugged and told her she didn't know. "I could never figure it out, but I tell you one thang," Cynthia said, "I asked The Father who told me He was restoring that place in me where that word was, to help me to never make you feel the way I did growin' up. That's why.... that's why I always tell you how beautiful you is, baby. It's the truth!" "Oh, mom," Holly said. She was crying again. "Even if you never told me how much you loved me and how happy you are about who I've become, I would have known from the look in your eyes." "Babygirl, I'm so glad you didn't take to your grandmother, Julia Reed. She's too much like Hattie May and Vanessa. Those kinds of folks don't know how to love, they only know how to keep prisoners. They need the Lawd!" "I know," Holly said softly. The two women embraced then the younger one asked, "Are you ever afraid?" "Of what, baby?" "Anything." Cynthia thought about that for a moment and shook her head. "No. Not even death because when I go. When the Lawd calls me home, I knowed I'm gonna get to see the Lover of my soul face-to-face and I'm gonna see your daddy again, too. My sweet, sweet David. My spiritual Boaz." As mother and daughter's tears rolled down their cheeks, Holly placed her hand at the back of the older woman's head to help it find her shoulder this time. It was her turn to be used by God to supply the comfort. Her turn to come face-to-face with her mother's "schoolyard bullies".

"Just put your clothes on," Cynthia emphasized to her daughter, who was giving her a hard time about the surprise she mentioned right before the young woman jumped into the shower. "I need to know what it is before I get dressed. This way I'll know what to wear. Should I put on some jeans or I don't know, a skirt and a blouse? What?" "Ask the Lawd, baby. He won't fail you. And that's all I'm gonna tell you," Cynthia said, pushing the towel-wrapped Holly into her bedroom and closing the door behind her. The older woman smiled and shook her head as she glanced at her watch. She made it down the hall into the kitchen. I'm gonna spank the surprises little buns if it doesn't get here soon, she mused. The phone rang. It was Peter notifying the Reed's of their surprise. "You know what to do," Cynthia said and hung up. She stuck her head out of the kitchen, peering down the hall at Holly's bedroom. Good, the door was still shut. She scurried the other way, getting to the front door before the doorbell rang. "Mama Reed...," the Latina woman said. Cynthia covered the young woman's mouth with her hand. Carmen nodded and stepped in. She set her luggage down and embraced the older Black woman after she had closed and locked the door. "Where is she?" Carmen Lopez whispered and Cynthia pointed toward the back of the apartment with her index finger. "These are the kinds of stories that books are birthed from," the Latina woman said with a frown. "Is she okay?" "She will be," the older woman said as she waved her daughter's best friend into the living room. "No, leave that right there," she added, noticing that Carmen was about to bring her suitcase along. "You sure brought a lot with you," Cynthia said. "Yeah," the Latina woman said as she entered the living room. She walked over to one of the straight-back chairs, sitting down. "I'd like to stay away for about two weeks." The older woman's eyes widened. "Praise the Lawd!" Cynthia said. She made herself comfortable on the sofa. "Holly could use a long break herself. These days off here and there will never give you the kind of refreshing she really needs," Carmen said, crossing her legs. "That's right. Those day's here and there ain't no vacation," Cynthia said, nodding. "And while the two of you are over there in the Bahamas, I don't want that law firm to come up one time, you hear me? Just have yourselves a good time. Keep yourselves prayed up," "Amen, we will," Carmen said, smiling and nodding her head. "You can rest. The Holy Spirit spoke to my heart and said that we will never be the same after this trip." "Shhhh," Cynthia instructed when she heard her child's room door open. "Baby, you dressed?" she hollered, holding her hand up to the Latina woman so she wouldn't say a word. "Yes. I was led to wear this little khaki wrap skirt and white tube top," Holly said. She was standing in the living room doorway, examining herself. "I'll carry a cardigan in case it gets chilly," she added, finally looking up. "Carmen, what are you doing here?" she asked, the perplexity on her face being replaced with a smile. The Latina woman stood up and both she and her friend met each other half way, hugging. Holly let her go and stared at her mother, who was smiling, too. "She's the surprise?" the hazel-eyed woman asked her. "Yep, but that ain't all, right baby?" the older woman said to Carmen. "No, it sure isn't." Holly turned her gaze at her friend with her eyebrows risen in anticipation. "We're going away," the Latina woman said. "We are?" "Yes, this is all Holy Spirit directed." "May I ask where?" "Yes, you may." Holly smiled. "Well, where are we going?" "Mama Reed, should I hold out on her till we get to the airport?" Carmen asked the older woman who wanted to say yes, but one look into her child's puffy eyes made her say no. "Go on and tell her," she said, watching as the two friend's gazes lock. "Sister Holly, we are going to the sunny Bahamas. The land of turquoise water and whatever else the Lord has for us there," she cleared her throat, grinned at Cynthia Reed, then looked back at Holly, saying, "Need I say more?" The hazel-eyed woman shook her head and let out an "I can't wait squeal," She gave Carmen another hug, blew a kiss to her mother and hurried into her room to pack.

Chapter Twenty-Eight

Holly and Carmen had awaken just as the plane was about to land. It was a pleasant flight. Free of air-pocket bumps and signs of rain. The Lord answered hers, her mother's and Carmen's prayer as the three women sent up a petition to their Heavenly Father before they left Holly's apartment. The hazel-eyed woman was assured in her heart as the aircraft descended, into Nassau's International Airport, taxing over toward the Gate, that she and Carmen were going to have a wonderful time. "Welcome to the Bahamas," the captain announced over the loud speaker. "The time is exactly 11:00 p.m. and the temperature is ninety degrees. Enjoy your stay and thank you once again for choosing American airlines," the deep voice added before signing off.

Holly and Carmen could hear the contagious beats of Caribbean music playing and the island patios coming from the mouths of the natives as they wandered further into the airport to collect their luggage. "Welcome to the Bahamas, pretty ladies," a tall, dark, slight Bahamian male said with his friend beside him. "I'm Delroy and this hear is Maxwell." Holly and Carmen exchanged brief glances and said hello to the men. "We want to know if we could be of service to you?" Delroy asked while Maxwell smiled and nodded his head. "Uh, I don't think so," Holly said, her eyes falling down toward the cart in Delroy's possession. "Don't you have suitcases?" Maxwell finally asked, "Or have you decided to leave behind your previous existence for one filled with pleasure and excitement?" "Yes, we do have luggage," Carmen said abruptly. She ignored the rest of the short, dark, red-eyed man's comment and told Holly to come on. As the two friends walked away, they both heard Delroy tell Maxwell, "American women don't know a good ting when they see it." We want a God thing, the Latina woman thought as she and Holly continued for their luggage.

The Dan Knolles Transportation bus dropped them off in front of the legendary, but newly refurbished, Paradise Cove Hotel, which was located on the breath-taking beaches of Paradise Island. When Holly climbed down out of the van, wind in her hair, lifting her suitcase to the floor, she began to look around. This was truly a palatial paradise, she thought. Everything from the swaying coconut palms trees lining the hotel courtyard to the canopy of stars overhead, told her she was in the right place. Yes, she was about due for a leisurely getaway. The timing couldn't have been better. "This is like heaven on earth," she mumbled, not realizing that the driver was hanging onto her every word. "It's the best resort on the island," he said, adding, "Next time let me do that." He was nodding down toward her suitcase as he set Carmen's down beside it. Holly smiled as she watched him board the bus again. "Enjoy your stay, ladies. And remember, call us at least a day before your departure." The two women nodded in unison. "Do you mind if I take these?" a voice well above Holly's head droned. She could feel Carmen poking her in the back as the silent seconds passed by. Holly gazed up at him and his hovering green eyes met hers. "I'm Jackson," said the hotel bell hop. "Well, would you?" he asked again in regards to helping them with their luggage. "Yes, you can take them. Thank you," Carmen said with a smile. "You are quite welcome," Jackson said, grinning in return as he bent down, picking up the luggage. When he turned to enter the hotel, Carmen fanned herself. "It is hot," Holly said with a smile. Jackson opened the door, holding it until the two women went in ahead of him. "If you need any type of recommendations, please don't hesitate to ask me," he said. Carmen nodded at Holly and told him that they'll keep that in mind.

At the front desk, Carmen introduced herself and the woman helping her smiled and typed something into the computer in front of her. She nodded when the information presented itself on the screen. "Okay, Ms. Lopez," she said, reaching under the desk and pulling out two keys with the numbers 455 written on them both. "Here you are," she said, handing them to the Latina woman. "The elevators are straight ahead to the right. I will have someone bring up your suitcases." "Thank you," Carmen said. "You're welcome. My name is Mattie in the event you need anything."

Standing in front of the golden-colored elevator doors, the two women started scanning the gargantuan lobby. The almond-toned marble floors beneath them blanketed the entire hotel. Holly spotted two restaurants: one proudly advertising the fact that they served *authentic* native food, and in fancy calligraphy on a gold-trimmed blackboard, it also read that they sold the best crack conch on the island. While the other mild-mannered eatery appeared much more confident, subdued, and upscale in its approach. It was more like a place for romance. It had tinted windows and a menu displayed to the right of the oak door, waiting for people to seek *it* out. Then down at the other end, in between a large circular-shaped valet stand, where Jackson dropped their luggage off at a nearby Concierge desk, and a gift shop was a club: The Blue Curtain.

Carmen's eyes widened more than Holly's. The writer within her had gone to work, passing right by the not so important happenings inside of the hotel. She tapped her friend, pointing toward the gold-tone trimmed glass doors leading to the back of the resort. "We could have breakfast out there tomorrow," she said, noticing the immense buffet setup. "Are you hungry now?" Holly asked. "Yes, I am, but I don't like to eat after eight o'clock. Let me think about it," Carmen said with a smile. "Are you hungry, chica?" The Latina woman asked her hazel-eyed friend. "No."

At 9:30 a.m., Holly rose to the sound of steel drums, and the cawing of parrots and toucans. She breathed and walked out onto the balcony. And the sight her eyes beheld could have never been imagined. Blue skies and a turquoise sea that looked as though one was the reflection of the other. Even the birds flew differently. Like the weight of the air was that of cotton candy. Light. Melting away as their wings carried them closer to their next destination. Holly inhaled. Was that how she wished she could feel? Sure, she was far away from the city. No one had her number except for her mother. But, she told herself, she'd still have to face both Philip and Vanessa when she returned. She would be foolish to think that this situation had been put to bed so easily. Last night in bed she prayed, asking her Heavenly Father to manifest His peace that surpasses all understanding as she felt so tense. Holly rested her hands along the railing and glanced down at the people on the beach. Some were moving at a snail's pace, their legs heavy with remnants of last night's partying, she thought. And then there were folks jogging and back-stroking in the swimming pool and ocean. Their day seemed to be getting off to a nice start. "This is the day that the Lord has made," she said softly. "You called it good, Abba Father and I agree with You." When Holly was about to smile at the way an elderly White couple had begun to enjoy the sounds of the steel-drum beat, she heard Carmen entering, her sneakered feet hitting the floor quickly, excitedly as she made her way into the hazel-eyed woman's room. "There you are!" the Latina woman said. She was nearly out of breath. Holly turned in her direction. "Don't you ever let someone tell you that the power of prayer doesn't work!" Carmen said with a huge grin followed by a joyful laugh. Holly smiled and furrowed her brows. "What happened?" she asked, her back up against the railing. "You are a woman of faith, so I'm not going to say that you won't believe who I ran into while I was jogging." "Who? Wait a minute. Are you okay? Catch your breath first." Carmen shook her head no. "I could not be better, sis. This is a longing pant that you're hearing." Holly smiled, holding up her hands, palms out. "Okay, who did you run into?" "Holly, Holly, *Holly!*" Carmen flopped down into a patio chair, raising her hands upward in praise. "Amen," the hazel-eyed woman said. "God is so faithful." "Carmen!" "Okay, okay. *Devin James,*" she said, looking at Holly. "Who?" Carmen stood up and said, "My mighty man of God! The one who our Padre in heaven had find me; his wife so he can get all that favor! No more Donald or So and

So situations for me! No more Ishmels! You had my Isaac find me! Hallelujah! Thank you, Mi Amour!" Carmen shouted with her arms raised in praise to God again. "What?" Holly asked, her mouth suddenly converting into a large O-shape, then, "The one from your building?" she added and the two women grabbed each other, shouting, "Yes!" "How did you find out his name?" Holly asked, her hands clutching Carmen's arms just above the elbow. "I asked. And that's not all." "What?" "He invited us to be his guest tonight at the club downstairs. His friend plays in the band." "The Blue Curtain?" Holly asked. "Yes. I'm led to go, sis. Devin told me that they rented it out. It's going to be a Christian celebration!" Carmen said. The hazel-eyed woman released her friend, averting her face back down toward the beach. "Listen," Carmen said. "I know you're hurting over what happened, but you have to let it go and move on. Do you want to pray about this?" Holly turned to look at the Latina woman. "I have peace about it," Holly said and smiled.

Before their evening plans, Holly and Carmen had gone snorkeling, took a cruise of the various islands and found themselves touring the streets of downtown Nassau. They both bought two hats and a couple of bags from the Straw Market. Their final stop before heading back over to Paradise Island, was into a quaint, little linen shop. Carmen hid beneath the brim of one of her new hats, browsing the narrow aisles, while Holly loaded up the register area with doilies, place mats and eyelet fabric-covered picture frames. Her mother loved these kinds of things and so did Helen. "Will this be all?" the cashier asked with a thick Bahamian accent and a welcoming smile. Holly stood there, her fingers pressed up against her lips as her eyes scanned the place one more time. She came across a table abundant with baby clothes. "Just a second," she told the woman and walked over to the infant wear. Carmen noticed the spot her friend had been led to as she admired a precious lace-trimmed photo album that had too few embellishments for anyone in the Lopez family to appreciate. She could hear her mother, saying, "Dis is so plain, Carmasetta," so she set it down while her eyes refocused on Holly. She knew her friend couldn't have been planning to purchase something for Vanessa and Philip's baby. Holly turned to Carmen, answering her question as if she had heard it in the spirit. "Helen just had a grandbaby. I can't remember if it was a boy or a girl. Could either wear these?" Carmen smiled and headed in Holly's direction. "Sure," the Latina woman said, feeling the fabric of the miniature clothing. "Cute, huh?" Holly asked and took the two tiny articles over to the register. "This will be all," she told the cashier.

The two friends managed their way out of the doors of the small establishment with shopping bags, two in each hand. They caught a cab back over the bridge to Paradise Island. "Where are you off to?" the driver asked. He was an older man, who looked as though he wanted to give them a guided tour. The gleam in his eyes told Holly so. "The Paradise Cove Resort," she said as she situated the bags on the floor in front of her and Carmen as they sat in the backseat of the taxi. "How did I guess?" he said, giving them a quick thumbs-up before turning back around and putting the car in drive. "Is it your first time here on the island?" he asked, his eyes leaving the road to find the rearview mirror. "No," Carmen said, "We've been here plenty of times." He smiled. "Good. Well, I'm glad to see that you liked it enough to keep coming back." The old man grinned again as they started over the bridge. Holly nodded and began looking down at the rippling water below them. Two jet skiers raced by while a party cruise took its time passing. Looking back toward Nassau, she eyed the Poop Deck, one of the islands famous restaurants, a place where many tourist would eat. Maybe she and Carmen would go there one night this week, Holly thought.

At the end of the bridge, Carmen passed the toll money to the driver. He paid and made a harmless remark to the young woman tending the both. She smiled without responding and the cab moved on.

In front of the hotel, Jackson came to meet them as he had done before, taking all eight bags at one time and carrying them up to their suite. At the door, Holly handed him a five-dollar bill and said they would take the bags from here. "There's going to be a celebration tonight down at the Blue Curtain. Just call to get yourselves on the list, if you want to go. The place crowds quickly," Jackson said as he slipped the money into his pocket, backing away for the elevators. The two women smiled. "We're already on it," Carmen said. He nodded, grinned back and he saluted them as the elevator doors closed.

"I didn't know it was open to the public," the Latina woman said to her friend as they entered their suite, walking into the living room. "I'm looking so forward to meeting the man that God chose for you," Holly said. "He is an Ephesians 3:20 Blessing and I'm going to honor what the Lord revealed to me. Deuteronomy 29:29 states: The secret things belong unto the Lord our God, but the things which are revealed belong to us and to our children forever, that we may do all of the words of the law," Carmen said. "This wonderful man is not a So and So. He's the real deal!" she added with a laugh. Holly paused and then she smiled. The Latina woman crossed the floor for her bedroom to check her phone service at home as well as her cellphone which was turned off. She called out to her friend and the hazel-eyed woman joined Carmen in her room. "Devin left me a message. He said he's looking forward to spending the evening with *us* and so is his friend." "Help me, Jesus," Holly said, shaking her head. "Please don't let me go around the same mountain," she added. Carmen gazed at her friend. "Rest."

Holly turned off the shower and sighed. She had been over thinking and found that she really didn't feel up to meeting anyone. Not even the man that God has for Carmen. This was supposed to be a getaway among friends. Time off to collect thoughts and maybe a sea shell here and there. She thought she and her best friend could reconnect. Discuss old times and a little of the new ones. Very little. Holly just wanted to go back. Be nostalgic. Laugh at the silly moments they both shared and the silly ones they'd braved alone. Holly sighed again, deeply. Why did Devin James have to choose this island? And more importantly, why did he have to be here with a friend? What would this guy's story be? "Well, whatever it is," she said to herself, "he better make sure he unpacks some of his "baggage" before he walks up to me tonight." And if he's too lazy or stubborn to open up one of his "overnighters" to shift some of the contents around, at least he'll be somebody to kill my pain for a little while, she thought. Holly wrapped her wet tresses up in a towel while she dried her body off. Then she moved into the bedroom, gazing at the two outfits she couldn't decide between laying across her bed. The chartreuse lycra dress hugged all of her curves just right. It was one of those things you wore to get attention. But it usually attracted the wrong type of man. Next to that was a burnt orange sheath with a matching tailored jacket.

Carmen knocked on the door. Holly told her to come in. She stood in front of the vanity, sliding the towel off of her head. "You're not dressed yet?" the Latina woman asked, her perfume coming all the way in while she stood at the door. "You look beautiful," Holly told her, avoiding her friend's question. Carmen smiled and glanced down at herself. "Thanks. You don't think I look too pale?" Holly shook her head no but the Latina woman didn't see her. She was still assessing herself. "While we were snorkeling, the Holy Spirit told me to lay out and enjoy the sun. "He truly loves you because you look wonderful," Holly said with a smile. She was still looking at herself in the vanity mirror. The Latina woman gazed at her friend, staring for a moment as she combed the tangles out of her hair. She was waiting to see her eyes. She had discerned some sadness stored in the container of her words. There they are, Carmen told herself. More hazel than ever. When Holly flung back her damp locks, the Latina woman finally walked in, sitting down in a chair near the patio door. "Other than the obvious," she said, "tell me what else are you allowing to trouble you?" Pausing, Holly brought the comb down from her hair, eyeing it in her lowered hand. She then turned to face her friend. "I know we came here to leave that incident behind. You prayed on my behalf on the plane before we went to sleep and you asked God to take the care of it." Holly sat down in the chair in front of the vanity, still positioned toward her friend. "But, I'm feeling so weak." "The joy of the Lord is your strength," Carmen said, "And in your weakness, His strength is made perfect." Holly sighed. "Yes, I know," she said, knowing how she hasn't been studying the Bible and also knowing how diligent Carmen is with her study of the Word. The Latina woman smiled. "Allow the Lord to cause you to rest in Him. Remember, it's by His Spirit." Holly smiled a little and shook her head. "Your strength, your ability to go on, the way you never give up on hope.... And then here we are miles away from where we live.... and you manage to bump into the man you've had your eye on from back home. That kind of thing never happens to me." Holly observed the deep breath Carmen had taken. "I know you know that this is God's doing." The hazel-eyed woman sat there with her mouth closed for a moment. "I need to change my focus. I need to believe the Lord for the time to study His Word," she said with a little sadness in her voice and facial expression. Carmen nodded her head. "Amen. He's not a respecter of person's. What He has done for one, He will do for another ... if we believe." "I feel like it is such a challenge to move forward," Holly said with tears forming in the bottom of her eyes. The Latina woman smiled warmly. "Did you die when you found out that Philip was the one who got Vanessa pregnant?" she asked. The hazel-eyed woman began to look at her with questioning eyes. "No." "Did you die when I told you that Bradford had another woman?" Holly paused and shook her head. "Are you on the verge of dying right now, as far as you know?" Carmen could see the puzzlement vanishing and a faint smile lurking behind the stubborn sadness dwindling on her friend's face. Holly shook her head no once again. "So, in other words, you are being blessed and highly favored by our Heavenly Father. The God of the second, third, forth and so on chance. He will never let you down. It's a guarantee," Carmen said, pulling herself up from the chair. "Listen, I'm going out into the living room, pouring myself a glass of iced cold water, and I expect you to be dressed by the time I've taken my final sip. Bien, sis?" Holly smiled and nodded her head.

Carmen sat out on the terrace sipping her water while Holly dressed. Although it was difficult to contain the euphoric feeling she had inside in regards to her meeting Devin James downstairs in a few minutes, she had to do it for Holly's sake. It was clear that she had to use most of the attention she had saved up to give Devin on her friend because she needed it right now. "Father, you have handled this just like everything else," Carmen said to the Lord among the warm, tropical breeze.

Next door, Holly slipped on chocolate-colored sandals, loving the way they complimented her mocha-manicured toenails. She stuck her lipstick and room key down into the tiny bag she was going to carry. And as she opened her room door to find Carmen, the telephone rang.

"Sweetie, I was just callin' to tell you I miss you," Cynthia Reed said, her voice sounding too far away. Holly smiled. "I miss you, too." "So, what's new?" "Oh, uh, Carmen and I were just about to go downstairs to the hotel club." "What?" the older woman asked. "They're having a private celebration and the man giving it is a Christian," Holly said with a smile. "Oh, that's nice, babygirl. I'm so glad you and Carmen are together. Most of all, sounds like the Lawd showin' His mighty Hand in a big way," said the older woman with a smile in her voice. Holly nodded. "He really is," she said and decided not to share her friend's good news with her mother. "Mr. Freeman wants to pay for me to take classes to learn how to talk … I meant to say to learn how to speak better. He told me he knowed somebody who is very anointed who could help," Cynthia said it and her daughter could hear the sound of joyful tears desiring to come forth. Holly smiled and paused. She remembered praying for God to help her mother with the way she spoke. The younger woman knew it made her mother feel insecure and less of who the Lord created her to be. "Were you comfortable with the way he offered?" Holly asked. "Never felt so comfortable. He said it to me with such a goodness coming from his heart. I heard the Lawd speakin' through him," Cynthia said. Holly knew she was crying now. "I never tole you this, babygirl, but that's why I did my bookclub. This way I could learn how ta speak right." "That's wonderful, mom. I'm so glad God answered the secret petitions of our hearts. And, Mr. Freeman is very sweet," the hazel-eyed woman said. "Just like honey," the older woman said.

Holly glanced into the living room where the Latina woman said she was going to be, then she found her, about to take her final sip of water, out on the balcony. Their eyes met and Carmen entered the suite, empty glass in her hand. "Babygirl," Cynthia said as she blew her nose. "Yes," Holly said. She looked away from Carmen to focus on her mother. "I have another praise report. Do you have time to hear?" The hazel-eyed woman glimpse her friend who smiled. She smiled back and said, "Yes, I have time. What is it?" Holly asked. "Julia called me ... she ain't got no cancer no mo'! God healed her, sweetie." The hazel-eyed woman froze and then she smiled. "Wow, that is good news," she said and swallowed before she could cry. "Okay, mom. I will speak with you soon," Holly said. She hung up after her mother stopped giving glory to their Heavenly Father and told her that she loved her.

"Well, well, well," Carmen said to Holly after she hung up with her mother. The Latina woman was admiring the way her friend was looking beautiful. "You look awesome." Holly smiled back, said thank you and told her that she was ready to go.

As the two women exited the elevators, they were both startled to see all of the people in the lobby. Some were about to patron the restaurants, some were clad in bathing suits and swimming trunks coming in from outdoors, some were sitting in the lounge/bar area that the two friends came across as they left the hotel that morning while the majority waited on line to enter the club. Holly and Carmen stood behind a young Black couple, who appeared to be honeymooners. They were exchanging such loving glances to eachother. Carmen and Holly looked at one another and smiled. "Praise God," the Latina woman said, "They're letting more people in." The long line proceeded in an orderly fashion, and when the two friend's got to the door, giving the host their names, Carmen spotted Devin James. The tall, beautiful man was seated at a table way off to the side of the stage, bringing a glass of something tropical looking, up toward his mustached lips. "There he is," Carmen whispered to Holly. "White shirt, chinos, dark, rich mahogany complexion, guarding three empty chairs." The host overheard the Latina women's quick description of the man in waiting and told the ladies to go in. "Is my dress riding up in the back?" Carmen asked Holly, whose eyes had settled on the performers on stage. She glimpsed the black stylish dress, said no and found the singer and her band once again. The songstress was a tall, big-boned woman with a pretty face, long flowing dreadlocks and a voice that carried those powerful lyrics by the Grace of God. She had wrapped her hands around the microphone and her throat around the words, like it was a war cry, belting out a very anointed song she must have written as she sang it with such confidence and joy. The hazel-eyed woman began to take In the psalmists' accompaniments, three brothers with individual styles. The one blowing the trumpet was wearing dark shades, an island hat, large and popcorn-shaped, with braids spewing out from under it and he had a nice beard. The other two men were less hidden. More clean cut. The one playing the piano was light in color and short in stature with neatly coifed hair. He was dressed in a white T-shirt, colorful vest and a pair of denim shorts. And the third musician playing the bass guitar was, now that Holly was getting closer, the spitting image of Gregory Hines in all aspects, hair, clothes and mannerisms. If he hadn't passed away, Holly would have thought that it was him.

"God's beloved's," Devin said as the two women approached him from behind. He was turned around in his seat smiling at the two friends. Holly averted her face to find Devin James setting his drink down. He stood up and extended his hand. She accepted it and told him her name. "That sounds very familiar," he said as he led them to their seats, one at a time, holding out their chairs. "Oh," Holly said. She shrugged and he smiled, shrugging, too as he found his seat, which was in between theirs. "Thank you so much for your voicemail," The Latina woman said to Devin who smiled again and told her it was his pleasure."Would you ladies like something to drink?" Devin asked. "Sure, I'll have a strawberry smoothie," Carmen said. "And you?" Devin asked Holly, who had been listening to the ministers of music on stage again. The woman's whispery voice had a range beyond measure. Her lyrics entered the atmosphere like the sweet smell of an old, familiar scent, leaving in the depth of Holly's heart a combination of loneliness and the considerate sense of being able to move on. I must keep going, she told herself, knowing that it was a spiritual thing. She began to refocus her attention onto the stage. There was a break in the song then the trumpeter came forward, standing center stage. He placed his instrument to his lips, capturing the audience. Everyone cheered when he hit a high note. Holly could only see the back of him, though. His braids were swinging and clapping behind him, applauding the grand sound he produced so well. "Sis, he asked if you wanted something to drink," Carmen said, nudging her friend in the arm. "Oh," Holly said, smiling as she looked into Devin's eyes. "I'm sorry. They're so good," she added. "Yes, I'll have an iced water with lime." Devin nodded and raised his hand, calling over the waitress. After he ordered, Holly asked him which of the musicians was his friend. "The trumpet player," Devin said, pointing up to him with his chin. "Why didn't you get a table over there?" Carmen asked. She nodded toward the two empty tables in front of the stage. "He," Devin said, referring to his friend, "said he flows better in front of people he doesn't know." The two women nodded in unison, understanding that they would probably make the musician nervous. "I told him that God didn't give him a spirit of fear but of love, power and a sound mind," Devin said and took a sip of his drink. "Amen," Carmen said. She began to gaze up at the stage.

The one-man performance was over and the music came to a momentary end. "Thank you," the songstress said, her dreads springing forward as she took a bow. Then, in the midst of the applauds, she extended her hand toward her band and the throng of people expressed their love once again. "Aren't they a Blessing?" the singer said into the microphone. You heard whistling and clapping. "Oh, you're too kind. Is everyone having a good time?" she asked. And the response was a resounding, "Yes!" And one man even shouted, "Feels like you were singin' to me," from the corner of the room that Holly, Carmen and Devin couldn't see. The woman smiled and told him, "I'm so glad the Lord used me on your behalf, my brother." She smiled again and peered around the crowded club as she said, "The band and I are about to take a little break." The crowd politely clapped their hands although the atmosphere spoke on their behalf, telling the anointed singer that they didn't want the praise and worship to stop. In her discernment, she raised her hands, smiling once again. "I promise it won't be too long, just about fifteen minutes or so. Then we will return *better* than ever ... by His Grace." Showing their approval and appreciation to the Heavenly Father that He heard their hearts by giving the dynamic musical group a huge round of applause, the crowd began to shout praises to God.

Devin smoothed down his mustache with his hand and told the two women that he would be right back. He went through a dark-blue door with the words *employees only* in gold embossed letters across it. Carmen took a sip from her glass and glanced at Holly. "What's wrong?" she asked her friend, who had obviously been waiting for this opportunity. "You know what." "No, I don't," Carmen said and Holly tilted her head, saying, "The trumpeter? I hope he's not interested in me because..." Carmen wanted to tell her friend to trust God in all things, but the Holy Spirit didn't allow her to say it. "But, I guess a hello is not going to take me off the narrow path ... once again," Holly said. She took a sip from her glass. "Only me. This type of thing could only happen to me. I need God to show me His power like never before," she said. Carmen had a very compassionate look on her face as she told Holly that Devin and his friend were coming. The trumpeter hung behind the Latina woman's love interest, saying something to two female admirers sitting at a table near the employee doors.

"He'll be right over," Devin said and sat down. Holly glanced back over her shoulder at the trumpeter. He was standing sideways, talking and smiling at the two women, who appeared to be clinging to his every word. Then Holly saw him shake their hands in turn, say something else as he waved and headed over in their direction. She spun around, hoping he didn't see her watching him. Listening for him, Holly could hear his footsteps, getting louder as he moved nearer. And then they stopped. But Where? And, why? She didn't see him from the corners of her eyes. There were no other tables or people who could have interrupted him behind them. Why wouldn't he come over? Focusing on Devin's eyes, Holly noticed the perplexity in them. They were filled with, what seemed to be, the same questions she had been asking herself. Devin stood up, waving his friend on, as if he needed a yank to continue. The trumpeter must not have been pleased with what he saw. Holly had spoken too soon, thinking that she would be the one avoiding him. I guess I'm not his type either, she told herself. Fine. Praise God. He heard her silent prayer. She could feel her shoulders shrugging as she brought her drink to her lips. Then Holly saw Carmen glance up at Devin, following his gaze. The Latina woman paused long enough on the trumpeter to allow a big smile to cross her face. Carmen stood, too, tapping her friend in the arm. Holly flinched because the drink in her hand almost spilled. She observed herself as she set it down on the table, making sure none of the lime water had gotten on her ensemble. The trumpeter's footsteps resumed. Faster in pace this time. And while Holly's eyes continued to scan her clothing, she heard his familiar-sounding voice speak. He said Carmen's name and told her how happy he was to see her as they embraced. Peering up at her friend and at the back of the trumpeter's head full of cluttered hair, Holly tried to get herself ready for the preliminaries as she wondered how her friend knew this man. She would have to conjure up some conversation is what she thought. "You know each other?" Devin asked, smiling. He was looking at Carmen and his friend. Holly decided to grin as well. There was no longer a need for her to give the musician the cold shoulder. "Yes," the trumpeter said in response to Devin's question. "For quite some time," he went on to say. Then the Latina woman gave Holly a look that asked, "Aren't you going to say hello?" and she mouthed back, "Who is he...." She was about to say more until the trumpeter turned her way. He just stared at her for a moment and the hazel-eyed woman wondered why he was gazing at her like that. She continued to stare back at him as he slowly removed his shades, revealing those eyes. Holly didn't realize she missed them so much. She closed her mouth, feeling her bottom lip tremble. The musician reached down, gently lifting her up into his arms. Holly could hear herself gasp as she embraced him and he whispered, "It's good to see you," into her ear. Pulling away a little and staring him in the face again, she asked Courtney Benjamin if he was okay and he smiled, nodded his head and held her in his arms again.

Chapter Twenty-Nine

The four of them sat around that small table fellowshipping for the entire fifteen minutes of Courtney's break. Holly and Carmen were so blessed by his testimony on how he came to the Lord. "God used my parents on good days," Courtney said, laughing a little, "as well as my God mother, Ms. Ernestine," he glanced at Devin, pointing at him with his thumb, "this faithful man of God ministered to me most of all. The Lord would have him watering and planting the Word in me for years and then the light shone so brightly, I couldn't fake it anymore, especially with what I'm going through right now," Courtney continued. He finished his lime water while Holly watched. She was feeling convicted about her knowing him for such a long time and how her life didn't line up with who God is on many occasions. She continued to watch Courtney and then he was called back up on stage. "The time of worship should be ending in another half an hour," he told the trio and glanced over at the two tables that were empty in front of the stage. There was still one available. He turned toward Devin and said as he pointed over at the table, "Bro, can you take the ladies over there? I'm good now." It surprised Holly when Courtney glimpsed her and smiled before he walked away. They all watched him take the stairs up onto the immense platform, whispering something into the songstresses' ear before taking position in the corner of the stage. She turned toward the crowd, telling them that her trumpeter had made a special request as Devin, Carmen and Holly moved over to the table in front of the stage. They saw the singer say something to the two other guys in her band and the music began. The song was entitled "Beautiful." It was indeed that, replete with a message that Holly, for some reason, took personal. It was ministering to her so deeply.

And she had a good reason for taking it to heart, she thought as her eyes met the singers. The dreadlock-wearing woman was flowing under the anointing so strong and powerfully. Her hand, lifted in worship to the Lord, seemed to be also pointed at Holly. The hazel-eyed woman felt her hand press up against her chest, unconsciously asking the songstress if the song was being dedicated to her. Holly's hand came down suddenly from her chest as she told herself that she needed to be asking God that question. What was Courtney Benjamin trying to tell me? Holly asked herself several times. She finally paused and took a deep breath. "I want to hear from You, Lord", she said under her breath. The hazel-eyed woman found herself glancing around the crowded club, seeing the people worshiping to the song that she had taken personally and she was surprised that by His Grace, she had finally wanted to hear from her God.

At nine forty-five Courtney made his way down to the table they were now sitting at. He was wiping beads of perspiration from his forehead with a small navy-blue towel, it was very apparent that he was free for the rest of the evening. Courtney sat down opposite Devin, who had an iced cold glass of water with lime in it waiting for him. "Thanks, man of God," he said and clinked his glass up against everyone elses before taking a sip. Holly saw him watching her over the rim of the glass and when he brought it down from his lips, placing it back atop the table, he smiled when he saw that she, too was drinking the same thing. "Seeing the two of you makes me forget the reason I came here," Courtney told both Holly and Carmen. The Latina woman rested her hand on his. "How are you doing?" she asked him, not wanting to question his appearance just yet. "Hey, all is well. Jesus, is Lord!" he said and nodded his head. "I know I did the right thing." Courtney took another sip of lime water, gazing at Holly over the rim of the glass once again. He brought the glass down from his lips and said, "I'm saved now. God led me to paradise and saved me. Don't you agree that all is well?" Courtney said and the hazel-eyed woman smiled at him and told him that it was very clear that he had done the correct thing, too. The sound of Christian music with an island beat beckoned their attention. On stage was an ensemble of two women and two men, natives of the Bahamas who started singing a song which thanked God for His favor. Courtney and Holly watched as a throng of people moved to the beat onto the dance floor. Some of the people were raising their hands while others were moving their bodies to the powerful sound. Devin finished his drink and asked Carmen if she wanted to dance. The Latina woman stood up and smiled "Amen," she said, moving to the beat as Devin grabbed her hand and led her toward a tiny space in between the elderly couple Holly had seen dancing down on the beach to the steel drums earlier from the balcony in her room and the honeymooners she and Carmen had stood behind on line before entering the club. "I can sense the Lord's presence so strongly," Courtney said. When Holly turned to look at him, she found him sitting there with both hands lifted and his eyes closed. She paused and quietly said, "Yes, I sense it, too." She watched Courtney for a moment as he continued to enjoy their God. She didn't know what to think or say or feel. Holly began to fan herself as it was a little warm in there for her. She was about to turn her head away from Courtney as she wondered why she really was not sensing God's presence. "Help me, Lord," she said and she saw him open his eyes. "Are you okay?" he asked. He lowered his hands and placed one on Holly's shoulder. She paused and then proceeded to fan herself. "I was feeling a little over heated," she said. "Do you want to go outside for some air?" he asked. "Sure." Courtney and Holly both stood up. The hazel-eyed woman was going to head toward the doors she and Carmen came through until Courtney gently patted her on her arm. "Let's go this way. It leads straight to the beach." Holly paused and nodded her head.

Outdoors, Courtney and Holly could hear island music playing in the distance, coming from the adjacent resort. "Let's go up there," Courtney said, pointing toward the boardwalk. "We'll sit under the cabana." Holly didn't oppose. She just let him lead the way. The setting was that of a midnight-blue sky, containing a wide array of sparkling stars. Unlike the back drop in New York which she usually loved but with so much going on, she couldn't enjoy it. Tonight, they both needed something special. The two of them being together the way they were, was different. It was the second time they had ever been alone, Holly thought, thinking about the time they were by themselves in her apartment on the day he left to come here. The water crashing up against the rocks beneath them, along the edge of the white-sanded beach made her begin to focus on it instead. Looking down onto the sandy shore, Holly saw that they weren't alone. A few other couples she had seen from inside of the club were walking barefoot in the water. "Oh," Courtney said, causing her to gaze at him. "I want to thank you for thinking about me when you gave me the non-alcoholic wine or was that champagne that you and uh Phil bought me for my birthday?" Courtney said. "I think it was wine," Holly said as she walked a little behind him. She felt a little foolish for not knowing for sure. He nodded. "Okay, well I also want you to know that the Lord told me not to drink any of it." Holly paused. She knew it was the same reason that God gave her. "It will beguile you to desire the kind with alcohol," is what the Holy Spirit warned her. "The Spirit of God spoke as clearly as we're speaking with each other right now," Courtney said. He turned to look at her as they walked. "He said that is would just drive me back to drinking the real stuff." Holly was quiet for a moment. "I'm sorry," she said as they stepped up underneath the cabana. Courtney was going to say that it was okay because she didn't know, but the Lord stopped him. He nodded and began to look around as he said, "Man, do I love it here." Courtney pulled a chair out from under a table so Holly could sit down. "I do too," she said, quietly as her hands smoothed the back of her dress before she made herself comfortable in the chair. She was feeling convicted about giving Courtney the non-alcoholic beverages. Holly watched him as he walked around, sitting in front of her, his back facing the ocean beneath them. He saw her blink and lower her eyes from his face. "I know what you're thinking," he said with a slight smile. Holly looked at him. "You're asking yourself. What happened to that clean-cut brother I used to know. Am I right?" She smiled, too. "I'm not saying this look is bad on you... but yes, I was wondering." Courtney laughed and removed the dark shades. Then, he got rid of the large hat with attached braids. Holly covered her mouth and chuckled. "They're not real?" she said, still giggling. He shook his head no and took his eyeglasses out of his pocket, putting them on. She is lovely, Courtney thought, wishing Holly could see herself through his eyes. He had often observed how she never relied on her beauty. It was like she didn't see herself to him. She noticed the change in his expression and she also noticed the way his stare revealed a bit of disconcertion. What was he thinking? Then she saw her reflection through his glasses. She needed to relax. She appeared stiff, her shoulders up high as if she had been shrugging. I probably did, she thought. She leaned back, feeling the support of the chair against her upper body. "Did you like my disguise?" Courtney finally asked as he placed the hat with connected braids and sunglasses down on the chair beside them. This time Holly noticed how the scar she had seen during his visit to her apartment had faded. It was still visible. but, instead of ruining his good looks, it added a certain distinguishing quality that was beautiful much to her surprise. Or was it because he was so beautiful that nothing could ruin him? In a secret place in her heart, she wanted it to go completely away. "Yes, I do," she finally said after taking him in, "but it hides you too much." Rubbing at his five o'clock shadow, Courtney said quietly, "That was the point." "Why?" "It was time for a change. I have been doing things too many other folk's ways for way too long." He paused and smiled a little. "I'm not saying that I'm going to put this new costume on forever. Just until I get Vanessa out of my system." He shook his head, adding, "I don't miss her. Trust the God in me... I'm just so mad at myself. Angry at me for staying with her for so long. I know that it's not right to hold a grudge ... I'm really depending on God." Holly nodded. "That's true and I also can understand why you feel the way you do," Holly said.

"Believe me when I tell you I've been there." "Bradford?" Courtney asked, and closed his mouth. He began to think about how much he wanted her to say Philip's name, too. Were they still together? is what he wanted to know. "Yes, and then some," she said and lowered her head. She lifted it back up to see Courtney nodding. He really wanted to ask her what she meant by that. He decided against it. He wasn't aggressive outside of business. But he was able to tell her about what God told him about the non-alcoholic beverage she gave him. "So," Holly said, "Is this where you've been ever since you left the city?" "Uh-huh, and to think Devin wanted me to meet him in Aruba. He was over there when I left and I asked him to come to the Bahamas." Courtney smiled and asked, "What brought you and Carmen here?" "Time. Let's just say it was *time* to get away. God's timing is perfect." Holly averted her face toward the beach. She could feel Courtney staring at her. Did her referring to the Lord appear false? She had been ignoring Him for too long. She would understand if it seemed phony. "Is everyone still wondering where I am?" he asked. Holly looked at him and nodded. "My mother has become your number one intercessor," she said, making them both laugh. "Uh, yes, Mrs. Reed," he said and got quiet. "All of this must make her feel like she's reading a book?" Courtney stroked his growing beard again and smiled. "But, I'm grateful for her prayers. How is she?" Holly smiled, too. "Mom, is just fine. And speaking of books, her book club has grown so now she has more people's businesses to mind *and* then she'll graciously minister to them as the Holy Spirit leads to keep things right." Holly laughed a little and then she smiled again. "She met someone as well. He sounds like a wonderful man of God who is encouraging her to speak better. My dad and I used to do it when I was a little girl, ... but again, God's timing is perfect." "Good for her," Courtney said. Just then the doors to the nightclub opened and coming out like a mighty rushing wind, was some of the Blue Curtains music. The foursome was singing "Lion of Judah" and the crowd was enjoying it, shouting, "Hail, hail, Lion of Judah!" as the doors closed "Carmen and Devin must be having a good time because she would have been looking for me by now, if they weren't," Holly said. "Oh, yes," Courtney said, smiling a little. "He told me that she was the one he had been trusting the Lord for when they ran into each other earlier today." Holly tilted her head, asking, "Did you know it was Carmen Lopez, my friend?" Courtney shook his head no. "DJ was calling her his woman of God. So, no, I didn't know." Holly smiled. "I have always admired him," he said. "He's been a Christian since he was a young boy and I could honestly say even though I know nobody's perfect but Jesus, I don't ever remember DJ compromising his relationship with the Lord. He's been the constant laborer in my field even though I didn't talk about him much." Courtney paused. He saw that Holly was getting uncomfortable. "How are you and Philip doing?" The hazel-eyed woman looked into his eyes. She wanted to know if he knew the whole story, that he was Vanessa's baby's father? "We broke up," she said and Courtney hoped he wasn't smiling on the outside. "It wasn't working and it was way too complicated to try to salvage the little we had," she added. Courtney was quiet. He just wanted to listen. Holly sighed. Should she tell him everything? The reason for their split? That the Holy Spirit had her lead him to the Lord? Later, she told herself. Holly shook her head and said, "I was prompted to have Philip pray the prayer of Salvation." Courtney shifted in his seat. She saw him do it but she could not make out why he had moved the way he did. Holly lowered her eyes when she saw the way he was looking at her. He looked like he was frightened, but she didn't understand. With her eyes still lowered, she said. "Sometimes I wonder if it would be better just to casually date, you know, go out with a different man every so often. This way we'd always be at that sweet stage when things seem to be at its best. Compliments are plenty, smiles are broad. Even if we're lying to ourselves." Courtney thought about what Holly said and he realized that what she said would not have made him smile and agree even before he was saved. Especially, because he was still with Vanessa. Yet, now having learned on the first day that he decided to go to church with

Devin, that marriage was of God and how He was the One Who chose Who He planned to be husband and wife to each other, gave him some hope in that area. And, the Lord called it good, he told himself. "If you did that you wouldn't have any memories *that* you want to hold on to. And what if you let the right one go too soon in the haste of hoping that you would probably be going out with somebody else when the opportunity presented itself?" She shrugged and lifted her eyes to look at Courtney. "Oh, well," Holly said. "Oh, well?" he asked and smiled. "Well, I want all that God has for me. I've done it my way for too long," Courtney said. The hazel-eyed woman opened and closed her mouth as she gazed at him. She saw that he was very serious. He was gazing back at her. "Don't you want God's perfect will for your life?" is what he finally asked. Holly just stared at him for a moment before she slowly nodded head. Courtney smiled again. "Good." "I was raised in the Word," she said. "I know. I remember you saying that before. Back in college." Holly paused and nodded her head. "I loved going to church and I also loved and enjoyed watching ministry on television when I was at home or just outside of the four walls of the church ..." "So, what or who did you allow to rob you of that which I'm finding to be the most important thing?" Courtney asked. He smiled and shook his head. "I was lost but now I'm found and there's nothing better. Vanessa would often say that I had no backbone. She'd call me out of my name so often it was as if those were my names to her most of the time. What she was really saying is that I had no Lordship over my life. No Jesus even if she didn't believe in Him." Holly just sat there quietly staring at Courtney. She was in awe of his transformation and she was now seeing God in a brand-new way. "I love the Lord," she said. "I believe I really do." He heard her words go down an octave. It was almost at a whisper. Although, he felt compassion rising in his heart toward Holly, he knew that being truthful was in greater manifestation in his heart and he was going to listen to that voice. "Jesus said if you love Me you will keep My Commandments. Do things His way," Courtney said. Holly paused and nodded her head slowly. "He did say that," she said and wiped away the tear that fell from her eye. "My mother had been asking me to come back to church, but she stopped asking after a while ... I chose to believe that it was God telling me that it was okay not to, that He understood. I've been so busy lately," she went on to say. Holly lowered her eyes and reached up to wipe away another tear. Courtney began to look around for a tissue then he patted his pants pocket, pulling out the small navy-blue towel he had used earlier to wipe the perspiration from his forehead. He was holding it out with a smile on his face when Holly peered up. "This is all I have on me." She glanced at the towel in his outstretched hand then into his eyes. She smiled, too and received it. "Thank you." As she began to pat around the bottoms of her eyes, she could smell the fresh scent in the cloth that came from Courtney. Holly tried to resist how it made her feel as she continued to gently pat her face, but she had to say something. "I love the cologne you're wearing." Courtney smiled and said, "Praise God." It sounded like he had known the Lord forever to Holly when he gave Him the glory the way he did. It came straight from his heart. "What is the name of the church that you and Devin have been attending here?" Holly asked. Courtney saw another tear stream down her cheek and he held out his hand for the towel. The hazel-eyed woman looked down at the navy-blue cloth, then back up at him. She lifted the hand holding it and gave the towel to Courtney. He took it, smiled, and slowly leaned forward toward her. Holly noticed the way she held her breath as he wiped away the tear that had fallen down her cheek. "That's better," he said and leaned back. She was focusing her eyes on the towel in his hand, near his lap. "Free Worship of the Bahamas," Courtney said. He glanced down at the cloth in his hand, knowing that Holly had stopped gazing at it. She was startled by the way he lifted his eyes to look at her. She never witnessed such a genuineness coming from a man before. "The services are so power-packed and the teaching is dynamic... We're going tomorrow. They're having an evening of praise and worship ... Why don't you and Carmen join us?" He smiled. "I have a feeling down in here," he said, touching his stomach, "That DJ will invite her, too ... he probably did already." Holly glanced at Courtney's mouth and then away toward the ocean behind him. He was still smiling. She saw him move a little like he had something else to say. Courtney had begun to think about the Lord and how He had Holly lead Philip to Him. But, He also realized how the Holy Spirit brought back what He had spoken to him through His Word that morning and then he was gently reminded about the way he found his smile and it made courage rise in him. He loved how God revealed that to him earlier that day as well. It seemed like he couldn't stop smiling once he began to play the trumpet two nights ago at church. The smile almost disappeared when he thought about how he had asked Devin to sit over in the pews in the section of the church that was to the far side of the pulpit where he could not see him. He was feeling like he could not play at his best in front of the people that he had known. The Lord revealed to him, before he went back up on stage inside the club, that he was blaming the people in his life for his not being able to enjoy the gifts of music that he had been Blessed with. Now, he knows that the Lord used that brother in church to lift his voice and shout, "Jubilee ... I hear the sound of a trumpet!" when he placed his lips to the trumpet, blowing it. That was a battle cry, the Holy Spirit told him. Tonight, he saw how the fear was a lie from the enemy. That fear that wanted him to shut out those who would lovingly support him. Courtney smiled again. He was enjoying the freedom to be who God created him to be. He thought about the sweetness he had experienced while Devin, Carmen and Holly sat right in front of where he was positioned on stage in The Blue Curtain tonight. Refocusing on Holly, he was led to share the awesome revelation God gave him earlier. "Um, I, uh, need some help," he said. Courtney placed the towel on top of the table and started to rub his knees. Holly was already looking at him. She could feel herself tensing up, getting on guard. And, he saw that happening immediately. "It's not bad," Courtney told her with a smile. "To me it's not." Holly paused and nodded her head. "Okay," she said and took a deep breath. "God is not surprised and if He has you telling me that you need help ... I'm going to believe that I can help," she said with those hazel eyes gazing at him, Courtney thought. He nodded. "When I was studying the Word this morning, the Holy Spirit revealed something to me ... I had been praying like I was taught to pray recently... I'm learning about how God is so purposeful and I love that about Him. I never knew how lost I was until I came to Christ. I was in desperate need of not only a Lord, but a Savior, too. And, I am so thankful to Him for all the times that He had people witness to me over the years, even while I thought I wasn't interested ... but now that I'm being taught about Him through His Word and by Pastor Charles and his lovely wife when they are teaching during service, I could only say Hallelujah as He truly is the only One worthy of the highest praise." Courtney stopped speaking for a moment. He lowered his eyes and took a deep breath then he lifted his eyes and began to look around. Holly was gazing at him as he did this. While she was marveling at how quickly the Lord had manifested this knowledge of Himself into Courtney's heart, she could see that he was a little uneasy, but determined to stand firm on his newfound beliefs. She felt herself slide back in her chair when he finally gazed back at her. Courtney managed to smile. "I remember when we had come together in a meeting regarding the Stephen Moore case. You, me, Vanessa, Tracy and Jeanne Landers. We had really come together on a friendly basis yet it was to know for sure if that case was something that Reed, Benjamin and Mann should be involved in. We all thought that it was going to be a quick and easy trial as the evidence against the boy's father was so clear, but it just seemed to drag on and on." Holly nodded. "Yes, I remember that," she said. "Good." Courtney said it so politely, she thought. "I also remember when you told us all that your mother would say "Everything happens for a reason" from time to time when you were a girl and that helped with the choice that was made on behalf of the firm." Holly smiled and nodded again. "Yes, it helped me many times." Courtney nodded too and took another deep breath. He pleasantly surprised Holly with a smile. "I really believe that everything happens for a reason," he said, still smiling. Then, the smile went away and he nodded his head again. He was staring at her and she saw a tear slowly stream down is cheek. Courtney grabbed the navy-blue towel off of the table before Holly could make an attempt to get it. He started wiping his face, where the tears were continuing to fall. He lowered his hand with the towel in it and began to gaze at the hazel-eyed woman again. "I don't know how I knew this back when we were in college and what I knew made me stay away from Vanessa, Tracy and ... you. I told myself to just work harder to build my career while I studied for the classes that I had. This would make what I knew go away." Holly nodded. "You were involved and very committed to the different activities and groups offered at school." Courtney nodded for what seemed to be a long time. "I know," he said. He smiled at Holly again and lowered his eyes. "Your presence is helping me," he said and cleared his throat. After taking another deep breath, Courtney looked over at the hazel-eyed woman. "The Holy Spirit told me through the Word of God, that you are my true wife, Holly. His choice for me." He placed his hand on his chest. "And, Pastor Charles told me that through the Word was the most authentic way to hear from the Lord. As soon as I read this verse out of I believe it was the book of Psalms. I would have to look it up, but I can tell you what it said..." Courtney was sensitive to the way she was looking at him, like she was trying to refrain from crying. He felt led to go on. "It said; He who finds a wife and true was in parenthesis next to wife ... He who finds a (true) wife, finds a good thing and obtains favor from the Lord ..." Courtney lowered his eyes and began to cry again a little deeper this time. "He is so good! He also healed my body. I'm not sterile anymore! I went for a second opinion and he told me that it was true that I was sterile, but after a minor surgery. I was in and out, Dr. Vincent told me that I should be able to have children now." "That's so wonderful," Holly said with a smile as she added. "My grandmother, wanted to meet me," she said as she began to cry. "She's my father's mother. Mom ran into her at the bookstore." She was still crying. Courtney peered over at her. He removed his eyeglasses and wiped his face with his hand. "Did you meet with her?" he asked and Holly took a deep breath and nodded her head. She wasn't looking at Courtney. "I didn't want to have anything to do with her, but ... she had cancer." "Had?" he said and put his eyeglasses back on. Holly nodded. "She asked for prayer after my mother and I were about to walk away from her ... mom prayed. She prayed such a powerful prayer and God heard and answered by manifesting her healing." She finally returned Courtney's tender gaze. "He healed her," Holly said. She sniffed and went on, "The cancer is gone. I have to forgive her and my grandfather," she said and started to cry again. "This is good news," he said and wanted to smile, but he began to cry again, too. After they poured out their hearts, allowing the Lord to cleanse them, she began to think about how she asked their Heavenly Father to show up strong on her behalf and she saw so clearly how He did on this day. Holly lifted her head and managed to stop crying as she said, "There is much restoration taking place... When I was nine-years old, I was bullied by this little White girl. She called me a nigger one day in the schoolyard. And, when I ran away from her, I thought I lost the bracelet my dad had given me. It was so precious to me. He had it inscribed to "Daddy's little sugar dumpling. I was his little SD. There was something very familiar about my new neighbor ... and then, I found out what it was." The hazel-eyed woman started to cry again. She was shaking her head. "It was that little White girl who called me that name. God had her find my bracelet and she kept it all of this time and then the Lord had us reconnect, but this time, it was on His terms. I got my bracelet back," Holly said. Courtney watched her cry and it made him cry again. The hazel-eyed woman gazed over at him and said, "I would love to attend church with you tomorrow." He swallowed, nodded his head and continued to cry as he whispered under his breath with a sigh of relief, "Praise God".

THE END

A bruised reed He will not break, and a dimly burning wick He will not quench; He will bring forth justice in truth. *Isaiah 42:3 Amplified Bible*

Review Requested:
If you liked this book, would you please provide a review at
Amazon.com?
Thank You

CPSIA information can be obtained
at www.ICGtesting.com
Printed in the USA
LVHW030806201119
637820LV00001B/39/P